BLACK ROSE

BOOK 2 - THE DRACULA DUET

KARINA HALLE

EVERY VAMPIRE HAS A SAD LOVE STORY TO TELL

BLOOD ORANGE BLACK ROSE

I'm more than just a little curious
How you're planning to go about making your amends to
the dead

"The Noose" A Perfect Circle

I found you in the water, you were soaking wet
Falling deep into your dripping heart again

"Vivien" +++ (Crosses)

Those who cannot remember the past are condemned to
repeat it.

George Santayana

PLAYLIST

"Vivien" - +++ (Crosses)

"The Vampyre of Time and Memory" - Queens of the Stone Age

"The Noose" - A Perfect Circle

"Last Cup of Sorrow" - Faith No More

"Sensation" - +++ (Crosses)

"Did you know that there's a tunnel under Ocean Blvd" - Lana Del Rey

"Some Kind of Ghost" - Black Rebel Motorcycle Club

"Bitches Brew" - +++ (Crosses)

PLAYLIST

"Born to Die" - Lana Del Rey

"Stripsearch" - Faith No More

"Ever (Foreign Flag)" - Team Sleep

"Sunspots" - NIN

"Initiation" - +++ (Crosses)

"Head like a Hole" - NIN

"16 Psyche" - Chelsea Wolfe

"Ultraviolence" - Lana Del Rey

"Change (In the House of Flies)" - Deftones

"Ashes to Ashes" - Faith No More

"The Hollow" - A Perfect Circle

"God Hates a Coward" - Tomahawk

"The Blackest Day" - Lana Del Rey

For a more extensive playlist please check my Spotify by clicking HERE or searching for "Karina Halle Black Rose" or scan this pic:

For Bruce: thank you for being the best doggo in the world. You are forever loved, my sweet boy.

CONTENT WARNING

Hello there, dear reader! Thank you so much for wanting to read Black Rose, and if you've been waiting some time for this book to release, I'm grateful for your patience! The Dracula Duet is now complete.

Just in case you picked this up on a whim, YOU MUST READ BLOOD ORANGE BEFORE THIS BOOK...Black Rose is not a standalone. But since you will have read Blood Orange already, you'll be familiar with the content warnings and there are similar warnings for Black Rose including:

Graphic violence, gore, blood, horror, harsh language, mild BDSM elements, sexually explicit situations, ghost of an unborn child, talk of suicide and pregnancy loss, death and grief.

PROLOGUE

THEN

"She is dead."

Bellamy grips the edge of his desk with bony fingers and thinks his heart might give out. It lurches in his chest, then seems to disappear entirely, as if erased. Her name doesn't need to be spoken because he innately knows the truth.

He knew it. He knew it even before Atlas Poe uttered the words, standing in the doorway to his office, afraid to step inside. He had felt severed all morning, blaming it on a dream he had, as if he lost some crucial part of him and couldn't remember it. But now he knew why. When you spent your years training a witch, shaping them to be another version of yourself, and take on the role of their guardian, they become connected to you in ways beyond what's natural. In many ways, she had become a daughter to him, though any love was conditional.

"What happened?" Bellamy asks, his voice barely audible in the vast depths of his office.

"She was killed," Atlas says. "Murdered."

Bellamy's eyes pinch shut. "By whom?"

1

"They believe it was the vampire, sir," Atlas says. He clears his throat.

Oh, *damn*.

Bellamy leans back in his chair, struggling to take a breath. There is a deep sorrow inside him that wants to rise but he never has room for sorrow in his life, so he pushes it away and lets the disappointment wash over him. He had given Dahlia one more chance to prove herself. During her last mission, the one that nearly got her ejected from the guild for good, she went and got too close to the female vampire she decided to befriend before killing, and the vampire became wise to her. If it wasn't for Bellamy rescuing Dahlia at the last moment, Dahlia would have died then.

And this time, Bellamy wasn't there to save her. He assumed he wouldn't need to. He thought that her desire to prove herself would have meant she'd taken extra precautions. But somehow her glamour must have slipped. Her truth must have come out. Valtu probably murdered her on the spot. The last he had heard from Livia was that the two of them had become very close. He almost smiles at the thought of Valtu suffering from the sweetest betrayal, but he stops short of feeling happy.

How can he be when his dear Dahlia is dead?

"This is my fault," he says quietly, mainly to himself.

Atlas hears him. "How so?"

Bellamy grunts and runs his hands over his face. They shake slightly as they do when his emotions become too much for him. All the magic in the world couldn't seem to get rid of them; neither did conventional medication like anti-depressants. He is a young sixty in every way except that. He hates to think what he'll be like in ten, twenty years. The thing he despises the most about vampires is that they don't have to suffer through aging. It is thoroughly unfair.

"She wasn't ready," Bellamy says, glancing at Atlas briefly. "I knew she wasn't ready. She was too foolish, too weak, lacked a sense of purpose and self. Too eager to make people like her. No doubt she threw her mission all away for that vampire. And look what that got her."

Atlas nods. He doesn't say much, which is why Bellamy likes him. Atlas is also a powerful witch in his own right. He'd been kicked out of the guild a couple of years ago for accidentally murdering a human, a civilian caught between Atlas and his attempt to slay the vampire witch Lenore. But Bellamy operated outside of the guild most of the time. He gave control to the new leader, Qiang, under the pretenses of his early retirement, but continues to run a sect outside of the guild, guarded by magic that Qiang, or any witch on the committee, can't see through.

It is in this sect that Bellamy welcomes witches such as Atlas Poe, who have been ostracized because of mere circumstances. Murder is often necessary for Bellamy to accomplish his goals, so why should he judge those who have done the same? The founding father of witches, Jeremias, the Devil rest his soul, welcomed the darkness, and so Bellamy wants to do the same. Especially now that Jeremias has been dead for some time.

Someone has to take his place, after all.

"I have more bad news," Atlas says.

Bellamy sighs. When it rains, it pours. "What?"

"Livia is also dead."

Bellamy feels flames building inside him. First Dahlia, now Livia? Both witches, both like daughters to him in some way.

"What about the book?" he asks.

"We don't have any intel on that. Yet." Atlas pauses. "There is something else. But it's good news. It's something you may want to take advantage of."

"And what is that?"

"The twins are unprotected."

That really gets his attention. He sits up straight, staring hard at Atlas's dark eyes which look like black holes across the dimly lit office. "How do you know?"

Atlas doesn't say anything for a moment. Bellamy knows he won't be forthcoming. Let him keep his secrets. Atlas has many connections to the city of San Francisco, ones he won't speak of, plus there is the magic that Atlas possesses, magic that even Bellamy doesn't fully understand the origins of. Something about his bloodline being connected to Edgar Allan Poe.

"Solon and Lenore are in Italy with Valtu," Atlas eventually says. "There is no real protection in the house with Solon gone. If I can get through to Ezra, then—"

"You're not doing this alone," Bellamy interrupts him, tapping his long nails against the worn desk. "Get us the first plane out of here."

"Sir, I can handle it—"

"No. I am not taking any more chances with my subordinates. Look what happened the last time I did. She's dead, Atlas. Do you want that to be you? No. We will take the twins, we'll take the mother, kill the rest. I'm going to personally step inside that blasted house." He pauses, his eyes going to the anemic sunlight coming through the stained-glass window. "Besides, it would be nice to trade in the gloom of Scotland for the gloom of San Francisco, wouldn't you agree?"

And so, they make their plans.

CHAPTER I

ROSE

NOW

T's funny how we're taught that the secret to life is knowing who we really are. That once we look deep, spend years soul-searching and find out who that person really is at the core of us, that the rest of our life will fall into place. Finding our "authentic, true selves" means we will finally find peace.

It's a lie, like all the other lies that our identity-obsessed society tells us.

It's not that we can't know who we are, rather that we are always changing. We are fluid. The moment we think we have figured out who we are and what we want, something inside of us changes. Always in motion, never in stasis. Even those that fear they are stuck are actually on the move, doing what they can to break free, flinging themselves against a wall again and again, hoping their confines will crumble.

My whole life I was told I had one identity: a vampire.

Or rather, that when I turned twenty-one, I would become a vampire.

So my identity has been someone waiting for that

clarity of self. I was Rose Harper, I moved around a lot, I had an older brother, parents who loved me, I spent my childhood as most humans did, and one day I would rely on human blood for survival. My biology and chemistry would change, I would go through The Becoming, and come out the other side as something more than I was before. I would finally be whole.

I had prayed my whole life, in silent, pitiful cries inside my mind as I lay in bed at night cast toward an unknown creator, that once I turned, once I became what I was supposed to be, that everything else would fall into place. That I would know peace, instead of this raging, turbulent chaos inside of me, one that jerked me from one emotion to the next my whole life. That the feeling of being incomplete, of missing something, of not being able to fit in with society, of being seen as an *other*, would finally go away.

I always felt there were different people locked inside me and I kept pinballing between them all, not knowing where I'd land.

But now I know the truth.

Now the truth has blasted through my veins along with the primal drive to drink blood.

I just turned into a vampire.

I just discovered who I *really* am.

And there will be no peace.

I'm standing in the garage, staring at the bags of blood in the fridge. I want to drink them all in one go because the need for blood is insatiable—like a painful combination of thirst and hunger that makes me believe I'll go mad without it. And yet the realization of who I am—who I have been—makes me feel just as crazed. I need the truth and I need it immediately.

I relent to my vampire instincts and grab the bags,

tearing them open with teeth that have turned into fangs, a process that's seamless, just a warm sensation in my gums as they sharpen in real time. The blood goes down my throat in seconds and it isn't until both bags are empty that I feel that incessant hunger subside.

Then I yank open the door with newfound strength and step into the house. I had been locked inside for the last few days, but my mother had untied me earlier when she realized that I was no longer a danger to myself or anyone else, and now I'm free to leave. I know I need a shower something fierce, my sense of smell is so strong now it's overwhelming, but all of that pales in comparison to the true need I have inside me.

The need for the truth.

I head right down the hall toward the kitchen where I can hear my mother laughing about something. I can hear my father talking as if he were right next to me. My senses are heightened to the point of being uncomfortable.

They both stop to stare at me as I barge into the kitchen and stop at the granite island in the middle, my hands gripping the counter like I'd crumble to my knees without it.

"Rose?" my mother asks, her violet eyes filled with worry. "Are you okay?"

"Where is Dracula?" I manage to say, my voice sounding foreign, deeper, like I'm hearing someone else speak.

My mother frowns. "What? Dracula? Honey, you should sit down, you're going through a lot. Have you had your blood yet?"

She comes over to me, but I hold my ground, my body starting to shake with rage.

"No!" I cry out. "No. Dracula. There's a real-life Dracula, I know there is, you've talked about him. Where is he?"

"Rose," my father says gently. "You've just transitioned. I understand you have a lot of questions right now. But your mother and I are going to help you through this. We both went through the same thing as you."

His words produce a sharp stabbing pain in my heart, because I know he's lying. I know it now. There were things that have thrown me off in the past, things my mother has said about her transition into a vampire that contradicted each other. But I can't focus on that right now.

I need answers.

I need to find Valtu.

A name that hadn't meant anything to me for the last twenty-one years and now, now that name means everything to me.

Because he was my everything.

Time and time again.

"You've told me that there is a vampire that inspired Bram Stoker to write Dracula," I say, trying to keep my emotions in check, even though they're coming in from all directions. I feel like a ship being slammed by waves, water pouring in through the portholes. "You said you knew him. That he helped you once. Where does he live? Is he...is he still alive?"

Oh god. What if he's not?

My father bristles, his hazel eyes flickering with a hit of discomfort. I've seen him do this before when Dracula was mentioned and there's something about that, something about all of this that feels like if I just thought a little harder, dug a little deeper, that I'd discover something big.

Bigger than the fact that I've just remembered all my past lives.

"I believe so," my mother says, sounding confused. "But we haven't seen him...it's been a long time."

"I need to find him," I tell her.

"Why?"

My father clears his throat. "Rose, what has gotten into you? Why are you so interested in Dracula? Do you think he's the king of the vampires? You know that's not the case."

I stare at him for a moment. I'm so used to never seeing my parents age, that sometimes I forget how close in age we appear. My father will never look a day over thirty-five. He will always look like a tall, Nordic guy with big muscles and thick dark-blond hair.

I look at my mother. She should look the same as me. Not literally, of course—she has violet eyes and black hair, I have green eyes and red hair, inherited from my father's side, I've always assumed. But she should look twenty-one, the age she would have transitioned.

But she doesn't. For the first time I'm realizing my mother looks older than twenty-one. Not as old as my father, but closer to thirty.

"Rose," my mother says, folding her arms. "I know you're going through a lot right now, but please tell us what's going on."

How do I even explain this? They're going to think I'm crazy.

I think I'm crazy.

I just know I have to find Valtu.

Suddenly more memories, more realizations flood my brain.

I remember the last people I was with as Dahlia Abernathy.

Lenore.

Solon.

The vampires from San Francisco.

They were with me when I died.

When my lover killed me.

Oh my god.

"Are you crying?" my mom asks, coming toward me again and before I can push her away, I realize tears are streaming down my face.

The anger in Valtu's eyes. How hurt he was at my betrayal, at finding out I was a witch. And yet he didn't know who I truly was. Not until I was dead. Not until my glamour had slipped away and he would have realized he just murdered his true love.

My mom's arms go around me and she holds me tight. "It's okay. I know it can be a lot."

"I'll go get my scotch," my dad says. "You need a little something."

"Wolf, she needs more blood," my mom says to my dad, calling him by his nickname as he leaves the kitchen. "Not alcohol." She shakes her head as she looks at me. "He thinks that's the answer to everything."

I pull back, unable to explain my emotions, but I have to try. "Lenore and Solon. They are vampire friends of yours, right? I've met them before, I remember."

"Yes," she says uneasily. "When you were young."

"How young?"

She frowns. "Rose, what is with—"

"How young was I?

"I don't know. Ten? Nine?"

That would explain why Lenore and Solon didn't recognize me. At that age I was moon-faced and gangly, not sharp-jawed and full-figured like I am now. They wouldn't have looked at me and seen Dahlia Abernathy as they knew her.

"Are they still in San Francisco?"

She stares at me for a moment. There's confusion in her eyes as to why I'm asking this shit, but there's also something else. Duplicity. Like she wants to lie.

"I think so," she eventually says. "But why are you asking?"

"You said they were your and dad's closest friends. Why haven't you seen them for the last ten years?"

She blinks, her mouth opening for a moment. "Oh, well you know how it is. We've moved a lot, Rose."

"And why?"

"You know why. We're vampires. People get suspicious if you don't age."

I know that's the truth, but I also know that there's more to it. That all of this is connected somehow, and I've been kept from a great lie my entire life, I just don't know what it is.

"Do you know who Dahlia Abernathy is?" I ask and the name, her name, *my name*, sounds like a powerful curse.

I watch my mother carefully for any hint of recognition. She seems to think it over, but her face is blank. "The name sounds familiar but I can't place it. Why? Who is she?"

I take in a deep breath as my father steps into the kitchen, a bag of blood in one hand, a glass of liquor in the other. "I couldn't choose," he says, coming over and placing both on the counter.

I don't even eye them. I don't want either drink right now.

"I think you're the one who will need the scotch," I warn him.

He frowns at that. My mom turns to him and says, "Do you know who Dahlia Abernathy is?"

My dad seems to recognize the name right away. "I didn't know her personally..."

Now my mom seems bothered by it, her shoulders straightening, eyes narrowing. She probably assumes it's some woman he knew. She always was the jealous type. If only she knew the truth, which she will any moment now.

"Well, who was she?" she asks.

"Dracula...Valtu," my dad says, his voice lowering. "She was his lover. The reincarnated one. The witch. The one he..."

"The one he killed," I fill in.

They both look at me. "Why are you asking about Valtu and his reincarnated witch lover?" my mom asks. "We never actually met her, we just heard about her from the others."

My eyes widen. "Did you hear about her from Valtu?"

My dad folds his arms across his chest. "Listen, Rose, you're going to need to explain why you're asking all these questions before we answer them. I'm being serious here."

I look between the both of them. There's so much I want to say and so much I want to know, that I don't know where to start.

But I have to start somewhere.

"Valtu killed Dahlia because Lenore had seen through her glamour," I explained, watching the confusion in their eyes grow. "Lenore saw that she was a witch in disguise, recognizing her as only another witch could. But what Lenore did not see was that Dahlia was not only a witch, but the reincarnated lover of Valtu's...and it was only just before that all of those repressed memories came back into Dahlia's head. Dahlia remembered all her past lives...but too late."

"How do you know all of this?" my dad asks carefully.

Another deep breath. It does nothing to calm my racing heart.

"Because it's happened again."

They exchange a bewildered look. "What do you mean?" my mom asks.

"*I* was Dahlia. And I was Lucy. And I was Mina."

They just stare at me for a moment. Finally my mother gives a shake of her head, puts her hand on my shoulder. "Okay, honey you need to sit down."

I stay rooted, grinding my teeth together. "I don't need to sit down. I need you to listen to me. I know this sounds crazy, but I am his reincarnated love. The minute the blood went down my throat is the minute I remembered everything. I remember every single life. Dahlia's feels like it happened yesterday, the others are more foggy, like a dream from long ago, but the emotions are still there. I'm not just Rose Harper. I'm everyone else as well, and I'm destined to be with Valtu."

The truth hangs in the air like fog. But I can tell neither of them believe me.

"You must have read about this online," my father says, reaching for the glass of scotch. I knew he'd need it. "Reincarnation...it's rare, okay, it happened to Valtu's lovers, but not to you. Not to our daughter."

"You don't want to believe me, because you don't like him," I say. "Because you're the one whose girl he stole once upon a time." And as those words leave my lips, the clarity of the truth hits me in the face like a cold shovel.

I feel my expression fall as the realization comes over me. "Wolf isn't your nickname. Wolf is your real name, isn't it? It's not John." I look at my mother. "And you...your name isn't Yvonne. Your real name is Amethyst."

Though both my parents are naturally pale, the color from their faces seem to drain in unison.

"Why did you change your names?" I lick my lips

anxiously, feeling like I'm on the edge of something, and that everything else in my life I took for granted is close to collapsing. "What are you running from?"

My father takes a step toward my mother, slipping his hand around her waist, steadying her. She already seems like she's going weak at the knees, and my mother is not the kind of woman to show weakness in any way.

I feel fury toward her that only a daughter can, a daughter that's been coddled and lied to her whole life. I want to maim her, to make the truth come out. Being a vampire has turned me into a monster already.

"You didn't even turn," I accuse her, wincing at how ferocious I sound. "You weren't born a vampire. You were made one."

"Rose," my father says sharply as my mother's eyes grow wet, full of pain.

"You both lied to me! My whole life!" I cry, throwing my arms out, feeling the anger coursing through me. "I never questioned it, but how could I? You taught me that vampires that were turned by another would not only turn into monsters, but could never procreate. So what is it?"

"Rose, you are my daughter," she manages to say, her voice shaking. "I can promise you that."

"But you weren't born a vampire. Lenore turned you into one. Didn't she?"

She presses her lips together into a thin pink line as tears run down her cheeks, her mascara running.

My dad leans in and kisses her on the head, giving her shoulders a squeeze. "Come on, baby," he says to her. "It's time we tell them the truth. Dylan, too."

So, it's not just me then. My brother has also been fed lies.

My god, so many lies. I was fed lies as Dahlia, too,

spending my whole life believing that my parents were killed by vampires when it was actually Bellamy, head of the witch's guild, that had them murdered so I would be a more dutiful soldier for him.

A sharp stab of fire emanates in my gut. They may have been my parents from another lifetime, but I remember them as Dahlia would, and their loss and the truth causes deep burning pain.

I have so much vengeance inside me, I don't even know where to start.

"Dylan!" my dad yells down the hallway.

In moments my brother appears, hair looking disheveled and his t-shirt askew like we just woke him up from a nap.

"What's up?" he asks, scratching his head as he stares at my parents with puzzlement. Then he looks at me and gives me a lazy grin. "Ah, hey Rose. You're up. You all vamped out now?"

"They've been lying to us, Dylan," I say to him.

His brows furrow as he looks at me, then them. "What do you mean?"

"I mean we're about to explain everything," my dad says.

"No," my mother says softly. Her hands grasp at my father's sleeve. "Honey, they'll be in danger if they know."

"Baby, they've always been in danger. It's about time they know why."

CHAPTER 2
VALTU
THEN

"Valtu?" Lenore says gently.

I've been sitting on the floor of the kitchen, cradling Dahlia in my arms like a newborn. But she is not a newborn. She is the opposite of that. She is dead and I am holding onto her because I know eventually I'll have to stop. These last moments with her, even though her heart has stopped beating and her spirit has moved on, are all I have left.

I want to hold her forever. Never let go, even as she's put into a grave with me and she rots in my grasp.

I woke up this morning a man in love. I felt something for Dahlia I never thought I'd feel again. I felt hope. I felt a future. I felt happy for the first time since Lucy died.

I was given a second chance at life.

But then it all came crashing down on me.

It all ended because of my own hand.

My own temper.

My own violence.

It never lets me forget the monster I have buried inside.

And now I see Dahlia for who she really is. The woman I

love now, but also the women I loved then. Love stacked on love stacked on love and I smashed it all to smithereens with my own hand.

I've lost her again.

"Valtu," Lenore says again, crouching down beside me. She tries hard not to look at Dahlia, even though she wants to. I know she feels guilty for what she did and I'm too drained to be angry at her. I know my anger will return and she might be on the receiving end of it, but until then, I just feel an emptiness so vast I fear I'll disintegrate into nothing.

No. That's not quite true. I don't fear that.

I *want* that.

To disappear.

To be with Dahlia in that vast nothingness.

"We have to do something," Lenore goes on. "I know how hard this is for you, but we have to do something about her..." she trails off, unable to finish her sentence. Unable to say the word "body."

"There will be people looking for her," she adds, with urgency in her voice now. "Friends, family, the school will notice she's missing. We have to cover this up."

I give my head a shake. It feels like the most energy I can spare. "She has no family."

"Are you sure? Are you sure that wasn't a lie—"

"She has no family," I repeat, my words sharper now. I stare at her hard enough that she flinches and moves back. "That wasn't a lie. You heard her yourself. Her parents were killed. By this, this *Bellamy*. There was no one else in her life. I knew Dahlia, I knew everything about her except that she was a witch. She wasn't lying. She had no one."

But, briefly, she had me.

Lenore presses her lips together for a moment, thinking. "Okay. I believe you. But I also know witches. Valtu, she was sent here to kill you. She wasn't alone in this. I know how they work. She knew someone else in this city. She had a friend, another witch, a contact, I guarantee it. They're going to sound the alarm when they find out she's missing."

"Maybe they won't. Maybe they figure Dahlia disappeared like so many other people have been doing in this city."

"Which is something else we need to look into," Lenore says.

I know there are pressing things outside of this moment, but I honestly don't care. Let Saara and Aleksi's demons eat the whole city. Let everyone rot. What's the point? What's the point of saving people in a world that allows something like this to happen?

But you have to avenge her, a voice inside my head says, and I stare at the freckles across Dahlia's nose. *You have to make sure her death wasn't for nothing.*

And yet I'm the one who killed her. Me. I did this.

How do I get vengeance on myself?

"Maybe we should go to her apartment. I take it you know where that is?" Lenore asks.

Of course. Her apartment. I never stepped inside of it. Never saw her place. I don't know why that didn't struck me as odd, but now I realize she was trying to protect herself, hide her true self from me. Which means there might be things there that could be useful.

"Whatever is there, we will have to remove it," Lenore says delicately, picking up on my thoughts. "We can make it look like she left on her own accord."

I hate this. I hate how quickly everything has changed. I can't even mourn her properly without having to cover our tracks and make it seem like I didn't fucking murder her.

Because that's what I am.

A murderer.

Not that it's anything new. I've murdered countless souls in my past, and I'll murder again. But this time it's something unforgivable.

"Valtu," Solon says, shutting the doors to the backyard and coming inside as he slips his phone in his pocket. "I hate to be the one who pulls you away from this and you know I always mean respect, but we have to decide what to do with Dahlia, and we have to decide now. Each moment we delay puts us all in direct danger. You don't want your life here to end."

I give him a look that says, *why not?*

He exhales heavily and I know he's trying to do what's best and what's right. He knows what to do—vampires are skilled at hiding the dead—and he wants to be able to do it without me getting in the way.

I look back down at Dahlia, at the dried blood splattered on her face, my blood that I had tried in vain for her to take. I need to leave her. I need to say goodbye.

I don't know how this time.

Solon comes over and puts his hands under Dahlia's arms and lifts her up and out of my hands. The feeling of her body, dead or not, no longer pressed against mine makes me instantly bereft. Hollowed out into nothing. Without her I am just a void.

"Where are you taking her?" I ask, my voice barely audible, my throat raw, my fingers curling over nothing into fists.

"We need to hide her," he says, staring down at me. The sight of her lifeless in his arms bleeds my heart dry. "We can have a service for her. But I think the only course of action is to put her in the boat, tie her down with bricks, and put her in the water. We'll wait till night, take her out past Lido."

The words are so callous.

"What are you doing with her now?"

"He's helping you," Lenore says, taking me by the elbow and pulling me to my feet. "You need to clean up. We all do. Then we need to go to her apartment. Okay?"

I nod and in a daze I let Lenore lead me up the stairs to the bathroom.

I let her clean me up, dabbing a washcloth to get off my own blood.

Then she leaves and I get changed into new clothes. I'm moving so slowly it feels like I've come apart from time as a whole. Like I'm operating just outside of it. Being a vampire means you're very in tune with your body and the world around you, but I've never felt more removed. Like the world is ticking on but I've stepped outside of time's path.

It's only when the three of us leave my house—Solon put Dahlia to rest somewhere until we get back—that I feel a little more life seep back into me. Purpose. Because if I can't have my love back, I can at least get started on making those that wronged her pay. She wouldn't have been sent to kill me, she wouldn't have been corrupted, had Bellamy and the guild of witches not killed her parents and forced her to be a slayer.

Still, the walk to her apartment feels like a dream. Not even a nightmare, because a nightmare would make things feel more real. But that terrible disassociation is back. I'm walking through my beloved city of Venice feeling like a ghost.

When we get to her apartment, just the sight of it makes me freeze. Suddenly the last thing I want to do is go inside there. But Lenore puts a cloaking spell over us to make sure we aren't seen, and somehow I find myself in the building. Though I'd never been in her apartment, I know which unit is hers and we head up the rickety staircase to the one at the end, facing the lagoon. I had told Dahlia that where she was staying was one of the most haunted areas in all of Venice, and now I'm feeling like hundreds of restless spirits are crowding around me, knowing what I did.

Judging me.

"What is this dark energy?" Lenore says, scrunching up her nose as she looks around the hallway, the floor tiles cracked in some places. "You'd think the guild with all their money would have put her up some place a little nicer."

"How much money does the guild have?" Solon asks.

"A lot," she says emphatically.

I stop in front of Dahlia's door, about to put my hand on the knob, despite knowing it will be locked, when I hear a faint noise from inside. And if I can barely hear it, that means whoever is there is really trying to be quiet.

I give the others a furtive look and put my finger to my lips. We all breathe in deeply in unison, expecting to smell a witch. But there's nothing.

There's a moment's pause before I pull back and then slam my shoulder into the door. It pops open with ease and I manage to see a woman going for the window, as if to climb out.

In seconds I'm at her, hand around her mouth, arm around her stomach, holding her in place.

"Who are you?" I seethe. I'm practically seeing red.

The woman squirms beneath me. She's strong but not strong enough to fight me off. I know that she might be a building manager, or maybe a classmate of Dahlia's, and that I'm dangerously close to hurting a civilian, but I can't think straight either. I just want answers. I just want the pain to go away.

"She's a witch!" Lenore cries out as Solon tries to close the door behind her. I know we're being loud, so I pray the cloaking spell holds. "She has a glamour on!"

The woman struggles even more and that's when I know it's true. Now that I know what to look for with glamour, it's something you can figure out. It's like staring at one of those paintings that look like something and morph into something else when the light hits it from a different angle.

"Search the apartment," I growl.

"What are we looking for?" Solon asks.

"The blade," Lenore says as they both start looking in drawers and under the bed. "That's probably why she's here too. She wants the blade of *mordernes*."

"So you're from the guild," I say to the girl, my words coming out like venom. "Tell me, did you set her up to fail? Was she sent here knowing she would fail in killing me? Was it a way for the guild to get rid of her, just as they got rid of her parents?"

"I found it," Solon says.

He's pulling a box out of the cupboard, hidden behind a fake wall. None of us vampires have to look at it to know what's in the box. We can sense the blade is there, its energy insidious.

The girl starts to struggle again. The stench of adrenaline and fear is high but that doesn't stop me from holding on so tight that I could break every bone with one twist of my hands.

"Where is she?" the girl manages to say. "What did you do to Dahlia?"

"You pretend to care?" I sneer. "You threw Dahlia to the wolves."

"And you are the wolves," the girl says through a gasp. "The wolves that tore her apart. I should have known she'd fallen in love with you. I should have known you were using her this whole time. I don't know how you vampires can live with yourselves."

I don't know how either.

The rage inside of me breaks and bubbles over and I'm not only seeing red, I'm feeling it too. Towards the witches, towards this girl, towards myself.

I take her head in my hands, palms pressed against her skin, fingers digging into her scalp, and before Solon has the chance to yell "No!" I twist my wrists quickly.

I break the girl's neck with a sickly crack that seems to bounce off the walls of Dahlia's apartment.

I step back and the girl crumbles to the floor, dead.

CHAPTER 3
ROSE
NOW

My parents gesture to the kitchen table. My brother and I sit down and my attention is briefly stolen by the clouds on the horizon outside the large bay windows. Our house isn't huge, but it's on the beach just north of Newport, and every day the view seems to change. I liked to think that I could control the weather with my moods and now, with the ocean roaring, dark gray and aqua curling into a powerful spray of white seafoam, I wonder even more. With the way the clouds are hanging low and charcoal gray, I feel a thread of electricity between me and the sky, like we are both plugged into the same socket.

Like it used to be, I find myself thinking. When I was Dahlia.

Did that mean that whatever witchcraft she had is still in my veins? God, I hope so.

"Someone tell me what's going on," Dylan says, sounding utterly annoyed.

"Rose," my father explains to him, "has discovered something about herself."

Dylan looks at me with a dry expression. "That she's a vampire?"

"I'm remembering past lives," I tell him, and his glassy eyes widen with disbelief. "But that's not the point of all of this. It's that I remember people, vampires, talking about mom and dad before I was born."

My brother slowly blinks. Even if he isn't drowsy from a nap, or possibly high, this would still be confusing to him.

"And," I go on, "I remember that their names aren't John and Yvonne. It's Wolf and Amethyst."

Dylan snorts. "Dad's nickname is Wolf."

"That's not his nickname. That's his real name."

"And who told you that?"

I glance at my parents who are hovering near the table, my father rubbing my mother's back.

"An old friend of mine," I say carefully, looking back at him. I don't want to bring up the whole Valtu/Dracula thing right now, because I know my brother has a fascination with him and all sorts of vampire lore, and I need things to stay on topic. I'm sure there will be endless questions in the future, and I'm more than happy to divulge them because I know the more I talk about it, the more I'll remember.

And the more I'll make sense of it.

The more I'll understand all the people I've been.

Because right now, it's just percolating beneath the surface, waiting to bubble over.

"Okay, so what's the danger then?" Dylan asks Mom and Dad. "If what Rose is saying is true, which is just far out, what does that have to do with us being in danger? You literally used the word *danger*."

I stare at my parents, waiting for the truth. My stomach

gurgles a little, a mild feeling of thirst passing through me, but I ignore it.

My dad runs a hand through his hair, a perfect mix of light brown and dark blond. I was always told that I got my red hair from his Norwegian side, but now I wonder if that's true. I'm starting to wonder if he really is my father. If what I remembered is true, how is it that they had me? My mother said I'm her child, but we were always told that vampires that were created by other vampires couldn't procreate.

"We may have been keeping some stuff from you," my dad says. "But it was for your own good."

"Okay...what stuff?" Dylan asks.

My parents exchange another harried look between themselves. Then my mother turns her attention to the window, watching as the storm clouds get closer. Rain starts to splatter against the panes and it's like I can feel that rain inside my chest, against my ribs.

She takes in a deep breath, brushing her dark hair behind her ear.

"I wasn't born a vampire," she says in a low voice.

I figured that, but to hear it is still a shock. And from the look on my brother's face, he's even more surprised than I am.

"What do you mean?" he asks. "How is that possible? Those that are turned, turn into monsters. You're annoying at times, but you're not a monster. Not to mention they can't, like, have children." A deeper look of horror comes across his face. "Are we adopted?"

"No," my father says emphatically. "You are biologically our children."

"Really," my mother says, her eyes full of tears. "You are. I was created by a vampire who is part witch. For whatever reason, she's able to turn people into vampires and not monsters."

"Lenore," I say, wondering if now that I'm a vampire, am I still part witch? Am I the same?

She nods. "Yes. Lenore. I asked her to do it."

"Why?" I ask.

She looks at my father. "Because I didn't want your father to go through life without me."

"I probably wouldn't have let her, had I known," my father says tiredly. "We had been friends for so long and had just gotten together..."

"My mother had just died," she explains. "And I was so broken. And Lenore...she brought back her lover, Solon, from the dead and he was fine so we took the chance. I almost died for good. But when she was done, I was a vampire. Of course, we didn't think I could get pregnant, but then I did."

"With me," Dylan says.

There's a flash of hesitation on her face. Then she smiles brightly. "Yes. You were born Dylan. You were a miracle." She looks at me. "And then you were our next miracle."

I frown, not liking the idea of being a miracle. "So then, why hide this from us? And why change your names? Our last name isn't really Harper, is it?"

My dad sighs and pulls out the chair across from us, sitting down, his tall frame making the chair seem tiny. "It isn't. Your mother and I never officially got married. But when we found out she was pregnant, we decided Dylan's last name would be mine. My real one. Eriksen."

"So why Harper? Why change?" I ask.

My mother comes over and puts her hand on his shoulder. "Word got out that I was an anomaly. Not only a vampire that was created and turned by another without going mad, but one that could have children." She takes in a trembling breath, her violet eyes filling with tears again. "We were afraid..."

"We thought it safest if we went into hiding," my father finishes for her. "It's not just humans we have to be cautious about in this world. It's witches. It's other vampires."

"Other vampires? Witches?" Dylan asks.

I try not to bristle at the way he said witches. We've been taught that witches are our enemy, not vampires. But because Dahlia was a witch, well, I know exactly why vampires fear them. Us. Fuck, this is confusing.

"Not all vampires operate with the same moral codes as us," my father explains patiently. "And I'm not talking about the occasional killing here and there in the name of sustenance. That happens. It's not something to be proud of or condone. But it happens. I'm talking about vampires who kill to kill. Who want to dominate the human species as a whole. Keep them as pets. That sort of mentality."

And that's when I remember why I was in Venice.

To get back the book that fell into the hands of Saara and Aleksi.

"The vampires!" I suddenly exclaim. "The ones in Venice. Saara and Aleksi. They had a book, that's why the guild sent me there, to get it back. What happened to them? What happened to the book?"

"Valtu killed them," my mom says, and a burst of pride goes through me.

"Well, he thought he did," corrects my father. "He killed Aleksi, but Saara is still alive. She managed to survive some-how. We think maybe she had learned some magic to thwart death, we aren't sure. She's now the head of that sect of vampires. The ones who want to enslave humanity and kill any vampire that resists. Her and another vampire called Enoch. They're trying to become the next Skarde with a vampire army."

I shudder. "And the book?"

My mother chews on her lip for a long moment. I'm about to ask again when she finally says, "Valtu has the book."

"What book?" Dylan asks. "Man, this is *crazy*," he adds, slapping his hands on his knees.

"The Book of Verimagiaa," our father says. "It's a book of spells made accessible to vampires, rumor has it that it was created by a vampire and a witch together. Very powerful if it's in the wrong hands..." his words trail off and his tone deepens, as if insinuating Valtu is the wrong hands.

"So, it's out of their hands," I say. "And out of the guild's hands, too. That's good news. Valtu will protect it."

My parents look at each other for a moment and something drops in my chest.

My mother clears her throat and looks at me. "A lot has changed since then, Rose," she says. "Valtu isn't exactly the same vampire that you...that he was."

I swallow. "What do you mean? What happened to him?"

"Rose," my father says gently, "you need to give us some time to come to terms with all of this. It's one thing for us to tell you why we're in hiding—"

"But you haven't *really* told us why," Dylan interjects, raising his hand.

"It's another thing," he goes on, ignoring his son, "it's another for you to tell us all about your ex-lives. I'm still not sure I believe it."

"You think I'm lying?!" I exclaim, pushing my chair back with such force I nearly fall out of it.

"Honey, please," my mom says, glaring at my dad for a second. "That's not it. It's just...maybe your wires got crossed. Maybe you were reading about Dracula, the real story, before the transition, and then all these hormones and chemical changes in your brain, maybe they—"

I get to my feet. "I'm not lying!" I yell just as a giant bolt of lightning hits the sundeck, frying the wood with an explosive bang.

"What the fuck?" Dylan yells, and now everyone is on their feet, staring at the fire as it smolders in the rain.

"Did you do that?" my dad asks me in a hushed voice.

I don't know what to say. Even as Dahlia I never had the magic to make lightning strike. Now it feels like my emotions are connected to the weather. An elemental witch? Something more? Something...else?

"I don't know," I whisper.

"I think we better drop this subject," my mom says nervously. "Before—"

"Hell no," Dylan says, pivoting his attention back to them. "You never told us why you changed your names. You said that you went into hiding because of other vampires. Or witches," he glances at me suspiciously. "Why would they care about you?"

"That's a conversation for another time," my father says.

"Another time? Why not now? It's all coming out, from the fact that you changed your names, to mom not being born a vampire, to us being in hiding, to Rose being reincarnated. Might as well tell us everything."

"Because of you!" my mother yells. "Because of you and Rose. Because I might have passed down the power that

Lenore gave me. That maybe *you* can create vampires that don't turn into monsters. That's exactly what Saara and Enoch would want. A way to have vampires take over the earth. They could do tests on you, force you to create more, add more minions to their army. Not to mention what the witches might do..."

"And maybe they want your mother for the same reasons," my dad says gruffly. "We couldn't take any more chances..." His eyes get misty and he looks away. Clears his throat. "Anyway. We did the best we could to keep all of us safe."

He goes over to my mother and puts his arm around her. "Now, if you kids don't mind, I need to talk to your mother alone. This is a lot to bring up in one go. We thought we buried this part of our past behind us, but I guess not."

He kisses her head gently and then guides her out of the kitchen.

Dylan watches them go and then shakes his head, going after them. "No way. I have too many questions."

"Dylan," I warn, wishing he would leave them alone, but he disappears down the hall.

I exhale, feeling weak and shaky, run my hand over my face as if it will clear the cobwebs. I stare out at the smoldering deck, the wooden boards charred. There's no more thunder or lightning, just rain and low clouds turning the day into twilight. I don't know if it's my witch side or my vampire side, but everything seems so much more alive.

And so much more painful.

There's more to what my parents just told me. Dylan suspects it too, but they won't give him anything. I've seen my father shut things down before when he gets that cagey look in his eye, and this won't be an exception.

What a fucking way to transition. My whole life I waited until the day I turned twenty-one, when I would finally step into the vampire I was destined to become.

Now it feels like destiny is fucking me over once again.

I've not only become a vampire, I've discovered I was and maybe am part witch. And that I am part of a long line of souls that keeps getting reincarnated. But brought back for what purpose? Is it as I promised Valtu, that my heart would always find his? Or is it something greater than that?

Why do I remember?

Why am I here *again*?

I close my eyes and a powerful surge of love washes over me, sinking into the marrow of my bones, making me feel borderline nauseous and dizzy.

I loved Valtu, and I still do.

I still do.

But where is he in this big bad world?

What has he done with the book? What has the book done with him?

And how the hell am I going to find him again?

...does he even want me to?

CHAPTER 4
VALTU

THEN

Two women died at my hand on the same day.

Two witches.

And yet, after the loss of Dahlia, I feel nothing for taking the life of the other witch. A sign that my humanity has been compromised, but my soul feels too ravaged to care. Frankly, it's hard to care about anything.

But Solon and Lenore care. They care about the bigger picture. To me there is no picture at all, just a negative, like watching film get developed in reverse.

So tonight we're getting rid of two bodies.

There is no moon, we have no lights, but we can see. The three of us living beings in my small motorboat with two dead ones.

We go past the long island of Lido, past the channel markers, out into the Gulf of Venice. The waves are big out here, and there are boats and ferries going back and forth, their lights bobbing with the swell, but we move easily through the dark.

I bring the boat to a stop when I think the water's deep enough.

It's cold. I shouldn't be cold but I am. It smells like snow and sorrow on the wind. I stare over into the inky depths and I wonder what would happen if I latched the bricks onto myself. If I sank to the bottom with my dove. Her wings may be clipped now but that doesn't mean I have to be without her.

"Valtu," Solon says gently, but there's a warning in his voice. He knows my thoughts. "We need you here."

Why? So I can kill someone else?

So I can lose someone else?

"We'll get rid of the witch first," Lenore says. She leans down and picks up the girl by the shoulders. I feel like this is the first time I'm getting a real look at her. I don't know her name but she's pretty, maybe late thirties, smooth skin and dark hair. I wonder if she was a true friend to Dahlia or if she operated under Bellamy's thumb. It's possible she was both.

Solon reaches down and takes her feet, the bricks resting on her stomach, and they unceremoniously dump the body overboard. The witch goes in with a splash then immediately sinks. I look away, not wanting to see her face as it disappears into the depths.

"Valtu?" Lenore says softly and I realize I've been looking off into the darkened distance for a while. "It's time."

I look down to see her and Solon holding onto Dahlia, this time with more reverence.

"Did you want to say a few words?" Lenore asks.

I shake my head. There is nothing to say. Nothing that I can say that would be a tribute to her, to our love, to any of this.

Once upon a time, I would have told her that I'd see her again.

This time I'm not so sure.

This time I feel, because I'm the one that killed her, that she won't be coming back.

If I were to say goodbye, it would be final.

Lenore and Solon hesitate, then they carefully place Dahlia in the ocean.

This time I watch as she sinks.

Watch as her pale face is swallowed by the deep, her hair flowing around her like silken seaweed.

And then the words finally come to me.

"I'm sorry," I say.

I'm so fucking sorry.

A FEW DAYS PASS. At least I think they do.

Time takes on a new form. No longer this thing that is on my side, a friend for eternity. Now it's the enemy. It flipped while it was in the trenches with me. Pulled a gun. Told me it was going to hold me hostage now, trapping me in it in never-ending agony.

Time has turned on me and taken me for a ride before. Then, I used the betrayal as fuel, as a springboard for my monstrous ways. I used it as much as it used me. But this time around, I am a slave to it, in the never-ending current that all immortals are blessed with. No. No, now I see it's not a blessing at all. But a curse, its roots twisting in deep, fastening me to eternity like a tree growing through stone.

"Valtu," Bitrus says in a gentle voice, an equally gentle hand placed on top of mine.

I swivel my head toward him, wincing slightly at the slice of sunlight bouncing off the windows of my neighbor across the canal.

"What do you want to do?" he asks.

I blink and adjust my sunglasses. Look around. We aren't alone. Sitting in my back garden in Venice are Lenore and Solon, as well as Bitrus and Van Helsing. It was only two nights ago that I said goodbye to my beloved Dahlia as she sank to the watery depths. There hasn't been any time for me to process anything, but I know my grief over my lost love has affected my cognitive abilities. I know of the pressing matter at hand, at the danger of having Saara and Aleksi in charge of the book, of monsters or whatever the hell is roaming around this city, but I simply do not care. I don't have it in me.

I manage to take in the faces of my friends. While Bitrus's dark face is looking at me with concern, taking his hand back gingerly, the others are talking animatedly. From the fury in Lenore's eyes, to the stern determination in Solon's, to the spark in Van Helsing's, I know their entire focus is on eradicating the vampires and taking back the book. The whole reason they have gathered here isn't because they feel I need companionship (I would rather be alone more than anything else), but because tonight they want us to ambush Poveglia, the island where the rogue vampires live.

You don't have to do this, Bitrus says to me inside my head. *I know Lenore and Solon are your friends, but don't you think they're a little too eager to get their hands on the book?*

I give Bitrus a steady look. *They are trustworthy*, I tell him.

The problem isn't them. It's me. I don't give a shit about anything anymore except for some way to end this constant pain and suffering inside me, this black and gaping maw that is eating me alive. Bitrus doesn't know Lenore and

Solon like I do, but even if they were planning on taking the book, they won't be able to. That book will be mine. Inside those cursed pages lay answers, keys to end my suffering. I know that if I get my hands on it before they do, I could possess more power than any other vampire, and I would use that power to bring Dahlia back from the dead.

There has to be a way. There has to be a spell to bring her back. Necromancy is one of the oldest dark arts, ones that vampires have never been privy to, for we're the ones who have never needed it, and it wouldn't be much of a grimoire if it didn't have a few spells for it.

Of course, being in possession of the book doesn't guarantee that the magic will work for me, and getting the book in my possession isn't guaranteed either. But that's really the only reason why I will be going to the island of Poveglia tonight.

Bitrus is still staring at me so I give him an even deeper look. *I'm fine*, I assure him. *And I'm going.*

Bitrus nods then takes a sip of his white wine and turns his attention to Solon. "Only Valtu and I will be allowed on the island. Perhaps it would be best if only the two of us went tonight."

"Absolutely not," Solon says firmly. "It's too risky. And Lenore and I are the only ones with magic of our own. You're going to need all the help you can get if you want them destroyed."

"You will be noticed," Bitrus counters.

"We won't," Lenore says, sitting up straight. "My cloaking spell will cover us. If Abe waits in the boat as getaway, it will cover him, too."

"Even with giant demonic plague doctors guarding the water?" Bitrus asks. For a moment I don't know what he's talking about, then it all comes flooding back. It's a risky thing we're going to do, and despite what Bitrus thinks, I know we need Lenore and Solon's magic to pull things off. It's the only way we can defeat Saara and Aleksi. Because Bitrus is right. It's not just the vampires we have to outsmart, we also have to get around the legion of demons and ghosts and monsters those two have been letting out into the waters of Venice, the same creatures preying on the humans in the town. We'd be foolish to think that we could do this without any magic.

"Her magic is strong," I manage to say, my eyes flitting briefly to Lenore. She looks both surprised and ashamed at my compliment, no doubt because of the guilt she still carries for Dahlia. "And Solon's is helpful. We'll need all the help we can get tonight."

Nearly everyone looks relieved. Probably because this is the first time I've really spoken about tonight, or really anything else for that matter. I see the look in their eyes, that little spark and hope that maybe I'll be okay, that maybe I'm on the mend, that there is this future where I am back to normal, back to the Valtu that they know, and this grief and sorrow will be past me once again. I'll get over Dahlia like I had to Lucy and Mina. *Oh Valtu*, they think, *thank god he's so resilient*.

I hate that look. I hate it because it reminds me that my grief makes them uncomfortable. That they would rather pretend it doesn't exist at all. That I don't exist at all. Because what am I without grief? There wouldn't be anything left of me. I would cease to exist. Grief is all I am.

"Then it's settled," Van Helsing says. Out of everyone, his expression is one of concern. He's the one who has been with me through grief before, and he's seen the animal I have become. I know he's waiting for the turn, wondering when it will happen. There is no relief in his eyes. "Tonight we'll head over to the island. Valtu, find some excuse to invite yourself over. If that doesn't take, we'll just have to chance it. We'll all go over on the boat, but only me, Lenore and Solon will be cloaked from the vampires and whatever else they have lurking on that island. We'll formulate a plan of attack so that they are surrounded. It would be helpful if we had some sort of plan or blueprint of the island."

"I'll see what I can come up with," Bitrus says. "I have a pretty good memory of how it's all organized. What we saw, at any rate. Since those two have a knack for torturing humans, they might use more sections of the island for it."

The rest of the afternoon melts into a blur again. There are voices and looks and plans and everything seems foreign to me, even the sun in the sky and the scent of muddied water and fish and oranges, and the taste of wine on my tongue. How quickly one's universe goes from familiar to foreign when loss has rearranged reality.

When night falls, I'm keeping myself going by focusing on the book. Focusing on Dahlia. I let my need to bring her back feed me, fuel me, until I want to kill Saara and her brother as much as the rest of them do, if only because I know they will never let me have the book willingly. It has corrupted them, and I know it has the power to do the same to me, but I know that once I get that spell I need to bring Dahlia back, I will gladly hand that book over to Solon for safekeeping.

It's a devilish night for our escapade. The moon is hiding somewhere, the city is strangely quiet and cold. There is fog just like there was fog before, a thick and damp blanket that snakes its hands down the canals. I think it has a few of us on edge, but to me it feels like we're doing the right thing. That this is an excellent night to kill some vampires, steal a tome of dark magic, and raise the dead.

I'm still nervous, though. Bitrus and I went to the Red Room for a while, to keep up appearances that everything is fine, that everything is normal, should someone wonder why I've missed teaching a class, and it was there that I happened upon Saara and basically invited myself over to their island under the guise of wanting a human to feed on and kill. Saara seems adept at reading others and I think I managed to block her from my innermost thoughts while letting her only see the superficial ones, ones I planted in my head as a decoy. It's not that hard once you learn how to do it, you just have to keep bouncing the same thoughts around inside your head like a ball.

That said, she invited me over with ease, which of course makes me suspicious that she knows something is afoot and this whole thing might be one giant trap. Especially as she was okay with the idea of me and Bitrus taking our own boat over instead of her sending out one of her plague doctors to collect us.

"We have to go into this thinking that they are onto us," I tell the others as we gather into my motorboat tethered to the canal behind my villa. "If we let our guards down for but a moment, I promise you it will be the end of all of us."

Solon gives me a funny look, his brows furrowing, perhaps wondering if I cared at all about the end of myself. Wheels are turning behind his stark blue eyes and I fear he may become suspicious of me, wary and watchful of my every move. Out of everyone here, I have the least to lose.

I have *nothing* to lose.

I stare right back at him, letting him know I'm not to be fucked with. He eventually blinks and looks away, though I feel some trust may have been broken. If not now, later.

I start the engine as Bitrus unties the boat and we motor quietly along the narrow *Rio Dei Frari*, the buildings looming over us like shadowy figures as we pass over the dark depths. I remember the demon in the water when I took Dahlia home after the recital, and even though the memory should have sent a wave of dread and trepidation through me, all it does is make fresh grief twist through my heart.

We are silent during our voyage, all of us scanning the opaque waters, peering through the fog. Even with our vision being better than any humans, the mist is still thick enough to obscure most things. I rely on just the mental map I'd made in my head from the last time I visited.

And then, when I start to fear that perhaps we overshot Lido and are out into the sea, a vision of Dahlia floating beneath the waves making my eyes pinch shut, Bitrus mutters, "There she is."

I open my eyes to see the faint outline of the island emerging from the fog. It still manages to send a shock of fear through me. Poveglia has so much history, sordid history, like most of the past, an island built on suffering and bones. The ghosts of that suffering still exist, haunting the island. It's not just the conjured demons and plague doctors that roam here, it's centuries of pain, humans discarded by their fellow men, isolated then tossed into plague pits to be forgotten. Ghosts have always fascinated vampires, but they terrify me. They're humans that have their own version of immortality, one locked in pain.

Perhaps they scare me because they remind me of myself.

I'm nothing but a ghost.

"We're here," Bitrus says softly, and I bring my attention back to the boat, moments before we nearly crash into the dock. We manage a smooth landing in the end, the waves rocking the boat, and then Saara, Aleksi, and two plague doctors appear out of the mist like shadowy phantoms, eyeing us distrustfully.

Here goes nothing.

CHAPTER 5
ROSE
NOW

"So, what does it feel like?" Dylan asks me as he drives his Jeep down the 101 into town, the beach to our right glowing pale while the crests of the waves catch the moonlight. It's been a few days since I became a vampire and we both learned the truth about our parents. In those few days I've done a lot of searching on the internet to find out more about what happened to Valtu, the guild, the vampires, anything. There's a whole lot of nothing out there, for the most part.

"What does what feel like?" I ask my brother, shielding my eyes as headlights from the passing cars blind me. Each day I'm finding it easier to be in my new, supersensitive skin, including eyes that hate bright lights and especially the sun, but I'm still not used to it yet. I'm not even used to drinking blood. Part of me craves it, the other part still finds it icky.

"What is it like to die?" he asks.

I glance at him. His expression is grave for once. I haven't really talked to him a lot these last few days. He's been keeping to himself, hanging out in the garage now that I'm not in there. The energy in the whole house has changed, becoming as somber as the gray clouds over the Pacific that only seemed to part tonight, and I know I'm to blame. I haven't been avoiding him, or my parents for that matter, just trying to figure out how to come to terms with everything the way that I normally do—alone.

But my parents, well, part of me thinks they might be avoiding me. There is a strange wariness when they look at me now, like they're waiting for me to lift up a mask and unveil someone else underneath. I don't know how to explain to them how I'm feeling or what I am, because I still don't understand it, but I do know that I can be Rose Harper, as much as I can be Dahlia, and Lucy, and Mina. My past doesn't erase who I am in the present. If anything, it adds to it. It gives me layers of life experience that weren't there before.

"You want to know what it's like to die?"

My brother nods. "Yeah. Who doesn't?"

Humans have been obsessed with death for all of time. I think vampires might share that same obsession. Vampires can die, of course, in three different ways—stabbed in the heart with the blade of *mordernes*, the slayer's blade; decapitation; or being burned alive. But I think the obsession comes with their own lack of real mortality.

I take in a deep breath, my eyes going to the stars that are peeking out from behind moving clouds. "It's peaceful," I admit. "The moments leading up to it can be awful, but all that awfulness disappears once you make it over. You realize how little that mattered. How little most things mattered."

"So what happened?"

"The first time I was Mina. And I died horrifically. At the hands of my father."

"Fucking hell." He whistles.

"Yeah. While my lover was feet away, held back by an army. My father…" I don't even want to finish it. Tell him what it really felt like to know the child inside me probably died moments before I did. "Anyway, uh, once I passed over to the other side, once I knew I was dead and made peace with it, I was in another plane. I was surrounded by family and friends, some that I hadn't even known in that lifetime." I pause. "You were there."

Dylan balks at that. "What? How is that possible?"

I shrug lightly. "I don't remember how. You learn everything when you're on the other side, but you forget it all when you come back here. I guess you have to, or you won't learn the lessons you're supposed to on this plane. But yes, bro, you were there. Time is a circle. All these lives are connected like a carousel around our soul. We can only see forwards and back on the circle but the soul is in the middle and it can see every life at once. It's too much for our brains to really understand but it's the truth. I think you were there, Dylan, because our souls know each other from this life and maybe others."

He's silent for a moment. "And to think I'm not even high yet."

"Well, maybe it will make more sense when you are," I joke.

"So what did it feel like? Being dead?"

"Like the biggest accomplishment," I admit, smiling a little. Because the memory of that feeling still lingers inside me. "Like…getting to the showdown with the final boss, after so many tries, and winning."

"You weren't sad after the fact?"

I shake my head. "No. Not really. There were things and people I missed but I knew I would see them again soon."

"And so how did you reincarnate? Does everyone?"

"I'm not sure. I think everyone can, but I also think it's a choice. For whatever reason, I kept choosing to come back, in the same body, with my same ties to Valtu. There's something I'm supposed to learn this time around that I never learned before."

"Maybe you were supposed to come back as a vampire so he didn't have to witness you dying again," Dylan says softly. "You're immortal now. You can be with him forever."

He's right. This time I don't have to die again. We don't have to be apart.

I just wish I had some sign in my gut that we'll find each other again.

Guess I'll have to find out.

"Can you do me a favor?" I ask him after we've sat in silence for a few minutes.

"What?"

"Take me to Eugene."

He blinks and takes his gaze off the road. "Eugene? Why?"

"I'm going to catch a plane to San Francisco," I tell him.

"What the fuck?"

I jerk my thumb at the backseat. "Already packed my bag, put it in the back before we got going."

He glances over his shoulder and notices my bag there for the first time. "What the fuck, Rose?" he repeats. He eyes me, bewildered. "Now? I thought we were going to 7/11."

"We can hit one on the way to the airport," I assure him.

"Why don't you take your own car?" he asks me.

"I don't know how long I'll be gone. It might be sitting there for a really long time."

"Rose," he says again, shaking his head. "I know you're going through a lot right now, with your whole vampire thing and your past lives thing, but this is nuts. Why are you going to San Francisco?"

"I want to see Solon and Lenore. They're the only ones that can help me find Valtu."

That's not one hundred percent true. During my research I did find Dr. Abraham Van Helsing who is a researcher at Oxford. One look at his photo and I know this is the same man I was friends with in the late 1800s in London, then in Venice twenty-one years ago. If he's still around, then he can help me find Valtu. But before I jet across the Atlantic to do that, I need to talk to Solon and Lenore and see what they know.

It wasn't easy to discover where they operate. I know from Dahlia's memories that they operated the feeding club called Dark Eyes in their house in San Francisco. The problem with vampires is that any human who knows the truth about them will never tell the general public. They're compelled not to. So if you search the internet for either a Lenore Warwick or an Absolon Stavig, you'll come up with nothing. It's so thoroughly wiped that there isn't even any record of Lenore, who went to Berkeley as a human, ever existing.

But I know that there was a club called Dark Eyes in the 1930s that old Russian czars used to hang out in and that the current club was modeled on that. I also know that club was located in the basement of the William Westerfeld House, which has some crazy dark past itself. Putting it all together, I'm guessing that's where Lenore and Solon live.

"What makes you think you'll find them?" he says. "Wouldn't they be in hiding if Mom and Dad are? You think they'll be easy to find?"

It's not that I think I'll be able to just waltz up to it. I'm sure there's a ton of security protocols in place. From what I remember about Solon in person, and what Valtu had said about him, plus all we had learned about him in the witch's guild, he has a lot of magic guarding him and that included intricate wards. But I still have to try. Maybe when they know who I am, if I can make it that far, they'll want to see me. I'm hoping so.

"Fine. I'll take you to Eugene," he says after a moment. "But I'm going with you to San Francisco."

I give him a look of surprise. "What? No."

"I'm not letting you go to that city alone. Rose, you haven't traveled anywhere alone."

"Neither have you." When you're a vampire, your social life tends to be a little sheltered. Sure, both my brother and I have friends but we've always held them at arm's length.

"Which is why I'm going with you." He sighs, slamming his palm against the steering wheel. "Actually, as the oldest, I should be reporting you to Mom and Dad."

"Oldest? You're twenty-two! You're a year older than me. And reporting me? What am I, twelve?"

"Then why not tell them? Why sneak off this way?"

I give him a steady look. "You know why."

Obviously they can't ground me. But I do live in their house and there is no way they would let me go. I might have newfound supernatural strength as a vampire, but I haven't tested it out yet, and there's two of them and one of me.

"Whatever," he says. "I'm going with you."

This is the last thing I want. This is something between me and Lenore and Solon. After all, I had met them before. But I have to admit, not only am I touched by my brother's protectiveness, it might be nice to have him there. I'm not worried about going places alone—he's right in that I never have traveled alone as Rose, but as Dahlia I was seeing the world by myself. Yet, I really don't know what to expect. Everything I know about these vampires is from twenty-one years ago.

"You didn't even pack," I point out.

"Then we're going to do some shopping once we get to San Francisco," he says with a twinkle in his eye.

THE DRIVE to Eugene took just under two hours, with the weather getting progressively colder as we got to the airport. It's late November, just after Thanksgiving, but the air smells like snow and I'm hoping it will hold off until we take off.

The flight I had booked for this evening luckily had an extra seat for Dylan I was able to snag from my app on the way to the airport. I wasn't sure what to say to my parents so I haven't said anything. It was just before we boarded the plane that my mom texted the both of us, wondering where we were.

Dylan responded that I was with him and we decided to go to Portland for the night and that we were fine. Then his phone went into airplane mode.

In just under two hours, our plane touches down at San Francisco airport. It's obviously not the first time I've been on a plane, my parents took Dylan and I to Disneyland when we were young, and also New York City one Christmas, plus all my adventures as Dahlia, but even so, I'm feeling both excited and nervous as soon as the wheels touch down.

It might be insane to do this, but it's taking me one step closer to Valtu.

I grab my bag and we get a cab, heading into the city.

The buildings get closer and my gut twists as I stare up at all the lights, the fog wisping past the tallest structures.

"Okay, now mom is really freaking out," Dylan says, waving his screen at me. I haven't turned my phone off airplane mode, all the info I need for our hotel and the Westerfeld House is offline in my notes section.

"Why?" I ask. "It's not like she really knows where we are."

The cabbie eyes me in the rearview mirror at that. I give him a dirty look in response. *Mind your own business, bud*, I think, and he flinches as if heard me, immediately turning his attention back to the road.

Oh yeah. I'm a vampire now. He probably did hear me. I probably compelled someone for the first time.

"Man, she is paranoid," Dylan says, texting something at the speed of lighting before shoving the phone in the pocket of his jeans. "And that's just with us being in Portland. You were right not to tell them about this."

I give him a look like, *I told you so*.

The hotel is where they filmed scenes from *Vertigo*, one of my favorite classic films. Like the original classics, stuff from nearly a hundred years ago. The hotel a little small and run-down, but it was cheap and not too far from where I believe Lenore and Solon are. We check in to our room and while I immediately want to go find the vampires, Dylan goes out to find some clothes and toiletries.

So I raid the mini bar. I have a small bottle of vodka that I take tiny sips of and I sit on the edge of one of the twin beds, staring at myself in the mirror.

I've been avoiding the mirror these last few days. I haven't put on any makeup. I look away from reflections. I'm finding it hard to come to terms with who I am.

But now I'm staring right at myself.

It's so weird to see the woman I've been throughout all these lives. And, yes, a woman, because even though last week I felt like a girl who barely stepped into adulthood, I know I've been someone in my mid-twenties and my late twenties as well. As Dahlia, I was nearly thirty. As Mina I was only twenty-three, but given my upbringing and the fact that it was the fucking 1600s, which seems absolutely unreal now, I had the mind of someone much older. Sometimes you have to grow up faster.

And yet here I am. Twenty-one. A vampire. My skin is clear, my freckles nearly faded overnight, perhaps because being a vampire gets rid of sun damage. My red hair is thick and glossy, my green eyes bright, teeth white (fangs or not). My body is still curvy and soft but I have lean muscle underneath that wasn't there before. I look like the best version of myself that I've ever been throughout the ages. But inside me, I've lived for at least eighty years put together. I feel older, wiser, different.

And totally unmoored.

I finish the rest of the vodka but it does nothing. Vampire metabolisms are so fast that you have to drink a lot to really get the effects and I'm broke, using my money that I earned over summer while working at an occult shop in town for this trip.

I worry about my parents a little. They can't know what I'm up to, I know it would hurt them if they knew. We've always been very close, our family very insulated. I've always felt it was a blessing of sorts to have family like this, even when I was a rebellious teenager and they annoyed me. I wonder now if deep down I remembered the trauma of what I went through as Dahlia, losing both those parents the way that I did.

Bellamy.

The thought of his name twists a knife in my gut.

I searched online for him, just as I searched for Valtu and the others. I found no record of Bellamy. I don't even know if he had a last name or if that was his last name, but regardless he doesn't exist. He would maybe be eighty years old now, so there's a big chance he's dead. If true, I hope that his death was horrible.

But he could still be out there. And if he is, I don't care if he's an old man now.

I want my revenge. For what he did to my parents, what he did to me, and all the other witches he manipulated into being weapons at the expense of their family.

The sound of a keycard in the door takes me out of my thirst for vengeance and Dylan comes inside with a bag from CVS.

"Back so soon?" I ask.

"Got everything I need right here," he says, pouring out the contents on the bed. There's travel toothpaste and toothbrush, body spray, deodorant, socks, a pack of cheap boxers and a couple of poorly made SF Giants tee shirts.

"Boys," I mutter under my breath. Only they could pack for a trip at a drugstore.

He shrugs and takes off his jacket and shirt, slipping on one of the Giants ones he just bought. "Okay. I'm ready to go."

I hesitate and glance at my phone. It's nearly eleven at night. Maybe it's too late.

"You think these vampires have a bedtime?" he scoffs. "Let's do the thing you came here to do."

He's right. If I delay it, I'll probably lose my nerve and head on the first flight back home.

We go out the door and into the night, getting a cab to

the house which is by the infamous Painted Ladies at Alamo Square.

"Which house is it?" Dylan asks as the car drives off.

"Shhh," I tell him, gathering my coat around me. It's foggy up here and the buildings look ghostly.

"You think they can hear me?"

"They're vampires," I remind him, looking around. The cypress trees in the park look like shadowy figures in the cold mist, and even though I don't see any people walking about, I feel like I'm being watched. This is a touristy spot, and yet tonight it feels like it's holding its breath. Even the sounds of the city stay muffled at the bottom of the hill.

The Westerfeld House is on the corner. It looks tall, narrow and foreboding, a slice of Victorian architecture that has survived the ages, but in the mist all the houses around it have a similar feel, their dark silhouettes against the white fog reminding me of a decaying jawbone.

I suppress a shiver and start walking down the sidewalk toward the building, Dylan trailing behind me. I stop right in front of the gates, a small garden with dying plants in the front, and crane my neck to stare up at the house. There are no lights on at all. There is no noise. The house feels dead in every way.

"Dude, I don't think anyone is home," Dylan says, thankfully his voice is quieter now. "Or maybe they do go to bed early."

I shake my head. "No. They're home." My instincts are different now, on high alert, and I can feel that they're in there. It's just that they're hidden. Perhaps if Solon has wards up around the house, they're powerful enough to not only fend off humans and witches, but other vampires as well. After all, if someone like Saara is still out there trying to be Skarde 2.0...

Well, I guess that means how the hell am I going to get in the house?

"You thinking what I'm thinking?" Dylan says as he stares up at the windows.

"Probably not."

"The house looks easy to climb," he says. Then his eyes widen and he looks to me. "Oh. Maybe you can fly now."

"Vampires can't fly," I tell him, kicking his foot.

"Some can. Some with magic."

"Sure, but the ones with magic are inside the house."

"Didn't you say you were a witch before in your past life? Maybe you have magic."

"I don't think it works like that," I say. "And Dahlia couldn't fly either. No witch can, not the ones I've known."

Who are you?

A voice sounds out but I can't tell if it's coming from behind me or in my head.

I whirl around and see a tall dark figure across the street, looming behind a car.

Dylan slowly turns around, though I'm not sure if he heard the voice or not.

"Is that a person?" Dylan asks, gesturing to the figure.

The person in question comes out from around the car with supernatural grace, stepping into the middle of the street where the streetlights weakly illuminate him.

I can't help but gasp.

It's Absolon Stavig.

And I catch the sharp sound of his inhale, his eyes widening with shock.

"This can't be," he says with a disbelieving shake of his head.

"Who is it?" Lenore's voice comes from behind me and I spin around to face her.

My eyes meet hers and I flashback to Valtu's kitchen in Venice, when she had me pinned against the fridge, wanting to kill me.

I know she's remembering the same thing I am.

"Dahlia?" she says in a harsh whisper.

Then everything goes black.

CHAPTER 6
VALTU
THEN

The mist whips between the vampires as they stare down at us on the dock, showcasing the ruined buildings of Poveglia behind them for a moment before covering them up again, like a sleight of hand magic trick.

"Professor Aminoff," Saara's voice comes floating over to us. "Bitrus. So delighted that you two could make it for the feast."

I nod at them while Bitrus climbs out of the boat and ties it to the dock. "Thank you for taking us up on such short notice." I must admit, it's hard not to look at Solon, Lenore, or Van Helsing perched warily in the boat, cloaked under Lenore's spell. I keep my eyes glued to Saara and Aleksi as much as possible and force myself into the role of a hungry vampire in need of real food. The last thing I want is to tip them off, even though I have to keep myself on guard as if I already have.

What I don't want to do is act any different toward them. They both know I despise them and what they are. I have to act like I'm here out of desperation and not because I've had a change of heart. They'd never believe it.

"I must say," Saara says as she walks toward us, wearing a black satin gown that's barely held together by ribbons. She's naked underneath and when the mist blows a certain way, she makes sure you can see every inch of her. "I didn't think you'd ever come back here. You seemed so..." she looks to her brother over her shoulder. "What was the word you used to describe him, Aleksi? Ah yes. Pussy."

She gives me a cunning smile. "I understood what my brother was trying to say, unfortunately he used a word that doesn't quite convey that meaning. After all, there's nothing weak about a pussy. Especially not this one."

She slides the slit in her dress to the side, giving me and Bitrus (and the invisible three behind us) a show. I can practically feel Lenore rolling her eyes at the scene.

I clear my throat and keep my gaze on Saara's cold blue eyes. "Definitely nothing weak about a pussy," I say. "However, I still prefer to feed in a more civilized manner. I figured that we could work something out."

She exchanges a look with her brother and chuckles as she turns back to me, one brow sharply raised. "It's a pity you haven't seen the way yet. Don't forget, you are on my turf here, not yours. I'm afraid if you want to feed from a human untethered, you must be prepared to do it our way. The humans never survive at the end. But isn't that the point of it all?"

No. That's not the point. But of course, I don't vocalize this.

"And you, Bitrus," Saara says to him. "Are you ready to partake this time?"

He nods determinedly. "Yes. I don't have the same qualms as Valtu."

She grins, showing her fangs. "Perfect."

Then she turns on her heel and crooks her finger over her shoulder at us. "Come along, now."

We follow her and Aleksi the same way we did before, the mist fogging the path and then lifting as we pass the crumbling building with rusted scaffolding outside, then past the faded sign that reads *Psychiatric Department* in Italian, until we're going through the main doors that have been left wide open, a large gaping maw that wants to swallow us whole.

I have no idea where the others have gone, if they're still on the docks, if they're following us silently, if they're going around the building. They could already be inside for all I know. I just hope that whatever they have planned works.

I don't even know what *we* have planned. It's hard to know when Saara and Aleksi are so unpredictable and we're in a place we can't control. I just have to figure out how to get my hands on the book and take it from there. If I have to kill a few humans to do so, I really don't care. Just add them to my recent tally.

I'd burn the world down for her if it meant bringing her back.

We step into the cold mouth of the building and follow a familiar path toward a large wooden door guarded by plague doctors on either side. I shiver despite myself, not quite used to their presence. I avoid the gaping holes in the mask they wear, not wanting to meet their eyes, though I wonder if that's really a plague mask at all, or their actual face. That makes it all the more disturbing.

The plague doctors move to the side gracefully and in one wave of Saara's hand, the door opens and we enter the chapel. As it was last time, it's a combination of white walls molding with green, with vines coming in through shattered stained glass windows, broken pews on either side with a few still intact, and a candlelit altar at the very front.

And like last time, there is a victim lying at the foot of the altar.

My heart sinks.

It's a girl in her early twenties, short blonde hair, brown eyes and a cherubic face. She's got duct tape over her mouth and her wrists and ankles are bound. She's been stripped completely nude and there doesn't seem to be a scratch on her body but that's not what has my chest going cold.

It's that I know her.

It's one of my students, Kate Rutherford, a piano player from England. I know I just said I'd kill whatever humans I had to in order to get my hands on the book, but I can't do that to someone I actually know.

I glance sharply at Saara. Of course she looks amused at my reaction.

"You did this on purpose," I sneer, gesturing to the girl. "You knew she was one of my students."

"Yes, well, rumor is that you're rather fond of your female students, aren't you, Professor?"

"Valtu," Bitrus warns from behind me. "Don't take the bait."

But I have to take the bait. She's talking about Dahlia.

"What do you mean by that?" My hands flex at my sides, a volcano of rage bubbling up beneath the surface, just ready to explode.

She shrugs and I glance at the girl again, Kate, her pleading eyes searing right into me, asking me to help her. I have to look away, back to Saara's smug face.

"Oh, not much. Just that I know you've been fucking

one of your students," Saara says. "Someone beneath you from the sounds of it. A human. A dirty *whore*."

"Valtu," Bitrus warns again but I'm lunging across at Saara in less than a second.

I wind up and deck the vampire right across her pretty face.

There's a crunch of bone under my fist and I hope I broke her perfect nose, even though it will correct itself in a minute, but god does this violence feel fucking good.

She goes flying to the tile floor, her face deformed and caved-in as she sprawls, broken and bleeding.

"What the fuck?!" she screeches, her words garbled as she presses her fingers to her face. "You fucking hit me!"

"And I'll fucking do it again!" I snarl at her, about to deliver another blow, maybe punch her head right off, but I'm suddenly held in place. I feel a heavy pressure around my chest, my arms pressing against me. It's like an invisible rope is being wrapped around me and before I have a chance to react I'm being yanked backward through the air.

And right into Aleksi. His arm goes around my throat, pressing in. I'd be able to fight him off but not this magic. "I can't pretend she didn't deserve that," Aleksi chuckles in my ear. "But I'm afraid you're not the type of person we'd have over at a dinner party."

"Fuck you."

"Uh huh. Mind telling us what you're really doing here?"

I meet Bitrus's eyes across the chapel, where he's now kneeling beside a sobbing Kate and quickly untying her bonds to free her. He's warning me not to say it, to hold up the lie, to keep things going until our backup gets here.

But I can't.

"The book," I plead, my voice sounding so desperate it makes me sick. "The Book of Verimagiaa. I need it."

Aleksi laughs while Saara slowly gets to her feet, leaning against a pew for balance.

"And what makes you think we'd give you the book?" Saara mumbles as she staggers to the next pew. "Especially now."

"Because you can't handle the burden of it. The responsibility of it. But I can."

Saara snorts, then spits out blood onto the floor. "Who are you, Tolkien? The book is no burden. And it belongs to us, fair and square."

"You stole it," I tell her. "You have no claim to it."

Give it to me so that I can bring back my love.

Give it to me so that it's not abused.

I direct my last though to the book.

Come to me and I'll swear my loyalty.

Aleksi lets out a dry chuckle and the magic pulls the ropes tighter, until I can barely breathe.

"We're vampires," he says. "We can claim what we—"

He's cut off by the skittering sound of a large, leather-bound book sliding across the tiles toward us. I look over to the shadows where the book came from and see red eyes looking back at me.

The bad thing.

Did a demon just throw the book to me?

I glance back at the book on the floor, right in front of me, and everything else seems to melt away. I'm immediately enraptured by it, the sight of the strange cover filling me with warmth and need and I find myself promising I'll do anything for it. Somewhere in those pages lies the secret to my salvation.

"Then I claim it for myself," I manage to say, my voice sounding hollow.

The world starts to move.

It shifts, like the whole chapel's foundation is collapsing, and suddenly the demon, the bad thing, is right in front of me, standing up on two legs. It's large, its hide so black and fathomless it's like looking into the abyss and I feel like I'm screaming.

It slides its long, thick leathery tail up the side of me, then along my collarbone and neck. It wraps around my throat, constricting slightly, and I can't look away from the void of its body. I hear Saara yelling something, I hear Bitrus screaming my name, and I'm slowly losing consciousness, being dragged into the depths of the abyss, a world of nothing but death.

Then Aleksi says something in a language I don't understand and the demon loosens its tail, whipping it right off me. It fixes its attention on Aleksi now and the tail that was at my neck is shooting past me.

Saara screams and I feel the magic in my bonds disappear, letting me loose. I stumble backwards, out of the way, falling to the floor and I watch as the demon quickly wraps its tail around Aleksi's neck, his blue eyes bulging out, his fingers going to the tail in a feeble attempt to get it off.

We all know it's useless.

With one tight yank, the black tail squeezes Aleksi's neck so tight that there's a crush of bone and then a loud popping sound and Aleksi's head flies clean off.

It lands on the ground beside me, staring up at me with eyes that blink once then close for good, blood pouring from the severed neck.

I yelp in surprise, scrambling to my feet, and look back at the demon, prepared for me to be next.

It's coming over to me now and before I can react, it picks up the book with its tail, holding it up in the air for a moment before it places it in my hands. Then it drops to all fours and turns back into a shadow, slinking back into the darkness from which it came.

I stare at the book in my shaking hands for just a moment but it's long enough for Saara to throw her magic my way. An invisible hand shoves me backward against the wall and she does the same to Bitrus and Kate, both of them thrown across the altar.

The book drops out of my hands and Saara is running toward me screaming, but then Lenore suddenly appears beside Saara and literally trips her up. Saara goes flying to the floor and Lenore gives me a nod before she loosens the spell that was pushing me back.

"Took you long enough," I say to her.

"You're the one who decided to go off script," Solon says, appearing on the other side of me. "We got here as quick as we could. Those plague doctors are something else." He glances at the floor and I watch as his eyes begin to glow, his pupils dilating. "Is that it? Is that the book?" he whispers, voice filled with awe.

Saara screeches something, stealing my attention but then Lenore is tackling her, the both of them rolling on the ground in an actual physical fight. "Solon!" Lenore yells for him.

Solon stares at the book, transfixed, then suddenly snaps out of it. He looks over and eyes them in surprise, perhaps enjoying the sight of the two vamps wrestling, but then jumps in to support Lenore.

I pick up the book and hold it to my chest and it requires a lot of effort to take in my surroundings and realize what's happening. Bitrus is with Kate and he's helping her to her feet, telling her—compelling her—to go to the docks at the far end of the island where there are a few boats, which she can take back to the city, and that she won't remember a single thing from tonight. She nods and runs off and I feel relief in knowing she's okay and that she won't remember any of this, but even more relief that I finally have what I came here for.

And the demon gave it to me.

It gave it to *me*.

That has to mean something.

It wants me to bring back Dahlia.

"Valtu," Solon says, and I look over. He and Lenore have Saara lying flat on her back, arms and legs spread like a pentagon. "What do you want us to do with her?"

I stare at Saara. I have the book now so I don't really care what happens to her and she knows it.

"Is Van Helsing ready at the boat?" I ask Solon.

"I'm hoping so," he says, wiping his hands on his coat.

I look to Lenore and raise my brow. "Got any gasoline?"

She nods, understanding. "Need a light?"

"No, I got one."

I go over to Saara and crouch down at her legs, tucking the book under my arm. I stick my hand out in front of her until flames appear on my fingertips.

"This is the only magic I know," I tell her, waving the flames over her as she stares up at me, her mouth moving but no sound coming out. "By tomorrow, I'll know a lot more. Too bad you won't be around to see it."

Lenore makes a small gesture with her finger at Saara and then walks away, Solon following. I place my fingers at Saara's feet and watch as the flames leap from my hands onto her calves, watching as the fire travels up Saara's thighs, to her stomach, then her chest, her body igniting.

She's screaming soundlessly, blue eyes filled with pain and horror as she's being burned alive.

I can only grin.

I walk over to Aleksi's severed head and pick it up, tossing it over to Saara so it lands right beside her. Only fair she doesn't die alone.

Then I turn and hurry after the others, knowing that Lenore probably has this whole island set to burn up. I can only hope Kate makes it off the island on time, though I know at least the other end of the island is far from the buildings.

We get outside into the fog and are just coming to the docks, Van Helsing starting up the motorboat, when explosions start and the buildings go up in flames. I swear I finally hear Saara scream, then nothing.

THE BOAT RIDE BACK to the city feels like it takes forever, especially as we have to take the back routes in. With the buildings in flames, fire boats will arrive shortly to fight the blaze and even with Lenore holding us under her cloaking spell, there's a chance we could collide with another boat.

All of that doesn't seem to matter now, not with the book cradled against my chest, hidden under my coat. I can feel its power seeping into me, something dark and smoky that leaches through my pores and into my bloodstream. It calls to me like a siren, seductive and destructive. Everything I need to get Dahlia back is right here in my arms. I have no need for anything else.

We've just docked the boat and stepped into my backyard, moving swiftly as to not call attention to ourselves while the misty air fills with the sounds of the fire boats, when Lenore's cell phone rings.

We all exchange a look, perhaps picking up on the strange energy of the call, and step inside the back doors to my kitchen as she answers her phone.

"Hello?" she says into the phone. "Ames?"

A shrieking sound emits from the other end and Lenore's eyes widen.

"What? Slow down," Lenore says, sounding panicked. "What happened?"

All of stop and listen, hearing Amethyst as clear as day from the other side of the world.

"They took him!" Amethyst cries out. "They took Leif!"

"Who is Leif?" Bitrus whispers to me. I'm not entirely sure myself but Solon quietly informs us, "Their son."

"Amethyst, who took him?" Lenore asks. "What happened?"

Amethyst just screeches and cries, a heartrending sound if there ever was one. I grip the book tighter to me, once again reminded what loss can bring us, how deeply it cuts and scars us.

There's a muffled sound and then Wolf's voice comes through, his voice deep but strained. "Lenore, is Solon with you?"

"He's right here," Lenore says.

"I can hear you," Solon says toward the phone. "Wolf, what happened?"

There's the sound of Wolf's ragged breathing while Amethyst continues to wail. I hear another male talking in the background, then a baby crying. "We were ambushed. They broke through the wards. Witches."

My chest goes cold.

Witches.

"Witches?" Lenore repeats. "Do you know who?"

"One knew who you were. Ezra says his name was Atlas Poe."

"Atlas Poe!" Lenore cries out, looking at us incredulously.

"And the other was an older man, wizard, whatever the fuck you want to call him. I think Atlas said his name, but it could have been a last name. Billings or Bellamy? Something like that."

A fist tightens around my heart at the sound of Bellamy's name.

"Oh my god," Lenore says, and I feel the world starting to tilt on its axis, enough so that I have to lean back against the fridge, my nails digging into the book's worn cover even tighter. I swear I hear the book calling to me.

Yes, yes, open me. I'm all you need, the book says. *None of this matters.*

"Do you recognize the name?" Wolf asks, his voice going louder with desperation.

"I recognize both their names," Lenore says grimly. "They're witches, Atlas was expelled from the guild years ago, and Bellamy, Bellamy is supposed to be the head of the guild. But I don't understand why they took Leif? Why would they target a baby? Is Liam okay?"

But now I'm walking away from them and around the corner to the living room, my feet moving as if on their own accord. There's a part of me that wants my revenge on Bellamy for what he did for Dahlia. And yes, of course the fact that the witches are now abducting vampire babies for no apparent reason. But mostly for Dahlia. That revenge has been burning in me ever since her death, because I know it's what she'd want me to do, I know she'd want me to avenge her parent's death, avenge the life of service and murder that Bellamy subjected her to.

Yet now that I have the book, the book has me. I won't dare be separated from it. This book holds the key to my future. It holds the key to what I really want, which isn't revenge, but actually bringing Dahlia back to life. Only then can the two of us seek out her vengeance.

Their conversation continues in the other room but I'm not listening. I already have the book on the coffee table, my fingers tracing the strange cover, made from some animal hide, both pebbled and smooth, with fine hair in patches.

"Valtu," Solon's voice says sternly and when I look up I realize that all of them are standing in front of me. From the look on their faces, I think they may have been there for some time. Perhaps I've been in a trance.

My throat feels thick and I attempt to clear it. "Yes?"

Van Helsing frowns. "Didn't you hear any of that?"

"Valtu, we have a problem on our hands," Solon says.

I can't help but laugh, the sound a boom echoing off the walls, making the string instruments sing. "Now you realize we have a problem? How astute of you, Solon. Yes, we have a problem, I believe it started when I accidentally murdered my wife!" I practically yell the last part.

"Hey," Lenore says softly, coming closer to me but I practically growl, swiping the book out of her reach. "We're not interested in the book, Valtu. We know that belongs to you now. You took it fair and square. But our friends are in a great deal of danger and we're going to need you—and the book—to help them."

I slowly shake my head, averting my eyes. "I don't think so."

"Valtu," Bitrus warns. "We have been working together like a team so far. No reason to stop now."

"Yes there is," I say with deliberation. "I have what I wanted. This book will help me bring Dahlia back. It *chose* me."

"Black magic isn't to be trifled with—" Solon says but then I'm leaping across the coffee table and on him like a flash, slamming him against the wall, holding the book under his chin like a knife. Sick of his fucking lectures.

"Don't you dare tell me what to do," I snarl at him, baring my teeth. "You've been collecting magic for centuries and everyone turned a blind eye. You barter with witches for your powers, you hand over vampires to them like a traitor. There's no difference between that and me using a book that is accessible to us, especially not one taken from vampires that were going to use that to destroy the human race."

His pupils go to pinpricks and I know what he's thinking. He's afraid I'm going to do the same thing.

"I just want Dahlia back," I add, rather pitifully, my voice cracking.

"And none of us will stop you from trying," he manages to say, his throat bobbing against the book's spine, "but this is about more than that. You want revenge for her, don't you? You want to kill the man that killed her parents, who made her into the witch she was, who did the same thing to many others who probably didn't deserve it? I know you do."

"Not as much as I want her," I say. I let him go and turn away, going to the end of the room, my grip so tight around the book that I feel my skin has fused with it. "I just want her."

"Valtu," Lenore says, her eyes wide and pleading, "Bellamy did all of that to Dahlia. But he also invaded our home. Wolf, Amethyst, and Ezra fought them off by the skin of their teeth. Those witches are powerful, powerful enough to nearly destroy three vampires in a ward-protected home and abduct one of their children. Look, we know this is bad timing, but we won't have any luck fighting back or finding them without that book's help."

I give her a tight smile. "You don't need my help. You're a witch. Solon has magic. You'll be just fine."

"We won't be," Lenore says. "I know when I'm outmatched."

"Don't turn your back on us," Solon says, more of a warning than a request.

"I'm not turning my back on you," I tell them, the guilt starting to creep up. "I want to help. I will help. One day, I promise. I pledge myself and the book to help with whatever you need. But right now, I don't even know how to use the book. It's too dangerous to travel with, and too dangerous to use. Solon, you just said that black magic isn't to be trifled with. I agree. Let me learn the book first. Then we'll talk about revenge."

"There is no time." Solon shakes his head and sighs in disappointment. "We're going to have to fly back. Tonight."

I raise my chin, having made my decision. "Then I wish you a pleasant flight."

Yes, the book seems to hiss to me. *You've made the right choice.*

CHAPTER 7
ROSE
NOW

I wake up in an armchair. I open my eyes, my vision momentarily blurred until a room comes into focus. There are candles flickering from sconces on teak walls, velvet-backed chairs and intricately carved onyx tables scattered throughout a large room, fine Turkish carpets on the floor. Everything is dimly lit and shades of red, brown, black, and gold.

This is Dark Eyes, I think to myself, the fuzziness in my head starting to lift. *This is the secret vampire club hidden in the basement of the house. They must have knocked us out and brought us here and...*

Dylan!

I jerk up, expecting to be restrained in my seat but there are no ropes holding me in place, just this feeling like I've been tied to one spot.

Fucking magic.

"Easy now," Lenore says, and she comes into view, eyeing me warily.

"Where is Dylan?" I cry out, but my voice is just a whisper. I try to look around but my head feels like an anvil, too heavy to move. "My brother?"

"He's with Solon in the billiards room," she says. "He's fine, if that's what you're worried about. I think he might even be winning."

I let out huff of air that borders on a growl, my brows lowering. "And I'm just supposed to trust that? The last time I saw you, you hand your arm against my windpipe."

She flinches at that. It's weird how she looks exactly the same. I know it's too be expected because she's a vampire and all, but other than my parents, I've never had that experience of being around those that never age. Hazel eyes, long honey-highlighted hair, pert nose. She's all light and ethereal but there's a toughness about her.

I'm not sure I like her very much. Some of that might have to do with the fact that she helped get me killed.

"I'm sorry about that," she says carefully. She comes closer, inspecting me. "But it really is you..."

"Surprised?"

"Your being reincarnated as a vampire? Yes. Very surprised. You're the last person I expected to see again."

"I want to see Dylan."

"Of course," she says. "Here, let me loosen your restraints. Just promise not to try anything."

"Why would I try something? I'm the one who came looking for you."

"Exactly," she says, and she closes her eyes for a moment and flutters her fingers in front of me. I can feel invisible ropes loosen and a vice-like pressure leave my head. "Can't help but think you might be a girl with revenge on your mind."

I slowly get out of the chair and follow Lenore as she walks past an old-fashioned looking bar with rows of glasses hanging above top-shelf liquor bottles. She gestures through a glass door to the billiards room where I can see Dylan playing pool with Solon. He's laughing and I can hear him faintly through the door, jabbering on about some TV show he's obsessed with.

"Want a drink?" Lenore asks, gesturing behind the bar. "Or would you like something more bloody? I could make you a real Bloody Mary. You're looking a little pale."

"I was pale even before I became a vampire."

She goes and grabs a vodka bottle. "I know. I see your freckles have faded a lot. Your skin has reverted to the way it used to be when you were born. When I transitioned, I lost every one of my tattoos. It sucked."

"Maybe that's for the best," I tell her, sitting on a bar stool. "Tattoos are great, but not for eternity."

She gives me a quick smile as she pours her vodka in a highball with ice. "So Dylan...that's his name, right? He said you didn't remember any of your past lives until you turned into a vampire. How long has that been?"

"Couple of days now."

"And your name is Rose now. Rose what?"

"Harper."

Her eyes turn into saucers and her hand starts shaking enough that she has to put down the bottle.

"Rose Harper?" she whispers, her brows knitting together. "Oh god. And...Dylan Harper?"

"Yeah," I say slowly.

"Your parents...I should have known."

And then I realize why she looks so shocked. Dylan didn't tell her who our parents are.

"They used to live in this very house," I inform her.

She swallows, shaking her head. "No way. It can't be."

"And yet it is. Of course, I didn't know that until the

73

other day. Dylan didn't know either. We didn't know that they weren't always John and Yvonne, but Wolf and Amethyst."

"Solon!" Lenore yells over her shoulder. "Get in here! You're not going to believe this."

In seconds there's a flash, the scent of warm tobacco filling my nose, and Solon is suddenly standing right beside her.

"What is it?" he asks, staring at Lenore with concern.

She points at me. "This is Rose Harper. *Harper*. She's... she's Wolf and Amethyst's daughter."

"The fuck?" Solon says, his voice gruff even in his faint British accent. "But we've met you before." He eyes Dylan as he walks out of the billiards room toward us. "We've met both of you before."

"That was like ten years ago," I tell him. "I've changed. I don't think you would have seen me and immediately thought of Dahlia."

He runs his hand over his brow. For such a distinguished and notorious vampire, I have to admit it's rather novel to see him reacting this way. "I don't understand. You're Dahlia. And you've been reincarnated into Wolf and Amethyst's child?"

I shrug. "I know."

"But don't you think that's a coincidence?"

"I don't know what it is. I don't know how reincarnation works. How did I happen to find Valtu again? Both times before?"

"It's a web," Lenore says. "And you keep getting tangled in it."

"By dying over and over again," I say grimly.

"Except not now cuz you're a vampire," Dylan points out, then notices the bar. "Hey, you got any beer?"

They ignore him. "I just can't believe it," Lenore says, wide-eyed. "You're their daughter. I never would have known. Do they know you're here?"

I wince. "No."

"Dahlia," Lenore scolds me. "I mean, Rose."

"You can call me Dahlia Rose if it's easier," I tell her.

"Why didn't you tell them?" Solon asks.

"Because they've been so cagey about the whole thing," I explain, exasperated. "They've lied to us our whole lives. I don't even know if Rose is my real name. Or if Dylan is his."

Solon and Lenore exchange a furtive glance.

"Oh no, don't tell me I had another name," I say, pressing my hand into the bar top.

"Well, you should be used to that by now," she says. Solon elbows her lightly and she sighs. "I feel like I'm stepping on toes here. Okay. You were born with the name Rose. But Dylan was born with the name Liam. And of course Leif's name was always Leif."

Leif? A cold sensation floods my chest. I look at Dylan who appears equally confused.

"Oh my god," Lenore whispers, her hands to her mouth.

"Leif? Who the hell is Leif?" Dylan asks.

"Fuck," Solon swears under his breath. He bites his lip, looking between my brother and I. "You don't know."

"Who is Leif?" I ask, my voice rising now.

"They didn't tell you everything," Lenore says as she looks pained.

"Obviously fucking not," Dylan says sharply. It's rare to see him angry, but I think the lies are finally getting to him too.

Solon swallows thickly, then leans against the bar, giving the both of us a grave look. "I don't know what Wolf and Amethyst told you, but I have no choice but to fill you in. I know they did it to protect you, I just assumed that when you found out the truth, you found out all the truth. Leif was your brother."

"Brother?" Dylan and I say in unison.

Solon eyes Dylan sympathetically. "You had a twin. Leif."

Dylan nearly falls backward. He reaches out and steadies himself on the edge of the bar top. "A twin?"

Solon nods while Lenore slides the straight vodka on the rocks over to my brother. "Yes, a twin," Solon says. "He was taken from you, from this very place, when you were only a year old."

Dylan's eyes are wild. Of course, this is all before I was born, so I don't remember it, but it might explain the many nights when I was younger seeing my mother red-eyed and crying over hushed and private things I didn't understand.

"Taken by whom?" I ask. "How?"

Lenore and Solon exchange another uneasy look. "Your mother and father were living here with us," Lenore says quietly. "As you saw tonight, the house has wards up. Most people can't get in or out, and that goes for witches and other vampires too. Solon and I were in Europe. With you, Dahlia. You and Valtu."

My mouth drops open. She goes on, "Amethyst and Wolf were here. They weren't alone, Ezra, one of the other vampires who lived here, he was here too. They came for them. Broke through the wards. Tried to kill everyone and take the babies. But your parents and Ezra, they fought back. Managed to save Dylan. But Leif...Leif was taken. And to this day we don't know where he is."

"Who took him?" I repeat, feeling fire raging in my chest, coupled with the sick feeling of knowing who it might be.

"Someone who took family from Dahlia," Lenore says with finality. "Bellamy."

It feels like I've been kicked in the gut, my hand instinctively going to my stomach, gasping for air. How could this man have taken so much from me?

"Oh my god," I gasp. "Oh my god." I can barely breathe. "He killed my parents and then he took my brother, even before I had a chance to become his sister."

When Leif was taken, I was still Dahlia. Fuck, this must have happened right after I died. I died as Dahlia and almost immediately would have been reborn to my mother. Like my birth was making up for what Bellamy took from me.

Tangled fucking web is right.

"I have to say, in all my years this is one of the most beguiling, mind-boggling scenarios I have ever come across," Solon says gravely. "I can't begin to make sense of it."

And yet somehow it does make sense.

"Is Bellamy still alive?" I ask.

"I'm going to fucking kill him," Dylan says after he finishes his drink, slamming it so hard on the counter that it nearly shatters.

"We've been keeping tabs on him throughout the years," Solon says, eying Dylan warily. "Lately though, we've lost contact. Or rather, we lost our contact. We assume he's still alive though. The kicker is…" He trails off, a grimace on his face.

"What?" I ask.

"He hasn't seemed to age," Solon says. "There's a whole group of witches that haven't aged at all. Their aging seems to have stopped twenty years ago."

"Twenty-one years ago," Dylan says dully. When he

meets my eyes, they're bloodshot. "They stopped aging when they took my twin."

Solon nods slowly. "Yeah. That's what we've been afraid of. We think the witches had an interest in you all specifically because you're the children of Amethyst, who was turned, and never should have been able to reproduce. We think they thought your blood holds special properties. They might be right."

"But you're the most valuable," I say, and point at Lenore. "You were able to turn Solon and my mom without creating monsters. Why not go after you instead?"

"As you can see, we don't have children," Solon says. "By choice. But they have come after me. They've come after Lenore, and they've come after your mother. That's why everyone is in hiding."

"Except you're hiding in plain sight," I say.

He gives me a wise smile. "That's the best place to hide. Not only does this house seem to operate as a museum during the day, we have it so that people think we live elsewhere. In fact, we do operate a feeding room here in the city, it's just no longer in Dark Eyes. It's in the decoy house. As long as the wards hold here, and they've never failed so as long as I've been in the house, then we're protected."

"They didn't hold up very well when they took Leif," Dylan says snidely as Lenore comes over and pours him more vodka.

Solon looks chagrined. "I know. Because I wasn't there. We believe it was an inside job. Someone that had already been in here before. We assumed it was Ezra at first, but I'm good at sniffing out the truth and he was telling the truth."

"Now you really look like you could use a drink," Lenore says. "Bloody Mary?"

I nod. "So, after that we went into hiding?"

"Yes," says Solon. "But not right away. Things were a mess. We all wanted to get Leif back. We did all we could think of. It wasn't until she discovered she was pregnant with you that they thought changing their names and hitting the road would be the safest option. They just wanted to protect you."

"And they did," Lenore says. I watch as she pours in tomato juice and then a few spoonfuls of dark red liquid. My stomach growls, immediately recognizing the smell and look of blood. She gives me an impish smile. "Told you. A real Bloody Mary. It will perk you right up. When's the last time you fed?"

I just shake my head. "I don't know." I look back at Solon. "My parents said Valtu has the book."

Solon nods at Lenore. "I think I'm going to need one of those too."

She passes the drink to me and he continues. "Yes. He has the book. We had hoped he would bring it here to help us with it, use the book to try and track down Bellamy and Leif in some way. But he didn't. He said he had to hide it to keep it safe. But it didn't matter anyway, because I don't think there was anything he could have done to help. Bellamy covered his tracks too well."

My heartrate has already increased since I said his name and I take in a deep breath to steady myself. "And where is Valtu now? Is he alive? Is he okay?" Solon rubs his lips together as Lenore hands him his drink. "You know that's why I'm here right?" I add, feeling frantic now. "I need to find him."

The tension in the room rises as he takes a deliberate sip of his drink, wetting his lips.

"I'm not sure you want to do that," Solon eventually says. "Maybe he doesn't want to be found."

I shake my head, not understanding. "I don't get. Of course he wants to be found. It's me. He was my damn husband at one point."

"Didn't he kill you?" Dylan points out softly.

I glare at him. "I'm sure he didn't mean to."

But even as I say it, I know the truth. He did mean to kill me. He meant to kill Dahlia, the witch who betrayed him, who was sent to slay him. He just didn't know it was *me*.

"He never would have killed me if I had dropped the glamour in time," I go on.

"Drink up, Rose," Lenore says, nodding to my drink.

I don't want to drink up. I don't want to be distracted or placated, not now. But the scent of blood is too irresistible. I take one sip and I feel all the cells in my body growing with life, as if being reborn, and that was just from a few splashes of blood.

I finish the drink in one gulp, my veins feeling warm and tingling, and my mind sharpens. No distraction here.

"Tell me why I shouldn't find him?" I say to them. "Give me a good reason. Is he..." I trail off, afraid to speak the next words, in case they're true. "Is he...married?"

Did he fall in love with someone else?

Oh god, I don't know how I'd be able to stand it.

"I doubt that," Solon says, scratching his chiseled jaw. "It's been a decade since we last heard from him, however."

"Then what's the problem?" I'm losing my patience.

"Valtu was living in Mittenwald, in the Bavarian Alps," Lenore says, her expression soft. "He's probably still there. He's got the Book of Verimagiaa with him. The book has an immense hold on him. We wanted him to help us in tracking the witches, but he never ended up doing so and..."

"Valtu just sort of...gave up," Solon adds. "He settled in Mittenwald. He has wards and spells all over the town to protect him, in case Bellamy or other vampires are hunting the book."

"Mittenwald," I repeat. "Then that's where I need to go."

"Listen," Solon says sharply. "It's not going to be that easy. Valtu doesn't want to be found."

"He'll want to be found by me."

"No. He won't." He closes his eyes and breathes in deeply through his nose. "Valtu was a broken man after you died. After Dahlia died. He was consumed by his sorrow and grief and that started to turn into anger. He always turned into a monster of sorts every time he lost you but this last time..." He opens his eyes and they pierce through me. I can almost feel Valtu's rage. "This last time was different. Because he killed you. And he couldn't live with that."

He swallows thickly. "He managed to find a spell in the book. A spell of erasure. A spell for forgetting. I was with him when he did it. I warned him not to do it. That doing so would erase his humanity, but he was in too much pain, he couldn't listen."

"A spell of erasure?" I whisper, my heart starting to sink. "What does that mean?"

"It means he erased you from his life. From his memory. There is no Mina or Lucy or Dahlia anymore. You're gone."

I stare at him, mouth agape, trying to understand the words he just said.

"He used a fucking *spell* to erase me from his memory?" I manage to say, my heart pounding in my throat.

"I'm sorry," Lenore says, eyes welling with sympathy. "I don't think he thought you'd ever come back. He thought because he killed you...that never seeing you again would be his punishment. That you would, well, stay dead."

"Now it's my punishment," I say to myself, feeling sick

and dizzy and trapped, like my skin is growing too hot and too tight for me. "Now it's my punishment because he won't remember me, but I'll remember him."

"Dude," Dylan says quietly, letting out a low whistle. "That's fucking harsh."

"I know it isn't fair," Solon says. "But Valtu chose the only way to make the pain stop. He's not been the same since you've been gone."

"He's not been the same since he got that book," Lenore says under her breath.

I refuse to believe it. I believe they're telling the truth, or what they believe is the truth, but there's no spell that will make him forget me, not for good.

"Then all the more reason I have to find him," I say, getting out of my seat. "The moment he sees me, he'll remember. I know he will."

"Your glamour prevented him from seeing you last time and that was magic," Lenore says, folding her arms across her chest. "What makes you think that this will be any different?"

Because I love him.

Because he loves me.

Even if he doesn't remember me right now, my love will awaken his memory. I know it will. He can't erase Mina, Lucy, and Dahlia.

Once he sees my heart, he'll recognize it for what it is.

His.

"I'm not staying away from him and giving up."

"But he gave up on you," Solon says and fuck, does that ever sting. I can't help but flinch.

"I'm going to find him," I glower. "He'll remember me. Like hell I'm just going to stay here and twiddle my thumbs and leave it at that. I'm going to fight for him."

"Once again, he killed you, Rose," Dylan says.

"He killed Dahlia," I correct him sharply. "And I'll make sure he remembers it."

I step away from the bar and take out my phone. It's one in the morning. I don't think I'm going anywhere right now other than the hotel.

"And how are you planning to get to...where? Germany?" Dylan asks. "With what money? You barely afforded the flight down here."

"*Flights*," I say, reminding him that I paid for both.

"Look," Lenore says, coming around the bar. "If you really want to find Valtu, we'll help you."

"Lenore," Solon warns.

"What?" she says, throwing her arms up and glaring at him. "Call me a romantic, but maybe she's right. Maybe Valtu will see her and..."

"The spell will break?" he suggests dryly.

"Yeah," she says, turning back to face me, her lips twisting sourly. "Something like that. And besides, this is my fault. If it wasn't for me, Valtu wouldn't have lost his mind. He wouldn't have...killed you. I've had to live with that ever since that day, you know. I know that was partly my fault and I've regretted the way I acted ever since."

Okay. Maybe I like Lenore just a smidge better now.

"So," she says, pressing her fingers together, her red lacquered nails catching the flickering candlelight. "As an apology, let me get you a flight out to Germany. Whenever you want to go."

Okay. Maybe I like her a lot better now.

"Tomorrow," I say.

"Rose," Dylan whines. "Come on. You can't just leave without telling mom and dad."

"And you don't know where you're going," Solon says. "*We* don't even know if Valtu is still there."

"Well, do you know who would? I remember he was friends with a vampire...Bitrus? What about Dr. Van Helsing? I knew Abe when I was Lucy too. I looked him up, he's still alive. At Oxford."

Solon doesn't say anything for a moment.

"You have his email," Lenore reminds him quietly. "We'll make sure Rose is set properly." She looks me up and down. "And I'm probably going to have to lend you some clothes for the mountains, and well, seduction efforts."

Fuck. Looks like I'm going to Germany.

CHAPTER 8
VALTU
THEN

"We're sorry to see you go, Professor Aminoff," Guido says to me with a sad twitch of his mustache. He offers his meaty hand to me and I shake it firmly. "It is a great loss to us and to the students, but we understand that change is an indisputable part of life."

"Thank you, Guido," I tell him. "And please, call me Valtu," I add with a wink.

I've been telling Guido to call me Valtu ever since I started at the music conservatory. I've been here for ten years and it's time for me to finally move on. It was always part of the plan, anyway. As a vampire you need to move every so often to avoid superstition over your lack of aging. The funny thing is, the last couple of years I do look like I've aged. I have dark circles where there weren't any before, and while I don't have any lines, I look tired. Like all the life has been drained from my face. It doesn't matter how much blood I have, nothing seems to nourish me anymore.

Not since I killed Dahlia.

I'm surprised I have stayed in Venice as long as I have.

My first instinct after the showdown in Poveglia was to get out of town right away. Leave my job and the Red Room behind, take off with the book and do what I could to try and crack the code.

But as crazy as it sounds, the book wanted me to stay in Venice. Every time I thought of leaving, I felt its weight like an anchor to this city.

And so I stayed.

I tried to shift through the rubble of my life and piece together something that resembled the person I was before I met Dahlia. I had been happy, hadn't I? I had lost her before, but the years passed, and I went on. I moved on. I had a life.

Then suddenly I didn't.

I spent my days teaching, going through the motions as music no longer soothed my soul. I went into the Red Room often to unleash my most depraved self. I fucked, I drank, I even hurt people for the sake of causing pain. I did all I could to try and channel my feelings, my most hated self, into some other place.

And the nights I spent with the book.

Pouring over the pages, trying to learn everything I could.

Everything it would allow me to learn.

The book has a mind of its own, you see. What it wants me to know, it shows. What it doesn't, it hides, the ink buried in the fabric of the paper, invisible to the eye. Every once in a while, I'll notice a page filled with ink that had been hidden before, and I dutifully learned the spell whether I thought it was relevant or not. Sometimes it was something bold, such as erasing someone's memory for a passage of time, almost as if someone was awake and yet under general anesthesia at the same time. Other times it was something as simple as creating light with a simple flick of the fingers. I already had knowledge of magic thanks to Solon, but it further solidified it.

And yet the spell I wanted most of all didn't seem to have a home in the book—or it's still being hidden from me. The spell of necromancy. The whole reason I took it. An attempt to get Dahlia back. It didn't matter how much time I spent flipping through the endless pages, looking for that particular spell, waiting for it to appear—it never did.

There have been some other complications with the book as well. Side effects, if you will.

The book has its own guardians.

I feel they are here to protect me too, since they haven't tried to do me any harm, but at the very least, they are here to protect the book.

One of the guardians is the bad thing, the infamous demon that killed Aleksi and practically handed me the book, and the same demon I had seen with Dahlia, that had been terrorizing Venice for a while there (people explained the murders as being the work of a serial killer who moved on to another area). Now the demon hangs around my villa, which is something I'm not sure I'll ever get used to. It doesn't make any noises, it doesn't say anything, it doesn't do anything except lurk in the shadowy corners, or sometimes lie flat against the ceiling. But it's always there, giving me the motherfucking creeps.

There are some other creatures or beings too, though I am unsure if they are guardians or just things I have inadvertently conjured with my usage of the text. They may even be leftovers from Saara and Aleksi when they opened a portal to the Red World.

One of them I call the pale man has an outstretched mouth and tiny black dots for eyes. He likes to appear in the corner of my eye, though he always disappears when I turn to face him. The other is harder to explain. It's always changing. I'm starting to think it's a physical manifestation of whatever you fear or are trying to escape from. Sometimes I see Dahlia's waterlogged corpse floating above my bed, her matted hair mixed with seaweed, eels coming out of her eye sockets. Other times I see a bloody, mutilated baby, crawling toward me with sharp snapping teeth. I often wonder if it represents the babies we had lost.

After I finish saying goodbye to others at the conservatory, I leave the building and step out into the streets of Venice. It's raining and it's February, as good a time as ever to leave the city when the crowds have descended for Carnival and *acqua alta* has flooded the streets. I manage to slide past tourists wearing festival masks, sloshing through puddles in their boots, before I get over the *Ponte dell'Accademia*. Normally the *Ponte di Rialto* is quicker, but that would mean walking straight through the heart of the tourists and I don't want to expose myself to that at the moment, not when the streets are so narrow already and so many of them have flooded.

So I ascend the quieter bridge and take a moment to look over the Grand Canal. With the *vaporettos* and gondoliers and motorboats sloshing through the gray waters, a dark mist swallowing the tops of the buildings and snaking through streets like smoke, Venice is at its most gothic, its most beautiful.

I will miss this place dearly. I think Venice will always have a piece of my heart. One day, when all who would remember me have died, I am sure I will come back. The world is small and my life is long. The only thing that worries me is that Venice might not be there when I do. At the rate the water is rising due to climate change, it's possible the city will be underwater by 2100. For the humans that exist today, it won't be around for their great-grandchildren and that makes me unfathomably sad. It's times like this that I feel immortality is a curse, particularly on this planet. To witness so much change and death and dying can take a toll on you.

I should know.

But tonight, tonight I have a plan. A solution to erase part of that toll.

It revealed itself to me a week ago as I sat by the roaring fire, the only light in the room. I was flipping through the book as I always do, filling that obsessive need to read it, touch it, be immersed in it. I know the demon was sitting on its haunches in the corner of the room, red eyes occasionally shining through the dark and I felt as if it were waiting for something. Suddenly, as I turned to a blank page, I watched it come to life before my eyes, the ink seeping up through the fibers.

A spell of erasure.

A spell for forgetting.

Tabula Rasa.

Blank slate.

I knew what I had to do to make all of this go away. Instantly I was filled with hope and a future and peace, for the first time in years.

The first step of course was to quit my job, give the Red Room to Bitrus to run, say my goodbyes. Then leave to start again.

Blank slate.

I keep repeating it through my head as I walk home, convincing myself I'm doing the right thing, when I come to a stop outside my villa.

Solon is standing there at the front gate, looking elegant

in a well-tailored coat with the collar pulled up. I haven't seen Solon since our ambush at Poveglia. Things hadn't ended well between us.

"Solon. What brings you here?" I ask, giving him a cautious smile though it's hard to hide my surprise.

His smile in return is cold. "I'm sorry to just pop by. Normally I would ask before I showed up at your door like this."

I nod uneasily, looking around. "And Lenore?"

"She's back home," he says.

"Everything okay?"

"For the most part," he says, and I can't get a read on him. I would try but he keeps his mind locked up like a safe.

I walk past him and through the gate to the front door, glancing over my shoulder at him. "Well, it would be very impolite of me if I didn't invite you in for a drink. Unfortunately, anything nourishing is at the club, but I do have a lot of wine."

"Wine is just fine. You have a better collection than I do," he comments, coming up the path, past the olive and fig trees that are laden with raindrops.

I have wards up around the villa so it takes me a moment to disarm them, muttering a few phrases under my breath.

"Wards," Solon says appreciatively from behind me. "I figured that's what was happening."

I narrow my eyes at him as I open the front door and step inside. "Why, were you trying to get in?"

"Get in? No. Just trying to see if you were home," he says, but I don't believe him. He probably was trying to get in and I know why. The book. It has been calling to him ever since he first laid eyes on it.

Speaking of the book, it's on the coffee table in the

living room, since I just read it last night, but I have no fear of Solon trying to grab it and make a run for it. I know the demon isn't far off.

"So I suppose this isn't a friendly visit," I tell him as we walk to the kitchen. I feel the energy of the book humming from the living room and the fireplace lights itself in response.

"What makes you say that?" he says mildly, following me.

I give him a tepid look. "Just a hunch. You weren't exactly pleased with me when we last spoke."

He grumbles though his eyes light up a little when I show him the bottle of 1965 Bordeaux that I'm about to open for us. "No, I suppose I wasn't. And that's partly the reason I'm here. To see if you'd had a change of heart."

"Ah," I say, uncorking the bottle with aplomb. I sniff the bottle lightly and can almost see the terroir and fields being worked decades ago, feel the waning sun on the day the grapes were picked. "I see. And I thought you just wanted my wine and company."

"Well that too," he says as I pour him a glass of the burgundy elixir before I pour my own. "We have a lot to catch up on, old friend."

I raise my glass. "*Salude*, anyway."

We cheers and I take a sip, savoring the explosion of grapes, then swallow and take a seat at the kitchen island across from him. "Let's get it out of the way then. What do you want? The book?"

He shakes his head. "Not particularly. I need you to use the book."

"For what?" I ask but I already know the answer from his weary expression. It's the same as before.

"To find Leif and Bellamy," he says.

I sigh. "Believe it or not, I'm not opposed to helping you. I want to help get Leif back as much as anyone. I may not really know Amethyst, and Wolf and I have had our differences, of course, but any vampire stolen by witches deserves revenge. But I have been over that book in detail for the last few years now and there is nothing in there that would help with tracking or locating him or any of the witches."

He studies me for a moment. "And you're sure?"

"Of course I'm sure," I snap, annoyed that he'd even suggest I wasn't thorough. "Don't forget the book was made by witches. Sure, they say a vampire was involved in it as well, but in the end the magic came from a witch and I'm sure they'll do anything to protect their own."

"Actually, no one really knows where the book came from," Solon muses. "Not even the witches. We only assume it favors them."

"Well it doesn't matter because what you're looking for doesn't exist. Not yet, anyway."

"Not yet?"

"It doesn't show its hand all at once. It slowly reveals itself to me. Most of the pages in there are blank. It's impossible to predict when a spell might finally appear."

He has a taste of his wine, still studying me closely. "Back when we asked you to help, you didn't even know that about the book. And yet you didn't even try. You know this isn't just about getting Leif back. It's about vengeance. Justice for Dahlia."

I swallow hard, hating the sickly pit of dread that forms in my stomach whenever I think of what I did to her. Thank god that will all be gone soon.

"There is no justice," I say quietly.

"You know you have to forgive yourself," he says.

I give him a sad smile. "I can't forgive myself."

"But you can't live like this forever. Shut away here. We've called so many times over the years. You never answer. I know that you barely have anything to do with the Red Room these days, that you're turning into a recluse, that you don't have time for your friends anymore."

"I'm not living like this forever," I tell him. "Actually, today was my last day at the school. Tomorrow I'm leaving Venice for good."

He blinks at me in surprise, straightening up. "What? Where?"

"I'm not sure yet," I tell him. "Somewhere cold and dark and hidden, so I suppose I'll still be a recluse after all. Anyway, if you know anyone who wants a villa in Venice," I gesture around me, "it's available. Well, Bitrus is moving in but I'm sure he'll share. He's taking over the Red Room for me." Outside of vampires, Bitrus has always kept to himself, so it will be much longer before the human population of Venice thinks anything is amiss with his lack of aging.

"Why?"

I give him a hard look. "Because I want a new life, Absolon. Surely you can understand that."

"I do. And I know firsthand you can't run away from your problems. Surely you know that too," he points out.

A sly smirk tugs across my lips, a feeling of elation at having found a loophole.

"Ah, but you see, I *can* run away from my problems. I can make them never exist in the first place."

His brows come together into a hard black line. "What do you mean?"

"Come with me," I say and take my wine around the corner to the living room. The room is mostly dark except for the roaring fire and the narrow shaft of light coming in through the closed velvet curtains. I take a seat on the sofa, facing the book on the coffee table, and gesture for Solon to do the same.

But he is frozen in the doorway, staring with wide eyes into the shadows of the room. "What the hell is that?" he whispers.

I don't need to turn my head to know what he's referring to. "I don't know. But I'm pretty sure it's here so that others like yourself don't try and take off with the book."

He swallows thickly and tears his gaze away from the demon, and then sits down beside me. "Wouldn't dream of it."

But when he looks at the book, I can see he's thinking of it a little. His eyes get this glow to it, the same glow I noticed in Poveglia. It's a look I'm sure I have in my eyes when I'm flipping through its storied pages late at night. Total enrapturement.

I reach for the book and it meets me halfway, lifting out of the air and flipping through the pages by itself, the pages flashing blank and full of ink alternatively, clearly showing Solon what I meant about the way it reveals itself.

Then it settles back down on the table, page flipped open to *Tabula Rasa*. Lots of detailed text, ingredients, and then a picture of a crudely drawn vial of liquid.

"What is this?" Solon says, attempting to read it. "It's Latin but...it's jumbled. Tabula Rasa is all I can understand. A blank slate..."

The book suddenly shuts itself, the show over.

"It's a recipe and a spell for a potion, one that I will drink tonight to make all my problems go away."

"I still don't understand," he says, displaying his hands in a show of confusion. "Why not get black-out drunk?"

I get to my feet and walk over to a music box that sits on top of the piano in the corner. I open up the music box and the ballerina on top does a little twirl, followed by a few haunting notes. A sad tune for a lonely ballerina. I reach in and take out a black vial that feels shockingly cold in my hands.

I turn and display it to him carefully, sure that it stays far out of his reach, even if he were to move fast. "A spell of erasure. A spell for forgetting. A way for me to live again without any memory of Dahlia."

His mouth drops open for a moment. "You're going to erase her from your memory?"

He looks so horrified that it's almost comical.

"Yes," I say simply. "It's the only way to make the pain go away. It's the only way to be free of her and what I did to her."

He shakes his head, getting to his feet, and the demon suddenly growls, low, raspy, and menacing. I hold the vial close to me just in case, even though Solon stays where he is.

"Valtu. Listen to me. We all go through shit in life. Some of us more than others, but believe me when I say that what I went through wasn't a walk through the park either. I was a monster."

"And so am I," I seethe. "We all have our battles. I know yours but this is mine and you can't possibly know what it's like to have had a love like Mina's and Lucy's and Dahlia's and have that love ripped from you each and every time. You can't know what it's like to have killed—"

"But I do know!" Solon yells. "I killed my first love and then countless others after, and I had to live with it. We all have to live with our choices, whether we meant to do it or not. That's how the world works. That's how we learn. That's how we stay human."

"Human?!" I scoff. "Are you kidding me? We aren't human, Solon, and it's a mistake to aspire to be one. We are vampires. We are killers."

"Then we should be making peace with that fact," he counters. "Not erasing it. Don't do this, Valtu. Dahlia doesn't deserve that."

"Does it matter what she deserves!?" I cry out, rage and grief crawling out of my chest. "What about what I deserve? She's dead. She's dead and I'm here and *I* have to live with it. More than that, I have to live with it forever! I'm tired of living with this grief. I'm so fucking tired, Solon. It's either this or I'm walking straight into a fire, because I can't go through this pain any longer. I just can't."

"It's a coward's way out," he says grimly, eyes burning.

"Then I'm a coward," I say. And I know it's true. I know I am. But the idea of being free from this weight, from these shackles, means I will gladly accept that title. "But at least I will be free."

"You'll lose all your humanity," he warns. "I know you just said it doesn't matter, that we shouldn't be like the humans, but we need to be, at least a little bit. If Dahlia and Mina and Lucy cease to exist in your life and in your memory, you will lose every part of you that has made you what you are. Every good part. She gave you goodness, Valtu. She gave you love. She made you care, she exercised your heart. If you erase all of that then you'll be..."

"Soulless?" I venture. "Nothing but a monster? I'm already those things, Solon. The difference is this time I won't be suffering any longer."

He shakes his head. "No. No, this is a mistake. This is a big mistake."

I give him a wan smile. "If it is, will it make a difference to me? No. She's dead and I need her to let me go. This is the only way I can let her go."

And even though I was planning to do it tonight alone, even though I planned to think about it a little more, I pop open the vial.

"*Hoc carmine te deleo, amorem deleo et incipio,*" I say, reciting the spell I had memorized by heart. "*Tersus. Tersus. Aeternum.*"

"Valtu, no!" Solon yells and he's coming toward me.

But I've already tipped the contents of the vial down my throat.

CHAPTER 9
ROSE
NOW

S oft murmurs of German fill my head followed by, "Miss? Can you put your shade up? We're landing soon."

I stir, my eyes opening slowly. I look up to see the stern-faced flight attendant gesturing to the shade at my window seat.

I nod. *"Freilich,"* I say, the German naturally slipping out of me, courtesy of both Mina and Dahlia knowing German, and fumble to raise up the window shade. Neither the god-awful bright light nor my use of German has put a smile on her face as she carries down the aisle.

This is the closest I've ever come to teleporting. The minute I got on the plane I fell asleep. I didn't even get a chance to eat my meal. Thankfully I had a window seat, so I was able to rest my head and just pass out. Lenore had wanted me to fly first class—to ease her guilty conscience for having me inadvertently killed, no doubt—but this flight was sold out in first and I didn't want to wait another day.

I'm not that surprised at how deeply I slept though. I

98

didn't sleep a wink the night before. Eventually Dylan ended up leaving Dark Eyes via the secret back entrance and went back to the hotel, and I stayed up talking with Solon and Lenore.

Despite the circumstances, it was actually really nice. Though Solon was the first vampire ever turned, by the now-dead king of vampires, Skarde, and had outgrown his monster phase over the centuries, Lenore was a natural-born vampire like myself, so we have a lot in common. She took care of me in ways that my mom might have, had I been at home and had our house not been filled with all this crazy tension, and made sure I was well-fed.

Which to them, in their old school ways, meant bringing in a human volunteer into the club in the middle of the night and putting them in the feeding room.

At first, I was totally squeamish and shy about the whole thing. I'd been popping the blood pills and drinking from blood bags ever since I turned. I hadn't sunk my fangs and fed from anyone. Ever.

But the volunteer was super excited to be there. Just some young man named Michael who was apparently a regular at the other "decoy" club Lenore and Solon ran in town, which turned out not to be much of a decoy at all. They took us into the feeding room, which is all stainless steel and leather mats and couches, everything that's easy to clean.

Michael laid down on one of the couches, then Solon held me back, which at first I thought was completely unnecessary, both his hands wrapped around my biceps. Lenore cut a gash on the guy's forearm and at the sight of his blood, I went completely nuts. I fought against Solon, testing my full strength for the first time, and if he had been just a regular man of his (quite large) size, I could have thrown him against the wall.

But Solon is unfathomably strong and he held me in place while I fed, so I didn't completely lose control and end up killing the guy. I totally understood why vampires had to be restrained by the chains inside the room.

I also understood why some vampires stayed alive on a diet of pills. It was addicting to feed from a live being. Lenore told me that the blood I had would sustain me for at least a week, and that regular food would keep my energy levels going, but within hours I immediately wanted more. Michael was already gone on his merry way, having got something out of having me feed on him, and I'm definitely not kink-shaming here, but it spurred something in me. Before I felt like I was still very much Rose Harper, just now a vampire, and now I feel like I'm a totally different species altogether.

Of course, remembering all my past lives doesn't help either.

When the sun came up, Lenore drove me to the airport. We stopped by the hotel to see Dylan, who was still angry with me that I was leaving. He was planning on staying in San Francisco for a few days, just to live it up, and apparently had enough money to do so from his part-time job as a bartender at the Rogue Brewing Company. Lenore promised me that she and Solon would keep an eye on him and that he would be safe.

I had to trust that. There was no reason for anyone to know who Dylan and I were and that we were in SF, but even so, I was a little paranoid, especially after learning what happened to Leif. But without going into too many details of the hows and the whys, Lenore assured me that he would be well protected. I guess the vampires have more security around them than I ever even noticed.

Lenore also promised to ring up my mom and tell her everything. I gave her our number and she said she would call from a secure line. It seems my parents got even more paranoid over the last ten years, hence why they pulled away from Lenore and Solon and why I hadn't seen them around. I have to wonder if some other incident happened, maybe there was an attempt to take me or Dylan and we don't remember it.

But all those questions have to wait for now. Now I only have one thing on my mind and that's Valtu.

Okay, there are two things on my mind. Valtu, and destroying Bellamy. But I can't do the latter without the former's help. He's the one with the magic book.

The plane touches down at the Innsbruck Airport and I shuffle off the plane with the rest of the passengers. Even though the sleep initially left me a little disoriented and groggy, now I feel that life force of last night's blood coursing through me. My mind keeps wanting to drift back and replay the moment my lips closed around Michael's skin, the way his blood flowed onto my tongue as I sucked it back, feeling his beating heart in every single drop.

But then I have to stop myself, because the more I think about it, the more of an animal I feel like. I don't want to be wild and unhinged. I want to keep my humanity as much as possible. I was a human so many times before I became a vampire, so I have to trust that my human side will always keep me on the straight and narrow.

My heart sinks when I realize how easy it is for someone like Valtu to throw all their humanity away.

Once I'm in the airport, the customs officers giving me a strange look for only traveling with a carry-on, I head toward the exit, hoping to get a taxi. Though I landed in Austria, it's the quickest way to get to Mittenwald since it's right by the border.

I see Dr. Van Helsing standing in the arrivals area and to my surprise he's holding up a sign that reads Mina Lucy Dahlia Rose.

I can't help but break into a grin at his familiar face. He looks just as he had the night I last saw him, twenty-one years ago during my organ recital in Venice. Tall, square-jawed, auburn-haired with twinkling blue eyes. He was wearing a suit then, and now is wearing a sporty-looking parka.

"Doctor!" I cry out and then start running toward him.

He's staring at me with a look of complete awe when I crash into him and throw my arms around him. "I can't believe it's really you," I tell him, giving him a squeeze. He smells Christmassy, like snow and cedar.

Dr. Van Helsing chuckles good-naturedly and pats my back. "Likewise." He pulls away as I release him from my grip and he studies my face intently, his eyes brightening as he looks over every crevice. "I have to admit, when Solon told me they found you, I didn't know what to think. I was sure they had been mistaken. But now that I see you, there is no mistaking it. It really is you. A little younger than the last time I saw you, but still you."

"I'm still not sure I believe it myself," I admit. "It's a lot to come to terms with."

"I can imagine. So, what do I call you?"

"Rose is fine," I say. "Dahlia Rose, if it's easier to remember."

He taps my current name on the sign. "I'll stick to Rose. I adapt easily." He peers at me. "So you really do remember me being your doctor, when you were Lucy?"

I nod. "I do. I mean, I don't remember *all* of Lucy's life, or Mina's...it's kind of like how you don't remember every moment of your childhood. But I do remember most of it and I remember you very well, Doctor."

He chuckles and gives me a dismissive wave. "Please. Just call me Abe. The days of me being your doctor are over." He pauses, his expression turning wistful and grim. "I must apologize for the way that you died when you were Lucy," he says softly. "If only I knew then what I know now, I could have saved your life. And the baby's."

I give him a small smile. "I know. It's not your fault. Even though all these past lives are still so new to me, I've made peace with their passing along the way."

His brow quirks up. "Even Dahlia's?"

I swallow, my throat suddenly thick. "Maybe not yet. But I will. That's why I'm here. To get closure."

"Is that all?" he asks carefully, eyeing me with discernment. "Just closure? You're not still in love with him?"

I let out a pitiful laugh, my heart feeling pinched and squeezed beneath my ribs. "How can I not be? I remember Dahlia's last moments. I remember being in love with him as Dahlia, and I remember being in love with him as Lucy and Mina."

"Moments before he killed you."

"Not something I need to be reminded of."

"But true all the same. So you do love him, even now as Rose. Very interesting." He strokes his chin as he thinks. "One would have thought the last twenty-one years in a new life with no memory of the others might have tempered that love a bit."

I nod slowly. "I guess we'll have to wait and see."

He gives his head a shake, making a low sound of disappointment. "Solon explained to you how Valtu is now, did he not? He doesn't remember you. He purposefully drank the formula to rid you from his mind, from his heart. The man you love, the relationship you had, that doesn't exist anymore. Not to him."

I can't help but flinch as if Abe just slapped me across the face.

"Sorry," he quickly says, licking his lips. "That wasn't very kind of me. I just don't want to see you get hurt. You've come such a long way and I'm afraid you're not going to get what you've come here for."

He looks around the airport, as if suddenly remembering where we are, and puts his hand at my back. "Come on, I parked in the short-term lot and I don't want to get towed. We'll get you into Germany, if this is still what you want to do."

I give him a steady look. "You know I do." Like hell I'm turning back now. "You think any of this is scaring me off?"

He gives me a sheepish smile, awe momentarily flitting across his face. "And there you have it. There's the girl I know. Coming through after all this time."

We start walking toward the exit. "Or maybe it's just me, Rose Harper, and I've always been like this," I point out. "You don't know." I may have lived many lives before, but the life I'm currently living is still my own, and still valid.

"Mmm. Very true. You know, one day, if you're ever up to it, I would love to have you at the lab in Oxford."

I stop dead in my tracks and give him an incredulous look. "You want to study me in a lab!?" My heart skips a beat. I'm remembering why Bellamy wanted Lenore, my mother, Dylan, and Leif. All for tests. Why not me next? I have the same genes that they do.

Good lord, is Van Helsing in on it?

His brows furrow at my reaction. "What's wrong? I

would just love to explore your past lives, your reincarnation. Why you and no one else."

"How do you know there isn't anyone else who has been reincarnated in the same body?" I say, folding my arms, still feeling cagey about all of this. "And what do you think science can do? You can't measure God that way."

He chuckles. "That I know, but it doesn't stop us from trying."

"You know, there are other reasons why scientists want to study me," I say, keeping my voice down, though the passengers milling about aren't paying us any attention.

He frowns for a moment then his eyes widen. "Ah. Yes. Of course. I take it you know what happened to your brother, Leif," he says solemnly. "Another regret of mine was being unable to convince Valtu to help. So strange how your lives are so intertwined, even moments after your death."

I don't want to think about Valtu somehow turning his back on my family.

I ignore it. "Do you know where Leif is now? Do you know if I'm in any danger, if my brother Dylan is? My mom?"

His head shakes and we walk through the doors to the outside, the frigid winter mountain blasting my face. Even though the cold doesn't hurt me as a vampire, it's still a shock to my senses and I'm finally registering that I'm in another continent entirely, in the Alps. I blink at the cloudy yet harsh light and take out my sunglasses, slipping them on.

"Bellamy's trail went cold not long after the abduction," Abe says.

"But how can that be? How can he have been gone for over twenty-one years without a trace?"

"I wish I knew," he says, guiding me toward the neatly plowed parking lot across the road. "The way I see it is it's not necessarily a bad thing. He's leaving us alone. If he had tried to come after any vampire again, we would know about it."

"Only because he got what he wanted," I say bitterly. "My brother. Dylan's twin that neither of us ever got to know."

He shoots me a thoughtful glance. "Careful there, Rose," he says. "Vengeance isn't all it's cracked up to be. Sometimes it's better to harbor justice in your heart than attempt to inflict it and fail."

I ignore that too. "Well, what about the book? The one that Valtu has. Aren't Bellamy and the covens trying to get it back? Or Saara and that other vampire? Solon said she's still alive, doing bad shit with someone called Enoch."

Van Helsing shrugs. "They're all probably trying to get it back. Or at least they were. But Valtu has it under lock and key. He himself is under lock and key. It's why I'm not taking you directly to him, but instead right into Mittenwald."

"You haven't been to his place?"

"I have," he says, flashing me a grin as he presses the key fob on his phone app and a car beeps its location across the lot. "I just couldn't tell you how to get there."

"Well, where does he live?"

"Let's just say Dracula finally found his castle."

A castle? I almost laugh. "A little on the nose, don't you think?"

"You know how he can get," he says. "Such a flair for the dramatic. Here we are." We stop by a flashy Mercedes.

"This yours?"

"A rental. I landed only a few hours ago, straight from

Oxford. Just enough time to get my favorite schnitzel in Innsbruck, then rent the car and come pick you up."

The doors unlock and I throw my bag in the back before sliding into the passenger seat. "It was really kind of you to pick me like this. I know you're busy, it couldn't have been easy to just drop everything and head over here."

"Not a problem," he says, turning on the car. It hums to life, electric. "As if I would pass up an opportunity to come see Mina Lucy Dahlia's latest reincarnation."

"Hope I haven't disappointed you."

"Not a chance." He gives me a kind smile as we drive out of the lot. "But I am afraid it's you that's going to be disappointed."

"We'll just have to see," I say, refusing to let him talk me out of this. "Did you tell him it was me that was coming?"

"Oh, *no*." He shakes his head adamantly. "That wouldn't have been wise. I didn't say much at all, except that I had someone he had to...meet." He pauses and squints at me. "You know how to block your thoughts from other vampires, don't you? Valtu can be very intrusive when he wants to be."

I laugh. "I've been doing that since I was eight years old and accidentally shattered my mother's favorite crystal. Didn't want her to know I did it. My brother got blamed instead."

"Good to know." He clears his throat. "Because I offered you up as a whore."

My eyes nearly fall out. "You what?" I exclaim.

Abe looks chagrined, but not enough. He raises one shoulder. "It was the only way I could deliver you to him."

"Do you often offer him whores?" I ask, though the second I say it, I don't want to know the answer. The jealousy inside me is acidic.

He bites his lip for a moment and gives me an uneasy look. "In some ways he's the same vampire you know. Well, perhaps closest to the Venice edition than anything else. He doesn't have a Red Room to run—Bitrus does that for him back in Italy—but his, uh, appetites haven't changed too much."

"So why are you his pimp?" I grumble.

He bristles at that. "I'm not his *pimp*. But he never leaves Mittenwald. Ever. And there are only so many people —and vampires—in this town. Even with the book and spells at his summoning, he doesn't get close to anyone without them being vetted beforehand." He clears his throat. "He's paranoid. Not just anyone is granted entry to his home."

"And I guess you can't just say, hey it's Mina Lucy Dahlia Rose coming to pay you a visit?"

He gives me a steady look. "If you had purposely erased Valtu from your memory and he showed up at your house, do you think you'd want him to stay? The minute he knows who you are, you'll be seeing the back of him." A dark cloud comes over his blue eyes. "Or worse. Possibly much worse."

"Don't tell me he'd try and kill me again."

I was joking when I said that but from the way Abe winces, I realize how serious it is.

"I wouldn't put it past him," he says, and I can't help but feel a little sick to my stomach. "Don't forget that you don't exist to him. He knows that there was a lover, that he erased that lover because he killed her, and because all her previous versions had died, but it's like being told a story to him. He doesn't remember it, so it doesn't seem real. Like you were something that happened to somebody else. Someone else's tragedy."

Someone else's tragedy. What a way to be thought of, to be reduced to.

I'm someone else's tragedy.

He goes on, voice firmer now. "I have no doubt he wouldn't hesitate to kill you, Rose. Valtu never let go of that monster. When he lost Lucy, he lost his humanity, became a dark and depraved killing machine, but after time, he found himself again, after the grief had loosened its hold. This time though...he never fully went back. Never returned to base-level Valtu. He's remained in this...other state."

"But he's not grieving. He can't be if he doesn't remember me."

"He's not grieving as far as he knows it," he says. "That doesn't mean he's not holding onto pain deep inside his heart, deep inside his psyche. The subconscious confounds most scientists, let alone me. When you add magic to the equation, something that has never been studied except attempts by rogue vampire outlier scientists and doctors like myself, then things get even murkier. I believe trauma is embedded in a way that our working mind can't easily access. In Valtu's case, it's locked in. How can you exorcise grief if you don't acknowledge it?"

I swallow uneasily at the thought of Valtu locked in deep grief and feel a sharp pinch in my chest. "So he's tormented."

"He's a lot of things," Abe says quietly. "But most of all, he is still Valtu. One version of him, anyway. I guess you'd know all about different versions of yourself."

The drive from Austria and over the German border to Mittenwald is fairly quick, even with early snow piled on the sides of the highway. We go along switchbacks and up through picturesque villages, passing under the shadows of the craggy mountains, mist hugging their flanks. Though the snow is bright even under the clouds, there is something ominous about it all. It's not just that I'm about to see Valtu for the first time in two decades, for the first time as Rose, and for the first time as a vampire. It's not even that there's an element of real fear now where there wasn't before. It's that I can feel something else here in the Bavarian Alps, something shadowy, dark and sinister. Like something is watching and waiting for me. My intuition seems to ratchet up a notch, my pulse thrumming in my neck. It's connected to Valtu and yet it's not him at all.

It's like all of this is about to be a very grave mistake, one I'll come to regret for the rest of my life.

I am doing the right thing, right?

But I don't dare voice my doubt to the doctor lest he turn the car around and drive me back to Austria.

Soon we're parking in a lot behind a row of buildings that look like colorful gingerbread houses and Abe shuts off the car. He shoots me a grave look, twisting in his seat to face me.

"Listen," he says softly. "I'm not going to bother warning you again. I can see you're stubborn and that's something that will never change, apparently. But I can tell you what to expect. I can give you advice. Naturally I'm not going to stick around here—"

"You're not?!" I jolt.

"I'll stay here tonight with you and Valtu, but then I have to head back to Oxford."

"For what? Work? Can't you postpone it?"

He gives me an apologetic look. "I do have important work back at the lab, yes. But more than that, it would be out of character for me to lurk around Mittenwald. If you want Valtu to believe you're a...well, who you say you are, it's normal for me to leave. I don't always partake in Valtu's parties, if you know what I mean. They can be rather distasteful."

I narrow my eyes at him. "Kink-shamer," I mutter under my breath.

"And so," he goes on, "I must go."

"And if something happens to me?"

"I'm sure you'll be able to handle yourself now," he says. "You're a vampire this time around. We're practically indestructible. In fact, part of my current research is trying to figure out if I can harness that gene. Make it work to our advantage."

"Like what? Someone chops off our head and we grow a new one?"

"Something like that," he says. "Vampires have a lot of enemies, including other vampires. If some of us were more immortal than others, truly invincible…"

I make a face. "None of this is making me feel better."

"I'm not trying to make you feel better. I'm trying to get you to reconsider." His gaze darts to outside the car, at the bundled-up tourists going past. "You still have a chance to change your mind. There's still time."

"I'm not changing my mind," I tell him evenly, but god, does my gut twist into knots.

He sighs, running a hand down his face. Then he reaches into the inner pocket of his coat and pulls out a business card, pure black with no writing on it.

"Look at this," he says, flipping the card so that it's right in front of my face, but there's still nothing to see. I'm about to protest when he adds, "Hold out your hand, palm down."

I do as he asks and he notices my hand shaking slightly, giving me a quick concerned glance before he drops the black card onto the back of my hand. I barely feel it land and then it starts to dissolve in front of my eyes, like it's sinking into my pores. I gasp as there's a tingling sensation and then the card is gone, as if it never existed.

"What the hell was that?" I exclaim breathlessly, staring at my hand in awe.

He grins, a twinkle in his blue eyes. "Magic."

"Valtu taught you that?"

He rolls his eyes. "Would it surprise you if it were plain old-fashioned technology? Anyway, at a certain angle, and to your eyes only, you'll be able to see the information you need."

I turn my hand one way and then the other, toward the light outside, and I can see a phone number written down, an iridescent collection of numbers that's barely visible.

"That's my number," he says. "Burner phone. Call it if you have a problem, but only in a life-or-death situation. I'll see what I can do to help."

"How long do the...how long do women...or whoever he's enjoying," I add, remembering how fluid Valtu's sexual attraction is, "how long do they stay with him for?"

"You might have a day, you might have weeks. It depends if he likes you." He shoots me a stiff smile. "And how much he likes you." Then his eyes widen. "Oh I just remembered." He reaches into his other pocket and pulls out a small black bag made of rubbery material. "Valtu doesn't always feed his guests though he'll feed *from* them. You'll need blood if he's not being generous. You have a few weeks' worth of blood pills in there. Totally new version I just created, hasn't even hit the black market yet. Keeps you full and energized for longer and the bag acts like a portable refrigerator. The cold is key to making the pills work better."

I take the bag in wonder, having briefly forgotten that Dr. Van Helsing is the one who invented blood pills to begin with. "Thank you," I tell him profusely as I slip it in my purse. "You know you're practically a hero for inventing these."

He gives me a dry look. "Depends on who you ask. Most vampires miss feeding on humans. It's the humans that should call me a hero for sparing the lot of them, but sadly most don't even know of our existence so..." he punctuates that with a shrug.

"So Valtu might not feed me?" Thank god I fed from Michael last night.

"He'll give you food. But I'm not sure about blood. You see, I don't think I've ever seen him have a vampire over for *this* sort of thing."

My brows raise. "Is the fact I'm a vampire going to be a problem?"

"Let's hope not." Then he opens the door and gets out of the car and it takes all my strength to take in a long, shuddering breath, then open the door and step into my cold and unknown future.

CHAPTER 10
ROSE

D r. Abraham Van Helsing places his fingers at my elbow and steers me down an icy lane toward the pedestrian street where people are walking, going about their daily lives in this mountain town, while I feel like I'm marching toward some uncertain doom.

I'm nervous. Not nervous enough to turn around and call the whole thing off, but nervous all the same, pins and needles inside my heart.

Will Valtu recognize me despite the spell?

Will he feel compelled to be with me?

Or will he be dismissive and cruel?

It feels like yesterday that I was in Venice with him, trying to figure out the game and how to play it, and yet that feels like it was a million times easier than what I'm about to do now, even with all that I know.

"Easy now," Abe whispers to me. "We'll be meeting him in the middle of a square. Knowing him, he's probably already there. Keep yourself together."

We round the corner, past red-faced skiers carrying skis over their shoulders, most likely having just come down a run from one of the giant mountains that loom over the town, and then the buildings open up into a snowy and picturesque pedestrian area.

And standing in the middle of it all, like a black smudge in a sea of white, is Valtu Aminoff. Sometimes my professor. Sometimes my husband. Sometimes my lover. But always Valtu.

He's not facing us, he's looking up at the mountains overhead, his hands in the pockets of his deep black coat. I come to a stop, wanting to stare at him and take him all in. His tall, powerful build, his luscious black hair, his disarmingly handsome face, forever staying the same through all my lifetimes. It's been so long and yet like yesterday since I last saw him, and it takes everything in me not to break free of Abe's grip on my arm and run toward him.

But I can't do that.

Because he doesn't know who I am.

And yet I still have faith. I still carry faith and hope inside my heart like a jar filled with fireflies. They burn there, fluttering against the glass, wanting to escape, but I can't let them loose yet. Not yet.

"Come on," Abe says quietly, pushing me forward gently, and then we're walking again and I keep alternating from feeling like my legs are full of lead or that there's a wind at my back.

The strange thing is that Valtu appears to be more than just a black smudge in the bright world—he's like a black hole. There's this dark energy about him, radiating from him and circling around him. People are walking past him, some giving him shy smiles, others glancing at him and keeping on their way, but no one seems scared or off-put by the darkness in his orbit. I wonder if only I can see it or if any vampires can. But Abe is looking forward, determined to stay in his role, and I know if I want this to work, I must do the same.

I feel like my life is bleeding back into Dahlia's. At least I've been through this before.

Yeah. And it didn't end well.

"Valtu," Abe greets him in a commanding voice as we approach, and Valtu slowly turns to face us.

His dark eyes go to Abe's first and I'm surprised to see he isn't smiling. Valtu always had a smile for his oldest friend. Often cheeky or amused but that smile was always there and freely given. Now though, Valtu's face remains completely impassive, even in his eyes.

Then his deep brown eyes move over to me and I suck in my breath because he finally sees me.

He sees me!

But then I'm only seeing what I want to, because his expression doesn't change at all. He looks me up and down, I guess to get an idea of the *goods* being delivered, but there's no recognition at all, only a hint of derisiveness.

"Doctor," Valtu says, the sound of his voice, low, rich and melodic, sending shivers in waves down my spine. "It's been some time."

He doesn't hug Abe, or shake his hand. Just continues to stand where he is, hands in his pockets, face blank. He doesn't even glance at me again, it's like I'm not even there.

Oh my god.

He really doesn't remember me.

I'm just some random redheaded whore that Abe brought for him to play with, and I'm not even sure he finds me attractive enough for that at this point. He doesn't seem that happy to have me there, then again he doesn't seem all that happy about anything.

Valtu, I think pleadingly and before I can finish that thought, he looks at me sharply, narrows his eyes.

Oh no. He heard that.

"And who did you bring me here?" he says coldly, his gaze flitting over my features as his attention is purely on me now. My heart pounds a mile a minute and I'm torn between feeling absolutely heartbroken over the fact that he doesn't know who I am, and completely smitten and joyous because he's here, in the flesh, standing right in front of me.

My heart found his again.

But his heart doesn't know mine.

"She's a big admirer of yours," Abe quickly says, and I know that's my cue to tone it down, but I can't. If anything, my pulse quickens, my nerves feeling shot and shaky.

I don't think I can handle this.

Valtu sniffs derisively, his nostrils flaring as he takes in my scent. "And a vampire. You couldn't find a human that was a big fan?"

"Vampires last a lot longer," Abe says to him with a knowing look in his eye, and I can't help but bristle at that, talking as if I'm just some cow on the auction block. "I know you don't care for humans, Valtu, but using them and discarding them as you do, really puts out a lot of, how should I say, bad juju into the world."

Valtu simultaneously sneers and grumbles and despite that, he's still the most beautiful creature I've ever seen. He always will be, even when I catch a glimpse of those dark eyes and I see nothing staring back at me. Just this void where his soul used to be.

And just like that, perhaps a moment too late, I'm suddenly afraid.

No, not just afraid. *Terrified*.

Because I realize how much heartbreak I'm setting myself up for.

Valtu, my love, doesn't know me. He doesn't remember me. Remember us. And worse than that, he's dangerous in a way that he never was before. Even when I was Dahlia and I was putting myself in harm's way by going after him, I never really believed he would kill me, not unless he found out who I was. He was Professor Aminoff. He was respected and kind and while his sexual appetites were on the kinky side (to say the least) I never felt I was actually in any danger with him. If anything, he went out of his way to not harm others, hence the creation of the Red Room.

But I can see with this Valtu, standing before me like a dark specter amongst the frozen snow, that he wouldn't hesitate to kill if he deemed it necessary—perhaps even if it wasn't necessary. And he wasn't one to feel remorse over it, or anything for that matter. I suppose it's hard to feel remorse when it can be so easily erased.

Because that's what I am.

So easily erased.

Valtu's eyes slide over my face again, then my body, despite it being covered by a winter coat (or partially covered, since I borrowed it from Lenore—it doesn't close over my boobs), then he tilts his head in consideration. I can only stand there on display, feeling like I'm being judged in the harshest way, my insides squirming with insecurity. If he doesn't deem me good enough for him, then what? What if he sends me back with Abe?

Then you tell him who you are, I think. *And hope for the best.*

But I know deep down that it would only end in more heartbreak. This man standing in front of me doesn't want to know who I've been. If I told him I was Mina and Lucy

118

and Dahlia, he would turn me away, and it would jeopardize his friendship with Abe, even though there doesn't seem to be much of a friendship left from the awkward tension between them.

Oh my love, what happened to you?

Finally, Valtu sighs and looks to Abe. "I suppose you've never let me down before." His eyes go to me again. "What's your name?"

"Rose," I tell him. If I say more my voice will start to shake. I raise my chin a little and take a firmer stance.

"Ah," he muses. "All petals or all thorns?"

"Depends on what you like," I answer.

Finally there's a hint of amusement in his eyes, the faintest ghost of a smile.

Winning that from him feels like winning the lottery.

"I like her," Valtu surmises to Abe. "A bit more fire than the others. I suppose she will do for the night."

The night? I look at Abe in surprise. Has that already been decided?

But Abe doesn't meet my eyes. "Shall I consider myself a guest for the night as well?" he asks Valtu.

"Of course," he says. "You know you never need ask."

From the tension in Abe's face, I can tell that's not true.

Valtu gives me another discerning look. "How are you for hiking a great distance?" Then he smirks, charming and acidic all at once. "Never mind. I forgot I'm not dealing with a human. Perhaps you're right, Doctor. Having a vampire might be a nice change after all."

"I can handle a hike," I tell him, pulling my bag further up on my shoulder. "Lead the way."

I guess Valtu's castle or whatever it is that he lives in isn't accessible by car. Maybe Valtu doesn't even own a car. I've actually never seen him in a car, which is funny. They didn't exist when I was Mina and Lucy, and in Venice Valtu only drove a motorboat. But still, being here in Germany, you'd think he would have some mode of transportation, though Abe did say he never leaves Mittenwald. I have to wonder if it's a great distance, how quickly he's able to get to the village. Vampires can move extremely fast when we need to but it's not something we can keep up for a long time. We're supposed to be more like cheetahs than an endurance racer.

Abe walks beside Valtu as we go across the square and I trail behind. I have to wonder why he decided to settle down here, but from the way that most people ignore him, or barely look in his direction, he must at least enjoy a degree of anonymity. Still, the Valtu I knew hated being cold. Italy, Greece, Croatia, those were the places he always found himself drawn to, even when we were in London he was always talking about taking me to the sun of the Mediterranean. The fact that he's in this village, in the dead of winter, is just another sign that he's changed.

It feels like I'm getting a tour of the entire village before we finally come to the edge of the gingerbread house buildings and pass over a river and there's just a faint trace of a trail heading up between the towering pines, the branches laden with snow.

Valtu comes to a stop in front of us, his eyes shining with faint amusement again as he looks us over, the mountain looming over him like a shadow and for a moment I'm afraid we're only going straight up.

"*Nunc vides*," he commands, his words in another language, maybe Latin. He holds up his fingers and snaps them. "*Nunc non faciunt*."

And suddenly the entire world changes.

I gasp, stumbling forward a step and Abe reaches out

and steadies me. Valtu is still standing in front of us, with his fingers in the air like he just snapped them, but the mass of the mountain and forest is no longer at his back. Instead, there's a sheer wall of rock with steps carved into it, leading to a door. The more I stare at the rock wall, the surface dark gray and shiny with snow clinging onto little ledges and outcrops, the more that it begins to resemble a house...no...a castle. There are arched windows cut right into the rock along the length of with stained glass inserts, and balconies built into crevices with gargoyle-laden stone railings, towers carved above.

Where am I? What the hell just happened?

I whirl around and gasp again when I feel the sharp breeze buffeting my cheek and realize we're hundreds if not thousands of feet above the village of Mittenwald.

Holy. Shit.

"What the fuck?" I exclaim breathlessly, feeling so dizzy at the sight of the valley no longer at our level but miles below us that I have to turn around again, vertigo taking over.

Valtu chuckles dryly. "I do enjoy this moment."

I look at Abe, still feeling sick, and he just shrugs. "It's the only way to get here."

"Yes, but how?" I ask.

"You must feel a little burn in your thighs, no?" Valtu asks, raising a black brow. "We just climbed all this way. Only took about three hours to do two thousand feet."

I blink rapidly. "I don't understand. I don't remember any of it."

"No, you wouldn't," he muses, then he turns around and heads up the stone steps that lead to the giant metal doors at the edge of the cliff face.

Abe puts his hand at my lower back and guides me

forward. He leans into me and whispers, "When I said I didn't know where he lived, I wasn't kidding."

I don't say anything to that since I know Valtu can hear us. I guess the words Valtu said when he snapped his fingers, the Latin, was some sort of memory spell. If he can erase me from his memory, surely he has the power to do the same to others. I feel like I'd been out cold the entire hike, but he's right, my thighs do burn a little and when I look down at my coat and my hands, they're dirty like I've been climbing up a mountain.

Fuck. The idea that I've had three hours of memory wiped doesn't sit well with me.

I'm still a little woozy and I'm grateful for Abe's support as he helps me up the slick steps to the metal doors that open automatically for us, no doubt thanks to some magic of Valtu's. Having that book for so long must mean he's learned every spell there is to know. Another shiver goes down my back, this one cold and unpleasant. The absolute power that Valtu has at his disposal is overwhelming to think about. The destruction that this vampire can do, if he hasn't done some already.

I try to keep my thoughts guarded and push them away. I focus on the castle instead. It's not hard to do. It's a marvel of engineering.

Everything inside is rock and stone. From the polished floor to the rough walls. There's enough light thanks to all the windows and the unobstructed view of the world beyond, but the place is still dark and full of shadows. It's a little creepy, if I do say so myself. There are some touches of warmth, like the blazing fire in the corner of the living area and the sconces lit all over, a mix of candlelit and electric bulbs, with some soft-looking Turkish rugs strewn about on the floor and rich tapestries and paintings on the walls, but even so it still puts me on edge. It certainly is the type of place that Dracula would find himself in. Cold, dark, and utterly Gothic.

"This is the main level," Valtu says, gesturing around. "The kitchen, which has more human food than you might imagine, the living area, the dining room, a couple of bedrooms down there." He nods to where a hallway snakes past the kitchen (which also looks straight out of the 1800s, except for the stainless-steel fridge), and disappears into darkness. "Then there's the upstairs."

He starts heading straight toward a wall and I fear he's going to walk right into it but then suddenly he disappears. I make an astonished noise and go after him, while Abe chuckles behind me, obviously having seen this before.

As I get to the wall I realize it's just an optical illusion in the rock and that you can actually walk around a corner. I follow Valtu as he heads up a flight of stairs that seem to zig zag through the dark, a few lone candles flickering on the walls, the wicks burning low. The air smells cold, like snow and frost and alpine, tempered with the scent of smoke from the fire and candles.

Most of all though, I smell Valtu.

His scent hasn't changed.

Walking behind him up these steps, it feels like my heart is being bled dry by the sight of him, the smell of him. Mint and oranges and something deeper, almost ancient, like santal or smoked oud. His scent seems to ignite every nerve inside, making my stomach do summersaults, my heart skip a few beats. Heat floods through me, enough so that he glances down at me over his shoulder and raises his brow, as if asking himself a question.

He can probably smell what my body is doing. I have to wonder if this is unusual for him, if the women or men that are usually brought here for his enjoyment have come so ready and willing, or if they've needed money or drugs to make it happen, to let their guards down and relax.

My stomach stops the summersault and starts to twist, the pit of jealousy hot and deep. I don't want to think about the others. It's ridiculous. I know vampires are a possessive bunch and that includes me now, but I also know that sex is just sex in many cases. Valtu has lived on and on while I have lived and died in my lives. To imagine he, of all people, has been celibate while I've been dead is ridiculous.

And yet the feelings persist. I have to do what I can to ignore it.

Valtu's attention turns back to the floor we step out onto. It's like a mezzanine that leads out through shuttered doors onto a large balcony. Several dark hallways lead off in different directions, disappearing into the rock. But the mezzanine itself catches my eye because as I adjust to the dim light, I see it's a music room of sorts. There's a few velvet and brocade couches and leather wing-backed armchairs, another roaring fire, then a piano on one side and on the other a massive organ that looks like it's been half-built into the rock wall.

The sight of the organ stuns me.

"Oh my god," I can't help but say and Valtu gives me an odd look.

"Never seen an organ before?" he asks and for a moment I think he suspects who I am, like this organ was put here as a trap. But then he walks over to it and lets his fingers trail over the keys without creating any noise. "I figured a proper vampire's lair would need an organ," he says lightly.

While he's staring at the organ, I look to Abe with my brows raised in question. Even if he doesn't remember

Dahlia, does he know that she played the organ and that's how they'd met? Or has he avoided all the details of our life together?

Abe just gives me a quick shrug, answering absolutely nothing, then says, "If you get Valtu drunk enough he might even play you something."

Valtu chuckles and turns around, giving me an apologetic look. "I'm afraid I'm not very good anymore. I was a music teacher at one point...that's one of the reasons I chose Mittenwald. Did you know that it's been famous for violin-making since the seventeenth century? I couldn't quite give music up..." He laughs again, though there is no humor in it. His tone is hard and bitter. "And yet I haven't touched any of these instruments in years."

He glowers for a moment and then seems to snap out of it. "If you wish to stay the night, Abe, your room is same as before, downstairs. But, Rose, yours is over here."

Valtu heads down one of the narrow hallways that twists and turns crookedly in the dark and I notice that Abe isn't following, which makes me uneasy. It shouldn't. This is Valtu. This is my love. And yet I can't help but be on edge.

"Here is your room," he says, opening a heavy wooden door with a creak. He gestures for me to step in.

I do so, looking around. It's relatively small and cold with one narrow window to a blur of white outside which I come to realize is a passing cloud. That's how high up we are.

There's not much else to the room, save for a large wrought-iron four-poster bed, a large rug, and an en suite bathroom. But when I look at the bed closer, I realize there are ropes and chains at each post.

I gulp.

"Now, be a good girl and stay here while I talk with my

friend," Valtu says as he steps back into the hall, his hand on the doorknob, "and figure out what I'm going to do with you."

His eyes go cold and crude, and then before I can protest, he shuts the door. A strange energy hums from it and I immediately go for the handle, trying to open it.

I can't. He's locked it with magic, which is smart because I'm sure I'd have no problem breaking the door down eventually.

I'm officially trapped here.

I sigh and sit on the corner of the bed and wonder what my fate will be.

CHAPTER 11
VALTU

I close the door to the girl's room and the wards come alive, their magic sealing the redhead inside. Normally I don't have to worry about humans breaking down the doors or busting through the locks in this place, but since this girl is a vampire, I'm not about to take any chances. I don't want her wandering through my house unaccompanied, and I'm not naïve enough to think she might not run. It's happened before, the human having changed their mind and gotten scared, trying to escape the mountain.

They never get far, though. If the mountain wolves don't get them, the demon will. Sometimes the demon is feeling especially generous and wants to share the human with me. I feed then let the demon do what it wants with them. Less messy that way and keeps my hands clean, for the most part.

The humans are always innocuous. That's one of the reasons I like them, especially the ones that Abe selects for me. He picks ones that are obsessed with vampires and feeding, that mourn the invention of the blood pills as much as I do. They scour the earth looking for the infamous feeding cages and Red Rooms of the glory days. When they're eventually brought here, they're ready to submit to me in any way I see fit, especially when they learn who I am and my history.

Everyone wants to suck Dracula's dick.

But vampires? Vampires have always had disdain for me. A century ago I would have said it was all Bram Stoker's fault. Vampires were jealous that I was the one who inspired the most famous bloodsucker of all time. Later, if they got a chance to know me, they then thought I was a joke, not worthy enough to be written about.

Now, though, it feels different. Not that I have a lot of interaction with vampires these days, but when I do I sense their animosity. Rumors had spread long ago that I was the one who let Bellamy and the coven on the loose, that I was the one who let Saara go (you can't blame me for thinking she was dead, that fire should have killed her) and that I was the one who had an infamous book of black magic that I kept hidden away. I get the impression that they think the book belongs to all vampires. Well, it's a shame for them that I don't share their ideals.

So the fact that Van Helsing brought a vampire here is very unusual indeed.

Even more unusual is the fact that I detect zero resentment or animosity in her.

Instead...I feel, well, something like love, if not infatuation. I can't explain it but when I look into her eyes, green eyes the color of faded moss in late summer, I see someone who has intense feelings of adoration for me.

Van Helsing did say she was an admirer of mine, and I have to believe him on that, it's just strange to be so openly adored by another vampire.

Hence why I need her to be sequestered away while I talk to him. Though she'll never get her hands on the book even if she tries, that could be the reason why she's here.

I head down the hallway and back to the music parlor where Van Helsing is standing at the window, looking out into the great beyond.

"Well?" I say to him, and he jerks around to face me, looking startled. He's a little jumpy today. Sometimes that happens after the journey here.

He clears his throat, composing himself. "Do you like her?"

I think that over, rubbing my lips. "I find her strange and peculiar."

"In a good way?"

"I'm not sure. Shall we have a drink? When's the last time you had real blood, Doctor?"

He laughs as we head down the stairs to the lower level. "I may have invented the pills, but I'm not a saint, Valtu. You of all people should know that."

"People change," I counter. "And you of all people should know *that*."

He takes a seat at the large chestnut table in the dining room. It's long and solid, the kind of table you would see used for dinner parties at royal palaces in the days of yore. Now it has a lonely existence, save for the occasional friend I may have over every other year or so. I haven't even fucked on it, which suddenly seems like a real waste of crafts-manship.

I bring him a bottle of red from the rack and then a bottle of blood from the fridge, along with two glasses and place them down in front of him.

"Which would you like first? Shot or chaser?"

"Blood before wine, as they say."

I pour us a glass of blood and clink mine against his.

"To your new gift," I tell him.

He stares at me blankly for a moment then smiles. "To *your* new gift. I hope you enjoy her."

"And I hope you enjoy this," I tell him, tapping the side of my glass with my finger before finishing the blood in one go. I've never been one for restraint and this blood is impossible to resist.

Van Helsing takes a sniff and then a tepid sip and I nearly laugh. I've had blood with the good doctor before, so I know he still partakes in it, but it still amuses me to see how much he fights his natural instinct to want blood. The pills only do so much. There's a real thirst inside of all of us vampires, one that can only really be quenched by the blood of a living human. Those that stick only to pills look gaunt and ashy, and deep down inside they know they're denying the most primal and basic part of themselves by abstaining from the fresh stuff.

Like Van Helsing here. The moment the blood hits his lips there's a chemical change. I smell it on him, I see it on him. His eyes light right up like fireworks. He has another sip, a little bigger now, his hands starting to shake, and then suddenly he's gulping the rest of the glass down. When he's done, red is running down his chin and he looks ravenous.

"There's the doctor I know," I exclaim, pouring us both another glass. "That's the one they called Jack the Ripper. Do you remember those days, old boy?"

He gives me a steady look before wiping the blood off his chin with his finger and then licking it clean. "*I* do," he says carefully, implying that I don't.

Memory is a funny subject for us. There's a lot of things

that we've experienced together that I don't remember. I'm guessing that when I had my memory wiped of the woman from my past, Dahlia, that a lot of events that involved the both of them disappeared. For example, once he talked about a play we had seen in London's West End, but I had no memory of it. Later he said that the woman was there with us, going by the name of Lucy at the time, which made me realize that by erasing her I had erased countless other things.

Sometimes I fear they were important things.

But we don't talk about what I went to such lengths to forget. I know her name was Dahlia and she had been reincarnated over and over. I know her other names from her other lives are Mina and Lucy, only because of Bram Stoker. I know I had loved her so much, and that too much death led to too much pain. At this point in my life I don't feel pain, so I can't even fathom it, but I know that I had to have been suffering in order to do something so drastic. Which is why it's not a subject I ever talk about, let alone think about.

It doesn't matter anyway. What's done is done. She's dead, whoever she was, and I have moved on in the only way I knew how. They say that grief is a thief of time because the pain of loss not only steals so much from the heart but so much from *life*. People lose months, years, decades of their lives to mourning. It is utterly unfair and I am grateful I don't have to lose anymore.

"So where did you get this blood from? Dare I ask?" Van Helsing says, reaching for the bottle.

"If I told you, you wouldn't like it."

He grimaces and puts the bottle back down. "Oh please. Don't say this belongs to a child or something."

"I'm not sure," I admit with a shrug. "I doubt it. But

what I do know is that I'm only brought the blood of the most, shall we say, succulent humans."

He stares at me for a moment then shakes his head. "Right. Brought. By your little friend. You're right, I didn't want to know that." He pours us both another glass and licks his lips appreciatively before he catches himself, looking guilty. He clears his throat. "Let me guess, you've got it trained like a dog now?"

Oh, how I wish, I think, and I don't dare say that out loud in case the demon is near. Even with vampire senses, the creature is invisible to me when it wants to be, and yet it seems to hear and see everything I do.

"Let's just say that sometimes it offers me a gift, much like you're doing tonight," I explain. "A way to make amends, or perhaps a way to get closer, to make me let my guard down. A way to take advantage with a little buttering up."

I squint at him as he swallows his drink, wondering if that's actually what he's doing here. The years have made my mind always jump to the worst conclusions, paranoid of even my dearest of friends. It's a potentially fatal flaw I can't seem to shake.

He raises his empty glass as a plea for more. "Well if you feel like buttering me up..."

I pour us both another glass and we toast before finishing the blood. Every cell inside me feels nourished and alive and I relish it. It's really the only time that I feel much of anything. I have my fits of rage and bitterness, but the blood soothes and calms like nothing else can. Except for a good fuck or two.

"So, tell me about this Rose," I ask him, feeling satisfied enough to move onto the wine. "Why did you really bring her?"

"I thought you could use a vampire for once," he says as I uncork the bottle of vintage red and pour him a glass, the burgundy swirling with the bright tinge of the leftover blood in the glass.

"And why is that?"

"You're a little rough with the humans," he explains with a wince.

"It's not *me* who is rough with them," I say, feeling mildly defensive as I sit back down. "Not always."

"Either way, it's been a long time since any of them left this place alive. You know that I invented those pills to help humans too, right? It wasn't sitting right with me to be leading so many of them like sheep to the slaughter."

I roll my eyes and have a gulp of wine, the grapes mixing beautifully with the blood, smoky and rich. "They know the risks in coming here."

"Regardless," he says steadily, "I thought maybe you could use someone who could take a, well, necessary roughness."

"If you think vampires stand a chance against my guardian, you are sorely mistaken." I saw the demon wrap its tail around Aleksi's neck and then pop his head clean off.

He clucks his tongue. "I don't know how you sleep at night."

I shrug, not knowing if he means with the demon here or with the way I conduct myself. Perhaps both. "Not well, thanks for asking." I sigh. "Anyway. So you think a vampire might handle my appetite better. Perhaps. But is that the real reason that girl is here?"

I stare hard at him until he flinches a little. "What?"

My brow goes up, suspicious. "I know why you brought her here."

He blinks and clears his throat and I know the truth

immediately. He is quite transparent and it's not because of his pale skin.

"Why?" he questions but I hear the reluctance in his voice, like he knows he's been found out.

I give him a triumphant grin. "You're trying to set me up. That's easy to see."

Van Helsing stares blankly at me for a moment before he says, "I'm setting you up..."

"Isn't it obvious? You bring an attractive vampire here, one that is already a fan of mine, so I don't have to win her over. You think I need the company beyond a quick fuck. You think I'm lonely up here, that perhaps if I had some other vampire in my life that it would tame me in some way." I have a sip of my wine and smirk. "Sorry, Doctor, but you're sorely mistaken."

A look of palpable relief comes across his brow. "Whew. Well. I'm glad I don't have to keep that from you anymore."

"It was a nice try," I commend him. "She's just my type. You know me well."

"But you *will* give her a try, won't you?" he asks.

I smirk at how eager he is. "I will give her a try tonight. Sure. But she'll be leaving with you in the morning."

He looks disappointed.

"Sorry," I add. "But the last thing I need is another complication in my life."

His look of disappointment turns into one of disbelief. "As if your life is highly complicated," he notes. "You're a fucking hermit."

I bristle at that. "You try living here with that *thing*."

"I'm sure your magic book makes it all better."

"It does," I tell him curtly.

I only wish that the pages would fill themselves in. I haven't seen a new spell appear in the book for over four years now. It's like whatever has been supplying me with magic, perhaps the book itself, has decided to withhold the last of it for reasons unknown. It doesn't stop me from pouring over the pages every night, wishing the pages would fill with ink before my eyes. There has to be more to it. There has to be some way to unlock more of it. But how?

Van Helsing steers the subject away from the book and back onto Rose.

"Just be nice to her," he says.

I let out a wry laugh. "Nice to her? Oh, I'll be nice to her. Where did you even find her anyway? Her accent is American."

"She's from Oregon. She came into my lab requesting to meet you."

"And you didn't find that odd?"

"At first. But you know how the young ones are. They want to know everything."

I frown mid-sip. "Young ones? How old is she?"

He shrugs. "I don't know, but she hasn't been around for all that long."

I swallow and think that over. Young blood. Young pussy. It's been a long time since I've experienced a vampire in their youth.

It's enough that by the time we have finished the bottle of wine, I'm excusing myself from the table. Van Helsing understands, of course, he knows what goes on here, and he retires to the living room with what remains of his wine.

I go straight up the stairs and down the hallway that leads to her room, the wards undoing themselves in my presence.

I open the door and step into her bedroom, the door closing behind me.

She's lying on the bed, staring straight up at the ceiling, and raises her head to look at me.

"Come here," I command her in a low voice, my eyes never leaving hers.

She hesitates for a moment, a strange look passing over her eyes, then gets off the bed and walks over to me. Her coat has since been discarded to the floor, her boots askew beside it, like she's accustomed to making a mess, and she's just wearing jeans and a thin sweater. I can see her curves more clearly now and my dick automatically hardens at the wide expanse of her hips, the pert shape of her full breasts, nipples already at attention.

She stops a couple of feet away and raises her chin to meet my gaze. I stare deeply into her eyes and take my time drinking in their vulnerability. Yes, she still has that glow in them that makes her iris's extra green, that look of love and affection, however misplaced it may be. But there's something else in them now. Fear. Just a touch of it. Just a kiss of terror.

It shouldn't turn me on, but it does. It always does. My cock presses against my fly, straining to be let out, and my jaw grows tight.

"Take off your clothes," I say roughly. "Let me see you."

She takes in a deep breath and reaches for the hem of her sweater, lifting it over her head. Underneath she's in a white cotton bra that she's barely fitting into, her full breasts spilling over. She's so pale and creamy and I'm practically panting at the sight of her.

Then she undoes her jeans and steps out of them and her socks. Her underwear is red and lacey. Strange, it's like she wasn't trying to make an effort at all. Usually the women that are brought here are very elaborately done up with makeup and lingerie. But not her.

136

It makes me want her even more. How incredibly easy it would be to defile her. How she might want to be defiled.

"All off," I say, my voice growing hoarse.

Her gaze doesn't leave mine as she slips out of her underwear and undoes her bra.

I have to tear my eyes away from hers and take in the sight of her body, nude and deliciously supple.

Fuck, is she ever soft. She has the muscle tone and strength that every vampire does, but she's somehow kept her plush curves intact. Perhaps she's even younger than I thought.

And when my eyes drop to her cunt, shadowed by hair, I realize I'm probably right.

"Where exactly did you come from?" I murmur, stepping toward her. I breathe in deeply, smelling her meadowsweet scent, something both familiar and not, and place my fingers at her waist, letting them trail over her delicate skin as I move around and behind her. She gasps, sucking in her stomach and my fingers go over her hips, then around the swell of her ample ass.

"Your body is unique for a vampire's," I go on. "How did you get to be so soft?"

She stiffens, and I realize she might think it's not a compliment. I forget how women can get and vampires are no exception.

"Don't worry, I like it," I whisper in her ear, leaning forward. She shivers now and I can smell the heat pooling between her legs, smell her musk as I'm turning her on.

Fuck, I'm going to take my time with her, even if it kills me.

I come back around to the front of her, my fingers slowly tracing up the skin of her stomach until they rise over the high mounds of her breasts. She gasps as I cup them, feeling the heavy weight of them in my hands, then gently brush my thumbs over her nipples until they're hard as pebbles. Her mouth drops open, a perfect pink tongue between her full lips, and her eyes pinch shut from the pleasure.

I can't stop touching her, I can't keep my eyes off her. Her face is so open and pure and pretty, something sweet and girlish, yet her jaw and her nose are sharp, a softness balanced with strong striking features. Her skin is smooth as milk, with only a faint scattering of freckles that remind me of the furthest stars in the sky. I keep my thumbs going over her breasts until her musk intensifies, until her breathing becomes shallow and I wonder if I can make her come from just her breasts alone.

But while I want to take my time, I'm also getting impatient.

I slip one hand down between her legs and find her soaking wet.

"Oh god," she says through a gasp and I barely have to touch her at all before she's coming right here and now, on her own two feet.

She's a firecracker. It's been a while since I've made a woman come in seconds flat.

Her hips jerk forward, knees buckle, and I quickly slip an arm around her waist to keep her upright, her clit throbbing beneath the slick rubs of my thumb. Her voice is hoarse as she cries out, the sound so sweet and warm in the austerity of this room.

I keep one hand at her breast while I slowly remove the other, sliding my finger over my tongue, tasting every inch of her. She's decadent and rich, like the most expensive wine, but fresh at the same time. The taste of youth.

"You're a good girl, aren't you?" I say, stepping back to

undo the fly of my pants, my cock twitching against the seam. "Coming for me so soft and easy like that. Such a good little whore."

Her eyes open and instead of giving me a look of annoyance, her expression is one of want. Fuck me. She *loves* this. Maybe Van Helsing wasn't all that wrong about me needing a companion.

I bring my cock out, hard as steel and pulsing hotly under my grip.

"Get on your knees."

To my surprise she grins, a beautiful smile that lights her eyes up in a wicked way, and does what she's told.

Once on her knees, she reaches for my cock and stares up at me with her big green eyes, her auburn hair flowing down her naked back. "Yes, my lord."

CHAPTER 12
ROSE

"**M**y lord."

The words just slip out. I couldn't help it, just like I couldn't help coming at his slightest touch. Because despite him not knowing me, it's *him*, and my body responds to his gaze, to his touch, to his voice, like a puppet on a string. I can't help but be pulled back through the passage of time to the ways we were together before, when he had the ability to make me see stars and take me to heaven with the flick of a finger.

And so I'm on my knees, the cold stone floor digging into my skin, my hands wrapped around the familiar heat and hardness of his cock, and I haven't felt this alive since... since the last night we slept together. That one night I was Dahlia and Lucy and Mina and I was so fucking in love with him, I thought my heart might burst like a dam and flood the both of us.

I would do anything to drown with him.

And just like those old times, I've reverted to calling him "my lord."

From the way he's frowning at me, his dark eyes being

pulled from molten need and into a state of confusion, I wonder if I've made a mistake. Does he remember the way I'd say it? Does he remember me? Does he know the truth?

"My lord," he repeats carefully, his tongue tracing his bottom lip. The sharpness in his eyes slowly melts into desire again. "I like that." His voice sounds like silk.

I hide my relief behind a teasing smile. "I only aim to please you."

He swallows audibly, mouth parting, then he suddenly reaches forward and grabs my hair, making a tight, painful fist of it at the top of my head.

I can't help but yelp, my grip on his cock loosening.

"Then start sucking me off," he growls, shoving my face forward.

Despite the pain, I eagerly accept his demand, gripping him expertly and savoring the taste of him as I swirl my tongue around his shaft, trying to relish every inch. I feel like I have waited for this for so long, this tease of intimacy.

Valtu groans loudly, a sound that tickles every pleasure point in my head, makes the heat grow between my legs. I have missed that sound so much, the way I'm able to pull it out from his cold and composed demeanor with just the pass of my tongue. It has always felt like a superpower, like magic, and now it's no different.

I open my mouth wide and envelop him, letting out a moan myself that I know he can feel vibrate along the stiff, hot length of him.

His hips buck against my face, and his grip on my hair tightens as I take him deeper in my mouth, my lips making a sucking noise as he passes through them with force. He groans and his fist constricts, pulling on my hair even harder.

I gasp around his length, the pain so sharp yet sweet at the same time.

God, I have missed *this*.

"You like that?" he asks huskily as he stares down at me. "Such a good girl choking on my cock like that. How deep can you take me, hmmm?"

His words make me shiver, my throat constricting in response. I can feel my arousal growing, threatening to overpower me as it spreads through my body. I know I already came from just the brush of his fingers, a hair-trigger to the extreme, but I feel it might be possible to come just from giving him head. My body is that ready.

I close my eyes and focus on the sensation, letting it take me over until I'm nothing but pleasure, until I'm nothing but his. I answer him with a moan, taking him as deeply as I can, wanting to give him all of me.

I'm yours to take, I think. *Yours to have. Forever.*

He releases my hair and grabs onto my shoulders, pushing me forward as he thrusts himself deep into my mouth. I can feel the muscles of my throat working over-time, accepting him with fervor as he pushes down deeper and deeper. If I was human I'd be choking on him, unable to breathe, but I can keep going for as long as I need to, as long as he wants me to. Another advantage of being a vampire, as I'm finding out.

He's groaning as he fucks my mouth, and I can feel his thighs trembling as he gets closer and closer to the edge.

I want to bring him there.

I quicken my pace, bobbing my head up and down as I draw him further and further into my depths. His fingers clench into my shoulder and he cries out, a deep bellow that rises from the bottom of his chest, his body tensing in the throes of his orgasm.

I swallow it all down, letting him release himself completely into me, ravenous and starving for him until his cock stops jerking inside me and I've worked him dry.

I stare up at him with big eyes, slowly pulling my mouth away from his cock with a wet sound, my lips feeling sore and bruised and yet I'm smiling anyway.

"Fuck," he says through a deep groan, gazing down at me in a hazy sort of awe. For a moment we're back in time together, me having just brought him this beautiful peace that I rarely saw in his eyes except when we were together.

That peace is here now, but only for a moment. Within moments the chill returns to his gaze, that hardness, turning him from the Valtu I know to a darker version of himself.

The version that has never known me.

But maybe, maybe if I keep trying, maybe if I play my cards right, he'll get to know me again.

Maybe I can make him remember.

If he'll let me stay, that is.

"Get up," he commands sharply and before I have a chance to get to my feet, he's grabbing me by the hair again and pulling me up.

I can't help but whimper, my eyes watering from the sudden pain. My Valtu liked to inflict pain but there was always pleasure involved, it always involved sex. This feels like something else entirely. Pain for his pleasure and no one else's.

"The doctor said you'd be able to handle a little necessary roughness," he says, suddenly bringing me forward until I'm pressed up against him, his cock still hard against my bare hip. His mouth is inches from mine, his eyes like earth frozen over as they peer into mine, searching me. "So far you seem to be able to take it. But how far will you let me go?" he murmurs. He reaches out with his free hand and runs his finger under my eyes until my tears run over them and it's only then that I realize I'm crying from the pain.

He tastes my tears, just like he did once upon a time, and he smiles devilishly, his eyes remaining hard. "Do you know what I taste in your tears?"

The world seems to slide backwards in time.

I swallow hard, not looking away. "Darkness," I tell him.

He blinks slowly, his control faltering for a moment. "How did you know that?"

Because that's what Dahlia's tears tasted like, I want to say. *Because we are the same.*

"Because I am made from the darkness," I tell him quietly, trying not to wince as he keeps tugging at my hair. "Just like you are."

His lip curls in disdain. "I am not the Prince of Darkness."

"I never said you were a prince."

Valtu stares at me for a moment, unsure of how to handle me, what to make of me. I can see the puzzlement in his gaze, and it's there even when he tries to hide it. "Fair enough, my dark rose," he eventually says, his focus now fixated on my lips and for a moment I think he's going to kiss me. But then he pulls back slightly. "So far you have more thorns than petals. It might just be enough to keep you. But we shall see."

He yanks me by the hair and throws me on top of the bed and I quickly manage to flip around to face him, my instincts telling me to flee, to panic, because even though this is Valtu it's also not. But he doesn't force himself on me.

Instead he grabs the chains and in mere seconds the

cold cuffs are placed over my ankles and wrists until I'm chained to the bedposts, naked and spread eagle.

"It's not just me that humans can't handle," he says to me, walking toward the door. "It's what keeps me company."

He opens the door and pauses, looking at me over his shoulder. "I'll see you in the morning. That is, if you're still here."

Then he shuts the door and the room goes black.

I WAKE UP WITH A START, my heart pounding against my ribs, adrenaline flooding through my limbs until I'm jerking at the restraints, the metal clanging loudly in the room.

It's full dark but my eyes are starting to adjust. The window shows dark clouds moving outside and the night sky beyond. I don't know how long I've been lying in this bed for but from the ache in my muscles and the soreness around my ankles and wrists, I'm going to guess it's been several hours at least.

I let out a heavy sigh and lift my head to look around, noting the emptiness with relief. It could be just after sundown, it might be the middle of the night. But Valtu hasn't come back for me.

What did he mean when he said it was his company that humans can't handle?

What company?

I thought he lived up here all alone.

I close my eyes and sink back into the bed, the cuffs cutting into my skin enough to make me moan uncomfortably.

I hate to say it, but maybe everyone was right. Maybe

this wasn't the best idea. I just don't know how I could handle being in the same world as Valtu and not being with him. More than that, I don't want to live in a world where people like Bellamy, people who take and take without consequence, are just allowed to get away with it. Not just get away with it, but actually thrive. If the rumors are true and he's not aging, that means he's cracked some sort of code and living his best life, perhaps an immortal like me.

No, even though I'm currently chained up to Valtu's bed in some secret location in the Bavarian Alps, and even though it's not the Valtu I've loved and lost, I know I don't have much of a choice here. I could have gone on as new vampire Rose Harper, but I'd never be able to live a long and happy life if I knew that my love was out there, nor would I be able to ignore the fact that justice would never be served. It's a big risk I'm here, and if there's even a small chance I might not survive the night, it's still a risk that needs to happen.

You don't just stop loving someone because they stop loving you.

You don't forget about a relationship because someone else forgets it.

No matter who he is now, what he's done, who he's become, he is still the man I love. It might not be on the surface, but it's still there, buried away. That man was my home. He is still my home. And I'm going to do whatever it takes so that he sees that, so that I can become his home again too. Our hearts belong together because we had true love, and true love never dies.

Except he did kill you, remember, a voice says inside my head.

That he did. I really thought I would feel nothing but anger and betrayal at the first sight of his face, but those feelings were so far away. They still are there, despite the circumstances, despite seeing firsthand again how easily he succumbs to the darkness inside him.

But, as he tasted, there's darkness inside me too. Maybe that's why we've always returned to each other.

The darkness in me calls to the darkness in you.

I sigh, my heart feeling especially tender. I know I'm doing this because I love him and I believe in him and I believe in us, but I can't pretend that it didn't sting while being with him tonight, tasting him, touching him, making him come undone like I have done countless times before, while he looked at me like I was nobody. He treated me like I was a snack or a toy for him to taste and play with before he gets bored. He looks at me and he only sees something to use and, fuck that hurts, and I know that pain is going to get worse the longer this goes on, I'm afraid I won't be able to—

My thoughts come to a sudden halt.

I go still.

There.

I can hear something in the room with me.

I hold my breath and concentrate, ignoring the sound of my heart which is starting to whoosh loudly in my veins. I lift up my head and look around but the room looks the same as before. Empty and dark.

But there's that sound again.

A cold trail of fear rolls down my spine.

It's a wet gurgling sound. Followed by a mewling sound.

At first I think maybe there's a kitten or a cat in the room with me, perhaps it's always been there, but then it doesn't quite sound like a cat either. It's more human and yet...not.

Suddenly there's a short gasping cry that echoes.

Oh my god.

It's...it sounds like a baby.

A human child.

"Hello?" I say, my voice sounding flat in the stone room as I keep searching the corners, wishing like hell I could move.

It lets out another cry again, not quite one of distress, but the happy, gurgling cries that a baby might make, only there's something off about it.

I feel a sharp pang in my womb in response, as if the baby is mine, and my mind wants to wallow in the pain for a moment and drift back to the babies I lost as Mina and Lucy. I didn't think I had any mothering instincts left since I never thought about being a mother as Dahlia, and I certainly hadn't considered it as Rose thus far, but it's rising up inside me sharp and powerful and primal.

Oh god, I think to myself, *I thought I'd made peace with the past.*

But the baby is somewhere in this room and it's making those gurgling sounds and in front of me the bathroom door is slowly opening with a drawn-out creak.

Holy *fuck*.

I suck in my breath, sorrow and terror fighting inside me for dominance, watching as the door opens wider, the low *creeeeeeak* filling my bones.

Then the door stops.

Nothing comes out, not that I can see.

But I can hear it.

I can hear something shuffling along the stone floor. It sounds wet and thick, like someone dragging a wet towel on the ground, but then I hear the occasional slap of flesh.

What the hell is happening?!

148

"Valtu?" I ask and it feels like the darkness of the room is swallowing up my voice, eating my strength, my nerve. "Hello? Please tell me who's there."

The sound disappears. I wait a moment, listening hard for its return. But there's only silence.

I breathe out in relief, relaxing back into the bed, hoping that this is all some horrible figment of my imagination.

Until I feel the covers shift underneath me.

I raise my head and look down at the bed and watch as the covers move back a little, as if being tugged, as if someone is lying at the foot of the bed and pulling at it.

Oh fuck. Oh god.

I keep my eyes glued to the end of the bed, right between my spread legs, a whimper escaping my throat as a tiny human hand comes into view.

A small bloody hand belonging to a baby.

I open my mouth to scream but no sound comes out.

The baby's head rises above the edge of the bed. Half of its skull is crushed in, like someone stepped on it, and I immediately know that it's my baby. It's the baby I carried as Mina, after my father had stepped on my stomach and before he chopped off my head.

It's me and Valtu's first child. And the first child to die.

The baby looks at me, one eye popping out, its mouth crooked and drooling blood. An aberration, and yet part of me loves it like a mother would love its child. Because this is my child, isn't it? A child I'd lost but had somehow found me again all these centuries later.

"Hello," I whisper, a sob falling from my lips. "Hello little one."

The baby opens its mouth wide, letting out a peal of

metallic laughter and bares its fangs at me. Fangs. Of course it has fangs.

I am cursed, Valtu, don't you see? I said that once to him, as I lay on my deathbed as Lucy, our second child still inside of me, dead. I see it now, clear as day. I'm cursed.

The baby starts crawling toward me, dragging itself along, and I realize it can't move its legs. It pulls itself up the length of the bed, heading right between my thighs.

Like it's heading back home.

Oh fuck. Oh no. Oh god no.

"No!" I cry out, trying to squirm, trying to move my body, but I can't. I pull and yank at the cuffs but they only cut into my skin and I'm trapped. I'm utterly trapped.

"Help!" I scream. "Help! Abe! Valtu! Help me!"

But my scream feels weak and flat, like it's contained in these walls.

And the baby keeps coming. Snapping its bloody fanged mouth, its eye nearly hanging out of its crushed skull, bits of brain matter leaking from its nose. It moves like a wet mop, these sloppy shuffles forward, all blood and other things I don't want to think about.

"Mother," the baby says, its voice positively deep and inhuman.

It reaches for me, heading right for my womb, its little hands grabbing my skin as it tries to force its way back inside me, and I'm unable to close my legs to stop it.

I scream and scream and scream. My body bucks and jerks, hips lifting off the bed, trying to stop it from coming inside but its little nails are digging into me as it reaches in deeper, grabbing a hold of my cervix.

I scream again until my throat is raw and the sound vanishes and I can feel the little monster pulling itself inside of me, feel its teeth biting at my insides until I'm bleeding profusely on the bed.

I'm going to die here. It's going to eat me from the inside, it's going to bleed me dry.

I throw my head back, ready to scream again in this never-ending horror when suddenly...

It stops.

The pain stops, the pressure stops, the sounds stop.

It all stops.

I look down and there's no baby. There's no blood. There's nothing there at all.

"Jesus," I swear breathlessly, beads of cold sweat rolling down my forehead. "What the hell was that?"

I keep looking around the room, thinking I'm going to see the baby appear somewhere, or see a tiny bloody handprint, evidence that it was here, but I'm utterly alone in the room again.

I put my head back down on the pillow and close my eyes, trying to control my heart and my ragged breath. If I were human, I think it's possible to have had five heart attacks by now.

How could my mind have conjured up something so real? I *felt* that pain.

And that's when I hear another sound.

A scraping of something rough against stone.

My eyes fly open and I look up at the ceiling.

I see the scaly black body of *the bad thing* lying flat against it, its xenomorph head tilted to the side to stare down at me with one beady red eye.

I suck in my breath, gasping in horror.

This can't be real either, can it?

But from the way it waits there against the ceiling,

silently watching me, I know it is. It's as real as it was the last time I saw it.

I try my bonds again but the metal remains as cold and unbreakable as before. Valtu must have magic on them to keep me tethered. A panicked vampire should be able to break through nearly anything.

The demon thing continues to study me and I continue to stare up at it in horror, caught in the path of its focused stare.

Then its long leathery tale twitches and it starts to pull itself along the ceiling with its six-inch claws and then down the adjacent wall, a skittling sound in its wake.

I pinch my eyes shut, hoping that when I open them again the demon will be gone just as the baby was.

But when I open them, the demon is still there.

This time it's closer.

Right by my foot.

It tilts its watermelon shaped head at me, as if in thought, and suddenly I know exactly what this hell beast is thinking.

It's wondering what I'm doing here.

Because we've met before. In Venice.

The demon knows me, has seen me as Dahlia.

And now it sees that I'm here, two decades later.

I'm guessing the reason it's here is either because Valtu befriended or trained it, or it has something to do with the book, since that's where the demon came from in the first place, summoned out of Hell by Saara.

How loyal is this beast? Will it tell Valtu? *Can* it tell Valtu?

Is it going to kill me instead?

Yeah. That's the more likely choice. After all, when it appeared in my bedroom in Venice after I was astral projecting, it tried to kill me. It was created to kill witches.

But I'm no longer a witch. Right?

At the very least, my vampire nature must override it. *Right?*

The creature looks at my foot and extends its bony leathery hand, the long black curved claws like a demonic bird's.

I flinch, watching in horror, waiting for it to bite my foot right off. Can vampires grow new feet?

But instead of sinking its claws into my flesh, it takes them to the cuffs and with a quick swipe it cuts right through the metal, like a knife through butter.

Part of the cuff clatters to the floor and suddenly my foot is free, the skin around my ankle aching profusely.

The demon slowly goes around the bed, doing the same to my other foot, then my hand. I can't help but stare at it with bated breath as it leans in to cut through the last cuff, both horrified and fascinated that this demon creature that once tried to kill me is actually letting me go.

Unless this is part of the game, I tell myself. *Maybe it just likes to hunt.*

Oh, well fuck that.

I carefully get off the bed, my legs shaking from disuse, not taking my eyes off the demon. I back up until my head hits the wall and I watch as the demon walks around on all fours over to the door, reaching up with its claws and carefully opening it. It disappears out into the hall, swallowed by the darkness, the door left open.

Panic prickles through my scalp and I feel like dry-heaving. I can't stay here in this room anymore, I have to make a run for it, I have to find Abe and leave this place, but stepping out into the dark void of the house feels just as awful. I know the demon just let me loose, but if it gets off on hunting down Valtu's guests, I'm going to be in big trouble.

I don't have a choice though. I quickly slip on my underwear and the sweater and then I'm heading out into the hall.

It feels like a million eyes are watching me as I scamper down the hall towards what I hope is the downstairs where I think Abe's room is, moving as soundlessly as possible. Yet as I move, I sense something large and dark behind me, tailing me.

It might be the demon, it might be some other horror that lives with Valtu—the company he keeps—but I'm not slowing down to find out.

I move faster and faster until I'm running, my bare feet slapping the floor, and then I'm moving past the music room and down the stairs and bursting out to the living area where I find Valtu and Abe, drinking and sitting by fire.

Both of them get to their feet, Abe looking concerned while Valtu looks completely flabbergasted. I swear that look on his face might have made all of this worth it.

"How the hell did you get out of there?" he asks incredulously. Then his expression grows even more surprised as he looks over my shoulder.

I don't even have to turn to look.

I know what's there.

CHAPTER 13
VALTU

I can't believe my eyes.

Somehow the redheaded girl has gotten out of her cage. I know the wards I have holding those cuffs in place are strong, but unless she's made of magic herself there's no way she could have gotten out of it on her own accord.

And that gives me cause for alarm. Though she looks deliciously scared, breathing hard, with her wide green eyes, wearing just the sweater and panties, I have to wonder if she's part witch. A witch is—

The demon appears behind her.

I stare at it, wondering what it's going to do. Did it free her from the room? Was it just chasing her? Was this all for its own pleasure, a need to hunt? Or is it some backwards way of showing me that it can fuck with my possessions, even those I'm not sure I want to keep. The demon has slaughtered nearly every human I've had in this place.

"Well," I repeat, my gaze flicking from the demon back to the girl. "How did you get out of there?"

"It, *it* freed me," she says, her voice shaking. She looks at me and then to the doctor. "This house is haunted."

I let out an empty laugh. "You thought it wouldn't be?"

"What do you mean it freed you?" Van Helsing asks. He's keeping a safe distance behind me, as he should.

She gives her head a shake. "It cut off the cuffs and opened the door for me."

Now this is hard to believe.

The demon starts to come toward her now, tired of waiting in the shadows. The girl's body stiffens and shakes slightly from fright and for once I'm not really enjoying this. It's not even about the mess that the creature would make in the middle of the living room, but that I don't want to see it devour her before I get to chance to fuck her.

"What do I do?" she whispers, eyes darting around her, knowing it's creeping closer.

"Valtu," Van Helsing hisses at me. "Control it."

"I can't," I say absently, watching as the demon stops right behind her and rises up on its back legs. It puts its inhuman claws over her shoulders, the tips of them pressing into the tops of her breasts, enough to draw blood that slowly darkens her sweater.

Christ on a bike.

Even though it's drawing blood, it seems to be gentle with her, its movements delicate and controlled.

Possessive.

The redhead looks pained and is trembling in terror but I'm staring at the demon's small red eyes, the empty inhumanness of them the epitome of cosmic horror.

Do you want her? I project toward it. *Why? Why her? What makes her so special?*

The demon doesn't answer. It never does.

But it's clear from the way it's cradling her from behind

that it does want her and it's showing me how easily it can take what it wants.

A hot burst of possession runs through me. It's been a long time since I've felt that way toward anyone. Controlling, yes, always, but I dislike the feeling of things belonging to me.

Except for the book, of course. There is no question that belongs to me.

And now, I guess, this girl belongs to me too.

"Get away from her," I command, my voice a fist. "She is not yours. She is mine."

The girl eyes me in surprise, a glimpse of that warmth in her eyes, that strange adoration that she has for me. She knows I'm trying to save her from a gruesome fate but I'm not yet sure she should celebrate.

But the demon doesn't put up a fight. It just stares at me for a moment, then removes its claws, one by one. The girl gasps, her hands flying to her chest where blood seeps over her fingers.

Then the demon goes back down on all fours and saunters off into the shadows, the clicking of its nails on the stone fading as it disappears.

The girl looks at the blood on her palms and then eyes me sharply, a darkness coming over her expression, reminding me of what I tasted in her tears. "Nice pet," she says stiffly.

"It let you loose, didn't it?"

"Are you okay, Rose?" Van Helsing asks, and she nods. Of course the doctor is always so caring and considerate. Makes me look like a real asshole for not asking.

You are a real asshole, I remind myself. *That demon would have shredded her to pieces and the truth is you probably wouldn't even blink.*

I sigh internally. Once upon a time I remember being someone who would care, but that person seems so removed from me now, it's like it happened in another life, to someone else.

And yet I did choose Rose. I told the demon that she's mine.

Now, what to do with my new possession?

But it is the middle of the night and I am tired, having talked and drank with Van Helsing into the wee hours. All this excitement has me riled up and yet I know I won't perform at my best with her if I don't get some sleep.

"Well, I best be off to bed," I say, clapping my hands together. "That's enough excitement for one night."

"Please don't make me sleep back in that room," Rose says softly, averting her eyes to the floor.

I fold my arms across my chest as I appraise her. I can't seem to figure her out. One moment she's gazing at me with affection, the next she's hard, the next she's aching in her vulnerability. It's making me feel things I shouldn't be feeling, and I ignore the faint pinch in my chest, this compulsion of wanting to protect her.

"She can stay with me," Van Helsing offers, a little too enthusiastically.

I cock my brow and eye him over my shoulder. "What?"

He raises his hands. "Why not?" he asks. *I know she sure as hell isn't staying with you*, he adds in his head.

He's got a point. I always sleep alone, and my bedroom is always off limits. I never let anyone over the threshold.

It's where I keep the book.

I look over at Rose, and she's staring at me with hope in her eyes. She wants to share his bed tonight. Whether it's out of a fear or for other reasons—after all I don't actually know if she and the doctor have anything going on between them—I can't let that happen. Not after I made a big show to the demon that the girl is mine and no one else's.

"I don't think so," I eventually say, and I watch the disappointment and fear cloud Rose's eyes as I walk over to her. I grab her by the elbow, my fingers digging into her sweater on the off-chance she decides to run. "You want to stay here? This is part of the package deal."

She gives Van Helsing a worried look as I lead her out of the room and up the stairs, back to the bedroom.

"Please don't make me go back in there," she says, her words trembling. "Please."

"The demon likes you," I say into her ear, catching the scent of her shampoo, that floral scent that instantly makes me hard. "I don't think you have too much to worry about."

"But there are...there are ghosts...of things from my past."

I pull her to a stop and peer down at her. The nearest light, a candle in a sconce, is further down the hall, putting her face into shadow. Here her features look harder, but her eyes remain wet and vulnerable, the light from the far-off flames flickering in them.

"What do you mean you've seen things from your past?" I ask.

She licks her lips and she's thinking something over and I try to push myself into her mind. But there's a wall there, solid black and as strong as the doors fortifying this castle. This girl knows how to protect herself. Another thing I find intriguing.

"What did you see?" I prod.

She swallows hard and I'm distracted by the way her throat moves. I have this brief urge to sink my teeth into the sweet soft flesh of her jugular and I don't know where that comes from since I've never been into drinking from other vampires.

"I saw...a baby," she says, and the word comes out in a hush.

The hairs on the back of my neck raise and I instantly see the baby too, the one that's been haunting me. How could she have seen it too?

"Are you sure it's from your past? Did you recognize it?" I ask carefully.

She gives a small shake of her head. "No. I didn't recognize it. But I think it thought I was its mother." She closes her eyes and to my surprise a tear rolls down. "I'm sorry," she whispers, keeping her eyes closed while she hurriedly wipes the tear away with the heel of her palm. "This is hard to talk about."

I swear I hear the way she wanted to end the sentence:

This is hard to talk about *with you*.

I have this sudden urge to put my arms around her and hold her close to me.

It makes me take one step back.

"This place," I say to her, my voice low, "it has a way of playing tricks on you. There are things that come alive here, fears that manifest." I pause, wondering how much I should say. "Maybe it's not so much this place, but me. They haunt me. And they'll haunt you too for as long as you're here."

There's no point in telling her that I've seen a baby too.

"So the baby...wasn't yours?" I go on. "Have you ever been pregnant?"

She doesn't say anything for a moment, but I swear I see her flinch. She opens her eyes and meets my gaze head on. "I'm only twenty-one."

Fuck me.

"Are you serious?" I ask.

Twenty-one? I knew she was young, but I didn't know she was *this* young.

"I just turned a couple of days ago," she admits.

"You what?" I let her go and run my hand over my face in disbelief. Van Helsing brought me a barely legal vampire. Hell, barely a vampire. "You've only been a vampire for a few days?"

She swallows and nods. "Yeah. Is that a problem?"

"A problem?" My dick doesn't seem to think so. It's harder than ever and it's taking a lot of effort to ignore it. I've never had someone so young before. "There's a bit of an age gap here."

The corner of her mouth lifts. "You're worried about an age gap? There are no age gaps with vampires."

"Considering I was born in the sixteen hundreds and you were born twenty-one years ago, yeah, I think that could be considered an age gap."

The fear seems to leave her eyes as she gazes at me. Something hot and carnal makes her pupils expand into black pools. "Are you having second thoughts about fucking me?"

Sweet Jesus. My dick practically screams for attention.

"I didn't think age gaps counted for much if it was just sex," she adds.

I swallow hard. Alright. Well, all that need for sleep has suddenly gone out the window, along with any resolve I was attempting to hold onto.

I lunge for her, wrapping her hair around my fingers like a silken fist, and I yank her head back so that her throat is exposed. I feel my fangs sharpen and I know she's a vampire and her blood won't give me what I'm looking for, but I want to bite and taste her all the same.

I place my lips at her throat, tasting the sweet sugar of her skin mixed with the sweat from her fear. She tastes so fucking new, the urge to come is threatening to undo me.

"Do it," she hisses, her throat moving against my mouth as she speaks. "Bite me."

I don't take orders well, but I obey her anyway.

My fangs sink into her skin, a snap of breaking flesh before her blood flows into my mouth, warm and intoxicating, sliding down my throat. She tastes almost human and it might be because she's so fresh and new, her humanity hasn't slipped away quite yet.

Thank you, Doctor, for finding this one, I can't help but think as I drink from her, pulling on her hair even more so that I can drink freely. With my other hands I slide over her sweater, still damp from where the demon spilled her blood, then between her legs. A quick jerk of my wrist and her panties tear apart, giving me full access to her cunt.

Fuck me. The insides of her thighs are damp with her need for me and I slip my finger along her clit, already hot and swollen and waiting for my touch.

She moans loudly, the sound bouncing off the walls of the narrow hall and vibrating against my tongue. I keep drinking from her, savoring her sweetness, feeling like I'm getting stronger by the second. Stronger and more turned on, which can be a rough combination.

But she likes it rough, that much I know.

I dislodge my teeth from her neck with a grunt and release her hair, shoving my hands under the firm contours of her ass and picking her up, whipping her around until she's slammed back against the wall.

Her legs wrap around me and I'm digging my cock out from my pants, positioning it at her cunt, just the tip pushing in. Her mouth drops open in another heady moan, and I'm tempted by her lips, how soft they are, what her tongue might taste like. But I try not to kiss my whores on the mouth, it feels too intimate for me to properly deal with.

So I bury my head into her neck, biting her where it curves into her shoulder. She cries out and I use the momentum to thrust into her fully, pushing her against the wall as I do.

"Oh fuck!" she shouts, her body tensing and I feel like I'm about to explode because she's tighter than a fist. I don't think I've ever had my cock squeezed into such a tight hole before, it's making my eyes roll back in my head and she's starting to tremble but I'm not sure if it's from pleasure or from pain. Even though she's wet, I feel like I'm pushing myself to the limit, crammed in so fucking tight, I can barely breathe.

Then it hits me. The tang of blood in the air, different from where I'm feeding at her throat.

I pull my head back and stare at her, at the way her eyes are pinched shut in pain, tears at the corners, and then I glance down at my cock where it's sinking into her.

It's red with blood.

Jesus Christ.

My eyes snap back to Rose's face.

"Are you a virgin?" I manage to ask, my voice guttural.

She presses her lips together and nods. "Yes."

Fuck me.

I look back down at my dick and pull out slowly and her body is quivering in response and oh fucking hell, I have never been so turned on before.

"Don't stop," she whispers. "Please."

I give her an incredulous look. "You want me to continue?"

"Don't you?" she responds, fixing her gaze on me. Her eyes have gained a bit of clarity, the pain dissipating. "Fuck me hard, Valtu. Make me see stars."

I can't help but blink at her. My cock is painfully stiff and I've never wanted to come so hard in my life and yet I'm confused as hell. She's been a virgin this whole time and yet she wants me to fuck her. She likes it. Needs it. Wants it. She gives expert head too, like she's done it a million times before.

"Fuck me, please," she whispers and her legs tighten around my waist, her heels digging into the back of my ass and she's pushing me forward until my cock is shoved fully back inside her.

We both gasp, her hands going to my back and digging her nails in, then to my hair, tugging on my strands, and now I think I'm the one who is about to see stars here.

"Fuck," I say through a groan and then I can't hold back any longer.

I thrust into her hard and fast, my hips slapping against hers as I take her with an intensity that over-whelms us. There's electricity that seems to form around our bodies, blurring the senses, and the pleasure is so unbearable, I feel it all the way down to the soles of my feet.

"Christ, Rose," I say through a grunt, pounding her harder until I fear I might be jackhammering her into the stone. "Such a good little virgin slut aren't you? That's exactly what you are."

I pull back, glancing down at my cock again, the blood along the length of it mixing with her arousal. "You see this? You see how much I turn you on, how your cunt is weeping for me, making such a mess?"

The look on her face tells me she does, her cheeks

burning bright red as her eyes hood and her body quivers against mine. "Yes," she whispers. "Please, don't stop."

"Ask me nicely," I say roughly. "Like you did before."

She nods, her breathing ragged, her eyes hooded with pleasure. I notice something else in there too, something that I don't understand yet, but I know I'll eventually figure out.

"Yes, my lord," she says breathlessly, her voice choking with need. "Don't stop, my lord."

Fuck. I love the sound of that.

I thrust into her again, the force of my body hammering her into the wall, her arching against the cold stone, and I know her spine will be bruised tomorrow. My hips slam into hers, each thrust taking us higher and higher until I feel like I'm flying.

Rose screams out and I can't help but grin as I feel her waves of pleasure wash over me. I continue to drive into her, each thrust almost too much to bear until I finally let go. White hot need explodes from within me and I swear I can feel every inch of Rose contracting around me as I come.

I cry out hoarsely, the sound echoing down the hall, and I can't seem to stop spilling into her, my balls emptying completely until I have nothing left to give.

Rose's legs wrap around me and she leans back against the stone, her eyes half-lidded, the little bit of strength she had left now drained from her body.

Finally, I pull out of her and she starts to slide down the wall, her legs too weak to hold her up.

But I'm not done with her yet. Not in her state.

When you've been around for nearly five centuries, it's not very often that a new experience pops up and I'm going to take it for what it's worth.

I tighten my grip around her ass and then I walk with her held up against me, through the door to her bedroom, then I'm dumping her on the bed, the chains rattling.

She bounces in surprise, a wash of fear going over her hazy eyes as she realizes where she is, but then I'm pulling off her sweater and parting her legs roughly.

I get on the bed between them and dig my nails into the side of her hips, smelling the fresh blood where I took her virginity.

"What are you doing?" she whispers, staring down at me.

I grin as I meet her eyes. "Enjoying all the fruits of my labor, my dove."

She freezes as I say that. Perhaps I'm being a little too crude for her liking. She'll have to get used to it if she wants me to make her come.

I lower my head and then I start to lick up the blood along her cunt, my tongue soaking it up as I lap at her, cleaning her up and moaning as I taste the mixture of her blood and my seed. Her want is leaking from her, soaking the covers and I can smell her arousal—she's still so fucking turned on, even after I've spilled into her.

"Valtu," she gasps, her hands digging into the bed. "Valtu, I—"

I grab her hips roughly and suck on her clit and she meets my eyes, her face flushed and eyes wide, clearly on the verge of an orgasm.

I want her to come again. I want her to come over and over again, in my mouth until she's dripping out of my lips.

My tongue works furiously against her clit in rough strokes and then I feel her body tensing beneath mine, her thighs squeezing the sides of my head.

"Valtu," she whispers. "My lord. Please make me come."

I groan in response and suck hard on her clit, thrusting my tongue deep inside her cunt, fucking it, and then she comes hard, making incoherent noises and grabbing fistfuls of the bedspread. Her hips raise and buck and she sounds like a symphony.

I release her clit and then I press my lips to her cunt, sucking the cum inside my mouth and moaning as the taste washes over me.

I don't stop. I can't stop. I just keep going until I feel her exhaustion sinking in. She's spent now, her whole body weak and trembling beneath mine.

Because she is mine, isn't she? That's what I declared. I don't know for how long, but for tonight at least, she one hundred percent belongs to me.

"Good, sweet girl," I murmur, pressing a kiss against her cunt. "I could drink you for ages."

Her eyelids flutter and she looks down at me with eyes that are hazy with pleasure. "My lord..."

A satisfied grin spreads across my face and I get off the bed and stare down at her, her body still trembling, her chest rising and falling with each heavy breath. With any luck she'll fall asleep soon and the demon and ghosts won't pay her a visit. Hopefully she'll just experience dreams of me and wake up only a little sore in the morning.

I go to the door before she has a chance to plead with me, before I have a chance of losing my resolve.

"This is your room now, for better or worse," I say as I open the door.

She sits up, her hair falling over her gorgeous tits, her eyes fearful. It's almost enough to make me stay and have another round with her. But there will be plenty of time for that later.

"You're not chaining me up?" she asks, her voice still thick with sex.

I manage a smile. "Chain you back up? I'm not an animal," I tell her. Then I step outside and close the door, making sure all the wards are activated so that she's locked inside.

"Goodnight Rose," I whisper before heading off down the hall.

CHAPTER 14
ROSE

My dove. He had called me his *dove*.

When I was Dahlia, he called me his dove all the time. I don't think it's a phrase he gives to everyone. He didn't call Mina or Lucy his dove either. But to Dahlia he did. He was my lord and I was his dove.

And yet here we are again, lord and dove.

Does he know? Is he remembering?

I'm not sure. Though this Valtu is harder to read, I'm still pretty good at getting a handle on him and I think I'd know if he remembered or suspected. Instead, I think he used the term without a second-thought, not realizing the importance and relevance behind it.

Even so, I took those words straight to my heart. I'm holding them there tightly, because in the end, they might be all I have left of what we were to each other. That little term of endearment could be the only thing remaining in the end.

I exhale heavily, my heart feeling damp, and look out the window. It's the morning and I'm still in this damn room with its chains and nightmares. Outside, the sun has risen above the clouds, a shaft of it coming in and turning the charcoal floor to light gray. In the daylight it doesn't seem scary at all. It wouldn't be a stretch to imagine this as some boutique hotel in the mountains or one of those crazy ass house rentals cut into a cave or something.

But last night told a different story.

The baby, the demon...

And the pure terror I felt when I realized that Valtu didn't seem to care what happened to me. I was still just disposable to him, like all the others were.

Thankfully I fell asleep right away last night and slept all the way in till morning, the sex having tuckered me out.

Because...holy fuck.

I had completely forgotten that I was a virgin.

Before I remembered my past lives, I'd always felt a little sheltered from the boys. Maybe it's because we'd moved around so much, maybe because I didn't know any vampires and so I knew I'd have to try and hide my true nature from everyone. How can you date someone when your relationship will expire when you turn twenty-one? So aside from a few kisses at a baseball game, or playing spin the bottle, or getting groped at the school dance, I didn't have any experience with sex at all.

But only my body carried that reality, not my heart and soul. I'd had sex as Mina, as Lucy, as Dahlia, and when it was Valtu it was the dirtiest most mind-blowing sex you could imagine. There wasn't anything that I haven't already done with him.

This body didn't know that though, not until he was thrusting inside me.

I'm tight and he's incredibly large and the pain took me by surprise.

What happened next, well, that should have surprised

me too. But it's Valtu, so it didn't. Some things never change. That man has to experience everything life has to offer, and he's always made sure to take me along for the ride.

Now, though, my body is sore. When I move there's a real tenderness between my legs. I know vampires heal fast —the marks the demon made on my chest are already gone, fully healed—but this feels like it might stick around for a bit.

I made it through the night, at least. He called me his last night, a hint of his possessiveness I once took for granted, but I don't trust him enough to know that it will last. He might have claimed me, called me his dove, but that was last night and I have no idea what type of person he'll be in the morning.

I decide to get up and find out. I pull my small bag of toiletries out of my pack and head into the bathroom to take a shower. To my surprise there's modern plumbing, which makes me wonder how exactly this place was designed. Did he create it out of magic, or had it been something else before?

There's hot water too, which feels like magic itself, and I find myself lingering in the shower, enjoying the warmth while trying to psyche myself up for the day. I have to think on my feet without giving anything away. This might end up being a very long game, but if I stay on Valtu's good side, I have a shot of accomplishing what I came here to do.

God, you sound just like Dahlia, I think to myself.

It's true. Our lives are overlapping in more ways than one. But Dahlia had to hide who she truly was—a witch. An assassin sent to kill Valtu. What I have to hide is, well, Dahlia. I'm at least free to be Rose.

In theory, anyway. What I want more than anything is

to text Dylan, talk to my mom and dad, let them all know that I'm okay. I want to know if *they're* okay. But I had to leave my phone in San Francisco. There was no way I could risk bringing it to Valtu's. Even though it's encrypted and protected by a password and facial ID, vampires have an uncanny knack for breaking tech to their advantage. And with Valtu possessing magic, well, it wouldn't be long before he'd be scrolling through my phone and wondering how I'm connected to Lenore and Solon and everything else. The cat would be out of the bag.

I get dressed, glad that I crammed a week's worth of clothes in that bag, though originally I thought I'd be in Northern California, not the Bavarian Alps. I slip on leggings and a tunic top of dark gray silk that shows off my breasts, then decide to take the leggings off in the end. I'd never go out in public without something underneath since the top barely covers my ass, but since it's Valtu and I'm supposed to be his plaything for the next while, I guess it can't hurt. I decide to forgo the bra and underwear as well in the end. They'd just get in the way.

Then I head to the door and pause, realizing he's locked me in here. Am I supposed to just wait until he comes to get me? Knowing Valtu, yes. He always liked to keep me waiting, especially when it came to anything related to sex.

I try the handle anyway and to my surprise it opens. Either he never locked it with wards at all, or he unlocked it this morning.

I make my way out into the hall, the floors cold against my bare feet, and head down the corridors to the lower level. This time I don't feel any eyes watching me or any dark presences at my back. The demon must be elsewhere.

The thought of it makes me shudder. The way it watched me, the way it held me from behind. The pain of its claws. It didn't say anything to me, just this low raspy breathing, but I could feel what it was thinking all the same.

The demon was showing me to Valtu.

It was saying: *this is the one you used to love. This is the woman you made yourself forget. What should I do with her?*

Valtu seemed to think the demon was claiming me as its own but that's something I wouldn't bet on. To do so could cost me my life.

The light at the end of the hall grows brighter and I find myself in the music mezzanine. There are two cigars in an ashtray, smoked halfway. Though no longer smoking, I breathe it in and smile. It's the same cigars that Valtu used to smoke.

I look around for him here but I don't see him. The view through the windows catches my eye and I open the shuttered doors to the balcony and gasp.

It is stunning out here.

I step out onto the dusting of snow, the chill biting through my feet, and into the cold wind and immediately feel like I'm flying. We're on top of the world and though I'm wary about getting too close to the railing, flanked on either end by gargoyles, I can see the mountain peaks across the valley, the clouds passing just below us. Twirling around I look up at the rest of the castle and the mountainside. I can see where the upper floors go, the row of windows, then two tower-like impressions above the rest that seem to push their way out of rock. The rest of the mountain goes straight up for another fifty feet or so until it ends in a craggy-peak, snow settling on the sides.

Suddenly I get the feeling that I'm falling and I stumble for a couple of feet, right up to the railing. I grip the edge of it and look over for a moment and see nothing but a sheer drop of two thousand feet, straight down into the forest far below.

The vertigo takes hold of me and I gasp and quickly move away from the edge. I know I'm immortal, but there's no guarantee that a fall from this height won't kill a vampire. Plenty of opportunities to get your head sliced off on the way down, not to mention the pain of the impact. We might not die from things like that, but it doesn't mean things don't hurt.

I'm just catching my breath and calming the spinning sensation when I catch a fluttery movement out of the corner of my eye. For a moment I think it's a bird that's come to perch along the stone railing.

But when I turn to look at it, I realize it's a bat. A small black bat resting there on all fours, sharp claws at the tips of its leathery wings.

"Hello," I say curiously to it. I had no idea bats could be found this high up and in winter.

The bat seems to stare at me for a moment and I get this peculiar feeling, like it knows me, or I know it, but that can't be possible because—

Suddenly the bat takes flight, going straight up in the air and down right in front of me and with a gust of wind the bat warps in shape and size and suddenly Valtu is standing right in front of me.

"Oh my god!" I scream, hands at my mouth as I stumble backward.

Valtu just dusts off the shoulders of his black coat and eyes me with a hint of amusement.

"Did I scare you?" he asks mildly.

"A bat...you just turned into a bat. That bat was you?"

"Of course." He gives me a ghost of a smile.

"We can *do* that!?" I exclaim.

"We? Oh you mean vampires. No, no, no," he tuts, looking proud of himself. "You can't. But I can."

"How?"

"A magician never reveals his secrets."

Of course. The damn book.

"Do you know magic, Valtu?" I ask, playing dumb for a moment.

His dark eyes narrow, brows snapping together. "You know I do. That's why you're here, isn't it?"

My swallow. "What do you mean?"

"There isn't a person alive, vampire or human, who comes here who doesn't know about the Book of Verimagiaa."

"And that's what you use the book for? Turning yourself into a bat? I thought you hated the fact that people called you Dracula?"

"Hated? No, that's too strong a word," he says with a shake of his head. "Let's just say it got tiresome after a while."

"And then after a while you decided to live in a castle and turn yourself into a bat. Is your life so boring these days?"

"These days?" he repeats, ice in his tone. His demeanor stiffens and I know I'm playing a risky game by getting him aggravated already, let alone on a balcony where he could easily toss me over the edge for fun. He'd probably laugh while I plunged the whole way down.

"People say you left Venice for the mountains because you were running away from something." And yet, there I go, pushing my luck.

His eyes narrow into dark slits. "I wasn't running away from anything. I was running to something."

"And what was that? Salvation?"

He lets out an acidic laugh. "Salvation? Oh, dear girl, there is no saving me. Not anymore. Thankfully I have no wish to be saved." He takes a step toward me, tilting his head as his gaze flicks over me. "Is that why you're here? You think I need saving?"

That's as good a reason as any. I decide to explore it, wondering how close I can get to the truth.

"I heard that you left because of a woman. Not just any woman either."

His energy changes like a cold front has just blasted in. "I will tell you this much," he says, his tone knife sharp. "There was a woman, but someone I went to great lengths to forget. As far as I'm concerned, the past has not only passed but it never existed in the first place. And if you dare to mention this woman, any woman at all that you think had some impact on my life, I will feed you to the demon and watch as it tears you limb from limb. You won't be the first person who has made such a dire mistake."

I swallow uneasily, my chest growing tight at his words.

I never existed in the first place.

Fuck if that doesn't hurt.

"Got it," I tell him, my cheeks going hot. I tear my eyes away from his gaze and glance back at the windows into the house. "Where is Abe?"

"The doctor left this morning," Valtu says, striding past me to the door.

"Already?" I cry out, following him inside. I didn't even get a chance to say goodbye! Now I'm truly alone here.

"Hmmm," Valtu muses, shutting the door behind me before shucking off his coat and laying it on the back of the couch. "I just got back. Decided to fly the way back up in case you got into any more trouble with my creature." He glances over at me. "Did you?"

I shake my head and make my way over to the piano, my fingers trailing over the keys. "No. Thank god. No bad things, no babies."

His gaze narrows. "Bad thing?"

Oh shit. That's what Livia had called the demon back in Venice. Is this information I shouldn't know?

"Yeah, bad thing," I repeat idly, pressing down on the D, E, and F keys. "I decided to call it—"

In a flash Valtu is on me, grabbing my face between his fingers and flipping me around so I'm pressed against the piano, the keys all crying out at once in cacophony of sound. "How did you know it was called that? Who are you? What do you want?" he hisses angrily, like a snake ready to strike. "Are you a witch?"

"I don't think so," I manage to say against his fingers.

His mahogany eyes search mine, his pupils angry little pin pricks. He blinks. "You don't think so?"

I don't say anything. It's hard to when he's holding me like he wants to snap my face in half. I keep staring at him, trying to figure out what I'm going to say, what my next move is.

He relents, just a little, moving his fingers down to my chin where he grips me hard. "What do you mean you don't think you're a witch?"

Does he know that Dahlia was a witch? Does he know the details of me?

"I don't know," I say again. "I know I'm a vampire, it's just, when I turned I felt this change inside me, some kind of connection to the earth."

He relaxes. "That's why you think you're a witch?"

"I made a lightning strike happen."

His eyes slide over my face thoughtfully. "Were you able to do it again?"

I try to shake my head though he's holding me in place. "No."

"Did you try?"

"Not really." That wasn't true. I made a few half-hearted attempts but it was nothing like when the lightning struck our deck.

Finally he releases my chin and moves back slightly. "You're not a witch, then. That just happens sometimes when you turn. You become more in tune with the natural world. It's not unusual to hear of vampires having supernatural abilities connected to the elements."

"Really?" I ask and I'm being genuine. This is the first I've heard of that.

"Really," he says. He gives me a quick smile. "Though if you did end up being a witch, I suppose it wouldn't be the worst thing in the world. You could help me decipher the rest of the book."

Now is my chance to ask him about it. To find out more about it. To see it, maybe even hold it in my hands. To find out where Bellamy and Leif are. Maybe even see if his spell of erasure can be reversed. But I know he's baiting me at the same time, and so I won't rise to meet it.

Instead I push it out of my head and let my body take the lead. A change in subject, a change in activities. I'm here for a reason. I shouldn't let him forget it.

And if using *my lord* had the power to bring back another phrase from the past, perhaps a musical instrument could do the same.

I let my body relax and gaze at him through my lashes, adjusting my body just enough for him to notice it.

He does. His eyes go to my breasts, then down to my thighs. If my tunic were any shorter, he'd be seeing everything. When he looks back up, heat has replaced everything that was cold and dark.

"You said you no longer play any musical instruments," I say to him, my voice growing sweet. "That seems such a shame to have them around, getting no use."

He raises a brow, trying to figure out where I'm going with this. "Sometimes it's nice just to look at things and appreciate their beauty. I have a tendency to *break* the things I touch."

I ignore the raw sensation in my throat, reminding me that I know firsthand what he means by that.

"You know, I play," I tell him, clearing my throat. "I could teach you the things you've forgotten."

His mouth twists into a crooked grin. "You think you could teach me things? Weren't you a virgin until last night?"

I bite my lip coyly, something I know used to get him all worked up in the past. From the flash of heat in his eyes, the flare of his nostrils, I know it still works the same. "I'm not talking about sex." I give him a cunning smile and slide off the piano, walking over to the organ.

I sit down at the bench and I'm caught by feelings of reverence and joy all at once. It feels good to slide my bare feet over the pedals, for my fingers to graze over the keys. I stare up at the pipes, the way they go in and out of the stone, and I can only hope that I remember to play as well as I think I do.

"You look like a natural," Valtu says, his voice low. He's not coming any closer though, just observing me where he is.

I shrug. "I'm sure I look like a lot of things to you."

Then I start to play.

The notes sing and come back to me as easy as breathing. I close my eyes and I slip back into being Dahlia, back to the time spent learning how to play, then my time at music school in Venice, Valtu being my teacher. Because magic had influenced so much of my ability, I feared that I would lose all my talent if I ceased to be a witch. But now that I'm here and I'm a vampire and I'm Rose and I'm playing, I realize that either the magic or the talent has survived death.

I'm playing Moonlight Sonata, a piece usually meant for the piano, and the stone walls vibrate with Beethoven's moody sounds, sounding all the more Gothic and deep when played through the organ. My feet know where to go, my fingers find their way, and I keep my eyes closed as I go. It feels like being swept along a sonic river, an experience that elevates me higher and higher until I'm one with the music itself.

When I finish the piece, I feel so unbearably alive that a tear is rolling down my cheek. My hands and feet are tingling, my chest feels effervescent, like champagne. The whole room seems to reverberate with the last notes, unable to let the song go.

Then I hear a slow clap.

I twist on the bench to look at Valtu with his hands together and he's staring at me with such awe and respect that I want to burst into tears. It takes everything in me not to leap to my feet, run over to him and kiss him, tell him that I love him and that I need him back. God, I need him back.

But that feeling of love stays in the back of my throat and I have to choke it down until I can breathe again.

"Did you like it?" I manage to say, my voice coming out in a whisper.

His eyes widen appreciatively as he walks over to me. "I

suppose I shouldn't be surprised since I know nothing about you, but yes. I liked it very much."

"Did you used to play the organ? When you were a teacher?"

He nods and slowly walks over to me, seeming to think as he goes. "Yes. I did. It was one of the classes I taught in Venice. Not always the most popular class, mind you."

"Perhaps you could teach me," I tell him.

He laughs and comes over to the bench. I scoot over and he sits down beside me, and I breathe him in deeply, the scent of him, of smoke and oranges, giving me goose-bumps. "Teach you? Looks like you could teach me a thing or two. I wasn't kidding when I said I haven't played for a very long time."

"How long?"

His brows come together and he stares blankly at the keys. "Nineteen years ago, maybe."

This surprises me. I would have thought Valtu would have played long after I departed this realm. "And yet you put an organ in here? In the rock?"

"Oh, I didn't do that," he says, staring up at the pipes. "This place used to be a monastery before I bought it."

"A monastery?"

He nods. "Believe it or not, they had a hard time attracting disciples. Something about the location..."

I can't help but laugh. "You don't say."

He returns my smile, his eyes lighting up, and my heart does cartwheels at the sight.

God, he is so fucking beautiful.

Please, please be mine again.

I feel the wish so acutely that for a moment I fear I projected it into his head. But his attention is back to the organ again. He tentatively sticks out his hands and presses down on a few keys, notes ringing out. The organ comes to life, as if it's been waiting forever to be touched by him. I have to say I can relate.

Then he snatches his hands back as if the keys burned his skin.

"I don't think I have it in me," he says, trepidation in his voice. "I don't remember."

"Sure you do," I assure him. "You just need a little practice, that's all."

I reach over and grab his hands, gently placing them back on the keys, putting my fingers over his in the correct formation. The feeling of his large, strong, cool hands below mine makes me feel dizzy and I have to close my eyes. "You can manage your feet," I whisper. "My legs aren't long enough."

He adjusts himself beside me on the bench, putting his feet on the pedals, and then I move his hands across the keys to the beginning position of Moonlight Sonata. I push down slightly, the keys depressed, and the pipes belt out with the moody tones. It feels so powerful to be able to make this instrument sing like this, like I'm some kind of god. I want him to have that feeling too. I guide his hands and fingers from one set of keys to the other, and we're playing together, the song slow at first as we find our footing together, a few wrong notes here and there, but then it's gliding along.

Eventually I take my hands off his and I just sit beside him, watching him play. My jaw tightens and my eyes burn and I have to keep breathing long and deep through my nose in order to hold it together, a deep ache forming in my chest. It sounds perfect and he looks perfect and everything about this makes sense and yet none of it makes any sense at all. I pray, hope, wish that somehow music can reach him, that it can travel somewhere deep inside, to wherever he harbors that trauma that Abe talked about, the one Valtu doesn't know is buried in his soul, and that it can bring him back to life, bring him back to me.

Please, please, please, I think, and the music continues to sweep us both away until the song is done and the room is so full of this wild, beautiful energy, you can feel it on your skin like melting snow.

Valtu closes his eyes and exhales.

I hold my breath and hope and wait.

"Thank you," he whispers, before rubbing his lips together. "Thank you." He breathes in deeply through his nose and straightens his shoulders before looking at me. "That took me back."

But from the way he's looking at me, like I'm some woman he still doesn't really know, I know it didn't take him back far enough.

CHAPTER 15
ROSE

Valtu clears his throat, stiffening a little and looking away. Whatever display of vulnerability I just saw from him has been shoved back to where he keeps the best parts of him, buried deep inside somewhere, like spring buds under a snowdrift.

But it's not just coldness that has returned to his demeanor. It's heat, too. He gets to his feet and stares down at me with a look that makes a thrill run down my spine, that look that tells me all the things he wants to do to me and then some. I used to provoke that look as much as I could. My eyes drop to his crotch, his erection large and hard against his black pants, as if I needed extra evidence of what he's feeling.

"Get up on the bench, on all fours, ass to me," he commands in a husky voice, his gaze penetrating.

"Yes, my lord," I tell him, relishing the feeling of saying those words, of seeing the way they affect him. They turn that carnality in his gaze to pure animalistic desire. The combination of wanting to fuck and to feed, the epitome of being the world's top predator.

I bring my knees up onto the bench and then get on all fours, my ass facing him.

"Jesus," he swears, and I know he can see I have nothing on underneath. Roughly, he reaches up and shoves up my tunic until I'm completely bare to him from the waist down. "Your ass is just as tempting as your cunt. Think I might spread you with my fingers and take it later."

I gulp and stiffen, preparing for him to touch me, hurt me, but then I hear him walk to somewhere else in the room and hear the rattle of instruments and strings. My heart rate increases and I have to wonder if he's about to do what I hope he's going to do. The music we used to make together.

"Ever play the violin?" he asks idly.

I hide a smile and shake my head. "No. And I haven't played the cello, either," I tell him, hoping it will jog his memory.

"Hmmm," he muses, and I hear the scrape of something being moved, the sound of strings being plucked, and I'm instantly turning into jelly, goosebumps flushing all over my body. My muscle memory is so strong with him, my skin already yearning for that sweet sting of his tender violence.

He stops behind me and I suck in my breath just in time. *Thwack!*

He brings a violin bow down across my ass in one sharp, hard hit. I moan loudly, a mix of pleasure and pain as the sensations flood my body, making me jolt, my fingertips curling into the bench.

"Beautiful," he murmurs, and I know he's staring at the red marks his work has left on my pale skin. "It's like watching a painting come to life."

There's another swoosh of air and then he spanks me

with the bow again. Stabbing heat flares up along my ass cheeks, the sting sharp, and then he's hitting me again and again and again.

Thwack!

Thwack!

Thwack!

Each hit harder than the last, much harder than he used to spank me. I taste blood and realize I'm biting my tongue and my vision is getting a bit spotty and then he spanks me with extra fervour, enough that I cry out and I'm sure he's cut the skin. It hurts and he doesn't seem interested in making me feel any better, not like he used to.

"I could do this for days," he says, his voice thick with lust. "But unfortunately you've broken the strings. No matter, it won't go to waste."

I hear a snapping, plucking sound and suddenly he's pushing between my shoulder blades so that my upper body collapses against the bench and I almost bite my tongue again, my teeth clacking together.

He reaches down and roughly yanks both my hands behind my back and then before I know what's happening, he's tying the violin strings around my wrists.

"You've been such a good girl, taking the pain like that. It almost makes me want to reward you."

I swallow as the sound of his zipper being undone fills the room, mixing with my ragged breathing and the erratic beat of my heart.

I feel the heat from his hips as they come up behind me, and his hand takes a rough hold of my hips, fingers bruising me, while his other hand rubs the swollen tip of his cock against my entrance. I can't help but moan and shift my hips to get more of him, but he's holding back.

"You're dripping wet," he says through a gasp. "And I

expect you're a little sore as well. No pain, no reward, as they say."

I brace myself but he doesn't push in yet, instead teases me, rubbing his shaft up along my clit until I'm pressing down into him, wanting more.

"Do you still want this?" he asks. "Will you beg me for it?"

"I do," I tell him, my voice breaking off as I suck in my breath. "I want everything you want to give me."

"I'm going to give you all I've got," he says, and before I can prepare myself, he's thrusting inside of me in one hard, painful stroke that knocks the air clean out of my lungs.

"Oh, God," I gasp, feeling full and stretched, and yes, there's pain, but there's also a burning desire in me that only grows as he starts to pump into me, making me rock back and forth, my back arching up and my cheek pressed against the bench.

"I don't know what it is about you," he grunts, his hands gripping me tightly, "but all I can think about is how to destroy you. How I'm going to fuck you to hell and back."

"Yes. Yes!" I cry out, the pain and pleasure of his words mixing together. I angle my hips back, wanting all of him, feeling like I can't get enough as he continues to drive his cock into me, deeper and deeper each time until I feel like my world is spinning.

"You should be careful what you wish for," he says, his voice rough.

"I'll take it," I tell him. I want everything he has to give me because that's the only part of him he'll give. It's the only part of him that seems to remember me, even if he doesn't know it.

"Yes, you'll fucking take it. Ask me nicely, like the good little whore you are."

"I'll take it, my lord."

"Take what?" he ekes out through a heady groan as he pushes into the hilt, his balls pressed against me. "You'll take my cock? You already are. I'm in your tight virgin cunt so deep you can feel it in your throat."

"Yes," I gasp. "Yes, I'll take your cock, my lord."

"Ask me to fuck you harder."

"Please, my lord, fuck me harder."

"Louder," he orders, and I obey, throwing my head back and moaning out loud, my cries echoing off the rock walls.

"My lord, please, fuck me harder!"

"Fucking hell," he groans, slamming into me, over and over, until I'm crying out and shuddering, my whole body on fire.

He reaches down and wraps his hand around my throat, making my back arch and pulling me up as he leans down to whisper harshly in my ear, his hot gasping breath tickling my skin.

"Good girl," he murmurs, "you take my cock so well. You were made for this, made for me."

I can feel my body responding to his words, my pussy clenching around him, urging him on. I can't help the moans and whimpers that escape me as he fucks me harder, faster, his breaths coming in ragged gasps.

"Say it," he orders, his grip on my throat tightening. "Say you were made for me."

"I was made for you," I gasp out, my voice barely audible. Part of me is panicked, having flashbacks of my death in Venice, but the memory is buried by how well he's fucking me. He's always been so good at making me forget.

"Again," he demands, his hips slamming into me.

"I was made for you!" I cry out, my body shaking with pleasure and pain, my mind consumed by the heat of his touch and the sound of his voice.

Because it's true. He doesn't know it, but it's true. I was made for Valtu, and he was made for me, and by some divine luck we've come together in the way we know how.

We are primal, we are raw, we are destined.

And even though he may not know me as I know him, I know that somewhere deep inside, he knows that I was made for him too.

And I have found him again.

He continues to fuck me hard and fast, his hand still tight around my throat, until I'm keening and moaning, on the edge of shattering into a million pieces.

"Oh god, Valtu," I cry out, and then I'm coming. I'm coming so hard my eyes roll back in my head and my mouth falls open and I clamp down on him, squeezing his cock as the spasms roll through me. I feel like I'm going to die from the pleasure but I'm too lost to care.

With his hand still around my throat, he wraps his other arm around my waist, dragging me down to the ground, continuing to fuck me hard and fast from behind. My cheek is pressed against the cold floor and I'm staring into the shadows, my vision blurring, my mind going numb.

I feel his cock twitch and shudder inside of me, his breathing ragged and his body beginning to shake. "I'm coming," he cries out roughly. "Oh hell. Fuck. Fuck."

I clench down tighter around him and he groans, pumping into me in short, sharp bursts.

I feel him release inside of me, the hot spurting of his cum. He pauses, shuddering, and then he pulls out of me and I feel him spill all over my back, the hot sticky fluid running down my ass and over my thighs.

I hear him panting, his whole body heaving from the exertion, and then I feel his hand on my shoulder, pushing me down to the ground.

"Good girl," he says, gently stroking my hair. "But a dirty girl. I need to clean you off."

I know exactly what he means to do and even though I am spent and exhausted, another thrill runs through me. He moves back and starts licking his own cum off my back, then spreads my legs and starts licking up my thighs, like a panther lapping from a stream, strong yet delicate passes of his tongue, until I've been licked clean.

Then he undoes the restraints, tearing the violin strings apart until my hands are free, and straightens up behind me, getting to his feet.

"Are you hungry?" he asks, and I hear him zip his pants back up.

I laugh. How could *he* be hungry when he just licked the hell out of me?

I pull my tunic back down and shake out my wrists, glancing up at him over my shoulder. "For what?"

"Whatever you want," he says, walking toward the stairs. "Food. Blood."

He goes down them and I take that as a sign he wants me to follow him.

I get up, my legs feeling a little unsteady, and go after him down the stairs to the lower level.

"When's the last time you drank?" he asks, heading to the fridge.

"The other night," I answer, knowing I have to be careful what I say.

"Were you with the doctor?" He opens the fridge door and starts placing things out on the counter.

Shit. I can't remember what day I was supposed to arrive in "Oxford" and I'm not sure what Abe told him.

"I wasn't," I say, praying it's the right thing. "I fed before I went to his lab."

"Pills, I'm assuming," he muses, taking out several steel bottles.

"No," I say. "I fed from a live human. At a feeding room. In London."

He chuckles and closes the fridge door, then looks over at me with his brow cocked. "Uh huh. I'm sure you, brand new baby vampire, could not only find a feeding room in London, but actually sink her teeth into a fucking live human being." He gives his head a shake, though he looks amused. "There's no use putting up pretenses at this point, though I guess I'm flattered you're trying to impress me."

I open my mouth to protest, then close it. Because I am lying about the being in London part. I want to tell him that I did feed from Michael, but unless I mentioned Solon and Lenore, there's no way he'd believe me.

I shrug one shoulder. "Can't blame me for trying."

He grins at that, looking boyish instead of brooding for once. "I'd prefer it if you tried to impress me in other ways."

"Are you saying I haven't been impressive so far?"

He lets out a small laugh and directs his attention to the steel bottle which he uncorks. "No, you have. You very much have." He raises the bottle. "I have fresh blood here." He waves dismissively. "Enough with the pills. That's no way to live a life."

Even though I did just feed, I have a hard time turning down what he's offering. Just the idea of drinking blood instead of swallowing a pill has my stomach churning hungrily, a deep addiction stirring inside me.

I watch as he pours the liquid into two goblets and I don't think I've ever felt as much of a vampire as I do right now. Drinking blood out of goblets with Dracula in his mountain lair? Suddenly this is my reality.

Valtu's always been your reality, I remind myself.

"Here," he says, walking over to me and holding out the glass. "To your health."

I gingerly take the glass, peering over into the blood like it's some magic elixir. "*Prost*," I say, cheersing in German. I take a sip and the moment the liquid hits my tongue I feel like another dimension has opened up inside my head. It immediately strokes the hunger inside me until it completely takes over and I finish the glass in one big gulp.

"Greedy girl, aren't you?" Valtu surmises over his glass as he stares intently at me. "Guess you're lucky you're with someone who can provide."

I don't want to lose control or appear desperate, but the blood is coursing through my veins and making them sing. I want to beg him for more and I'm practically panting trying to keep myself in check.

But he notices. This is what he wants. Me to submit to him, to succumb to him, to beg for him in more ways than one. It's all part of the power play.

"Look at you," he says richly, his eyes flicking over my face. "How hard you try to hide it, to deny what you really are. Tell me, Rose, is your family a slave to these pills as well?"

I try to swallow, my mouth and throat feeling desert dry. "Every vampire is."

"Not every vampire." He raises his chin.

My eyes flick back to his glass which he still hasn't

finished. "We can't all live in isolation. Murder is a thing you know. And the feeding rooms are hard to find. They definitely don't exist where I'm from."

"And where are you from? Answer some questions and I'll let you have more blood."

I pause, taking in a deep breath to steady myself, hoping I don't fuck up. "Okay. I'm from Oregon."

"That's what the doctor said. Where in Oregon? I've spent some time on the west coast."

"Newport?"

Valtu nods. "Fishing village. Big bridge. Bigger surf."

I stare at him in surprise, totally forgetting about blood for the moment. "You've been?"

I had no idea that Valtu had been there. Then again, it's been a long time.

"I've been around," he says. His eyes narrow thoughtfully. "But of course, you haven't lived there your whole life. Your parents would have to move a couple of times if they don't want the humans to get suspicious."

"That we did." I motion for the glass.

He keeps it closer to him. "Siblings?"

"A brother," I say. "Older but he hasn't turned. You?"

He blinks at me in surprise. "Me? Do I have any siblings?" He has a sip of his wine. "I was adopted but had a brother, briefly, but he died when he was very young. You know how things were back then, especially before turning."

"Well I wouldn't, because I wasn't alive back then," I say, even though it's a lie. Because I was alive back then too.

He takes a step closer and hands out the glass. "Are you sure? Because sometimes when I look at you, I see an old soul."

I eagerly take his glass from him. "They say that's just a

trauma response." I tip the glass back and let the blood flow down my throat, swallowing it all down greedily. My god, it's almost as good as sex.

"A trauma response?" Valtu says with an air of disbelief.

"Yeah," I say, wiping my mouth. "They say when you meet someone who you'd call an old soul, it usually means you're just seeing the trauma from them having to live through shit and grow up fast."

"And who is *they*?"

"The internet," I tell him, then glance around the dark medieval looking room. "Though I guess you don't get a lot of that here. If I didn't know any better, I'd say the lack of internet helped you become a well-rounded individual."

He lets out a dry laugh, his eyes crinkling at the corners. "Then I'm glad you know better."

I'm about to laugh too but then the hair on the back of my neck stiffens and I feel a cold draft pushing at my back. It's not the alpine winds blowing in through a window though, it's a cold that comes from the depths of some place dark and evil and cosmic.

Valtu's expression darkens as he spots something over my shoulder. I have no doubt it's the bad thing, coming to pay us a visit.

I keep my eyes focused on the floor. "It's behind me, isn't it?" I whisper.

"It is," Valtu says carefully, his voice equally low. "But it's just looking at you. If I didn't know any better, I'd think it was infatuated with you."

"It's always the ones you're not interested in," I say as a joke, though he doesn't know how painfully true that actually is for me.

Then the cold horror at my back disappears, the energy in the room lifting, and Valtu visibly relaxes.

"It's moved on," Valtu says with a huff of relief.

I wish I could be as relaxed. I'm not sure I can when I'm reminded the bad thing exists. "Moved on where? Do you know? Where did it come from?"

"So many questions," he says, taking the glasses and bringing them over to the sink.

"And worthwhile questions," I point out. "If I'm going to be living here, I think I deserve to know what I'm dealing with."

Valtu suddenly tenses, his back to me, and he lowers his head for a moment before turning around and leaning back against the counter, his arms folded across his chest, a piece of his black hair flopping over his forehead. "You think you're living here?"

I rub my lips together, not sure what to say.

"You're not living here, Rose," he adds, his tone unkind. "You're just staying here. And not for long either. You might be a damn good fuck, but I'll get bored of you sooner rather than later."

It's like a shotgun blast to the fucking chest.

I swallow painfully and raise my chin, pretending that this isn't a surprise, that it doesn't bother me. "Of course," I tell him. "Whatever you'd like."

"Whatever you'd like, my lord," he corrects me.

"Whatever you'd like, my lord," I tell him.

Though I feel whatever he'd like involves breaking my heart over and over again.

CHAPTER 16
VALTU

The girl has become a puzzle to me. One that I both want to solve and yet am afraid to look deeper into, because the deeper I go, the more I might like having her here.

And that can't happen. I don't let myself get close to people. I specifically never let myself get close to the people who have been brought to my place as a blood slave or a whore. Why should I when they almost never make it out alive?

I may have forgotten large chunks of my life, but their absence only tells me that erasing love, forgetting relationships, is the only way to survive in this world. In my world. Other people seem to handle love and loss as easy as they do breathing. They accept it and they take it and they suffer and they act like it's just part of life and it's okay.

But it's not okay. And most people haven't suffered what I had to. Grief took from me, it took *everything*. And as a vampire, we're just supposed to deal with loss and sorrow for eternity?

It doesn't seem fair now and it didn't seem fair then. I

don't remember the pain that I was in, just as I don't remember the woman and our love, and it's only been a blessing in my life. Yet I'm aware of how easily things could change again. Every time you get close to someone you open yourself up to pain. Because eventually they will die or leave you and you'll be a husk of your former self, discarded, left behind, and scattered by the wind.

But you do have a solution, I remind myself. *It's right over there.*

I look over to my desk by the window. On top of it is the book. The cover was always worn, since it's been around for a long time, centuries maybe, but the new wear and tear is due to my hands, the countless hours I've spent every day for years as I've flipped through the pages.

Beside the book is a music box, and inside that music box is a vial.

When I made the potion for myself all those years ago, I ended up making two just in case one broke or something went wrong. Now that extra vial is in the box, safe and waiting for the worst-case scenario, which is that there might be someone else in my future that I'd want to erase from my mind.

You're getting way ahead of yourself, I think as I lie back in my bed. *Rose is just a girl. Have fun with her while she's here, then say goodbye.*

But then I'm struck with a terrifying thought.

I don't want Rose to be slaughtered by the demon. Call me sentimental. But now I'm thinking that if the demon is truly possessive over her, it might not let her leave here at all.

And then what? What power do I truly have over it? It seemed to leave her alone when I claimed her as mine, and then yesterday when it appeared behind her, I was able to ask it to leave with just my eyes. It disappeared into the shadows and I haven't seen it since. But when it's time for her to go, will my claim on her still hold? After all, if you possess something you generally don't let it out of your hands. It's possible that the moment I do, the demon will jump in and snatch her for his own.

I guess I'll have to cross that bridge when I come to it.

I sigh and stare up at the ceiling, aware that even the slightest complication in my well-preserved life is throwing things off-balance. I had a system to things, an order. My life has been lonely, but it's at least made sense. Perhaps it's best to get her to go now before I get attached. I didn't think it was even possible to feel a sense of attachment, affection or possession for anyone, but there's something about her that is slowly getting under my skin and I don't like it.

I know she's young, but I wasn't kidding when I said she seemed like an old soul. Whether online shrinks call that a trauma response, she really does seem like someone who has seen a lot, been through a lot. On the surface she comes across as your average young vampire, but I don't know how many of them go through *The Becoming* and then immediately fly across the world. Especially to find me.

The more I talked to Abe before he left, though, the more he explained Rose. That she was always obsessed with Bram Stoker's Dracula, then became obsessed with the idea of *me*. When she turned, she decided to finally take the leap and seek me out. Abe didn't elaborate too much, but it seemed that her parents were controlling and didn't approve of her seeking out the true meaning of being a vampire.

I think I know what she's looking for. It's not me—she doesn't know me, and the idea of me probably doesn't match what I really am. What she's looking for is an excuse to return to basic instinct. To become the primal version of herself, the real version. Vampires have been slowly sanitized over the last two decades, no thanks to my oldest friend and his pills. What Rose wants—and what she's afraid to ask for —is to let herself go. Not just to me, she's been very apt in showing how easily she'll submit to my wants and demands. No, she needs to submit to herself. To what she really wants. Once she does that, then I think I'll have her figured out. The puzzle will be solved and I will be rid of her. I have already put a plan in place to make this happen.

But it will be such a shame to see her go. Everything about her is a maze of contradictions. She is both soft and hard at the same time, in her body, her face, her soul. She's inexperienced sexually and yet gives her body to me so readily. She enjoys sex more than anyone I've ever come across, and more than that, she enjoys it the way I like it: rough and raw and completely uninhibited. Whatever I want to give she takes and she takes it eagerly, so open and wanting with her need, and she's giving in return. Not just because I command her to, but because she loves it. She loves seeing me get off.

Just the thought of her has me reaching down into my pants, making a fist around my cock which is already hard as the mountain around this room.

I pull it out and start stroking myself, thinking of the way she looked this morning with my cock in her mouth, when I paid a visit to her bedroom and made her suck me off. The way she looked when she pulled me out of my fly and stared at my length like I was a fucking lollipop, her lips parted, her eyes glistening, her pink tongue darting out to lick her lips in anticipation.

I groan, my hand moving faster. I think about making her say it.

I want you, my lord.

I want to hear her mouth say the words, begging for my cock. I imagine the look on her face, how her eyes would light up with desire, her mouth parted with primal need.

I want to see her open her legs, pull down her panties and say it.

Say it or I'll spank you harder.

Say it or I'll tie you up, force you on your knees and fuck your mouth until you choke.

Say it or I'll lock you in a room alone and fuck you in the night when you're sleeping.

My lord, my lord, yes, my lord.

I'm so close to coming now. Why does that phrase sound so good?

I'm picturing her now tied to a chair and spread wide open, my cock in her mouth, her plump red lips wrapped tight around me.

I think about her tied up on my bed, getting ready for me.

I think about her tied up and tied down and spread open, completely at my mercy.

I think about her bent over the couch with her bottom raised, begging me to fuck her.

Why on earth do I want to see her go?

I moan out loud, my hand moving faster and faster, the pressure building. I'm so close to coming. I don't want to do it without her. I want her to be here.

But that want is enough for me to climax. I gasp and then through a stifled groan, I come, the weight of it pouring out of my cock, shooting out onto my stomach, coating my shirt and making a mess.

I try to catch my breath, to slow my heart, to clear my head. I don't know why I'm so worked up over her. Centuries of women and this is the one I can't get out of my head.

It makes no damn sense.

I groan and get out of bed. I've been lying here most of the afternoon, trapped in my thoughts. There's a snowstorm raging outside, the window turning into a blurring white of frost on the panes and the snow beyond. I told Rose that I wanted to have a proper dinner with her tonight, and that's when I'll really put her to the test. She probably thinks I'm serving up food and blood, but she won't be expecting the main course.

That is if she's still here. There's a kernel of unease in my stomach. It's nearly dusk but I haven't seen her since this morning. I thought she would be safe in her room but considering the demon can go into her room when it wants to, I'm not sure she's safe anywhere in this place, even though I sent the demon out of the house earlier.

It's enough to get me moving. I change my shirt—I still have some class—and put on a charcoal grey dress shirt, then black pants. I spend more time than usual in the mirror, fixing my hair and I have to stop and pause as I stare at myself. I can't remember the last time I've even looked in the mirror—honestly, what's the point when I never see anyone, and those I see I don't care what they think about me? Besides, my ego has always been healthier than most.

Yet, I'm inspecting my face for flaws. My skin is a little gray, my cheeks gaunt and I'm wishing I had some kind of grooming cream for my hair, which has gotten wavier, almost curly in places. I haven't changed my appearance in centuries, my hair has always been about chin-length and wild and now I'm wondering if it's appealing to her, if she likes it.

Get a fucking grip. She's just a whore and you're thinking about hair gel.

I shake that off and leave the room. My bedroom is located up one of the towers, so it's a long narrow flight of stairs down to the maze of lower hallways beneath where her room is located. I believe my bedroom was once used as a chapel, and the disciples would have to pilgrimage up the stairs, but I've seen no signs of salvation in there.

When I get to her door, the candles on the walls flickering as I pass them, I'm surprised to see it ajar. A wash of fear stiffens my chest and I quickly push the door open, expecting the worst.

Her bed is messy but empty and there's no sign of blood or a massacre.

I exhale in relief, looking around. I should probably go and find her but instead I go straight for her bags, hoping to find some sort of clue to who she is. I rifle through her clothes, none of which seem appropriate for the mountains, but then again vampires never really need warm outfits. There's nothing else there though, in there or in her purse. No phone, no wallet.

I see her coat rumpled on the floor and pick it up, finding her wallet in one pocket and her passport in another. I flip the passport open and see her pretty face all serious in black and white overlayed with identity holograms.

Rose Harper.

Born May 19th, 2023.

San Francisco, California.

A true west coaster.

Her wallet gives the same information, except her driver's license has her address in Newport, Oregon.

I guess she has been telling the truth. I'm pretty good at seeing through fake documents and the like and these seem as legitimate as anything.

The fact that I can't seem to find a phone though feels odd.

I go through the rest of the wallet, trying to see what I can glean, but it's the type just made for holding her money and key cards, all under her name as well. The only clue I have is a key card for the Hotel Vertigo in San Francisco, but that doesn't strike me as too strange considering that's the city she was born in. Perhaps she has family or friends there and goes back often. Though for some reason, Rose strikes me as a lone wolf.

I put everything back and am about to head back out into the hall when I see a black bag shoved behind the sink's faucet. I step into the bathroom and retrieve it, looking inside. It's cold to touch and when I open it, chilled air seeps out. There are blood pills inside, a kind I've never seen before, no doubt given to her by the doctor.

Exhaling in disappointment, I shake my head, then I turn the bag over the toilet and watch the pills fall out into the bowl, and flush them down. Now she won't have a choice.

I go back out into the hall and start looking around for her. I finally find her in the living room, sitting primly by the fire and staring at the flames. She doesn't seem to hear me approaching and I take a moment to take her in. She's dressed for our dinner, wearing a green dress with thin straps over her shoulders, making her pale skin glow. Her hair is down, waving around her shoulders and looking like amber on fire, thanks to the roaring flames.

She's absolutely stunning, the kind of beauty that feels like a punch to the gut.

"Rose Harper of 267 Cliff Street, Newport, Oregon," I say from behind her.

She whips her head around, caught off guard, her eyes wide and mouth open, hand pressed at her chest.

"How long have you been standing there?" she says breathlessly.

"Not long."

Then she frowns, realizing what I've said. "How did you know my address?"

"I went through your wallet," I tell her, not ashamed in the slightest.

She looks aghast. "Why?"

"Why not? I like to know as much about my guests as possible. You can never be too careful."

Now there's a hint of a smile on her lips, making her eyes dance in the firelight. "I can see that. Why else would you have a demon as a guard dog?"

There's something that's been nagging at me for the last few days. "You called that demon the bad thing. You never did tell me how you knew that name."

I study her carefully but she remains composed. "Doesn't everyone know that name? That's what the rest of the world calls it. You can't keep that thing a secret. You know it's part of your *mystique*."

I nod, liking the sound of that. I hold out my arm in offering. "Why don't you tell me more about this mystique over dinner."

Her brows go up in surprise. "We're eating already?" She cranes her neck to look over at the dining room table and the kitchen. "I haven't seen you prepare anything."

"Never underestimate a vampire with a magic book," I tell her as she gets up and comes over to me.

She takes my arm, giving a look that's both shy and warm, like I just presented her with a bouquet of flowers instead of my arm, and I try to ignore the pleasurable feeling it creates in my chest. I lead her to the table where I pull out her chair and she sits down.

"You sit and behave," I tell her, pushing in her chair before heading to the kitchen.

"Don't tell me you use magic to prepare your food," she says, sounding less than impressed.

"Actually," I say, opening the fridge and bringing the premade charcuterie boards out onto the counter, "it was the deli people at the Aldi in Mittenwald."

I shut the fridge and take the boards over to her and place them on the table. She looks them over, finally impressed. "You hike up and down the mountain with your groceries?"

I nod my head toward the front door. "There's a cable car on the other side of the peak out there. Easy to get a ride up and down if you know how to cloak yourself."

She laughs. "Must be fun being an invisible man, even if you are just getting wine and cheese," she says as I walk back to the counter to pick up a bottle of cab sav. "Ever think of teaching your guests some of your tricks?"

"Nice try," I tell her, unscrewing the bottle. "I can't tell you the number of people who think I'm about to give them all my secrets."

"They're not really *your* secrets. They're the book's."

I give her a steady look. "And the book lets me know what it wants me to know. No one else. That's not part of the deal," I tell her, taking out the cork with a satisfying pop.

"What *is* the deal?"

I shrug and pour us both a glass of the wine. Usually I don't like discussing the book, but I feel I can divulge a little with her. "I'm not really sure. I just know that it feels safe with me, and it gives me the information I need."

"So you've memorized every spell in the book?"

"Every spell I've been able to," I admit. "It doesn't show me everything. Half the book is just blank pages. Over the years spells will appear in ink, but lately the book seems to think I've gotten all I need to know."

She thinks that over as I take the seat across from her. "And do you? Do you have all you need to know?"

"I'm starting to think so." The whole reason I took the book in the first place was for the spell of erasure. There wasn't even a reason to keep the book after that and yet I did. I couldn't part with it. More than that, I couldn't imagine it in anyone else's hands. Perhaps someone more noble than me, like Solon, would make a good guardian for the book. He would no doubt use it for all the right causes, like tracking down Bellamy and finding Leif, the stolen vampire child, or destroying Saara for good. But I don't have a reason to care about any of that anymore, and the book wants to stay in my company. If it didn't, I'm sure the demon would abscond with it all together.

At least, that's what I tell myself.

"Don't you wonder why you have the book?" she says, taking a sip of her wine. "Why it chose you?"

I clear my throat. "Yes. All the time." Then I take a mouthful of my drink and switch the subject. "I don't know how satisfied you are with food, but since you've only recently turned, I'm guessing you still have an appetite for the stuff."

"I do," she says, reaching forward with her knife to slice

off some of the soft cheese and spread it on a cracker. "I'm always hungry." She gives me another one of those shy smiles, the kind that makes my dick twitch. The innocence of her face plus the sight of her breasts spilling out of her dress that's a little too small for her is like a fucking wet dream.

I'm tempted to throw her down on the table, right on top of the food, and have my way with her, but I need her to be ravenous for the main course and I need to focus.

We both eat a little and drink a lot of wine, until I know she's feeling pretty loose, her inhibitions melting away dabbling in small talk which is easy and enjoyable for once and not torturous. Then I decide it's time.

"Now, onto the main course of the evening," I announce, getting out of my chair.

"That wasn't it?" she asks.

I just give her a faint smile and tell her I'll be right back. Then I go up the stairs all the way back toward my bedroom. There are two towers located next to each other, and I make my way to the higher one above my room.

This place was never a chapel. Never a place of salvation.

It was a place where they'd put the disciples when they needed to be punished. It was their own personal hell, locked away in the dark tower with nary a god to hear them.

It is here that I am keeping the boy.

CHAPTER 17
ROSE

I watch as Valtu walks off and disappears around the corner, going upstairs. The moment he's out of sight, I breathe out a sigh of relief.

This dinner has been nice. Unexpectedly so. This morning when he came into my room, I expected the blow job. I had no problems making his eyes roll back in his head. But when he told me after that he wanted me to join him at dinner, and to wear something nice, it threw me for a loop. I remember Abe specifically telling me he wouldn't feed me, whether it be food or blood, and yet Valtu requested my company.

I'd be lying if it didn't warm me from the inside out.

He was choosing me without even knowing my past, without knowing who I really am to him. Does that mean that in some way, we'll always find our way back to each other? Is it possible for Valtu to want me on an emotional level just as I am now, as Rose Harper and no one else?

It gives me hope. Because even if he doesn't remember our past, I'll take any version of love. I tell myself that to love me as Rose is to love me as Dahlia, Lucy, and Mina, because we all are one and the same.

But I'm so wary of how fragile that hope is. With each second I'm with Valtu, my heart is constantly in free-fall. I never know when it will land, how much it will hurt. It's a special kind of agony to be so deeply in love with someone, your actual soulmate that you've found through death time and time again, and for them to be so indifferent to you.

I think that indifference is slowly melting away, though. Perhaps the sex is getting to him—he always was easy to assuage in that way. Or maybe it's the fact that it's been ages since he's had anyone to really talk to or confide in. I know Abe told me he wishes they were closer but ever since he got hold of the book, he's become a pariah on purpose. Perhaps he feels others judge him for the choices he's made. All I know is that even though Valtu acts like this life here, hidden away alone in the mountains, is something he prefers, I can sense the loneliness deep inside him. I can *see* it, this emptiness in the blackened recesses of his eyes.

There's a darkness in both of us but at least I understand why I am the way I am. Dying repeatedly has something to do with it. Yet Valtu isn't conscious of why his darkness is there. Everything that has made Valtu brooding and cold and dark is because of *me*. It's been because he's lost me so many times. Now that he doesn't remember me or any of his past, he doesn't understand his own darkness. He can't face it. And so it sits there and festers and he believes he's completely fine.

In some ways tonight has felt like old times and there's an ease to the way he is around me. He's quicker to smile, quicker to laugh, to joke. The hard shell of him is starting to crack in places.

But he's not completely comfortable. Something has

him on edge. Maybe it's that he's aware that his shell has weak points and his guard is up to prevent it from cracking all together. Maybe it's something else. Whatever it is, it reminds me to keep my own guard up, despite how many glasses of wine I've had.

It feels like Valtu's been gone a long time and I'm starting to think he might not be coming back, when I hear the sound of chains.

I automatically sit up, on alert, wondering if he's thinking of chaining me to the table. I wouldn't mind, of course.

Then I see him appear from around the corner.

I stiffen.

He's not alone.

Behind him, with a chain around his neck, is a naked man. No. More like a boy in his late teens.

Valtu holds onto the chain and jerks it forward, yanking on the boy's neck. The boy looks around him with wide eyes, his mouth clamped together into a hard line, and he doesn't make a noise, though I can tell he's screaming inside.

I get to my feet, feeling panicked. I don't even know what's about to happen, but it feels wrong. This isn't a sex thing; this is something else.

"Who is that?" I manage to say as Valtu leads the boy over to me. I can feel the heaviness of whatever magic Valtu is using.

"I don't know," Valtu says simply, looking the boy over as if it's the first time seeing him. "I asked for a human in their prime and this is what it brought back."

I don't even have to ask who *it* is.

"Brought back for what?" I ask, though I know it's a pointless question.

Valtu just grins at me. Devious and cold and lacking any of the empathy I once saw in him. I almost don't know him at all.

"I brought him back for you," he says with flourish. Then he throws the chain on the table where it lands with a clunk, knocking the food and wine everywhere. "I thought you could use a real feast. There's a lot of firsts for you while you're here." He nods at the boy. "Get on the table. Lie on your back."

I gulp and watch as the boy obeys and climbs on top of the table, lying down on his back. His movements are stiff and controlled and I have the feeling that Valtu has him like a puppet on a string.

I stare into the boy's eyes and see them pleading with me to let him go, to end this nightmare. I look up at Valtu. "I don't want him," I say adamantly, shaking my head. "No. You have to let him go."

Valtu sneers. "Don't be ridiculous. You're not a real vampire until you've fed from a human."

But I've fed from one, I want to yell, but I tried to tell him that before.

"I have blood pills," I quickly say. "Abe gave them to me."

All I see is a cold, cunning smile. "You don't have them anymore. I flushed them down the toilet."

"You what!?" I exclaim, my face going hot with rage. "How could you do that? I needed those!"

"And if the doctor hadn't given you any, then what would you have done? Did you think you could rely on my generosity? You're lucky I'm being this hospitable with you. Normally I'd keep this human for myself."

"Then keep him for yourself! I said I don't want him.

He's not a volunteer, he didn't consent to this. You had him abducted!"

"Consent," he scoffs and his lip curls in another sneer. "Now you're pretending to take the high road. You realize you came here to be my fucking whore. To get fucked, to get used, to do whatever I please. You think you have some kind of greater moral standing than I do? You're just as bad as I am."

I am not! I want to yell but I know that would be a mistake.

"I consented to that. Not to this," I tell him, my eyes darting to the boy and back. God, he reminds me of Dylan when he was eighteen. I can't look at him anymore.

"Does it look like I'm forcing you to do anything?" Valtu says snidely.

Then he walks over to the table, picks up the knife and slices along the boy's artery in his arm.

I scream as the blood spurts out and I know I need to put something there to stop the bleeding, maybe my dress, or a dishrag, but the will to help the boy is fading away and being replaced by something else.

The smell of blood.

Young blood.

Fresh blood.

My tongue starts to tingle, my stomach starts to ache as if I haven't eaten in years, my mouth goes painfully dry and I'm remembering Michael, remembering how good it felt to feed from a human.

But Michael volunteered. This boy didn't. And he's scared to death.

"You're just going to let him bleed out like that?" Valtu admonishes me. "Tut tut, that's very wasteful of you, Rose."

I glare at Valtu with all the fury I can spare, wondering

why the sight of blood isn't doing the same thing to him, how he can keep so cool while I feel my hunger is ripping me apart at the seams.

"I don't want him," I manage to say, but my words are so weak that Valtu doesn't believe me and I don't believe it, either.

"You do," he says, running his fingers over the blood in the wound and bringing it over to my face.

I shrink back from his hand, trying not to breathe in the blood, and pinch my eyes shut. Inside I feel like I'm on fire, like I'm going to go insane.

"You've submitted to me, my black Rose," he murmurs, his voice filling my head. "Now submit to your darkest instincts."

I open my eyes to see him sliding his fingers into his mouth, the blood pooling between his lower teeth and his bottom lip. I can't look away as his fangs sharpen into existence.

Then he grabs me by the back of my neck and kisses me.

Valtu *kisses* me.

His mouth envelopes mine, strong and commanding, his lips soft yet firm, and blood spills onto my tongue while the heat of it all takes my breath away. It awakens a yearning so sharp, so deep, that I fear it might never abate.

I press my hands on his shirt, wanting to push him away because to keep his lips on mine, his tongue fucking my mouth with such fierce urgency, is only making me hungrier. It's making me into an animal, a predator at the top of the food chain, and I want nothing more than to fuck Valtu, then rip that boy apart.

Instead my fingers curl around Valtu's shirt as I attempt to hold on to him, keep his mouth on mine, and our kiss deepens in its intensity. He lets out a moan, sounding almost surprised, then tightens his hold on my neck to keep me in place as he kisses me harder. My lips respond in kind, having wanted to kiss him for so long. The blood is gone now, swallowed down my throat, and yet we're losing ourselves to this, to *us*. I've slid back in time and I'm Dahlia and Lucy and Mina and he's kissing me like he kissed them. I might just melt on my feet, I'd forgotten how beautiful and dizzying it was to be kissed by him.

But when he pulls back, breathing hard, his wild eyes staring into mine with need and something else blurry and warm, my stomach twists sharply, and the urge to feed takes over even my feelings for Valtu.

"I hate you for doing this," I snarl, breathless and feral and slowly losing control.

"About time you started hating me for something," he says. His hand goes to my jaw, holding me until it hurts, his fingers bruising. "You know that you can't stop it now, can't stop it once it's in motion. If you don't drink from him, you'll die from the agony and he'll die for no reason."

"Okay," I whimper, trying to swallow the sawdust in my throat. "But promise me you'll let him go after this. That you'll compel him to forget this and let him go."

"I promise to let him go," he says, running his thumb over my chin. "Now go get your fill, my dove."

He moves out of the way and pushes me a step toward the boy. The boy is staring at the ceiling and for a moment I fear he's dead, but then he blinks and tries to look at me.

I avert my eyes. I look at the blood leaking onto the table and spilling onto the floor.

And I let myself go.

I rush to the boy's side and grab his arm and sink my teeth over his wound. The blood, so fresh, so young, fills my mouth and I drink, insatiable and unrepentant. I feel all my humanity drain out of me while my veins fill with this stranger's blood and in my heart of hearts I realize what I am and what I know I'll spend my life trying not to be.

An animal. A creature. A monster.

Not a human being. I'm not Dahlia Abernathy anymore. I'm Rose Harper. I'm a vampire and I drink the blood of the living in order to survive. No, not even to survive but to *live*. Valtu was right in that I can't go back to those blood pills, not after this. Michael was just a taste but I tried my best to pretend it would only be a one-time thing. Now I know it can't be. I must feed and I hate myself for it, hate what I've become.

And I hate Valtu for making me this way.

I let that hate simmer inside me for a moment and then I use it to stop. It takes all my willpower but I can't let him win. I can't let his depravity push me to these depths. I can't kill this boy because if I don't stop, I will kill him.

I unhook my fangs and stagger backward from the table. The boy is barely breathing, his skin ashen and blue. In my trance, I don't know how long I've been feeding from him but I think I've nearly bled him dry.

The boy jerks and then turns his head, manages to look at me with pleading eyes and I feel my humanity come rushing back.

It's a relief. He's alive.

"You said you'd let him go," I say to Valtu, my voice cracking.

He's been watching me this whole time, a glint of pleasure in his eyes.

"And I will," he says simply. "A promise is a promise."

He walks over to the boy and grins down at him, removes the chain cuff around his neck.

"You're free to go," Valtu says to him, brushing the boy's

hair off his forehead in a strangely tender gesture. "Thank you for your sacrifice."

Wait. Sacrifice?

The boy is finally able to open his mouth, free from whatever spell Valtu had him under, and he lets out a weak but haunting scream that I know I'll hear in my nightmares.

Then Valtu picks up the knife from earlier and in a blur of movement, stabs the boy right in the heart. The crunch of bone and a squelching sound.

The boy's hollow scream dies in his throat.

But I'm screaming now.

"No!" I yelp, hurrying back to the boy. I push Valtu's arms out of the way and place my hand around the hilt, pulling out the knife, yet only a little blood leaks out. There's nothing left.

The boy just lets out a gasp, a wheeze and then he's still.

He's dead.

I look up at Valtu, shaking with the horror of it all.

"I let him go," Valtu explains carefully as he eyes my rage. "He was dead the moment I cut his artery. I let him go, Rose."

I blink at him in disbelief, trying to find the words. He's excusing himself. He's making it sound like killing him was the noble thing to do, ignoring the fact that he got his demon to abduct this boy and bring him here so we could feed.

"You're a monster!" I scream at him.

His features harden, eyes turning to ice. "Isn't that why you're here? To fuck a monster? Or to become one yourself?"

Fire rages through me and I turn on my heel and run, my footsteps echoing against the stone. I go to the stairs, then up them to the second floor, needing to clear my head, to scream, to come to terms with what he did, what I just did.

He's a monster, but now I'm one, too.

I run through the music mezzanine and straight to the shuttered doors that lead to outside, then fling them open and stumble out onto the balcony.

I'm met with a rush of snow, the wind driving it hard into an arctic swirl of white. I run to the edge, to the railing, wanting the vertigo to bury everything else I'm feeling. My hands clasp the stone railing and I stare out into the white nothingness. It's cold, even for a vampire, and I welcome it, needing it to cleanse me of my sins.

I open my mouth and scream, letting out all the horror I just witnessed.

I scream for all the deaths I've had to go through, all the lives I've lost, the women I've been.

I scream for the pain in my heart that I know will never go away so long as Valtu doesn't know who I am.

And I scream because the man I loved has become a man that feels so easy to hate.

"What are you doing?" Valtu's voice breaks through my anguish and he grabs me roughly by the arm, spinning me around until he has me pinned back against the railing.

I cry out, painfully aware of how high up we are, how easily I could just fall backward over the railing and fall through a blizzard to my death, or something even worse than death.

"Get a hold of yourself," he says and through the passing white flakes I see the worry in his eyes, like he thinks I've actually gone mad. Maybe I have. Who could blame me after all I've been through? Only a fucking mad woman would end up here with him.

"Fuck you," I practically spit at him.

"Yeah, that's just what I was thinking," he growls.

Before I can say anything else, he's kissing me again. It's a brutal, punishing kiss, one that I feel all the way to my toes, and I try to put my palms against his shoulders to get leverage but his mouth overtakes mine. His hands slip to the hem of my dress and he hikes it up to my waist, all while pressing me even harder against the railing.

Then he's lifting me up, so the railing is no longer supporting my back and I feel the dizzying drop of space behind me.

I gasp and he buries it with his lips while one hand goes to my upper back, holding me in place, and the other unzips his pants.

"You're here to fuck the monster, aren't you?" he rumbles against my mouth, his lips and teeth trailing roughly along my jaw. "Isn't that what we are?"

I push against his chest, trying to break the kiss, but his grip is too strong. My heart is pounding against my ribs, not just from the height but because of all the emotions whirling through me, pummeling my heart like the blizzard.

I love him. I loved him. I hate what he's become.

I hate that he's right, that I am a monster too, and that terrifies me because I don't want to be like him. The Valtu I loved had his darkness but he was also filled with light and I am so terrified that I won't find that with him, not here and not with this life.

It's breaking my heart into pieces.

"Tell me you want this," he says, positioning his cock at my entrance. "Tell me you still want me despite everything I've done."

"Or what?" I say, trying to hold onto his biceps, the fear

of falling making the edges of my vision blur. "Or you'll let go? Or you'll kill me too? You'd like that, wouldn't you? You'd like to just let go and never have to see me again."

It's a rhetorical question but he stares at me in such a way it's like he's actually seeing it happen. A faint look of horror comes across his brow.

"The darkness in me calls to the darkness in you," he says roughly, and I have to bite my lip from crying at hearing those words out loud. "If you want me, you'll want me as I am, right here, right now." He brings his face in closer until I can see the gold flecks in his eyes. "So, do you?"

I search those eyes, looking for a sign that the man I love is still there, that he's worth fighting for.

I'm not sure if I find him.

But I decide I want him anyway.

"I do," I say, my voice barely above a whisper.

"Good," he snarls and then with one violent thrust he enters me, pushing the air from my lungs and almost sends me over the edge and into a freefall.

I gasp in fear and pleasure and he's holding me in place with thousands of feet below my back, the wind whistling past.

He groans, rough and guttural, and then his mouth is on mine and his tongue sweeps over my lips, claiming me with a ferocity that matches the storm around us.

I'm his and he's mine, not just now but always. If I'm going to stay by his side like I have before, then I have to accept him now, as he is.

But what if accepting him means that I'll lose my humanity too?

The blizzard whips around us, snowflakes sticking to our skin as we move together, his hips pumping against me, a rhythm as old as time. I'm lost in the moment, lost in him, lost in the memories of the man he was before this new darkness took hold. But for now, all that is pushed aside as I focus on the pleasure coursing through me, on the way his hands hold me so tightly it's almost painful.

"Val," I whisper to him and he pauses for a moment, lifting his head back to look at me, a strange look of awe in his molten eyes.

"It's been a long time since someone called me Val," he says, his voice low and nearly swallowed by the wind.

Right. My old name for him. I don't want to give anything away so I skirt around it. "Do you prefer that, or my lord?"

He gives me a wicked grin. "Oh, definitely my lord."

I feel my entire body burn with want. "Then, my lord, it would please me if you finish what you started," I say with a coquettish smile.

He growls and adjusts himself, pulls my leg up, putting me off balance then thrusts his cock back into me in one stroke, all the way to the hilt, letting go of me just enough that it feels like I'm falling.

I cry out, the sensation almost too much to bear, like he's fucking me into space, but then his grip is back, strong and hard and I shift my hips against him.

"That's it," he says, his lips hot against my ear, his cock even hotter as he pulls out and thrusts back in, his large hands on my hips helping me find the rhythm.

"Harder," I whimper, digging my nails into his arm with enough force to draw blood, my other hand braced against the railing. "I want it harder."

"As you wish," he rumbles and starts moving faster, slamming into me with a force that makes me moan with pleasure and pain. The wind howls around us, the snow falling faster now, like it's racing my heartbeat, and in this moment it's just him and me, lost in the storm and each other.

I feel myself getting closer and closer to the edge, my body shaking with need as he drives into me relentlessly. Then, with one final thrust, I come undone, my body convulsing around him.

"Val!" I cry through a ragged gasp, his name coming so easily to my lips. I see stars and feel heat and I'm breaking into a million pieces, carried away with the snowflakes.

He follows shortly after, his body shuddering with release as he empties himself inside me.

For a moment, we stay like that, holding onto each other as the wind and snow swirl around us. Then, with a final kiss, a kiss of sweetness, of tenderness that disarms me, he lifts me up and back onto the floor of the balcony.

My legs give out, the vertigo finally taking over, and I collapse, wanting to be as far away from the edge as possible.

Valtu just scoops me up like I weigh nothing at all and brings me to my feet, ushering me back inside the building.

The storm rages on outside but I have a feeling the storm between us is only just beginning.

CHAPTER 18
ROSE

Back inside the building, my head starts to clear a little. I brush the snow off my shoulders and glance warily at Valtu who is doing the same to his.

I'm still mad, despite all that. I'm still horrified at what just happened downstairs. A good fuck doesn't erase everything. It's not magic.

"What should we do about the body?" I whisper, swallowing hard.

He gives me a curious look. "The body? There is no body left. It will have been disposed of by now." He clears his throat and he quickly loses his impassioned look, composing himself. "I should go downstairs and clean up the rest of the mess."

His dark eyes pierce into mine and I know he's wondering if I'll join him.

But I need time to be alone, to think.

"I think I'll head to bed," I tell him.

There's a flash of disappointment on his face and then it's gone, his face beautiful but blank. "Then I shall see you in the morning," he says, his voice clipped.

He turns and strides off across the mezzanine, disappearing down the stairs.

I glance over at the darkened hallway that leads to my room and sigh. Even though I do want to be alone, I hate the idea of being alone in *that* bedroom. When I'm with Valtu I feel fine, or something close to that, but when I'm alone, everything about this place gives me the creeps. And obviously for good reason.

I tell myself that the bad thing is currently taking care of the boy and that it shouldn't be bothering me. As if a demon devouring an innocent human is something I can use to assure myself.

But it's not the bad thing I'm afraid of.

I'm afraid of myself, of my own judgment.

Because that boy I just fed from, that I helped kill, he had a home. He had a family. He had a life and I just...I just ended it. It doesn't matter that I didn't think he'd die, my actions led to his death. If Valtu hadn't stabbed him in the heart, he would have eventually died anyway. I had drained all his blood, sucked him dry.

And it felt good. It felt so damn good to drink from him that it makes me sick.

Who am I? What have I become? No wonder my parents tried so hard to keep the idea of feeding rooms and the old ways out of our lives. They didn't want me to turn into a monster because they both knew how easy it was to become one.

I make my way down the hall, past the flickering candles on the walls. They never seem to go out, another product of magic inside these walls. I go inside my room and turn on all the lights. Then I strip off my clothes and get in the shower to wash away all the blood but when I finally emerge, I don't feel any cleaner. I don't feel any calmer. And now the lights seem too bright, the shadows too dark, and I shut the lights off again, slip into the old Cherry Coke T-shirt I sleep in, and get into bed.

My thoughts eat away at me like termites. I think about my parents. I was too hard on them. I wish I could go back and erase what I said to my mom. I know why she lied about how she became a vampire and I know that my parents did everything they could to protect us. I wish they had told us the truth but, at the same time, I could see how it would be so much easier to just brush it under the rug. Had I not remembered all my lives when I turned, I would be back in Newport right now, drinking from blood bags and popping pills and living a safe and sanitized life. I would have kept my humanity. I wouldn't have known this hurt, this *shame*.

Perhaps it was destiny, though. Maybe each life with Valtu was always nudging me toward my true self, toward that true darkness. Valtu has always been a bit of a bad influence on me. When I was Mina, he charmed me. He wasn't even a vampire yet—neither of us had any idea of what he would become. But he was one hundred percent him and all that he is. Witty, charming, and leaning on the side of deviant.

As Mina I should have played it safe. I was the general's daughter after all and I was destined to be with someone that would have pledged allegiance to Russia, someone under my father's tyrannical influence. But that wasn't my destiny at all because the moment I laid my eyes on Valtu, a peasant, I knew he would corrupt me. That he would be the answer to everything I had wanted. I was so ready to flee with him, to run away, to give up the safe and secure life I was accustomed to. I would have gone anywhere with

Valtu. But we weren't given much time together in those early days.

As Lucy, I was an upper crust Victorian lady and Valtu pursued me with everything he had. Of course, Valtu knew I was Mina and I didn't, so he wasn't taking no for an answer when it came to me. He knew I would be his. Meanwhile, I barely knew of sex and yet I was willing to let him do anything to me. He pulled loose the threads that held me tightly together, he turned me from a lady to something wild and completely his. Another step toward something feral and free.

Then Dahlia. Oh, Dahlia. I had just one goal. I had one mission. And I threw it all to hell the moment I fell in love with him again. I went from a vampire slayer to a vampire lover in what felt like no time at all, and then he's the one who ended up killing *me*. The ultimate corruption.

I let out a heavy breath and sink back into the bed, my emotions pulling me in every which way, like a whirlpool that keeps changing direction.

I must fall asleep with these thoughts in my head because suddenly I wake up.

My eyes snap open and I look around the dark room, feeling the heavy pull of sleep alongside my erratic heartbeat, adrenaline on high alert, wondering what just woke me up.

I hold my breath and listen.

Please don't let it be the demon, please don't let it be the demon.

There's no sound except for the howl of wind outside the window, the patter of thick snow on the pane.

Then I hear it.

The *creeaaaaaak* of the bathroom door.

I watch as it slowly opens.

Opens.

Opens.

Oh fuck no, not the baby again.

Thank god I'm not chained down this time.

I'm about to get out of bed and go for the door when something drips on my arm. I stare at it, a dark splotch of foul-smelling blood spreading on my skin, then look up.

The boy is staring at me.

His back is on the ceiling, his arms and legs splayed in broken angles, his mouth open wide in a silent scream. Blood drips down from the gash in his arm, splattering cold on my forehead.

You did this! his voice screams inside my head. *You did this! You did this!*

I yelp and throw back the covers, leaping out of the bed. They tangle around my legs and I stumble to the floor, my hands taking the brunt of the fall.

You did this! The boy keeps screaming and suddenly he falls from the ceiling onto the bed, as if gravity lost its hold, and I'm scrambling to get to my feet. I reach for the door and fling it open just as I hear his bloody feet hit the ground behind me.

Holy fuck!

There's nowhere for me to run but to Valtu and I don't even know where his room is in this maze of hallways, but I head down a passage I haven't been through before, running as fast as I can. The candles quiver in my wake but thankfully don't go out and from behind me I hear that slap of his bloody feet on the floor, coming after me, closer and closer. My vampire speed is put to the test, but the boy keeps up with ease.

Finally I come to a set of stairs and head up it just as I

feel a whoosh of air, the boy lunging for me, just grazing the ends of my hair as I fly around the corner.

I yelp and run up the stairs two at a time, my thighs burning, up up up until I'm wondering if it's a trick, if there's a door at the end of this all and god help me if it's not Valtu's room.

Then I see the door, metal and heavy, faintly lit by one flickering wall sconce.

"Valtu!" I scream. "Help me!"

I reach the door, going for the handle and pushing and with a heavy groan the door opens a crack. I throw my weight against it, aware that the boy is running up the stairs on all fours like a rabid dog, snapping at my heels.

The door opens more, enough for me to slide on through, and I launch myself into the room, expecting to see the type of bedroom that Valtu would have.

But it's not a bedroom at all.

It's a literal torture chamber.

There are chains hooked up to the walls, blood stains splattered all over the floor, and there's even one of those stocks that you'd find a medieval criminal in, with holes for the head and hands.

"What the fuck?" I whisper out loud.

I have no time to ponder it. The door flies open further, banging against the wall hard enough that dust floats from the ceiling, and the boy comes staggering into the room, raging blue eyes fixed on me.

I'm fucked. The room is circular and there's nowhere for me to go, the window a narrow slit that I wouldn't even get my head through.

"Valtu!" I scream again, praying he hears me through the house. Praying he cares.

The boy takes another step forward, his ankles broken, his movements like a zombie.

You did this! You did this!

I back up against the wall and look for a weapon. The chains. Maybe I could wield the chains.

I make a go for them, all the while hoping to hell that this boy is only an apparition just like the baby was, that he'll suddenly disappear and I'll escape unharmed.

But he doesn't disappear.

Instead, he grabs me by the throat, his fingers cold as ice and nails cutting my skin and drags me right up to his face.

You did this! he screams, and his mouth gets wider and wider and wider until it's just a big black hole with teeth that's taking over his face and I'm being sucked into it, being sucked into this never-ending abyss, this cosmic world of horror.

I feel so much fear, so much terror, that I cease to exist at all and I'm just this ball of horrible energy, reaching, spreading and—

CRASH!

Suddenly the room explodes in a flash of light. There's the sound of glass breaking, shards of it cutting my skin, frozen air mixing with white hot heat and a burning smell.

The abyss falls away and the boy is no longer holding my throat.

He's not touching me at all.

Instead, he's a thin stalk of charcoal, the floor beneath him marked in a black pentacle, and suddenly he collapses into ash and dust until he's just a burnt mess that billows across the floor, mixing with the snow coming in through the window.

I gasp, staring at him in confusion. My eyes go to the

228

window which has shattered, the clouds whirling outside, and it feels like my brows and lashes have been singed. The smell of burnt flesh lingers in the air, making my nose crinkle.

Then my focus goes to the door.

Where Valtu is standing. Eyes round, mouth open, staring at me like *I'm* the ghost now.

"What the hell was that?" he asks, his voice higher, his tone careful, as if he's actually afraid of me.

"You tell me!" I exclaim. "It's you that's causing these ghosts to appear!"

"No. Not the ghost," he says flatly. "*You.* I just saw lightning pierce through that window and strike him. You did that. You made that lighting strike happen."

I can't argue with that because it's exactly what it looks like. "I don't know. I don't know how I did it. I was just so afraid. You said yourself that it's normal for vampires to be locked in with the elements."

"Not like that," he says, and his gaze hardens as it falls to the floor. "And not like *that.*"

I follow his eyes to the black pentacle on the ground. It's not that the ground is burned in such a way that it *looks* like one, the way you might see shapes in the grass after a lightning strike, but that there are five clear points and a circle in the middle. A symbol that Dahlia was very familiar with.

I blink, shaking my head, not understanding it. "I don't know. I didn't do it on purpose." I look up at him with pleading eyes. "I really don't know what happened."

His expression is cold and wary as he stares at me, his jaw tight. "Who are you, Rose? Who are you really?"

"I'm Rose Harper," I tell him, placing my hands on my chest. "I swear to god I am."

"*What* are you?" he whispers harshly.

"You know I'm a vampire. You saw it today. You know your own kind."

"And you're also a witch."

I give my head a more violent shake. "I'm not. I'm not a witch. I can't be. You'd be able to tell, you know you would. Unless I was wearing a glamour..." I trail off.

His eyes narrow at that thoughtfully. "A glamour. I've been fooled by one before."

"You remember that!?" I exclaim and for a moment I'm filled with hope.

Now his frown deepens, the line between his brows a hard line. "No. I don't remember. I was told. How come you know about it?"

I fumble for the words, panic rising in my chest like a caged bird. "I just knew, I don't know, I heard it somewhere, I—"

"Enough with the lies!" he roars.

I go still. My heart feels like it's crawling up my throat, it's going so fast.

"Tell me who you are, or I'll kill you," he says, his tone a steel blade. There is no mercy in his eyes. They look like black holes to nowhere. "I'll kill you right here and now."

I swallow, gathering resolve from somewhere in my veins. I raise my chin and look him dead in the eyes and decide it's time to put a stop to the charade. "It wouldn't matter if you did. I'll just come back." I pause. "I always do."

Clarity slowly washes over him and his eyes widen. "Y-you..." he stammers, mouth dropping open. "You're *her*."

The way he says *her*, like it's some sort of disease, feels like he's ripping my heart right out of my chest and spitting on it.

And yet...and yet, telling him the truth, ending the lies,

feels better than I could have imagined. I only wished Dahlia had the chance to tell him the truth, too.

"Why are you here? What do you want?" Valtu manages to say, sounding so distraught and pained that it breaks my heart. But I have to remember what he's capable of. Right now, he reminds me of a cornered animal. A dangerous one that's ready to snap.

"I'm on a fool's errand," I tell him. It takes all my strength to say it. "I was hoping I could make you remember."

He looks vaguely horrified at the idea. "You thought you could make me remember? I'll *never* remember you." His words are sharp and quick, a wasp's sting to my chest.

"I know that now," I say, my voice going quiet as the dejection becomes hard to ignore. "But it was always worth a shot."

He closes his eyes, running his hands down his face, shaking his head. "None of it...none of it was real."

"It's all been real, Val!" I protest.

His head snaps up, dark eyes blazing at me. "Don't call me that," he seethes.

"My name is Rose, and I do have a brother and my parents live in Newport, Oregon. But I'm also Dahlia and Lucy and Mina. Val, I know you better than anyone else on this planet."

"You know nothing about the person I am now," he snarls, storming over to me, clouds of ash rising up as he stomps through the pentacle. He shoves his finger under my chin, forcing it up, his nail almost piercing my tender flesh.

I stand my ground, refusing to back down and keep my eyes on his. "I think I do," I say carefully. "You've shown me plenty of what a monster you've become."

"A monster because of you!" he screams, flecks of spit landing on my cheek.

I bristle, my face feeling tight and red. "Hey!" I snap. "You're a monster because you erased me. I kept you good. I kept you whole."

He removes his finger and steps back, laughing, a sharp and acidic sound that echoes around the room. "You kept me good? You? Who helped kill an innocent human today?"

"That isn't fair!" I cry out. "You did that on purpose. You tried to corrupt me."

"Corrupt you? You're the one who has been here under a lie, fucking me left and right to get what you want. And what *do* you want, your revenge? You want to murder me for murdering you? You want the book too, is that part of your deal?"

"No." Then I stop and close my eyes, breathing in sharply through my nose. I can't lie anymore. "Yes." I look at him, pleading. "I also came here because I need your help, and yes it involves the book."

"Well, you're not getting my help," he says and takes another step closer until there's barely any room between us. His breath is hot on my skin and his eyes are fire. "You're not getting anything else from me. I *erased* you. I got that damn cursed book to forget you. How fucking dare you show up here and hide who you are? How fucking dare you think that this was the right thing to do?"

I grit my teeth, trying to keep it together. "I did it because I love you."

His head jerks back, his features distorting. "Love? This is what you call love? If you truly loved me, you would have stayed forgotten!" He averts his eyes and shakes his head back and forth. "No. This can't happen. I will not make all my sacrifices for nothing."

"Your sacrifices?!" I explode. "I'm the one who died!"

"Then you should have stayed dead!"

I blink. Inside I'm plummeting like an elevator, the cable snapped.

I stagger back a step and realize that this is the end of it. That I had a chance and now it's gone and now Valtu will never, ever want anything to do with me.

I'm not getting the book.

I'm not getting him.

I'm getting nothing.

I'm staying forgotten.

Valtu looks at me with violence in his eyes, breathing hard, nostrils wide, his teeth set in a sneer. "You need to go," he ekes out in a low, threatening rumble. "You need to leave right now. And pray that fucking demon lets you go. Because if he doesn't, I'm not going to save you."

Valtu points to the door, his message more than clear.

I know protesting or pleading will make no difference.

I can't stay.

I fucking blew it all.

I look at him for the last time and he has the audacity to look away, as if he's so ashamed and embarrassed of me he can't even look at me. Maybe I feel I deserve some of it. Maybe I deserve all of it.

I stride past him and quickly go down the stairs. It's going to be a long hike down that mountain, and though it's probably the middle of the night, I'm going to have to hurry if I want to escape this place unscathed. I still don't know what the bad thing thinks of me or wants from me, but I have a feeling if it sees me leaving, things will be different.

I go to my room and slip on jeans and boots and the coat, then cram everything in my bag and go. I don't have a phone but as soon as I get down to the village, I'll call the number Abe left for me on my hand. If anything, he can help me figure out what to do next. He certainly expected that this would happen.

That's right, keep telling yourself that, I think while I hurry through the halls and to the front door. *Think of the next steps. You need to get Leif back, you can't give up on that, even if you have to do it without Valtu's help.*

I keep that going in my head, over and over, because the moment I stop thinking is the moment I start feeling and I know I'm going to start crying and never ever stop.

My love. My Valtu.

He really is gone.

And I will never be his again.

I open the heavy front doors, the metal creaking, and step out into the night. I have no idea how to get to Mittenwald, but I figure if I head straight down the mountains toward the lights below, I can't go wrong.

I hurry down the steps, careful in places where it's icy, then start down the worn path that snakes along the crags of the mountainside. I'm a single thought away from breaking down in tears, a single thought away from dissolving completely.

But then there's a raspy wet snarl behind me, reverberating through the chilled air.

A snarl that can only belong to one thing.

It found me.

CHAPTER 19
VALTU

I stare at the charred pentacle on the floor, my mind reeling so much that I have to press my fingertips into my temples, as if that will stop the contents from shifting.

I knew there was something off about Rose. I thought tonight I had her figured out. I thought that she was just repressed, suppressing herself from her darkest desires of being a vampire. I thought that real human blood would awaken what she clearly tried so hard to hide and I wanted to be the one to open up that world for her.

What a fool I was. It was just an act, a role. She knew how to work me, how to play the part. Nothing she said was real. I don't care that her name is Rose this time around, nothing was real. She played me like a fucking puppet.

She didn't get any of you, a voice says. *You haven't lost a thing. Just a week of your time.*

I try to hold onto that but I can't.

I feel betrayed. It's such a new feeling to me that I'm not

sure how to handle it, what to do with it. But I feel it deep in the marrow of my bones.

Betrayal.

And all because I had let myself get too close to her. Despite my best efforts, I got close. She got under my skin and into my blood. The way she looked at me. The way she said my name. The way she knew exactly what to do with her body. She knew how to do that because it worked on me before, over and over again.

But then there was the way she made me play music, the first time I had felt in tune with anything in years. And then there was the darkness inside her that so clearly wants to play with mine. And then there was the closest feeling to salvation I'd ever had when I was buried deep inside of her, losing my mind to her body and heart and soul.

Fuck.

Fuck, fuck, *fuck.*

I throw my head back and roar, the sound multiplying to deafening levels in this room. The room where the disciples sought punishment. A testament to the universe's sense of humor that Rose and her ghost would go straight here of all places. Then again, it was the ghost of the boy we just killed. I suppose it was an act of revenge to make all of this unfold, to torture us in retaliation.

And then there was this damn lightning. Rose did that. I saw it with my own eyes as the ghost had a hold of her. Yet I'm inclined to believe her when she says she doesn't know *how* she did it. Dahlia had been a witch, that much I knew (a witch sent to kill me, I know that part too). Is it possible that Dahlia's magic got reincarnated as well? Or has Rose been a vampire witch from day one, just like Lenore?

Lenore. The key card in San Francisco. Is it possible that Rose knows her? Was she visiting her and Solon before she came here? Is that how she really found me, or Abe? And why did she wait until she was a vampire to come and meet me? Why not earlier?

I have so many questions. Too many questions.

The biggest question of all is: if Rose really is a witch and has innate powers, is it possible she can read the rest of the book, the parts that I can't?

But I won't get any answers to my question if the demon finds her. I don't know what it will do if it sees she's no longer under my command. Will it possess her for itself? Or will it kill her because it finally has permission to?

She had called it the *bad thing*. She had seen it before.

Does that mean it knows who she is?

Thinking about it won't do shit. I can let it take her or I can do what I just told her I wouldn't do, which is save her.

Fuck me.

I used to be a man of my word.

I snap into action and bolt out of the room and down the stairs, moving so quickly that I'm passing through walls. In seconds I have searched the house and the demon isn't here.

Then I'm outside, into the whirl of the winter storm, and I see them.

The demon is a blackened blot in the snow, an alien perched on the edge of our world.

My heart leaps inside my chest.

In his arms is Rose.

One long bony black hand is spread across Rose's face like a cage, its claws curving over her chin and into her throat. The other hand is wrapped across her chest, gripping her hard enough that blood is soaking through her coat.

He's seconds away from tearing her head right off.

"Stop!" I yell. I want to run to her, I could be at her side in the snap of my fingers, but I'm afraid any ambush would result in her death, so I stay where I am.

The demon raises its oblong head and fixes its beady crimson eyes on me.

"She is mine!" I boom, though the storm seems to swallow the sound. "Release her!"

The demon continues to stare at me.

It's thinking.

"She is mine," I repeat, my voice louder, steadier. I raise out my arm as if to smote it. I have tried in the past to use the book's magic on the demon, to destroy it, but nothing has ever worked. "She belongs to me and only to me."

I add, "She always has."

I can barely see Rose's eyes through the cage of claws but they widen at my words. I may not remember her, I may not *want* to remember her, but the truth is the truth. This is a woman who has belonged to me during various points throughout my life, and if that doesn't lay claim to her, then I don't know what does.

But the demon continues to stare. It tilts its head, seeming to consider.

Let her go. Let her go.

It has a mouth of tiny shark-like teeth that seems incapable of smiling and yet I swear it's grinning at me. The kind of grin that only means one thing.

"No!" I holler just as Rose lets out an ear-piercing scream and the demon begins to pull at her, muscles flexing, claws digging and—

A lightning bolt comes out of the clouds in a jagged white-hot line and strikes the both of them, appearing to eviscerate them in a cloud of black smoke.

"Rose!" I scream and start running toward them, expecting the worst.

The smoke is thick, filling my lungs, and I can't see a thing, even the snow seems unable to penetrate it.

Then it becomes transparent, just enough that I see a flash of red and, fuck, dear god let that not be blood. Let Rose be alive.

The smoke starts to clear and with relief I see the red is actually her hair and as the tendrils lift, I'm staring at Rose.

She's on her knees, her head down and her hair flowing forward, most of her clothes blasted away by the lightning, leaving only singed scraps behind that flutter on her body. Behind her is the demon.

Or what is left of the demon. Just a pile of charcoal and ash until the wind blows that away too.

It's gone.

I can't believe it.

The demon is fucking *gone*.

"Rose," I whisper in shock and then drop to my knees beside her, placing my fingers under her chin and lifting it up. Her hair falls around her face and she opens her eyes, her beautiful green eyes that remind me of buds in the spring, and she looks right at me, and I can feel her in my soul.

"What happened?" she rasps. She's shaking slightly and I reach out with my other hand and push her hair back behind her ears.

"You destroyed it," I tell her, gripping her shoulders now. "You did what I could never do. You destroyed the demon."

She stares at me, bewildered. "I did?"

"The lightning. Did you do it on purpose that time?"

Her swallow is audible in the storm. She nods. "I did. I

figured I had one last chance. I just asked and then there was noise and heat and I felt like I was on fire." She looks over her shoulder at the ashes. "It killed it. But it didn't kill me."

She seems so confused, so surprised by her power, that it only solidifies what I thought. That she wasn't born a witch.

"You're new to this," I say, "aren't you? To being a witch in a vampire's body."

Her tongue darts out to lick her lips and it never fails to surprise me at how fast my thoughts with her turn sexual at the most inappropriate times. "I swear to you, I haven't had any sort of powers or magical ability my whole life," she tells me. "This only started the day that I turned. The day that I got my memories back."

"So you remembered Dahlia and somehow your subconscious remembered her magic as well," I muse. I don't like saying Dahlia's name for fear that I'll remember her, but now that she's right in front of me, I don't think that's going to be a problem.

"Maybe my subconscious remembers, maybe my body does, but when I was Dahlia, I didn't have this sort of power either. This is next level shit. This is the stuff that..." she trails off and looks away, her face looking pained.

"The stuff that what?"

She frowns as she looks at me. "I know you don't remember me or us, but do you remember who Bellamy is?"

"Head of the witch's guild," I say. "At least he was. He operates his own sect now. They've found a way to become immortal," I add bitterly.

She grimaces, her lips curling. "Yeah, I've heard. Do you know how a bunch of witches managed that?"

I can't tell if she already knows or she's asking. "There are rumors," I say carefully.

"Of what?"

"That a baby vampire was taken. Experimented on. That they were able to use that vampire's blood and isolate the genes it had, use it to make themselves immortal."

Tears well in her eyes, her lower lip trembling, and I'm about to wonder what I said when she suddenly gets to her feet. "That baby was my brother."

"What?" I get up, staring at her in confusion. "It couldn't be your brother. The baby was Leif. He was the son of Wolf and Amethyst. Vampires I personally know."

"Yeah, well, I know them too," she says. She gives me a faint smile. "They're my parents."

I can't help but look at her, absolutely dumbfounded. "They can't be your parents. That's impossible."

She folds her arms across her chest, which causes a scrap of material to fall from her, and gives me a steady stare. "Tell me how that's impossible."

I quickly try and calculate but all the years seem to be a blur. I haven't talked to Wolf in, well, a very long time. They went into hiding after Leif was taken from them. "Leif was a twin..."

"At the time it was Leif and Liam," she says, and it catches something in my memory. "But they changed his name from Liam to Dylan a long time ago. Right before I was born."

I have to shake my head, all of this seeming too impossible. "You can't be their daughter."

"But I am."

I run my hand over my face. "Christ on a bike," I mutter. My brain hurts. "How?"

"It's a tangled web when it comes to me," she says.

"Don't you think about how impossible it was for you to find me again after the first time I died? All the people in the world, and you run into me in the British Museum. Had you gone earlier in the day or the next day, had I not gone at all, had I just bent down to adjust my dress at the very moment you were looking my way, we would have missed each other. But we didn't. And how impossible is it that I was sent to Venice to kill you, that I had a glamour on that prevented you from recognizing who I really was? All of this is impossible, Valtu, and yet it's happened. The universe keeps finding a way to put us in each other's path, no matter the circumstances."

I had no idea we had met at the British Museum. There is so much that's been erased because I erased her.

Because you had to. You lost her.

And yet she's here.

"The universe also keeps finding a way to torture me," I tell her gravely. "Because it also finds a way to make you *die*."

It even had me kill you, the last time, I think and for once I feel a touch of guilt. Guilt that had never been there before. What is happening to me?

She gives her head a shake. "Nope. I'm a vampire now. I'm not going anywhere."

"You almost did," I point out, gesturing to the ash.

"Perhaps I'm lucky this time around."

"When you live long enough, you learn everyone's luck runs out eventually."

Rose raises her shoulder in a shrug. "Perhaps. But for now, I'm alive and I'm standing right in front of you." She looks again at the ash on the ground. "I'm assuming you didn't have any emotional attachment to the demon?"

"Me? Fuck no." Then terror floods my mouth, a sour

taste. "Shit. The book!"

I turn and run toward the house and after a beat I hear Rose coming after me.

I throw open the front door, then speed through the house and the halls until I'm bursting through my bedroom, my eyes flying to the book.

It's sitting there, on my desk as usual. Destroying the demon didn't destroy it as well.

Still, I have to be sure.

I go to it and flip open the pages. To my relief the spells that were there before are still there, though there's that touch of disappointment in that no new ones have appeared.

"What happened?" Rose says from behind me, and I look over my shoulder to see her standing in the doorway. She steps on through and I realize for the first time ever, someone else is in my bedroom.

She comes to my side and lays her eyes on the book. "Is this it? The Book of Verimagiaa?"

I snatch the book away from her and hold it to my chest.

"Okay, Gollum," she says with a snort. "I'm not going to take it from you."

I can't be too sure of that. She's a witch after all. "I met Tolkien, you know."

She rolls her eyes. "Oh god, please don't tell me you were his muse too. Did he and Bram Stoker hang out in the same circles or something?"

"Not as far as I know."

"Good. Wouldn't want your ego to get any bigger."

Despite myself, I find myself smiling at her, our conversation melting into something of comfort and ease, like I'm slipping backward into a past that I don't remember.

"Why do you care about reading the book if you've already found all you need to know?" Rose asks, putting a hand on her hip that nearly causes the last piece of fabric to fall, a thin charred piece that runs from her breasts to between her legs and around her hips. "You wanted it to erase me, right? Well, you've done that."

"And yet here you are."

"Yes. Here I am."

My throat feels thick with sudden need.

She eyes me for a moment and then walks closer. I flinch and hold the book away from her, operating on some deep instinct to keep the pages safe.

"I don't want the book, Valtu," she says quietly, pinning me with her stare. "I want you to help me get Leif back. I want you to help me destroy Bellamy. I want my revenge."

"You don't need me to destroy Bellamy. You just obliterated that demon. You have more power than you think."

"Bellamy is immortal now and has powers I can't pretend to understand. My lightning might not stand a chance against him or the others. On top of that, I don't know where Bellamy or Leif are. If they're even together. You have to help me track them."

"First of all, I don't have to do anything," I remind her curtly.

She glares at me. "I'm aware. That's why I am *asking* you."

"What makes you think I can find them? There's no tracking spell or magic in the book. There wasn't when Solon asked me for a decade ago, and there isn't now."

She looks away and makes a tiny growl of frustration.

"I'm sorry," I tell her.

"No, you're not."

But I am. It catches me by surprise. I actually want to

help her.

I've turned into such a fool, I barely recognize myself.

So I put the book down on the desk and I kiss her instead.

She gasps in shock as I cover her mouth with mine, my hands disappearing into her hair, pulling her close until I feel the rest of her clothes fall away and she's soft and naked and in my grasp. Her lips open to mine, kissing me back with a sweetness greater than honey, and my cock is instantly hard, my tongue exploring her as our kiss deepens.

"Is that all you want?" I whisper against her lips, my voice tight and hoarse as the need sweeps through me, held back by the finest thread.

She shakes her head, sadness making the green in her eyes deepen. "I want you to remember."

"And if I never remember?"

"Then I just want to love you."

Fuck me. Her words pierce the skin. "You shouldn't love me, Rose. I don't want your love. I'm not worthy of it." My gaze drops to her mouth. "I have shown you nothing but hostility."

A tiny smile flits across her lips and she places her hand on my cheek. She's warm, so warm, and I am so cold. "You underestimate yourself. There is good in you. I have seen it before and I see it now. You have more dimensions than you think you do."

"You're remembering a man who doesn't exist anymore."

"I'm not remembering anything. I *know* you, Val."

Val. Val. Only my closest friends have ever called me Val. But those friends aren't so close anymore. No one is close anymore. It's by design.

Push her away, the voice in my head says, the voice of all my fears. *Push her away before you start falling for her all over again.*

I close my eyes and breathe in deep, trying to gather the parts inside me that make me hard and cold and strong. I need to tell her to go, to walk, to leave. But I can't. The pull she has on me is too great, even without remembering what we were to each other.

Then erase her again, the voice says. *Help her get her brother back, destroy Bellamy, learn the rest of the book with her help. And when it seems like you're falling over the edge, drink the vial and erase her once more.*

I open my eyes and stare at her. The relief inside me is palpable.

Yes, yes that's the only way I can do this.

I will erase you again, I think, keeping my thoughts on a short leash so that she can't pick up on them even if she tried. *I will give in to you and then I won't know Rose Harper ever existed. And I will be free once more.*

"Val," she whispers, searching my face. "Help me."

Such simple words and I'm already being undone.

You will be erased.

"I will do all that I can," I tell her.

Rose breaks into the widest smile, so bright and brilliant that it nearly brings tears to my eyes. I can feel the hope in her expand, like a blooming flower in her chest, and then she's kissing me back.

I let out a soft moan against her lips, unable to resist.

I spin her around and her hands go to my shirt, unbuttoning it, her movements fast and frantic and I'm taking off my pants, moving her backward until she's pushed up against the end of the bed.

Then I'm on her, pressing her down against the

mattress and her legs wrap around me, pulling me in close. We're both naked together for the first time and I'm startled at how warm she feels, like a soft dream that I never want to wake from.

"You're a dream," I murmur to her and I can feel her heart thundering in her chest. I want to ruin her and I'm afraid she's going to ruin me.

But I need to feel this.

I need to feel her just like this. To be deep inside her knowing that she truly does belong to me, not just now, but in so many times throughout my life.

I need to feel everything before I take it away.

I'm almost shaking as I cover her completely, my lips against hers, I've never wanted so much from anyone and suddenly I want it all from her.

You can erase her after this. It's okay to let go.

"Are you okay?" she breathes, her fingers tangled into my hair as she stares up at me.

"Perfect," I say, my voice rough. I break away to kiss her neck and Rose is wound so tight that she's already whimpering, trembling slightly under my touch.

"Val..." she manages to say in a husky voice. "Fuck me."

I move lower, kissing the swell of her breasts. Her fingers tighten in my hair, urging me further.

"Fuck me, *my lord*," I remind her as I cover her nipple with my mouth. She quivers beneath me and I suck at her, roll my tongue against that perfect little bud.

"Fuck me, my lord," she whispers as she arches beneath me, as if she can't help herself. I move to her other nipple and her body is trembling. I blow against her nipple and she makes a sound that causes my cock to jerk.

I grin against her breast. "Say please." I suck at her again, running my fingertips over her ribcage, drinking her in with my eyes. She's so beautiful, so raw and open and pure and yet I know of the darkness underneath. I saw it today, this woman of mine with the power to destroy demons.

She might even destroy my own demons.

She moans. "Please, my lord," Rose pleads. "Please. Fuck me."

I don't hesitate to sink into her.

I swear I can hear the world breaking open as I push into her tight, wet heat. My eyes roll back and I'm gasping.

She's so amazingly, beautifully wet that it takes me all I have to keep from coming.

She's mine. Mine now. All of her.

Even if she won't be mine in the future, in this moment she belongs only to me.

I move slowly to try and keep my control from slipping. Rose's body is still tense, still gripping me hard, and she's so damn tight that she's milking me in the best way possible. Every thrust of my hips and it feels like my cock is seconds from coming.

"Oh, fuck," I say through a grunt. "Fuck, Rose. You're so good, so fucking good."

She's hissing and mewling, crying out as I push into her and withdraw, watching where I sink into her, where she's so damn wet, she's coating my shaft until it's dripping.

Despite my resolve to slow things down and keep control, I can't resist slamming into her over and over, wanting more of her, more of that.

Her arms wrap around my head, her legs are shaking and she's breathless. I can feel how close to the edge she is, and I know that I won't last much longer. She gasps, her breasts bouncing with each powerful thrust of my hips, the sounds coming from her mouth dirty and obscene.

"Val!" she screams. "Oh, my lord."

I'm about to destroy her. I can feel it, feel her winding up tighter and tighter.

"Rose," I say in a desperate voice. "I need you to let go."

I sink down, kissing her hard enough to bruise, drinking in all that she's offering. She arches into me and her body becomes a living flame under my touch.

Over and over, I push into her and she's so tight that I can barely breathe and she's trembling now, mouth open. I'm shaking with the effort of trying to hold back and I watch her face as she comes beneath me, the orgasm ripping through her like a wildfire.

It's beautiful. So fucking beautiful and I'm going up in flames.

Rose's body takes mine over the edge and I'm coming so hard, I can't even breathe.

My head goes back and I bellow, a deep guttural roar that tears out of me. She's screaming and I'm shaking, I'm shaking so fucking hard that it feels like my bones are rattling and when I come to, I can't move and I'm staring into her eyes and I don't want to look away but eventually I have to. I collapse against her, sweat pooling between our bodies, our breath ragged in unison.

The orgasm is so intense that I fight to come back to reality, to pull myself together. I'm shaking and shaking and I feel lightheaded. I've never had so much pleasure in every inch of my body.

Because she knows you better than you know yourself. And deep down inside, you know you know her, too.

That's what I'm afraid of.

CHAPTER 20
ROSE

I wake up in an unfamiliar bed, a shaft of sunlight poised on my face. I wince at the light, despite how good it feels, then roll over to see Valtu sleeping soundly with his back to me, his back rising and falling.

Holy shit.

He's here. I'm here.

I'm here in his bedroom.

I glance around his room, curious to see what it looks like in the daytime. The bed is large and draped in black sheets, the room is circular much like that torture chamber I found myself in from the other night. Thankfully, there are no chains, but a few things that seem very Valtu. There are a few bookcases crammed with old editions, some which I recognize from back in our London days, and a small velvet loveseat beside it. There's a fireplace but it doesn't look like it's been used in years and a couple of items on the mantle above: a venetian mask, an original printing of Dracula, a figurine of a raven, a tired looking music box, a human skull which I have no doubt is real, even some crystals, including a black tourmaline sphere and a gray lithium scepter.

Apparently, all of Dahlia's crystal knowledge is deeply ingrained.

At that thought my eyes go over to his desk by the window. The light that's coming in is also hitting the desk, illuminating the book. I feel it calling to me, something quiet yet persistent and I have to wonder if it's looking for a new owner, if that's even how it works. I'm the one who destroyed its demon, its own personal guardian. Does that mean the book is mine now?

Of course I would never take it from Valtu. I think it wants me to, I think it's trying to promise me things, but Valtu's attachment to that book is very real and very strong. It means something to him still and I don't want to fuck with that. I just want to use it. There's a chance that maybe the book will show new spells to me. Maybe it trusts a witch. Maybe I just have to ask it properly.

Valtu stirs from beside me, shifting so he's facing me. A strand of unruly hair falls across his forehead and I can't help myself. I reach over and brush it off his forehead.

He lets out a small, sleepy moan and his eyes slowly flutter open.

I hold my breath, praying and hoping that when he sees me, he really sees me, that somehow all the events of last night rewrote the past and freed him from his spell.

His pupils focus and widen, his eyes bigger as he takes me in. I hope I don't look like a wreck first thing in the morning. It's not lost on me that this is the first time we've slept together in a bed, the first time he's been completely naked, and the first time he's fucked me with just a bit of affection.

"Hi," I say softly.

He blinks at me. I don't see any love in his eyes, but I don't see any fear or anger either. I'm not a lover from his past, just a lover from the present. And that has to be good enough for now.

"Hi," he says back, voice throaty with sleep. He gives me the faintest smile.

I trail my fingertip over his nose, his perfect nose, his beautiful lips, his strong chin where the ever-present stubble scratches my fingertip.

"Not a monster in the morning, am I?" he asks with a small yawn.

I grin. "Not even a little. What about me?"

"If you are, I wish all monsters looked like you," he says. He shifts his head so that he's lightly biting my finger. "And of course you taste like heaven," he adds, placing a kiss on my palm.

Then he's reaching out and cupping the side of my face and pulling me to him and kissing me.

It's not the hard, demanding kiss that he's been known to give, but a soft, easy one. It's not a kiss of hunger or lust but one of lingering affection, and I'll take what I can get, whatever he's willing to give me. His softness stirs my heart.

His lips melt against mine, his tongue is gentle and warm, and even though we have yet to get out of bed, he tastes faintly like mint. We kiss, slowly, deliberately. We take our time, as if we're kissing each other for the first time, until the flames start to build between my legs and I feel a deep, hot ache inside me. Our kiss deepens and my body shifts, thighs squeezing together to quell the throbbing that's building and building. His grip on my neck tightens and he tilts my head to take me deeper, and I moan into his mouth.

He pulls away, breathing hard.

"Get on my face," he murmurs, eyes unfocused with lust. "I want you coming on my tongue."

My mouth goes dry. "Okay," I whisper.

He rolls onto his back, his head on the pillow, and I climb up over his face and hover over his mouth. I feel his hot wet breath and I have instant goosebumps, every nerve in me dancing like a livewire and he hasn't even touched me yet. He's using one hand to position me, the other stroking his cock slowly.

And then I'm sinking down, feeling his lips part slightly, the rough rasp of his morning beard scratching my inner thighs.

The sensation is so raw, so carnal, it makes me clutch the iron headboard.

The second he starts to suckle my clit, I know I'm a goner.

You like that?

It's his voice in my head. He's projecting his thoughts, because of course he can't talk with a mouthful of pussy.

"Yes," I manage to say, shifting my hips against him.

Of course you do. You like your tight pink cunt fucked by my tongue. Look at you. You're honey pouring into my mouth.

I smile, biting my lip, loving how he sounds in my head, loving how he fucks me with his mouth, his dirty fucking words. He licks slowly, deliberately, his tongue dipping in and out and over the cap of my clit and I'm gasping.

You feel me, sucking your sweet fucking honey down my throat?

Oh god.

This man, this man.

I'm panting and gasping, so full of desperate arousal, my thighs quaking. I slide my hands down into his hair and grip hard as I grind against his mouth.

He flicks his tongue over me, his cheeks hollowing as he sucks hard.

I'm so fucking close.

Let go Rose, he says.

But I don't want to. Not yet. It's torture to hold myself back when I'm such a hair-trigger with him.

I glance down at him and his eyes flash with stark determination. He sucks me harder and harder, his tongue swirling around and around until I might go insane.

You're so goddamn wet for me. Look at you. You're soaking my face, fucking drenching me. You love my tongue thrusting in your cunt, don't you? Can't get enough of it.

"Yes," I moan, pinching my eyes shut as another wave of primal pleasure takes over.

He laps at me, quick and shallow, his tongue flicking over my clit.

I'm so fucking hard, swollen, and ready to burst.

"Yes," I breathe. "More, please."

God yes, yes.

Take it. Take it, Rose. Fuck, I could eat you for days and never get full.

He growls in his chest and his lips tighten around my clit and he sucks hard.

I arch my back, my body flooding with pleasure as my orgasm slams into me.

It takes my breath away, strips me of all control, until I'm a gyrating mess.

I'm sobbing, gasping, all my muscles clenching hard.

I moan and grip his hair, hips bucking against his face as he sucks every last drop of my climax into his mouth and I fall against the headboard, gasping and shaking.

I writhe on his face for a moment and then lower myself, feeling his tongue slide out of my pussy.

Then his strong hands are wrapping around my waist and he's lifting me up and he adjusts himself so he's sitting up, his back against the headboard and he's lowering me onto his lap.

Right onto his cock, which is hard and thick, pushing into me as he slowly presses me onto him.

"Oh fuck," he moans, fingers digging into my waist until it hurts.

I slide down, watching his jaw clench and his eyes glaze over as he sinks deeper and deeper inside me and I'm completely straddling him.

"Fuck," he says again, his hands on my hips, holding me still. His gaze is intense and burning as it locks me in place and I'm unable to look away, our noses brushing against each other, our breathing hard and shallow.

Then he's lifting me up and lowering me again, thrusting his hips up into mine until he's in so deep I can't breathe, I can't speak.

I can only gasp, my hands clutching the hard curve of his shoulders, the taut muscles of his biceps, holding tight as I begin to rock back and forth on him, our bodies finding that easy rhythm.

Effortless.

When we're like this, it's effortless. As if we were made to be together like this, as if this is all we were ever meant to do, as if this is how we were meant to live the rest of our lives, if only they weren't always cut so short.

I glance down at him and his eyes are shut firmly, his jaw clenched, his nostrils flared.

He's not just holding on to me, the way he's digging his fingers into my hips. This is his way of holding onto himself.

His way of keeping his control, even though I can see for myself that it's already slipping.

Just having me in his bed like this, our faces close, our bodies naked, after learning the truth...he's giving me more than I thought he would. Last night when he banished me, I thought I was done for and would never see him again. I really believed that.

But he came for me.

He told me he wouldn't save me, but he came to save me anyway and claimed me as his and despite my lies, despite our past, despite the fact that he doesn't want to remember, I'm here.

I'm here with him in the most intimate way I know.

And we're both going over the edge.

Together.

"I'm going to come," he mutters, his voice thick with desire, his eyes wild as he looks at me. "I'm going to come so fucking hard."

He kisses me, hard and deep, the taste of me still on his tongue, and thrusts up into me with a few final pumps, and then we both let go.

I pull back, my neck and back arching, and cry out his name as I come harder than I've come before, like I'm being torn apart on every level.

Valtu grunts loudly and his cock jerks inside me, his hips shoving up against mine, and he comes with a hoarse gasp.

His warmth spills into me, not stopping.

He crushes me to him, my breasts pressed against his damp, hard chest and he's growling and grunting against my ear as he continues to fill me up, all slick and hot.

Holy hell.

I'm spinning.

I lay my head on his shoulder and the sweat-slicked skin feels good against my cheek. His heart is pounding against my chest, and it takes a while to catch our breath. The world seems fuzzy and distant and cold and there's nothing out there except our two bodies, deep in connection and wrapped together.

He lifts me up suddenly and I gasp in surprise as I slide off of him, but he wraps an arm around my waist, then he rolls onto his side and pulls my back into him.

He holds me like I'm precious, his grip strong and possessive and I listen to his breathing as it slows.

I close my eyes and I let myself pretend that we're in the past. It feels so right, so good, that I wonder if I'm becoming delusional, how easy it might be to live in another reality. I could live a whole life just on this edge of what's real and what's not. At least here, in bed with each other, fucking each other, it's as real as it gets.

I hold onto that and fall asleep in his arms.

When I wake up again, the sun is in a different position and fainter, and Valtu isn't beside me in bed.

I raise my head, propping myself up on my elbows and see Valtu at his desk, his head down, intently flipping through the pages of the book.

I get out of bed, my legs sore from our earlier activity, and grab one of his shirts from the back of the loveseat, slipping it on and doing the middle button before walking over to him.

He hears me but he doesn't turn around. I put my hands on his shoulders and he melts into my touch, ever so briefly, and it feels like a win.

"Any luck?" I ask, peering over his shoulder at the pages. I'm staring at a bunch of Latin and though I haven't read Latin since I was Dahlia, it comes easy to me. "A spell to walk through walls," I read out loud.

He turns his head slightly to glance up at me. "You can read Latin? Wait. Of course you can." Then he shifts over in his seat, the chair moving out slightly and then pats his thigh.

I beam at him, feeling like I've crossed a new threshold yet again, and come around, sitting on his lap. He slips one arm around me and with the other sweeps my hair forward and plants a kiss on the nape of my neck.

"Good morning, by the way," he murmurs against my skin, his lips warm, breath hot. I can't help but shiver, though I'm trying to keep my attention focused on the book. "Or afternoon, I should say."

"How long have you been awake?" I ask while trying to read over the spell. I want to walk through walls, too.

"I never went back to sleep," he says. "My mind kept turning and you were out like a light. I think harnessing that lightning took more out of you than you realized."

He's right. Though I'm awake now, the groggy feeling is lingering. "What have you been doing all day?"

"This," he says, reaching out and flipping the page of the book.

"Wait, go back. I'm not done."

He looks at me for a moment, impressed. Then he turns the page back and I finish reading the spell, putting it away in a compartment in my brain and memorizing it.

"Okay, now you can turn the page," I say with a satisfied nod.

"You memorized all that?" he asks.

"I think so."

"You're a wonder, Rose Harper," he says appreciatively, brushing my hair behind my ear. "Let's see if having a real witch here pleases the book. I assume if it didn't want you to know the spells, it wouldn't have let you read it."

"That's what I figure," I admit. I don't add the part where I'm wondering if I'm also the book's new guardian. Does the demon need to be replaced? Or was the demon always holding the book hostage? Did I free it?

Valtu starts flipping through the pages, some with text, some blank. With each blank page we see, his shoulders deflate more and more. "I just don't get it."

"Maybe the book is done," I say, but I don't want that to be true either. How else will we find Bellamy? How else will we defeat him?

"Maybe," he says quietly, sounding dejected.

"Can I ask you something?"

He glances at me through his lashes, eyes skimming over my face. "What?"

"If you only took the book because you wanted to erase me..."

He sucks at his teeth, his gaze darkening.

I peer at him. "That was why you took the book, right?"

"Actually," he says carefully, "I've been told the reason I took the book was to bring you back from the dead."

"You were going to bring me back from the dead?" My brows go up.

"A spell for necromancy." He licks his lips, and I can't tell if he's burdened or relieved by the confession. "That's all I ever wanted. And when I couldn't find it, the spell of erasure appeared. Tabula Rasa. I knew what I had to do."

I can't pretend that it doesn't hurt. That erasing me was something he had to do. On the otherhand, I do understand. Valtu lost me twice before, we lost our baby twice, and on the third try at our destiny, he killed me. I can't imagine trying to live with that kind of guilt. I understand why he chose not to live with it all.

But it does have me thinking: how will I die this time around? I know I'm a vampire, but last night I came very close to dying again. I said it's luck but I can't expect luck to keep me alive forever.

Is my destiny to always be with him?

Or is my destiny to always die?

"What's wrong?" he asks softly. I blink and look at him while that new revelation sinks in and he gives me a strained smile. "You have to forgive me when I talk about these things so matter of fact. I just don't..."

"I know. You don't remember. It's fine."

I switch the subject by leaning over and flipping the blank page and as the page is turning, I swear I see ink starting to form on it.

"Wait!" Valtu cries out and he immediately flips the page back.

Ink is filling up the page as we speak and we both watch with open mouths as it forms into legible text.

"*Cantatio Pro Vertitate*," Valtu reads in a deep voice. "A spell for the truth. It says it will cause the recipient to be unable to lie." He gives me a sidelong glance. "Good thing you told me the truth last night." His words are sharp but there's a glint in his eyes, giddiness over finding a new spell after so long.

"Check the rest of the book," I tell him, tapping his hand.

He flips the pages but the blank pages are still there. "Oh," he says despondently. "At least it gave me one more."

I feel a strange pull inside me, the urge to touch the book again, so I reach over and turn the page, slower this time. Just like last time ink begins to bleed through the fibers and I flip it back over as a new spell forms.

"You want to know why I keep the book around?" Valtu whispers in awe. "It's because I had a feeling that one day it would show me something else I would need to know. *This*."

Together we read the new text that's forming before our eyes.

"*Movere Aliquid*," we say together. A spell that allows one to summon objects.

"This one is very handy," he says. "I could bring the rest of the books over to me without having to get up."

"Or a bottle of wine," I say, grinning.

"You turn the page," he tells me, looking absolutely boyish in his excitement. "It's you that's doing this, you that the book is responding to. You're the magic, my dove. Not me."

And so I start flipping through the book, watching as page after page goes from blank to Latin text. There are new spells for levitation, and causing blindness in your enemy. There's magic for unlocking doorways and incantations for bringing to life inanimate objects. There's one for an invisible shield and another for freezing someone in their place. There's even one for teleportation, albeit with some caveats, like you have to have been to the place before.

But despite all we read through, there isn't the one that we need.

There's nothing about tracking or finding people.

And there's also nothing that can reverse a spell. I don't dare tell Valtu this, but this one is as equally important as the other. If I could only find a spell of reversal or a counterspell, then I could undo the *Tabula Rasa* and he'd finally see the real me. I don't even feel guilty, well not much, about going against his wishes because I know the Valtu I'll see on the other side, the one who loves me, will be overjoyed at seeing me again.

At least, I hope.

Fuck. Even if there was such a spell, I guess there's still a chance that after all that, after everything, he might not feel the same way about me. These twenty-one years may have altered him in ways that can't be fixed.

But that's neither here nor there right now. I'm just happy that he seems just as disappointed as I am that the spell we really want hasn't appeared.

"Well, I guess that's that," I say sadly, shifting on his thigh. "All the pages are full."

He leans in and kisses my neck. "I'm not going to give up. We're going to get your brother back and we're going to get you the justice that you fucking deserve."

I give him a steady look, staring deep into his rich eyes. "Why are you being so nice to me now?"

His brows go up. "Am I being nice?"

"You are being *very* nice. It's quite un-Dracula of you."

He gives me a quick smile. "Must be the sex." He clears his throat and looks back to the book. "I don't know," he says, his voice dropping a register. "I just feel that maybe the reason I've held on to the book for so long is because of you. Maybe you were the key to show me the rest. And maybe the spell I really needed was the one to help you find your brother."

"Well, if we do somehow end up finding him one day, at least we'll have a shit ton of magic to destroy Bellamy once and for all."

"Provided he doesn't know all of this already. Don't forget, he is immortal."

"And don't forget that so are we. In the end, he's still

just a human. We are vampires. Top of the food chain. Doesn't matter what that bastard thinks he knows."

He kisses my cheek. "All this talk about being top of the food chain is turning me on, you know." He adjusts himself and I feel the hard press of his cock against my ass.

I giggle. "Yeah, what the hell doesn't?"

He smiles back at me, eyes going hazy with lust, but then they suddenly clear, like a fog has lifted. "The beginning," he whispers harshly, brows up.

"Huh?"

"Of the book!" he exclaims. "There's some blank pages at the beginning!"

Hastily, I reach for the book and flip the cover closed. Then I open it to the first page, a blank page, and touch the edge of it. Slowly the words seep onto the paper.

Exponentia Pro Somno.

A spell for sleep.

I flip through a few more pages that are already filled, coming across ones for walking through walls and keeping candles lit, stuff that Valtu already knows, as well as opening a portal to another world, the Red World, which I don't think either of us will touch with a ten-foot pole.

Then I come across a single blank page.

It's practically calling for me.

Please let it undo his spell, I think. *Please bring back the man who loves me.*

I touch the paper, pressing my fingers down on it and wishing.

I feel energy seep from my fingers onto the book and then back again.

The letters start to form.

Carmina ut Aliquem.

An incantation to find someone.

"This is it!" Valtu practically shouts. "This is what you're looking for."

I let myself feel sad for exactly one second before I push my own personal feelings away and focus on the news. The good news. The spell that not only I wanted, but that my parents and Solon and Lenore wanted as well, is finally right in front us.

"We can find him now," I whisper. "I'm going to get my brother back."

"Then we're going to rip Bellamy's fucking head right off and piss on it," Valtu snarls. "Let's see him still be immortal after that."

CHAPTER 21
VALTU

"Bellamy is in Istanbul?" Van Helsing asks over the phone. "Are you sure?"

"They're both there," I correct him. "Him and apparently Leif. And I can't be one hundred percent sure until I actually see them, but yes, that's what the magic has revealed to us so far. We're still getting a hang of how the spell works."

"So now what?" he asks.

"Now you better get a hold of Solon and Lenore and whoever else you can think of and get them over here. Despite all the magic, we're going to need reinforcements. We can't do this alone."

"Wolf and Amethyst will want to be a part of this," he says. "And what do you mean here? You want us to meet you in Mittenwald?"

"No, in Turkey," I tell him. "I'm already here."

"Valtu!"

"Just get a hold of them. I'll call you back when we have a plan going."

"Valtu, wait—"

But I hang up on him and slip my phone into the locker, locking it using my mind before I grab my towel and wrap it around my waist.

I step out of the change room and into the ancient Roman cistern that the hotel has turned into a spa. Huge arches of stone converge in the middle above the pale blue waters churned by jets and in the middle of it is Rose, looking around her curiously. We're the only ones in here.

"Built during the Byzantine Empire," I tell her as I go down the steps and enter the hot water. "Amazing that this is still standing."

"Way before my time. And yours, I guess," Rose says, and it strokes my ego to see the lust in her eyes as her gaze goes up and down over my body. "Does it bother you that there's so much history you missed out on?"

I shake my head and dip into the water, lazily swimming toward her. "Not at all. I like the fact that there's so much mystery still. In the past and in the future."

Right now, the future has never seemed more mysterious.

It was only yesterday that we discovered that Rose had the power to bring the pages of the book to life and make the rest of the spells appear. With each one that revealed itself to us, I felt my feelings for her grow, like a flower blossoming in a graveyard. My first instinct was to push back against the feelings, trample them underfoot. They didn't belong here, not with me, and not for her.

But I couldn't help myself. I kept repeating in my head that I have the spell of erasure and I can rid myself of her after all of this is said and done, and that gave me permission to try and enjoy it for once. I've always kept people at arm's length, but knowing that what I feel now and what I might feel tomorrow could be forgotten makes letting her in a little easier.

And then we found the spell. Finally. A chance to get her brother back, a chance to destroy Bellamy and whoever else is in that sect of his. The so-called immortal witches.

I know that my interest in all of this is purely selfish. I have harbored guilt on behalf of Solon and the others for decades now. I have had to live with the fact that I never helped them when I could have. And no, there were no spells at the time to locate him, but in those early days, it may have been easier, and I didn't even fucking try.

So when the spell leapt onto the page, I knew that I would try and help Rose, as much for her as it is for my own salvation.

It took a while to learn the spell. It wasn't as simple as learning a few lines or creating a potion. It's a highly mental thing that takes a lot of focus in your own head on the individual you're seeking. I wasn't able to bring up Bellamy or Leif at all.

But Rose was. She was able to see Bellamy in her head, clear as day, and with that clarity she could glean his surroundings as well. She'd never met Leif because he was gone before she was born, but she says she saw him. He looks just like her brother Dylan.

I'm sure Rose was able to do it because she said that when she was Dahlia, Bellamy had been like a father to her. A father that had murdered her parents, but still a father figure all the same. The connection was strong.

Though I'm starting to wonder if Rose has taken the demon's place. The book obviously favors her, it only comes alive now at her touch. Is it possible that when this is all over, and I have forgotten her, she'll take the book with her?

My gut clenches and I have no choice but to ignore it as

I swim over to Rose. Perhaps I'll have to use the spell to forget the book, too.

"Did you talk to Abe?" Rose asks as I swim up to her and press her against the edge of the pool, bracketing her in between my arms. I can't help but stare at her breasts that are nearly popping out of the bikini she bought at the gift shop in the hotel lobby. A three-hundred-dollar bikini and one that doesn't fit, but fuck if she doesn't look delectable in it.

"Please don't talk about the doctor when I'm admiring your breasts," I murmur, dipping my head to lick along the firm swells of them.

"Val," she warns, trying to move out of the way but I have her pinned in place. "We're in a public pool."

I grumble and kiss up toward her collarbone, then her neck, her jaw, her chin, her lips. "So we are," I muse against her skin. "You don't seem like the type that's squeamish about fucking in public."

She lets out a breathy huff of air and when I pull back, she's chucking in amusement. I don't want to touch the memory at all and I don't want to ask, but I have a feeling I've probably fucked her in public before.

See how nice it would be to remember? a voice says inside me. This voice is quiet and rarely ever speaking but sometimes it makes its point. *What would be the harm?*

But even if I wanted to remember our past, I can't. There was no spell in there that would undo it. What I chose is what I am stuck with, and I am not about to feel bad about something I *had* to do.

"What did Abe say?" she asks again pointedly and I sigh, pulling myself together. I guess we do have a rather large mission at hand, one that neither of us are prepared for at all, hence why we need enforcements.

"I told him what's going on and that he needs to let everyone know."

"Do you think they'll come all the way out here?"

"We did," I point out.

We would have used one of the new spells, the one for teleportation, but it only works if you've been to the place before. I've been to Istanbul plenty of times, even living here for a brief period of time in the 1920s, but Rose had never been as herself or in any of her past lives.

"And you know that your parents will be on the first flight over," I add. "Leif was taken from their arms. They want their revenge more than you probably even know."

She swallows hard and worries her lip between her teeth. "And Solon and Lenore?"

"Solon has been asking me to use the book to find Leif for years. And the doctor is willing to help out whenever he can. Even my friend Bitrus might be of use."

"Bitrus," she says brightly. "That's a name I haven't heard in a long time. How is he?"

I blink at her for a moment, wondering how she knows him, and then of course I remember that Dahlia must have met him.

"He's good," I say carefully. "Though now that I'm thinking of it, perhaps it would be better if he stayed in Venice. He has a business to run."

"Is he running the Red Room?"

I stare at her for a moment. "You've been there?"

A coquettish smile appears. "Remember when you said I didn't seem squeamish about fucking in public?"

I attempt to smile back but it falters on my face. So I had fucked Dahlia in the Red Room in front of everyone and I have no memory of it. I *want* to have a memory of that. I want to have a memory of her face, what she looked like, the way everyone else watched. I want that and I can never have that.

The realization is a kick to the gut.

I erased my grief, but I also erased my *life*.

"Val," she says in a hush. She places her fingers at my cheekbone. "It's okay."

"What happens when I want to remember?" I ask her, my jaw going tight.

"Then I'll tell you what happened," she says. "More than that, I'll help you remember."

"I won't..."

"But I'll still show you," she says softly, gazing at me with such tenderness that I feel even weaker than before.

Somewhere in this large cistern there's the sound of a door opening, and I know other hotel guests are coming to enjoy the hot bath, ruining our privacy.

Rose's eyes go over my shoulder to the door and her eyes crinkle at the corner impishly.

"What?" I ask and then her fingers flutter in the space between us and I know she's just used a cloaking spell on us.

"Did it work?" she whispers. "I'm kind of new to this."

I glance over my shoulder at the couple that just walked in, both guys in their late forties. They should be able to see us but they don't and they place their robes on the benches before going down the steps into the tub, wearing Speedos so bright it hurts my eyes.

One of them remarks on how hot the water is, and the other mentions how nice it is to have the whole place to themselves.

I look back at Rose. "I don't think they can see us."

She bites her lip for a moment, her eyes going a warm green. "Good."

Then she reaches down and grabs my cock, giving it a squeeze through my swim shorts, which I admit leave nothing to the imagination. I haven't been swimming in one hell of a long time, so naturally I had to pick up a pair at the hotel gift shop too. Seems the swimwear in Turkey has gotten a lot more risqué since the 1920s.

"Rose," I say through a gasp.

She just grins and looks over my shoulder again while her grip on my cock only gets tighter. "Don't worry, they don't seem to hear us either."

"They're going to see the whirlpool forming when I fuck the hell out of you."

She brings my cock right out, running her hand from base to tip. "Then we'll do what vampires do best and compel them to forget. Otherwise they'll be saying this place is haunted." She pauses, giving the head a squeeze and causing a moan to fall from my lips. "Besides, what were you just saying about fucking in public?"

"I was saying I'm fucking good at it," I growl, grabbing her by her hair and pulling her face toward mine, kissing her so hard I know I'm leaving her breathless.

Rose moans into my mouth as I press her up against the wall of the pool, our bodies pressing together as I deepen the kiss. My hands roam over her body, cupping and squeezing her breasts through her bikini top, feeling her nipples harden under my touch.

She lets out a whimper as I break the kiss, trailing my lips down her neck and collarbone. My hands slide down her body, gripping her ass as I lift her up, her legs wrapping around my waist as I press her harder against the wall.

I grind my cock against her, feeling how wet she is through the thin material of her bikini bottoms. She gasps, her nails digging into my back as I reach between us, pulling the material aside to slide two fingers inside her.

Rose moans loudly, her head falling back against the wall as I pump my fingers in and out of her, my thumb rubbing circles over her clit. I can feel her getting close, her walls clenching around my fingers.

"That's it, my dove," I murmur, feeling her body tense up as her orgasm approaches. "Come on my hand."

And with that, Rose lets out a loud moan, her body shaking as she comes hard against my fingers. I keep pumping in and out of her, prolonging her pleasure as much as I can.

When she finally comes down from her high, I pull my fingers out of her and lift my head to look at her. Her eyes are still closed, and her lips are parted as she tries to catch her breath.

I lean in and kiss her gently, my tongue tracing her lips until she opens up to me. I deepen the kiss, my hands roaming over her body once more and now she's grabbing my aching dick.

"Please," she whispers. "I need you inside."

I give her a salacious grin. "Okay. But when you come again for me, you're also coming for them."

She eyes the couple over my shoulder, her lids growing heavy with lust. "Then make me come, my lord."

I waste no time in positioning myself between her legs, my cock pulsing with need as I line it up with her cunt. I thrust into her with one swift motion, filling her completely as she lets out a loud moan.

The water around us churns as I start to move, my cock sliding in and out of her with increasing speed. Rose's legs are still wrapped around my waist, her arms around my neck as she kisses me deeply.

I can feel the eyes of the couple on us, probably watching the whirlpool I'm creating, but I don't care. I'm lost in the feeling of Rose's body around me, the way she moans and writhes beneath me.

I pull back slightly, holding her hips as I start to drive into her harder, deeper. She gasps and arches her back, her nails digging into my skin as she claws for purchase.

The pressure is building steadily in my balls, the need to come overwhelming. I start to pump harder, faster, my breath coming in short gasps as I chase my own pleasure.

Rose's body tenses up again, her walls clenching around me as she comes for the second time. The sight and feeling of her orgasm is enough to push me over the edge, and I pump my hot cum into her, filling her up as I roar out my own climax.

I collapse against her, our bodies still joined as we catch our breath. The water around us is still churning, evidence of a ghost.

Rose leans up and kisses me softly, her eyes sparkling with satisfaction. "That was fun," she whispers.

I grin down at her. "You're telling me. Now I only wish they were able to see us."

We both turn towards the couple, who are staring at us in only mild confusion.

"That jet looks extra powerful," one of them says, gesturing to where the water still spins, and they both start making their way through the water toward us.

I quickly pull out of Rose and I take her hand and yank her out of the water with me. We watch as the couple looks around the pool, wondering where the whirlpool went, and we laugh as we run off together.

I WAKE up from a nap feeling hungry. It hasn't been long since I fed—both Rose and I had bottles of blood before we got on the plane, the last of the fresh supply I had at the house. But even so, my stomach growls. Though feeding from vampires doesn't do a lot to curb hunger pangs, I find myself craving her blood. Or maybe it's just her in general that I'm hungry for.

I get up and see her through the open French doors standing on the balcony, looking out over the busy waters of the Bosphorus. She's wearing just a robe, her hair blowing back in the wind and catching the last light of the sunset and I think I've never seen such a beautiful sight.

This woman has fused herself to me in so many ways, and every time I'm surprised at the depth of my feelings for her, the way they keep building moment by moment until I'm afraid of the crescendo. I shouldn't be surprised at all. There has to be some level of me that is head over heels in love with her and that's constantly bubbling to the surface, threatening to breach. Maybe I don't remember her and what we were to each other but I'm starting to *feel* what we were. I'm starting to feel not just her love for me, but I may be feeling love for her.

It's just every time I think about it, the feeling leaves. It's nebulous and hard to pin down and it leaves me all the more confused. All I know is that if I'm not careful, and I give myself to Rose like I had in some distant past, I will end up heartbroken all over again.

She will leave me again. Somehow, I fear she'll leave me.

What if death is her destiny?

And if she doesn't die, then I will be with her but never remembering her and that's a special kind of hell of its own.

A hell you willingly walked into, I remind myself. *A hell you welcomed.*

Fuck. I am a mess. It's the worst time to be a mess too, because I need to stay sharp. I can't let the past and the lack of it fuck up the job we came here to do. That takes precedence over everything else, especially my feelings for her.

So I shove those feelings aside and I try to pretend I don't notice how goddamn ravishing she is and I join her on the balcony.

"It reminds me of Venice," she comments without turning around. "But fewer tourists and more real people. And I love the sound of the mosques." As she says that, a call to prayer rings out from the nearest mosque, filling the air at sunset.

I go and stand beside her, leaning forward so I'm resting my arms on the railing. It's December now and the nights are getting cold here, but for us it's the perfect temperature, warm with a bite to it. "It's one of the reasons I love it here," I tell her. "The culture, the history. Glad I had a chance to come back. Even if it's under the present circumstances."

"Speaking of," she says, turning to face me. "I think I got an idea of their location. I can't be sure because it keeps changing."

"Where?"

"So you know this morning I kept seeing what I'm assuming is the Grand Bazaar, though I'm sure there are a million markets like that here? It's like I'm looking through Bellamy's eyes when I'm doing this, so I can't quite see him. But I see what he's seeing. And I'm seeing Leif with him wherever he goes. He's a little fuzzy, like looking through a staticky TV, but he still looks like Dylan to me."

"Do you have any idea yet what they were doing in the market?"

She shrugs. "I don't know. I still think it was spices but maybe materials to make magic with? This city does feel like it's brimming with it."

"And you just tried again now?"

"Yes. It works a little better when I'm out here. I don't know if it's me being in nature or what, but it's like the wind and the river help bring me clarity. So this time I saw them inside an old building. Almost like a mosque but not. It had the look but not the reverence. It was Bellamy and Leif, but also two others that I vaguely recognized. One ended up being Atlas Poe, a witch that I knew of back then. The other was a witch I think I went to school with. Celina something. They were discussing stuff, but I don't know what. Business, I guess, I couldn't make out what they were saying most of the time."

She turns her attention back to the city and gestures toward the Asian side of the Strait. "But I feel a magnetic like pull to that area. Kind of where the docks are. I think if we went there tomorrow and got closer, maybe I could pick up more details, and maybe I could actually pinpoint where they are."

She turns back to look at me and her cheeks are flushed, she's practically glowing. She's proud. Proud of the magic. When I first learned my spells, I wasn't proud, I was just smug. I used it to feel better about myself. But with her, she's becoming alive before my eyes.

"What?" she asks.

I swallow thickly. "Nothing," I say quietly, clearing my throat. "It's just that the magic suits you. And so does being a vampire. You're so incredible and I'm not even sure you know it."

Her brows go up. "I know I'm incredible enough to keep getting reincarnated."

I chuckle. "That's very true. So maybe you do know."

She puts her hand on top of mine. "I want to know why *you* think I'm incredible. To have Dracula say that is no small feat."

"You're incredible because you're you," I tell her, my chest twisting into knots. "And you have me under a lovely spell."

A spell there's only one way to wake up from.

She staring at me with tears in her green eyes and I'm thinking of breaking the emergency glass.

There's a vial in my suitcase.

Waiting for me.

CHAPTER 22
ROSE

"I still think we should wait for the others," Valtu says to me under his breath as the taxicab careens around a corner, honking at people spilling onto the street. We've just left our hotel in the Sultanahmet district, the cab driver expertly navigating the chaos of the Old Town, and are about to head through the Eurasia Tunnel to the other side of the Bosphorus Strait.

"You said that Abe couldn't get a hold of my parents," I point out. I tried to get in touch with them through Valtu's cell, but they didn't answer me either. "Who knows how long they'll take. Maybe they won't even come. I know my dad will want to come and fuck things up, but I don't see him letting my mom do this. He's very protective of her."

"He also said that Lenore and Solon were on their way to Oregon. They stayed in touch with Dylan," he says.

"But again, we don't know when they'll get here," I tell him. "Anyway, I'm not planning on doing anything now. I just want to see if I can pinpoint their position. If the witches are still in that building, and perhaps that's where they always go, then we can ambush them."

He gives me a stern look. "I mean it, Rose. No ambushing until we know what we're up against and until we've got enforcements. We may have the power that the book gave us, but we haven't been wielding it long and we have no idea how formidable they might be."

I glance at the cabbie in the rear-view mirror. He's humming along to the music on the radio and not paying us any attention, the air freshener swinging back and forth as he drives.

"Fine," I say. "I don't want to do anything either."

Though I can't promise that I won't strike Bellamy with lightning if I see him. I honestly don't know what I'll do if we come face to face. Just thinking about it I feel my chest going tight with bottled rage and I want to tear him apart, limb from limb. What did Valtu say he wanted to do the other day? Rip off his head and piss on it? Yeah, that seems about right.

I take in a deep breath and Valtu puts his hand on my leg, giving my knee a squeeze. I stare out the window just as we head into the tunnel and I'm looking at my own reflection in the glass. Sometimes I wonder which version of myself I'm looking at. We left Germany so fast that it's taken a couple of days to actually let it sink in that I'm in Turkey.

Not only that, but that I've actually seen my brother through Bellamy's eyes.

The end is near, I can just feel it.

The problem is, I don't know if it's the end of us or the end of Bellamy's reign.

Or the end of me.

Once again.

"And voila," Valtu says as we start to climb out of the

tunnel, now on the other side of the water. "Welcome to the continent of Asia."

I look behind me at where we just came from, the European side. Just wild.

Another five minutes, and the cab is dropping us off by the water, along a mix of industrial buildings and shipping containers and the occasional café that looks closed.

We step out of the cab and it drives off, the driver giving us a funny look as he goes. Maybe we're in a bad area. Too bad he doesn't know that *we're* the bad things that other people are afraid of.

"Well, as far as evil villain lairs, this seems to be pretty spot on," Valtu says, looking around the warehouses. "Though I would have thought witches would have picked a more aesthetically pleasing area. You know how they love their goth shit."

I laugh. "Excuse me, Mr. *I Live in a Monastery Carved into a Mountainside with a Literal Torture Chamber*. The only thing you're missing is a coffin."

His brow goes up in amusement. "You ever try sleeping in one of those things? They're actually quite comfortable." He sticks his hands in the pockets of his leather jacket. "Well? Where to?"

I close my eyes and try to get a read by clearing my mind, which is easier said than done. I focus on Bellamy and my hatred for him, the betrayal, zeroes in on him like a laser. It's easier now that we're closer to him and I feel a little sick at being so close to his presence. "It feels like he's coming from over there," I say, pointing to the left, my eyes still closed in concentration. "And I think he's in the same building as I saw before."

"Do you see Leif?"

I try to look around but I'm seeing through Bellamy's

eyes and he's looking at an apple, of all things, turning it over in his hand as if he's pondering whether to eat it or not. What a psycho. "No. I don't see him."

"Okay, well let's go over there then, see if you recognize anything." Valtu puts his hand at my lower back and guides me along the street as we pass a building. On the other side is a narrow road that goes between a mix of brick two-story businesses and metal warehouses and there's something pulling me down it, like an invisible tug.

"Down here," I say, leading Valtu now. It's strangely deserted though I can hear metalwork and chatter in Turkish and other noises coming from inside the warehouses. We're a couple of hours away from sunset but it feels dark as the buildings loom over us, and the street gets more narrow as it leads to the docks.

"Where are you taking me?" Valtu asks as I grab his hand and pull him down a narrow alley. When we approach the next street, I recognize one of the buildings further down the road. It's got the look of a small, old cathedral. Very old, considering the front has crumbled away, the remains spread out on the street, like there had been recent earthquake damage that no one bothered to fix.

"I think that's it," I whisper to Valtu. "Come on."

He reaches out and grabs me by the elbow, yanking me back into the shadows of the alley. "What do you think you're doing?"

I glare at his grip and shrug out of it. "Well, I need to see if they're there."

"And then what?"

I open my mouth, then close it, thinking of what the next move should be. Kill Bellamy? I don't know.

As I'm doing that, I see Dylan stepping out of the door to that old cathedral and start walking down the street toward the water. Except it's not Dylan of course, but it's Leif, his twin. He's wearing army green head-to-toe, like a uniform of some sort, and looks exactly like a bulkier version of my brother. His hair is the same gold brown, eyes the same hazel, and he has an impressive beard that Dylan would be extremely jealous of.

"What the hell," I utter, not believing my eyes. But it's *him*.

I twist around to Valtu. "Stay here!" I hiss at him. And then I'm bolting across the street to Leif as he continues to march past, not even looking in my direction.

"Rose!" Valtu whispers harshly after me but he's staying where he is for now.

I keep my focus on my brother. Because it is my brother. It has to be.

"Leif!" I call out as I jog toward him.

Leif stops and looks at me in confusion just as another person exits the same building, walking toward us quickly.

"Do I know you?" Leif asks, brows furrowing.

"Uh..."

He gives me a puzzled look and then keeps walking toward the docks, glancing over his shoulder at me, then over at Valtu, as he goes.

"Rose," Valtu hisses.

"Hey!" the guy approaching me says and I look to see who I assume is Atlas Poe. I'd never met the witch, but I knew of him. He looks like a pale, sniveling moody mother-fucker, dressed all in black but not making it look half as elegant as Valtu does. "What do you want with him?"

"That guy? Oh, he, uh, he just looks like someone I know," I say, staring at Leif as he walks off in hopes he somehow remembers me, but of course he doesn't have any idea who I am. We've never met before.

"Then how did you know his name?" Atlas asks, his eyes narrowing and growing hard. Suddenly he breathes in sharply through his nose and the hardness in his eyes turns to flint. "*Vampire*," he seethes.

Oh fuck.

I turn to run but Atlas is on me with such force that we go flying through the air.

"Rose!" I hear Valtu scream just as Atlas slams me back against a building across the street, the plaster crumbling from the impact, and he whips out the glowing silver and blue blade of *mordernes* from inside his coat.

And so this is how I die this time around, I can't help but think, the irony not lost on me, even now.

I scream, trying to struggle, but Atlas is fast and he plunges the blade right into my chest where it glows blue and hisses and burns and I'm screaming again, bloody murder.

Then Valtu is there, tackling Atlas to the ground with a primal roar, and then suddenly it's just Valtu, Atlas having disappeared completely beneath him.

"What the fuck?" Valtu cries out, searching for Atlas and finding nothing, then gets to his feet and staggers over to me. "Rose," he says tightly as he grabs my shoulders, helping to hold me up. I already have my hand around the hilt of the blade. I remember it like it was yesterday, how easily it was to wield this thing as Dahlia and I'm aware that I probably should be dead right now. The blow is instant when it comes to vampires.

"Oh god," Valtu whispers his face wrought with horror as he stares at the blade. "Rose, Rose."

"I can pull it out," I say, wincing hard as I try to yank it out of my chest. It's not budging. The pain is excruciating, hot tears spilling over and streaming down my face. But underneath the agony I can still feel my heart beating. "I think he missed," I manage to say.

Valtu's eyes fill with hope and he puts his hands over mine and with one sharp tug we manage to get the blade out of my chest.

I grip it hard in my hands, the handle seeming to fuse to my palm, while he takes off his leather jacket and presses it against my chest to staunch the bleeding.

My eyes are locked on the blade in my palm, glowing blue, the handle silver and intricately carved, and I know every slayer's blade is different but it looks similar to the one I used to have.

"Stay with me Rose," Valtu whispers, keeping the pressure on. He looks around but in this dim and industrial area there's no one else around. Both Leif and Atlas are completely gone, like they were never here at all.

"I'm okay," I assure Valtu quietly. "I think I'm going to be okay."

"Are you sure?" He lifts away the jacket and the blood has spread across my top but it's not pouring out anymore. "I can't lose you, Rose. I can't."

"You won't," I reassure him, turning the blade over in my hand, relishing the feel of it.

He doesn't seem to believe me. He looks around and then puts his arm around my waist. "We're going to try teleporting," he says.

"What, now?"

"We need to get out of here."

"And run from a fight? They came from that building. Bellamy is right in there!"

"Rose," he says sharply, his eyes like daggers, "we are going to continue the fight, but not alone and you can't fight like this right now. You may be alive, but you're still wounded. Next time you may not be so lucky."

"But I know he's in there!" I protest but I sound weak and I start coughing. Maybe the stabbing did more damage than I thought.

"Just close your eyes and think of the hotel room," Valtu whispers and I force my brain to cooperate, to picture it the way we left it this afternoon. I picture the book resting on the desk. "*Accipe nos ibi nunc,*" he recites.

There's a sudden snapping sensation against my body, rattling my head, and swiftly the world shifts around us until the streets disappear and we're standing in the middle of the hotel room, right in front of the book on the desk, holding onto each other.

Holy fuck. It worked.

"That was interesting," Valtu muses, looking around our room in surprise. "Fucking terrible headache though." He looks at me through a grimace. "Are you okay?"

I let out a shallow breath and nod quickly. "Yeah, just a little nauseous. Probably a combination of teleporting and being stabbed."

The worry never seems to leave his face. "Let's get you cleaned up and see what we're dealing with here."

He leads me to our bathroom, large and intricately decorated with a mosaic of teal tiles, and I hop up on the counter. He takes off my top and grabs a towel, wetting it under warm water and pressing it gently to my chest. "You're already healing but it's not as fast as it should be."

"I think getting stabbed with the blade of *mordernes* causes wounds to linger," I tell him. "I've seen it before. When I first started slaying, I was stabbing vampires in the back, just doing anything to get them to stop. It definitely slowed them down."

His black brows knit together, eyes roaming over my face. "Sometimes I forget you were a vampire slayer before."

I give him a small smile in return. "You're supposed to forget. Remember?"

He rubs his lips together and swallows. Something dark washes over his eyes. Something troubling. I don't like it. It makes my scalp prickle with unease.

"I'm *fine*," I tell him again. "Atlas missed."

"By a millimetre," Valtu says tightly, his jaw clamping together as he stares down at the wound. Little black and blue lines are snaking out from the wound, but I know they'll be gone by tomorrow.

"I'll take what I can get," I say dryly but the gravity is etched on his face. I clear my throat. "I think I'm going to take a shower. Can you get me that bottle of vodka from the mini bar?"

He frowns. "For what?"

I shrug. "To help process the trauma."

He leaves into the room and I hop off the counter, staring at myself in the mirror. I look like shit. But I guess when you come that close to dying again, you're allowed to look like shit.

Valtu comes back in and hands me the bottle of vodka. He tries to smile but it doesn't reach his eyes, and the dark energy that's rolling off of him is palpable and chaotic and makes me instantly afraid.

"Are you okay?" I ask him softly, reaching out for his hand.

He lets me hold it for a moment, fear coming across his brow. Then he nods stiffly. "I will be. And so will you. Remember that, my dove." He pulls his hand away and I feel strangely bereft without it.

He goes to leave and pauses, one hand on the bathroom

door, ready to close it. He's looking off into the room, and from the way his focus intensifies I know he's staring at the book. "I'm going to call Abe and Solon and see what's what," he says quietly. He swallows hard. "We are going to get your brother back, Rose. I can promise you that."

Then he closes the door.

There's something so final about it that I feel panic rising through me.

You've literally just been stabbed, millimetres away from death, I remind myself. *It's okay for the both of you to be on edge right now.*

I take in a deep breath, then unscrew the vodka cap and take a swig of it, enjoying the burn. Then I turn it over and pour some of it on my wound, hoping some disinfectant won't hurt. But of course, it does. It stings like hell.

"Son of a bitch," I swear and step into the shower, moving back from the stream as I turn it on.

I don't know how long I spend in the shower, soaking in the hot water and using all the luxurious toiletries, but by the time I finally turn it off, I'm completely pruney and the blue and black lines have faded a lot. The wound itself is pretty much closed, though it's red, raw and ugly.

I sigh, shaking my head. I can't believe that just happened. I can't believe I actually saw Leif, actually found the very place we were looking for. And I can't believe I ended up getting stabbed. Like, right away. The worst part is that now Atlas knows something is up. He's going to go back to Bellamy and tell him what happened, that he saw some vampires. Now I can only hope that Bellamy won't have a clue who I am. That's the only surprise I've got at this point. But I'm sure with Atlas' description of Valtu, he'll be quick to recognize Dracula.

I dry off and blow dry my hair, then put on my robe and

step out into the suite, feeling a million times better than before I went in.

The balcony doors are open, cold damp air flowing in, and I think I see Valtu outside. I walk over to him, passing by the book on the hotel desk.

Something catches my eye. Beside the book is a pen and a pad of paper, the hotel's stationary, covered in tightly scribbled writing.

I stop and pick it up, wondering what Valtu's been writing, and read it.

A letter to myself,

You're going to be disoriented. You don't know who the woman is in front of you, you don't know how she fits into your life or what she means to you. This is by design. By your own design.

My hand starts to shake as I read on.

You are Valtu Aminoff. It is December. You are in Istanbul, Turkey. You may remember most of this or maybe none of this, perhaps the potion takes more from you each time. The reason you're here is of most importance and something you can't back away from. I won't let you. You're here because you have finally tracked Bellamy and his secret sect of immortal witches, as well as the stolen vampire baby Leif, who is very much a twenty-two-year-old man now. It's hard to tell if he's still a vampire, or a witch, or what has been done to him but make no mistake, though he is not on your side, you must protect him and rescue him from the sect. This is the most important goal.

The second most important goal is to destroy Bellamy.

The third most important goal is to get out of there as soon as you've accomplished both.

The woman in front of you is a woman you have decided to erase. You don't need to know her past or her details. Her name is Rose Harper and though that name means nothing to you now, she is the reason you have erased her from your memory. It was the only way.

Oh my god.

"Valtu!" I shriek, dropping the papers on the desk and running for the doors to the balcony.

Oh god, oh please no, please don't let him have done it!

"Valtu!" I cry out again and he turns around to face me, his back to the railing, the sounds of the city rising up on the sea breeze.

To my relief, there is recognition in his eyes.

Guilt.

And then I notice the black vial in his hand, halfway to his mouth.

"No, stop!" I make a move for him, but he holds out his other hand and that pushes me back with invisible force.

"I'm sorry," he says pitifully, his words barely audible. "I can't afford to lose you again."

"Valtu, please!" I screech and it feels like my world is seconds from ending. "Don't do this. Don't erase me again!"

He gives his head a shake, a tear rolling down his cheek. "I *want* to remember you. I want to remember us. But I can't. So I have to forget."

"Please!" I plead again, my voice going hoarse, the panic a vice inside my chest. "Don't. Don't, just don't do this. We can start over, it's okay, I'm okay with us just having what we are to each other right now."

He shakes his head. "I'm a coward, Rose. You know I am. I won't be able handle the pain. I've lost too many years to grief. It steals from you. It shows no mercy. It takes and it takes and it never gives anything back," he says, grinding his teeth together.

"Grief only exists because of love!"

"And to erase the love is to erase the pain. Don't tell me you wouldn't do the same."

"I would *never* do the same!" I yell, struggling against the invisible force, but it's no use. I'm trying to think of magic from the book but now of all times my mind is blank. All I can feel, all I can focus on, is the horror of being nothing again. "Loss is the risk you take when you love someone, but it's always worth the risk, Valtu." Tears are spilling down my cheeks now, sobs stretching my chest. "I have loved you and lost you and I'll do it again and again because loving you is everything. Loving you is everything!"

He looks down at the vial, gives his head a slight shake. "That's where you've made your biggest mistake. Loving me is a mistake. You should never love a monster."

"Please," I plead, praying, hoping, wishing he can see how badly I need to stay in his mind and his heart and life. "Don't do this. I love you. I love you and...don't you think maybe it's worth loving me too?" A sob escapes me, tears burning. My heart twists tighter and tighter into a knot so small I can't even breathe. "Couldn't you just love me back?" I whisper. "Can't loving me be worth the loss?"

He sniffs, pressing his lips together firmly. "I'm sorry, Rose. I guess I'll never know."

Then he opens his mouth and pours the contents of the vial on his tongue.

And swallows.

I scream his name.

Drop to my knees.

My heart discarded on the floor.

CHAPTER 23
VALTU

My head explodes in pain, shrapnel stabbing my temples and I press my hands over my eyes, as if they're going to start leaking out of my head. A certain pain I've only felt once before.

Oh fuck.

I go still, my breathing ragged and adrenaline pumping through me, and there's a taste of bitter floral in my mouth, violets and dandelion greens, and I instantly know what I've done. The sense of dizziness, of emptiness, of having your brain scooped out, is prominent.

I've used the spell of erasure again.

Why the hell would I do that again?

I hear a sniff and I slowly take my hands off my face.

There's a girl kneeling in front of me, dressed in a bathrobe.

She's bawling, like an animal in pain, tears flooding her face.

The air smells like oud and salt.

Something is very wrong here.

It's the girl that's wrong.

Her head snaps up and she stares at me and I realize I'm staring into the eyes of a witch, her power brimming off of her.

I don't need an explanation.

She's done something to me.

I launch myself at her, grabbing her by the throat and forcing her on her back.

She yelps and tries to scream and I have my fingers wrapped around her neck, squeezing harder and harder as I bear down on her.

"Who are you?" I growl, feeling her cartilage breaking under my grip.

Her hands are at mine, trying to pry my fingers off, and she looks scared more than anything. A wild kind of fear that kicks more adrenaline into my system. She could be unpredictable.

And she is, because she suddenly does something I didn't expect her to.

She goes limp. Relaxes completely. Stops fighting me.

But she's not dead, nor dying. Not yet.

Her eyes, a brilliant green, stop flashing and go hazy, her expression as if she's resigning herself to this fate.

As if she doesn't want to fight.

As if she expects to die.

Her hands drop away and she's staring up at me.

Go ahead, Val, she projects into my head. *Do it. Rip my head right off*.

I blink at her, my fingers loosening slightly. Rip her head off? That's a little extreme.

And that's when I realize she's not using parlor tricks to get into my head. She's just thinking. Because she's a vampire. And that's why no matter how hard I squeeze, she's still breathing, her chest rising and falling, and when I look down I see an ugly fresh wound near her heart with faint lines radiating outward. Like she had been stabbed with the blade of *mordernes*.

I quickly remove my hands and straighten up, rocking back on my heels.

"You're a vampire," I whisper.

I blink at her and it's all coming together, at least a little bit. I don't know who she is, but I know I have the taste of erasure in my mouth, and there's a woman here that knows my name and seems to be both a witch *and* a vampire. I breathe in deeply and I'm getting both scents, one of power and magic, and the other of ancient blood. It reminds me of Lenore.

"I'm sorry," I quickly say, getting to my feet. "I..."

I look around. I'm standing on a massive balcony that juts out over a crowded city, a river flowing nearby. Then I realize it's not a river and I've been here before. We're in Istanbul.

Why am I here? I think, looking around frantically for the proof of what I've done. I spot the empty vial on the ground and go over, picking it up. So much power in such a little thing.

Why did I do this? Again? Why is it so hard to remember anything?

"Who are you?" I ask hoarsely, turning to face the girl again.

The girl slowly sits up, rubbing at her throat. Red hair spills over her shoulders, beautiful red hair the color of autumn leaves and sunsets. Now that I'm able to get a better, calmer look at her, I realize she's the most stunning woman I've ever seen.

She fixes her eyes on me and I'm immediately pulled into their depths, my heart skipping a beat, and I immediately know why I don't know her. I know why I chose to erase her.

Because how could I not have been in love with her?

And from the way she's looking at me, absolutely broken, like she just watched a loved one die, I realize that she's in love with me.

"What have I done?" I ask.

"What you do best," she says quietly, getting to her feet. "But if you want a real explanation..."

She walks a little off-balance through the French doors and into a hotel room.

I follow, enraptured in a mystery of my own doing.

She stops by a desk and tightens up her robe, then hands me a pad of hotel stationary and then quickly steps back, as if needing to keep a safe distance from me. I don't blame her.

I briefly eye the book on the desk, a sense of relief at the sight of it, then proceed to read the notepad.

It's in my handwriting, a letter addressed to me, perhaps only written moments ago.

It explains most things. Where I am and why I'm here. And a little bit about the reason I took the potion. The reason for the spell.

"Rose Harper?" I ask her, looking up from the paper. "That's your name?"

Her face contorts, her jaw quivering but she nods. "Yes."

"But you're not dead," I say. "In the past, when I erased...someone else, it was because she had died. You're alive."

She lets out a sad laugh, looking at the floor. "Yeah, well, I suppose this time you wanted to do it before it got that far along." She sniffles and wipes away a tear with her fingers. "And once again I'm here to sift through the pieces of what we could have had."

I frown, wishing my headache would go away. "Once again?"

The girl, Rose, she just shakes her head. "Never mind."

She turns around her back to me and puts her head in her hands.

I feel like I should go over there and comfort her, but honestly I have no idea what I would say. How do you comfort someone you just purposefully forgot?

"Well, I guess I should probably figure out what to do next," I say. "You can keep this room, I'll go to the front desk and get myself another."

"That's it!?" she shrieks, whipping around to face me. Her eyes are on fire. "That's it!? You just go and get another fucking hotel room and that's it?! Like everything is back to normal for you? Oh, it must be nice to be Valtu Aminoff, motherfucking coward of the year, keeps running from problems that don't even exist yet, just another clean slate and another clean slate, never having to be the one left behind when someone erases your existence!"

I put up my hands, taken aback by her rage. "Hey. Listen, Rose, I don't know what to say, I didn't choose this—"

"Yes you did!" Her face flames with anger as she storms over, getting right in front of me. "You chose this! Don't pretend there are a million different versions of yourself because there's only one and he's a fucking coward that puts the title of Dracula to shame. You're pathetic, you know that? Absolutely pathetic and selfish and a gutless, scared little boy. You're all of those things and yet I still love you and I fucking HATE you for it! And I hate me too! And all of this, I hate all of this, all of this!"

With a final shriek that nearly blows out my eardrums she picks the book off the desk and grips it hard between her hands. "I hate this book for coming into our lives, for ruining our love and what we had and making you believe that living without love was the only way to live. You are so wrong, Val, so fucking wrong, and one day you'll see it. One day, centuries from now, you will be so alone it will curdle your blood and hollow your bones and you will wish that you had someone you could love. And there will be no one there! You will live forever with only your own emptiness for company and it will be what you deserve!"

With another scream she raises the book high above her head and stares up at it with fury so strong that her whole body starts trembling violently and she's levitating off the ground.

"I wish this book never existed!" she howls, her voice bouncing off the walls. "I want it destroyed!"

"Wait, what are you doing?" I ask, fear clutching my chest. "I need that to—"

Lightning jolts through the open doors of the balcony, hurtling right into the room, right into Rose with a fiery CRASH.

Everything explodes into white.

I go flying backward, hit by a ball of spreading nuclear light, my back slamming against the wall where I get the wind knocked out of me and fall to the floor. I hit my head on the tiles, wincing, covering my face as smoke fills the room, the smell of burned pages.

Shit.

I cough, and try to sit up, to look through the smoke. Pieces of burning paper rain down from above, electricity crackling around us.

The book.

I feel it in the very depths of me, like someone removed one of my organs in my sleep.

It's gone.

The book is *gone*.

She destroyed it, she...she...she...

Suddenly a figure steps out of the smoke.

A woman. A naked woman.

I stare at her open-mouthed. Not because she's naked, but because I know that body. I know those hips and that stomach and that warm spot between her thighs. I know the curve of her breasts and the slope of her shoulders. I know that neck, a neck that I've drank from, blood that made me more alive than anything else in this world.

I know that face. The strong jaw and nose, the soft lips, those cheekbones and those eyes.

I'm staring up into eyes the color of March leaves and late summer moss and they're staring back at me.

I can't breathe.

This can't be.

"Dahlia?" I manage to say, and she flinches like she's hit by another bolt of lightning.

And then they all come back to me.

She all comes back to me.

Mina. Lucy. Dahlia. Rose.

Rose.

"Rose?" I ask, her name feeling like honey on my lips.

I can't breathe. This can't be.

Now her mouth parts, her eyes wide and she presses her hand to her chest and she's gasping. "Val?" The hope that spreads across her face is like a firework.

I try to say something, anything, but I can't because all at once every single memory that I had so selfishly erased comes pouring back over me like a tidal wave. It drowns me, crushes me, bombards me from all angles until I am given no choice but to remember.

My mind flips back in time, back to when I killed her, then to a burial at sea, then the taking of the book. Then the night in Venice with Solon when I took the potion and erased her.

Then I'm living my years without any knowledge of her, unaware of the simmering pain and grief that was collecting in my soul. I lived a life so selfish and cold and isolated that I lost all parts of my humanity, all those tiny good parts that were binding me together like a rag doll, a monstrous creation of my own doing.

Then I'm in the square of Mittenwald, waiting for Van Helsing to deliver me a whore and then I see her, I see Dahlia walking toward me and I see the pain on her face when she realizes what I've done, how it's erased her, and then I see how awful I've been treating her, so cruel, so callous, and, and...

I see myself falling in love with her despite all my best laid plans. I see myself falling in love with Rose, because it's my destiny to love her, no matter what her name is, no matter where we are in time.

And then I see what I just did today. I see myself getting so damn scared of feeling pain again, of losing her and feeling grief, that I erase her yet again.

A heavy cloak is lifted from my head and I can see clearly for the first time.

And what I see is my reflection looking back at me.

I really am a fucking monster.

"Val?" Rose says again, taking a tentative step forward, wounded inside and out. "Please don't be fucking with me, please."

I get to my knees and try to get up but I can't. The

weight of guilt and anger and disappointment keeps me where I am.

I stare up at her, at my dove, my love, at her goodness and her loyalty and the fact that she's in my life again, she's alive and she's here and I burst out into tears.

"I'm sorry," I say through a sob, the sorrow wracking through me, hollowing me out. "I am so fucking sorry."

"No," she says, and she drops to her knees beside me, her fingers going through my hair. "Val, please, you have nothing to be sorry for."

I raise my head and look at her, my vision blurred, the guilt tearing me apart. "Nothing to be sorry for? Rose, I have everything to be sorry for. I treated you so horribly, I...I don't understand how it all happened."

"You were in pain," she says, crying now too. "You were in pain and you couldn't bear it. I don't blame you for what you did, you were just trying to survive. We have such long lives and there is so much pain in this world."

"You would have never done that to me," I tell her, unable to escape the agony while at the same time, fuck, *fuck* I am so goddamn overjoyed that she's alive and she's here.

She's here!

"You're alive," I add, shaking my head, the tears spilling onto the floor. "I can't believe you're alive."

"I told you my heart would always find yours," she says, her hands now at my cheeks, wiping away the tears. "And it did. It did."

"I love you." I take in a deep, shaking breath. "I love you, I love you. As Mina and Lucy and Dahlia and Rose, I love all of you."

"I love you," Rose says, smiling so sweetly it breaks my heart. "You know I do."

She leans in and kisses me.

This kiss is also a spell of erasure.

In this kiss it feels like she's erasing my sins.

I feel like I'm being saved, and I never knew I needed saving.

"My love," I whisper against her mouth, trying to get a hold of myself and failing, so I hold onto her instead. I grab the back of her neck and hold her tight, I grip her waist until she feels fused to me. "I love you and I don't deserve an ounce of your love."

"You deserve all of that and more," she says, placing kisses on the corner of my lips, my chin, my nose. "I was never going to give up on you."

And I know she's right. She wouldn't have. She didn't. Even after I fucking killed her, she still came back in love with me, willing to risk it all in case I still knew her heart.

"Dahlia...I didn't know who you were until the glamour slipped," I try to explain. "It was too late. I tried to save you, I tried to give you blood..."

Her head quirks to the side. "You tried to give me blood?"

"I tried to create a vampire. I wanted Lenore to do it, but she said it was too late. I gave you my own blood but it did nothing. You were dead."

"You gave me blood..." she muses. "Perhaps that's the reason why I came back a vampire this time around."

"This time?" I shake my head adamantly. "This is the only time. You're a vampire now and we're going to do whatever the fuck we can to keep you alive. I promise I won't erase you again, but I am not going through losing you again either. Even if we always do end up finding each other."

She grins. Pure, beautiful joy that radiates outward. She is the sun.

"My god, I have missed you," I tell her, kissing her again, my tongue searching her mouth deeply, as if I'm trying to meld with her permanently. The hunger starts to burn through me, the urge to pick-up where we left off, or close enough, but I swallow it back for now.

I pull back, breathing hard, and rest my forehead against hers. "I may have not remembered you, but I was suffering so deeply, there really was no escape. Grief will get you one way or another. For me, it was like a shadow in the room. It followed me wherever I went, always visible out of the corner of my eye." I'm suddenly struck with pride and rub my thumbs along her cheekbones. "There had been an actual shadow too. But you destroyed the demon."

"And I destroyed the book," she points out gravely.

"And I'm eternally grateful for that," I tell her, my eyes searing deep into hers. "It was the only way to set things back to the way they always should have been."

"Yeah, but what about all of the magic? All the power you've been stockpiling for the last two decades is just gone."

I take my hand off her face and hold it between us, my thoughts creating flames along the fingertips. I wave the flames back and forth. "I still know a few party tricks that Solon had taught me. And you're still a witch. You may have learned some spells from that book, but you already had a few in you to begin with."

"I'm not so sure. Yeah there's the lightning, which I'll admit, has been three-for-three for being handy lately, but other than that I don't really remember any of the things I was taught as Dahlia. Honestly, most of the stuff I learned at the academy was just how to kill vampires."

She leans down slightly and blows out the flames on my fingers.

I can't help but smile. In some ways I think I'll never stop smiling. "Just because you don't remember doesn't mean you don't know. It will come back to you. Lean into it. Think like a witch. And knowing how to kill vampires is not nothing. Witches might be our enemy at the moment, but generally whatever you do to kill a vampire will kill a human as well."

"How about an immortal human? We have no idea what Bellamy and they have done to themselves to make them immortal. I expected to see Leif as some sickly patient that's been experimented on for years, but he didn't look that way at all. He looked normal." Her nose wrinkles. "And, fuck. Now we can't track them."

I reach out and cup her face in my hand and she automatically closes her eyes, leaning into my touch. "Right now, all of that is something else to worry about some other day. All that truly matters to me is that you're here. Maybe that's because I truly am a selfish bastard but that's the truth. You're here, my darling. And I will walk to the ends of the earth and through to the end of time in order to never lose you again."

I dip my head and catch her lips in a soft kiss, one that seems to slide backward in time and forward again, wrapping us together like a bow. "Tell me I'm yours, my dove," I plead softly, my lips brushing against hers.

"I am yours, my lord," she whispers.

"And you still would fuck a monster?" I venture.

She laughs. "You're not a monster, Val." Her eyes dance. "You're just an asshole."

"The question still stands."

Another breathy laugh. "Yes, my lord."

CHAPTER 24
ROSE

He's here.

He's here.

Valtu. The Valtu that I met as Mina.

It's not just that he knows my names, he knows me. I see it in his eyes, I see the man I love and the man who finally loves *me*. His love is strong and good and powerful, and I feel it from the way he's kissing me, touching me, the depth of his words, the gravity of his pain, and it's here and it's mine and it's *real*.

"Will you forgive me?" Valtu asks me softly, his hand trailing over my collarbone, skirting around the healing wound on my chest. "Will you forgive all that I have done to you?"

My breath hitches as his fingers dip lower, down between my breasts, and goosebumps rush across my skin. "There is nothing to forgive," I say, my voice hushed as I try to soothe his soul.

And I'm telling the truth.

The man that was acting the way he was—he was a different man than the one that loved me. We are all made up of the sum of our parts, of our experiences, from whatever life throws our way. That includes the good and the bad, the joys and the sorrow. If we erase the sorrow from our lives, we erase part of the process, the part that makes us human. Even for vampires, being human is still a worthwhile goal.

And if we erase the sorrow, we might erase the love as well, because love and grief go hand-in-hand. It doesn't make you feel any better, it doesn't make it hurt any less, but the fact remains that you only hurt because you loved that person so much. Valtu erased me because that erased the pain but it also removed his love for me. That love is what made him who he is.

It made him the person on his knees in front of me right now, his fingers delicately brushing over my breasts.

I gasp at the feeling of the cool air wafting over my skin, my nipples already hard as pebbles. The look in Valtu's eyes isn't just of love, because there is *so* much love, but it's of want and need and raw hunger. And as his heated gaze scorches over my body, I feel like every cell inside of me is coming alive. I burn to be with him.

"Fuck me," I whisper to him.

His pupils expand, his breath catching.

Then he's on me, hands in my hair, moving me backward until the hard tiles press into my back.

Valtu positions himself over me, his mouth descending on mine with a hunger so fierce that it steals the air from my lungs. I moan into his mouth, my hands roaming over his chest, feeling the muscles tense and flex beneath my touch. I undo the buttons on his shirt as swiftly as I can and then he's shrugging it off until I'm touching the bare heat of his skin below.

He pulls back, his eyes blazing with desire.

"I need you," he growls, his fingers already working on the tie of my robe. "God help me, I've never needed you this much."

I arch my back, helping him ease the garment off me until I'm completely naked beneath him. His gaze rakes over my body, the heat of his stare igniting a flame deep within me. I reach for him, my fingers tracing the lines of his body, feeling the hard planes of his chest and the taut muscles of his arms.

You, you, you.

I belong to you. You belong to me.

Valtu's mouth finds mine again, his kiss deepening as he presses his body against mine. I feel his thick, hard length against my thigh, his stiff need for me evident in every touch and every caress.

"Please," I pant, "I need you inside me."

He lets out a tight noise of want and then starts moving backward down my body, licking and kissing and sucking as he goes. His mouth is hot and wet and unbearably soft as he dips lower and lower down between my breasts, over my stomach, lower, lower. He traces the curve of my hip with his tongue, then moves towards the juncture of my thighs. I spread my legs wider, my breaths coming in short gasps as I wait for him to touch me where I need him the most.

He doesn't waste any time. He buries his head between my thighs, his tongue flicking over my clit with an expert touch.

Oh god, *yes.*

I moan loudly, my hands pressing into the tiles behind me as he works me to the brink of ecstasy. He knows exactly how to touch me, how to make me come undone with pleasure. This is the difference now. He remembers. Yes, he's had no issues in getting me off before, but now he knows my body and the way it responds to him, knows it as well as he knows his own.

He possesses me thoroughly.

"Valtu," I whimper, my body trembling with need. "Please, I need you inside me now."

I feel him grin against my pussy. He's not going to let me go until I come.

Say the magic words, he says inside my head.

Please come inside me, my lord, I answer back.

Not until I feel this hot pink cunt come around my tongue, he says.

It's a lovely threat.

He plunges his tongue deep inside me and I moan, my hips bucking up into his face as he continues to fuck me with his mouth. My body feels like it's on fire, and I know that I'm close. So close.

"Valtu," I gasp, my voice shaking. "I'm going to come."

He growls in response, his fingers digging into my thighs as he redoubles his efforts. And then it happens. My orgasm slams into me, ripping through my body like the very bolt of lightning that struck me earlier. I cry out his name, my body convulsing as I come hard around his mouth, my limbs convulsing.

He doesn't stop until every last tremor has wracked my body, until the aftershocks have faded away and I'm left panting and gasping for breath, my body boneless. And then, finally, he pulls away, a satisfied smirk on his face, his mouth slick with my desire.

"Fuck me," I whimper, my mind still reeling from the intensity of my release.

"That's coming," he warns, his eyes dark with lust as he unzips his pants and takes out his cock, the tip swollen and shiny with pre-cum. He positions himself between my legs.

I feel the head of his cock probing at my entrance, which is still sensitive and throbbing, then he slides inside me with one smooth stroke, filling me completely.

We both gasp, his mouth falling open with a look of utter awe, as if he's fucking me for the first time.

Then his mouth comes crashing down on mine, the kiss a mixture of the old Valtu—hard and demanding—and the new Valtu, who has a softer touch, still tentative, as if he can't believe I'm still here, that I'm not a ghost. With his lips he shows me what his body is already doing, his tongue and lips matching the thrust of his hips.

I moan into his mouth, my nails digging into his back, my legs wrapped around him, pulling him deeper and deeper inside me, until I can feel him all the way to my core.

He feels so good, so big, stretching me until I'm sure I'm going to split in two. He pushes deeper, my body yielding to his as he moves inside me, the friction of our bodies making me groan, the tiles hard against my spine.

My hands reach for his back, his cool skin beneath my fingers, feeling the way his muscles ripple and tense as he works me so thoroughly. He fucks me like it's his job, his one purpose, so deliberate and intense with every single drive of his hips. He fucks me so hard that we're beginning to move across the floor, until we're surrounded by the still smoldering ashes of the book, faint dust rising in the air.

There's something so poetic about this, fucking on top of the very thing that took him from me.

"Val," I moan quietly, not wanting to disturb the moment. He feels so good, I'm suddenly emotional, a wave washing over my chest, covering my heart.

He's here. He's here. He's mine.

He knows me.

He sees me.

He *loves* me.

He breaks the kiss, his mouth moving to my neck, and I arch myself, offering my throat to him.

"Taste me," I whisper. "Drink me."

He hesitates for just a moment and then he brushes his teeth against my skin before biting down. The bite is slow and sensual, his fangs breaking through my flesh with just the softest touch of pain.

"God, yes," I say through a gasp.

He grunts and begins to drink.

Heat like I've never felt before flames through my body, every nerve alive with sensation. His mouth so hot and wet against my neck, drinking me in, and his cock thrusting hard and fast inside me. His thrusts echo the rhythm of his mouth, hard and fast, making me gasp with every thrust.

It's too much. I can't take it.

My lord.

I feel as though I've made contact with a livewire, every sensation of pleasure tinged with pain. My orgasm slams into me, hard and fast, burning through my limbs, my heart, my soul. I cry out his name as I come, my fingernails clawing into his back, his name falling from my lips over and over again, my tongue forming it into a prayer.

And then he's thrusting inside me, again and again and again, until I can feel his cock grow even harder and I know he's close.

"Come inside me," I whisper, my voice ragged from the orgasm.

Valtu growls, a low, guttural sound of pure pleasure. He thrusts deep and hard, like I'm being nailed to the floor, and then he comes like a freight train, every muscle in his body taut with the effort, his neck corded as his head is thrown back.

"Fuck!" he bellows, the sound hammering the room.

Holy fucking shit.

I watch him come undone and he's buried so deep, my body a tight fist around him, my pussy clenching him, making him moan, that I don't know if we'll ever come apart. I feel him shoot inside of me, white hot and heavy and I'm bucking my hips up so that he keeps coming and coming.

Then he's gasping, chest heaving and his thrusts slow and we're easing down together into this heady, luxurious kind of heat.

But it's not enough, I need more, I need—

I need his blood, too. I want to feed from him for the first time, to taste him. I just don't know how to ask for it.

And though his cock is still hard inside me, he pulls out and gets to his feet, his pants falling to the floor.

"Come here," he says, stepping out of them and crouching down to scoop me up in his arms. "I want the world to know you're mine."

He picks me up and carries me out to the balcony, the both of us naked, and he takes me over to the railing. He places my ass on the edge and I'm having a flashback to Mittenwald. That feels like a different time because it *was* a different time. He was a different Valtu, and I was different too. I had no idea of the powers I possessed, no idea that I was about to destroy the demon, let alone the book.

And I had no idea that Valtu would ever come back to me.

But he has. He's here and he's roughly spreading my legs with one hand, holding me secure with the other.

I look around, at the other hotel room windows, at the city streets below me, at the lights reflecting on the water between the continents, and while night has descended, we're very much in public.

"You belong to me, my dove," Valtu says gruffly, and with his grip strong on my hips, he pushes back inside me. "You always have. From the very start through eternity."

I gasp as he thrusts up into me, feeling the height of the world below. But the thrill of being watched, the danger of falling, only adds to the intensity of what we're doing. Valtu is claiming me, showing the world that I'm his, and I revel in it.

"Yours," I breathe, my hands gripping the railing behind me. "I'm yours."

He grinds his hips against me, his cock filling me up completely, and I can feel him getting harder inside me. His fingers dig into my skin, leaving crescent-shaped marks on my hips, as he fucks me harder and harder, his breath coming in hot, panting gasps.

"Fuck, you feel so good," he growls, his eyes locked on mine. "Such a good girl, aren't you?"

I whimper in agreement, my body writhing against his as he drives into me, deeper and harder with each thrust. I can feel the heat building inside me again, the familiar coiling sensation, and I don't think I'll ever tire of this, of him.

"You like that, yeah?" His voice rumbles. "You like getting fucked in front of the world like this? Look at you, letting everyone know that it's my big cock that claims you. Such a good fucking girl."

Jesus. My whole body flushes hot and tight. I could hear his filthy mouth forever.

"Val," I whisper to him, the pace of his hips quickening. "Can I ask for something?"

"Anything, my love," he says, kissing my neck.

"I want to feed from you," I manage to say, feeling shy all of a sudden, which is an odd feeling when you're being thoroughly fucked above a bustling city.

He pulls back enough for his dark eyes to search mine, surprise flickering. "I would be honored."

He tilts his head to the side, his jugular exposed, and I automatically feel my canines sharpen into fangs, the hunger for his blood coursing through me. There are so many smells around us, the scent of our sex, our sweat, the diesel and spices and incense of the city, but it's his blood I suddenly smell most of all.

He smells like home.

My mouth waters and I grab his neck and bite him sharply. He hisses as I sink my fangs deep into his neck. The taste of his blood is like nothing I've ever experienced before. It's warm and thick, with a hint of sweetness, and it floods my mouth, filling every corner of my being with its essence. Even after all these lives and years together, we have found a new first.

I suck greedily, my body pulsing with a hunger that I never knew existed until now. Valtu moans, his fingers tightening around my waist as he continues to thrust into me, his own pleasure building to a fever pitch.

The combination of his blood and his cock inside me is almost too much to bear. I'm on the brink of another orgasm, my body coiling tighter and tighter with each passing moment.

"You like this, don't you?' he says through a throaty gasp. "Being fucked and fed at the same time?"

"God, yes," I moan, my body arching against him, as a few trails of hot blood spill down my chin.

"Then come for me, my dove," he whispers. "Come for me, and drink me in."

And with those words, I shatter into a thousand pieces, my body flying apart from him, from his cock, from the feel of my teeth in his neck, his blood in my throat. My climax spirals out of control and I can feel it from every extremity, from my fingers to my toes, until it takes over every inch of my body and everything lights up with ecstasy, and I'm screaming out his name as I come. My back arches over the railing until I think I'm free falling and I submit to it.

But his grip is strong, his arms are safe, and I am his.

Everything goes hot and cold at the same time, my blood racing and pounding through my veins, a mixture of the two of us together.

"I'm coming," he groans, his body straining, his muscles taut and tight.

He lets out a low grunt and his cock throbbing and jerking within me, his blood rich and red in my mouth, and even though I'm still flying high with the aftershocks of my orgasm, I can feel the connection between us growing. I can feel the bond that I thought was severed beginning to reknit, to form anew between us.

Then time seems to slow. It wraps itself around us, holding us in place, him inside me, while I'm holding his head to my chest, letting our breath return.

Anyone looking out of their hotel rooms could see us right now and frankly I'm surprised that the fire department hasn't been called because of the lightning strike, or the police because of all our yelling and screaming, but I guess people just accept the chaos that comes with a bustling old city such as Istanbul.

Valtu pulls his head back and gives me a most satisfied grin. "So how did I taste?"

"Amazing," I tell him, grinning back at him with a blood-stained mouth.

"I could tell. You're a greedy little girl, you know that."

"Would you have me any other way?"

He laughs and kisses me.

My heart is full.

He picks me up off the railing and sets me down, then pulls me to him in a sudden embrace, his hand cupping the back of my head and holding me to him. I wrap my arms around his waist and grasp him tight. His heart beats steadily in his chest and my heart matches his rhythm in return and even though he's no longer inside me, I still feel like we're one.

The wind whips off the water but it's warm this time and I close my eyes to it, inhaling him, us, and the scents of the city, feeling so infinitely alive.

Alive and powerful.

"They're out there," I say quietly, determination hardening my voice. I turn my head against his chest so that I'm looking across the water. "Somewhere in this city, my brother is out there. And we will find them again."

"The chances of them staying at the same place are low," he says, kissing the top of my head. "And I don't want to do anything that will put you in harm's way."

"Then we'll wait for the others."

"And if they don't show up? Without that book, Rose, I don't think we can do this alone."

I know he's right. And yet I still regret nothing.

"We will find a way," I tell him.

I have to believe it.

CHAPTER 25
VALTU

The LED clock face glows 5:00 AM when my phone rings.

I groan, being pulled from the darkest depths of sleep. I can't remember the last time I've slept so soundly, so solidly.

It's been decades.

I open my eyes and see the reason. My love of many names has her back to me, her red hair pooling on the sheets between us. She stirs a little and I wish for nothing more for the both of us to go back into slumber.

But the phone doesn't stop ringing and I remember that there's a pressing matter out there that's bigger than our complicated love affair.

I roll over and grab my mobile from the nightside table, answering it.

"Hello?"

"Valtu," the deep and steady voice of Wolf comes over the line. "Did I wake you?"

I blink and sit up, rubbing the heel of my palm between

my eyes. I was expecting to hear from Van Helsing, maybe even Solon, but not Wolf of all people.

"Wolf," I say, and Rose suddenly jerks herself awake, staring up at me in surprise. "How are you?"

He lets out a dry chuckle at my attempt at small talk. "Just about as well as I could be, considering you're sleeping with my daughter."

Oh. Fuck. Right.

That.

I clear my throat. "Uh, well, the world's a funny place, Wolf. You never know what it's going to throw your way."

He grumbles. "Who won the last time we fought? Pretty sure it was me."

"It was too close to call," I remind him carefully.

"You know, I've had some time now to think about what Rose told us, about how she was Dahlia and all her past lives and how they all wrap around you, and I have to admit, even still, I don't understand a fucking ounce of it." He pauses. "But I'm guessing you don't understand either."

"I got my memories of her back," I tell him. "Last night. The spell reversed."

"Oh. Good for you. Guess I'm alone in my confusion."

"Perhaps there are some things in life that are best not understood," I suggest.

"Valtu, cut the shit," he says. "You know why I'm calling."

"I do?"

"Put my daughter on the phone."

"Sure." I give Rose a wild look and hand her the phone. "Guess what, it's your dad."

She gingerly takes it from me, a look of trepidation on her brow, and puts it to her ear. "Dad?"

315

Man, I don't know if I am ever going to get used to this. Of all the families she could have been born into...

"Daddy," Rose sniffs into the phone and then she starts crying. "I'm so sorry."

Alright. This is definitely weird. And personal.

I decide to get up. I won't be going back to sleep after this. I putter around the suite making coffee, trying not to eavesdrop but it's extremely hard when your hearing is as good as mine is.

Their conversation is a lot of Rose crying and apologizing and asking about Dylan and her mother and then a lot of her trying to convince Wolf of something and I have no doubt that it's about me. I don't think I will ever get used to Wolf being her father but he will *definitely* never get used to her being with me.

Finally, as I place her cup of coffee beside her on the nightstand, she starts telling him about Leif and Atlas, and then how she got stabbed. The wound is nearly fully healed now, just a faint red mark where the knife went in, but that doesn't erase how horrific it was in the moment.

Wolf practically roars in response. I knew he would. As weird as it all is, he does seem to be a good, protective father.

"He *was* there, Dad," Rose says in my defense, glancing over at me with furrowed brows. "He tackled Atlas to the ground. Who then disappeared in thin air."

I don't blame Wolf for wondering how this happened. Of course I didn't *let* any of that happen to Rose. I was on Atlas in seconds. It's just that when Leif appeared, I was as surprised as she was to see him there. It caught me off-guard and I was slow to react to Atlas' approach. I didn't even smell that he was a witch; he must have some sort of glamor on him at all times.

Seeing Rose get stabbed with the blade put the fear of god in me. I can't make any excuses for how I used that fear. The man who erased her for the second time was a different man than I am right now, shaped by different experiences (or rather, lack of experiences), and he was too weak to endure what he assumed would be another loss. He thought Rose was dead when she was stabbed and that felt like the end of the world to him, so he took the easy way out.

They say what doesn't kill you makes you stronger. I think that's a lie. It's how you choose to deal with things that makes you stronger. I went through all the tragedy in the world and it made me stronger...until it didn't. Until it made me weaker. Until I took the easy way out by erasing her the first time.

To say I feel shame is an understatement. I chose to forget her in the first place and I'll be trying to come to terms with that for the rest of my life. In the end, I have to take responsibility for what I've done, no matter who I was at the time. The excuses don't matter.

What does matter is that I have a chance to get it right again. I have a chance to be with my love for eternity, if the fates allow.

Naturally, I am a little wary about this whole Bellamy thing. I know she wants her revenge and I want her revenge for her. I'd say there's nothing I want more than to torture the guy who killed Dahlia's parents. But what I want more than that is for her to remain safe. The other day was too close of a call. The both of us had the book's magic at our disposal at the time we saw Atlas and Leif, and yet we were totally blindsided. Even if the others join us to help, I have a bad feeling that things aren't going to go the way we want them to.

And selfishly I don't want anything to happen to Rose. I would rather take her back to Mittenwald or...no, not even there. We need a fresh start together. I would go wherever she wants to go in this world. Some place where we can just be together in a whole new life. Letting her try to find Bellamy again feels like we're putting everything at risk, everything we worked so hard for.

I go take a shower and when I come out, Rose is making another coffee.

"So?" I say, leaning against the desk. "What was that all about? Is he coming here?"

"He's already here," she says.

"What?!"

"Yup. He was calling from the airport. He, my mom, Lenore, and Solon all flew from Portland. Dylan stayed behind. They're just waiting for Abe to arrive and then they're coming straight over here."

I gesture to my phone on the bed. "He could have told you all that in person."

She shrugs and lifts her coffee cup to her lips. "He wouldn't have though. It's hard to get Dad to open up about most things. He says he just wanted to be able to talk to me before all the chaos started."

"And he's okay with you taking part in this, getting Leif back?"

"I wouldn't say he's *okay*," she says with a small smile. "But I think he knows he can't stop me, and he knows that this is as equally important to me as it is to them. What did he say to you? Do you think he's going to kill you?"

I laugh and I go over to her and kiss her forehead. "We'll see. Considering I once stole his girlfriend, and now I'm stealing his daughter..."

She laughs. "It's going to be an adjustment for a lot of you."

"It's okay. I always felt I missed out on the *stay away from my daughter* phase. Feels like being in a movie, and your dad plays the role very well."

Her lips twist sourly. "I don't know, I think you got a lot of *stay away from my daughter* from Mina's father."

I try not to remember that moment. Time usually fades the sting, but the day I lost Mina is something that will never stop aching, like a sliver you can't dislodge. Maybe because it was before I was a vampire. Maybe because it was my first time loving her. Having erased that moment for decades has only made it hurt even worse.

"I'm going to be honest with you, my dove," I tell her, cupping the back of her head and staring down at her. "I would rather the two of us leave your parents to the battle. I would rather take you away, safe and sound, somewhere far off. I think if we bowed out, everyone would not only understand, but be relieved."

She stiffens. "We can't bow out. This is my fight, Val. It's their fight too, but it's also mine. I have to do this."

"How?"

"How are *you* of all people running from a fight?"

"Right? I usually cause the fights."

"Val," she warns, and I know from the jut of her chin that she is not going to back down.

"I want to rip his head off and I want you to get your revenge," I tell her. "But I am terrified of losing you again. I finally have you, all of you, in my grasp and it would be foolish for me to even think about putting you in harm's way."

She gives me a bone-dry look. "You didn't seem to feel this way when we first came here."

"Because that was a different me," I tell her. "And he was afraid. He just didn't know what to do with that fear..." Well, actually he did.

She studies me carefully, lips pursed in thought. "You know, all this time I thought your erasure of me destroyed all of your humanity. But I don't think that was the case. In the end, you took that potion because you were so afraid to love and to lose. There's nothing more human than that."

I don't know if that was her intention, but I'll admit that does make me feel a little better.

"Still an asshole though," she adds, biting her lip.

"Yeah. But I'm your asshole." I grab her and she's giggling, trying to run away. I throw her on the bed, then pounce on top of her, and give her all of my humanity.

THE TWO OF us are still entwined in each other's arms, thoroughly sated and exhausted from each other's bodies, when there's a knock at our door.

"Fucking hell, this can't be them already," I grumble, throwing back the covers and getting out of bed. "I'm not prepared for this."

I start for the door and Rose calls out, "Val, you may want to uh," she trails off, gesturing to the fact that my half-hard dick is swinging about.

I grumble again and grab the towel from earlier, wrapping it around my waist. Could be a housekeeper and I don't want her to get the wrong idea.

But when I glance through the peephole, I see Wolf's big fat head on the other side and I know that things are about to get nuts.

I sigh heavily and Wolf says, "I can hear you Valtu," from the other side. He sniffs. "Smell you, too."

Here goes nothing.

I open the door and see Wolf, tall with all that Scandinavian burliness. From behind him Amethyst pokes out her head.

"Where is she?" Amethyst says, her violet eyes sharp and demanding. Then she eyes my bare chest and my towel and her eyes grow even sharper.

"Well hello to you, too," I say, as she pushes me to the side and barrels past me into the room, her black hair trailing behind her.

I look back to Wolf, grinning.

I only see his fist.

He punches me right in the face. Pain explodes as my bones crunch beneath his hand.

"Fuck!" I yelp, stumbling back against the wall, holding my nose. "What was that for?"

"For everything."

"Everything?" I repeat, trying to move my nose. "Oh. Right."

"Yeah. *Everything*," he says. Not just the fact that I'm with Rose, but the fact that I never helped them when I first got the book.

I rub at the bridge of my nose, feeling the bones go back into place. "I guess I deserved that."

He glares at me but there's just a tinge of sympathy in his eyes. It makes things a hell of a lot worse.

Meanwhile, in the bedroom of the suite, Amethyst and Rose are sobbing away during their reunion.

"Coffee?" I ask Wolf walking toward the machine.

"*Please*," he says emphatically. "I am jetlagged as fuck."

"Where's the rest of them?"

"Solon and Lenore are exploring the area. Wanted to give us some time alone with Rose."

"And I'm right here," Van Helsing says loudly from the other side of the door.

I go back over to it and open it, still wiggling my nose back and forth.

Van Helsing glances at my towel, a brow raised. "All of us catching you at a bad time?"

I roll my eyes and usher him inside. "Get in here."

Wolf is now with Amethyst and Rose in the bedroom, their reunion continuing. I'm not about to intrude, lest I get punched in the face again.

"Help yourself to some coffee," I tell the doctor, gesturing to the machine which is currently brewing Wolf's cup.

"Don't touch my coffee!" Wolf roars from the bedroom.

I shrug. "Careful, he'll fight you for it," I comment and then drop my towel.

Van Helsing winces and turns his attention to the espresso machine. "I don't care how long we've known each other, Val, I never need to see that."

"Phhff," I snort. "You're a doctor, you should be used to the human anatomy. Also..." I lower my voice as I slip on my boxer briefs. "Got any pills?"

The doctor turns around and looks at me in mock surprise. "I can't believe it. You, Dracula, Prince of Darkness, King of the Undead, who would rather starve than take pills, is now asking *me* for that very thing."

I give him a tired look. "Yeah, well, I'd watch your mouth if I were you. After all, you did bring Rose to me under false pretenses, you lying motherfucker. I should be punching *you* in the face."

Van Helsing looks chagrined. "I do apologize for that.

But in the state you were in, I thought it was worth a shot if Rose could make you remember. At the very least, I thought if you would have some sort of affection for her, it could soften you."

"I'm afraid it worked, for better or for worse."

"Well, I do have to say, it's for the better. It's good to have you back," he says solemnly. "I mean, have you *really* back. You were a changed man, Val. It wasn't a good change." He pauses. "I'd hug you, but I'll wait until you put on pants."

I take the hint and grab my pants, slipping them on. I'm buttoning up my shirt when the Doctor comes over, holding out a black pouch, the same one he had given Rose. "Here," he says, opening the pouch and takes out a red pill. "This will help."

"You gave the same ones to Rose," I say, taking one from him.

"Did she like them?"

"I don't know. I flushed them down the toilet," I admit.

Oooh, he doesn't like that. His eyes narrow. "You're a fucking dick, you know that?"

"I'm very aware. Come on." I pop the pill in my mouth and then pull my oldest friend into a big bear hug, squeezing him tight.

"At least you're wearing pants," he mutters against me.

I laugh and release him, slapping him hard on the back just as Rose, Wolf, and Amethyst come out of the bedroom. The girls' eyes are red and puffy and even Wolf's look a little bloodshot.

Rose's face lights up when she sees me and she goes straight over and into my arms, occupying the spot that Van Helsing was in, who quickly steps aside.

"Hey, darling," I say to her, wrapping my arms around

her and kissing the top of her head, unable to ignore the fact that Wolf and Amethyst are staring at us with blatant disappointment. I don't blame them. On paper, I am the worst vampire in this world for Rose to end up with. But it is what it is.

And it's beautiful.

"Oh, hey Abe," Rose says, pulling back to greet the Doctor.

"Ms. Harper," he says with a tip of an imaginary hat. "Oh," he says and then takes another blood pill from the pouch. "Apparently your boyfriend approves of these now."

I roll my eyes at the term *boyfriend* while she takes the pill from him and puts it in her mouth, swallowing. I don't want to admit this to Van Helsing, but I can already feel his blood pill working through my system. It doesn't have that taste, that physically addicting feeling you get from drinking straight from a human, but it is making my cells replenish, giving my mind and body a boost. I'd compare it to vitamins—you're better off eating a healthy diet but supplements will help you when you can't.

I'd say it's already taking the edge off my hunger, but I think I'm still hungry for Rose. Her blood last night was exquisite. It tasted like Dahlia's blood but different now. It's both fresher because of her age and headier because she's now a vampire. If I could only feed off Rose for the rest of my life, I would be a very happy man.

"So what's the plan?" Wolf's voice booms across the room, taking a wide stance and crossing his arms. If he thinks he's trying to intimidate me, he's got another thing coming.

"I don't know," I tell him. "Shouldn't we wait for Lenore and Solon to figure this out?"

"Doesn't hurt to get it started," Van Helsing says and

ticks off his fingers. "Let's see, we have two vampires that are witches, two vampires that know some party tricks, and then—"

"Then the rest of us normal fucking people," Amethyst pipes up dryly, arching a black brow.

"And you both remember where Bellamy was located?" Van Helsing asks us.

Rose nods, absently rubbing at the scar on her chest. "Yes. But that's all we know now. Without the book, we can't tap into their location. I doubt they'd still be there now that we know."

"Except we don't know what they know," I point out. "You're a vampire now. That might prevent Bellamy from knowing that it's you, that you're his Dahlia. They definitely know who I am though."

"Like you're really so distinctive," Wolf mutters under his breath.

"And they think you have the book," Van Helsing points out. "We could use that to our advantage somehow."

"I still don't think they'd be there," Rose says. "And if they are, they'll be waiting for us. And anyway, I don't think you can really count me as a vampire witch. I don't know any spells or how to use magic other than killing things with lightning bolts."

"You can do what now?" Amethyst asks, her eyes going round.

Rose gives her a hangdog look. "Remember when the lightning hit the deck when we were fighting? That was me."

Wolf sighs loudly. "I've spent days trying to replace the boards," he says with a groan but there's just a touch of pride in his eyes.

"That's not nothing," Van Helsing says. "I'm counting you as a witch."

"Speaking of witches," Lenore's voice rings out through the suite. Okay, this hotel room is officially at capacity.

Our heads all swivel toward Lenore and Solon who've just come inside, the sound of the door closing behind them.

"How did you get in here?" I frown.

"Magic," she says with a smug smile, wiggling her fingers in a manner that's both saying hello and showing off her abilities.

Even though I haven't seen Solon for a long time, and Lenore for even longer than that, it feels like no time at all. There's something to be said about being immortal and everyone always looks the same.

Solon and I nod at each other.

Valtu. It's been awhile, Solon projects his thoughts.

A little too long, I tell him. *That's on me.*

He nods. *I can see that you're back.*

I grab Rose's hand and give it a squeeze. *I am.*

Better late than never, he says. *Bit of a trip dealing with Wolf, no?*

I can't help but laugh at that. *You can say that again.*

"Okay boys, enough with your private little convo," Lenore says to us with an air of impatience. She looks at everyone else. "We were just in the Spice Bazaar down the street and holy fuck, did I ever feel a presence."

"What do you mean?" Rose asks.

"We both felt it," Lenore says, gesturing to Solon and he nods. "Witches. At least two. And I swear I picked up on a vampire as well. It was all a little muddled, there are so many rich scents in there, but there was the vague smell of a bloodsucker."

"Are you sure it wasn't Solon? He did get off a long flight," I point out.

Solon glares at me.

Lenore rolls her eyes and ignores me. "Maybe it's nothing. I'm sure a city as rich in history as Istanbul is just teeming with vampires and witches and who knows what else. We're always a little egotistical aren't we, thinking we're the only ones that matter."

"Well, I am the only Dracula," I say, half-joking, and that brings out a communal groan and eyeroll from everyone.

"Wait a minute, this spice bazaar," Rose says to her, "it's like a market?"

Lenore nods. "Yeah. You know, mounds of saffron and cumin and whatnot."

"See, when I was able to track them before, I saw them in this market," Rose says, getting excited. "Maybe that's where they are. We should start there."

"Except you could be describing all the markets in Istanbul," I tell her.

"It's still worth a shot, don't you think?"

"No matter what," Solon speaks up, "I don't think it would be wise if we all went to the spice bazaar together. The five of us leaving the airport together was a bit much for the humans. You know how they can get. Seven of us together would cause problems."

Right. As a rule, vampires tend to travel in small groups. Generally, the more vampires together in a cluster, the more it starts to affect the world around them. Most humans don't believe in vampires, but put them in a room filled with them and things start to get really weird. You attract a lot of attention, and not the good kind. The kind that will get you in trouble and fuck up all your plans. The last thing we need is to get hauled off by the police.

"So then we split up," Wolf says. "Half of us will go check out the place you saw them at before. Just to put eyes on the building, scope it out. The other half will go to the market and see if it correlates with what Rose saw." He pauses. "Of course, now the question is, who is going with who?"

CHAPTER 26
ROSE

"Rose and I will go to the industrial area," Valtu says. I slap him across the chest with the back of my hand. "I'm going to the spice bazaar. You don't get to make my decisions."

"That's my girl," I hear my mom say under her breath.

Valtu balks, staring down at me. "I'm not letting you out of my sight and they don't know where the location is."

"And I need to lay my eyes on the bazaar to see if it's the same one I had seen through Bellamy's eyes," I counter.

"How about we go to the industrial area later?" Van Helsing says, attempting a compromise. "That way we can all go together."

"Nah," Wolf says. "I feel like we're running out of time here. Amethyst and I will go to the industrial area. I'm sure you both can tell us exactly where to go and how to get there. That is the last place you saw Leif, so I'm going with that."

"You shouldn't go without a witch," Lenore says. "I'll go with you." She looks to me. "You okay with that?"

I shrug. "Guess it's hard when there's only one witch to go around."

"You're a witch, my dove," Valtu says, giving my hand a squeeze. "Whatever magic Dahlia had in her veins runs in yours now. Just believe in it."

I sigh tiredly. I wish I could. Aside from the lightning, I feel totally lost. If only the spells I had memorized from the book still worked, but I guess those spells were tied to that book and that book alone.

"I'll give you some pointers before we split up, okay?" Lenore assures me.

I give her a grateful smile. "First I borrow your clothes, then I borrow your magic?"

"What's mine is yours," she says, and I know she *still* feels guilty for her hand in Dahlia's death.

You've been wearing her clothes this whole time? Valtu asks in my head. *That explains so much.*

I glance down. Even now, Lenore's shirt I'm wearing is stretched across the chest and a little tight across the stomach. *God damn boobs*, I grumble.

Don't you dare ever speak that way about your breasts, he rebukes me.

"I'll stay with Valtu and Rose," Solon announces. "I don't have a witch's arsenal, but my magic might come in handy."

I breathe out a sigh of relief. Going anywhere with both Valtu and Solon would make any vampire feel protected. I'd say the same about my dad, but I'm glad he and my mom won't be with me. Things get so complicated when they're around as it is, and they hate the idea that I'm taking part in this to begin with.

"Then I'll go with the others," Van Helsing says. "And so

it's settled." He takes out his phone and gets Valtu to show him exactly where to go on the map.

Shit. I'm nervous. I'm really nervous. I don't actually think my parents will be in any danger because I just can't imagine Bellamy hanging around, but if that building really is their headquarters or something, they might not leave so hastily. I feel a lot better with Lenore going with them, especially if Solon is with us. But still, it's just going to be the three of us in the spice market. I both want to see Bellamy and also hope it's a fool's errand.

We say our goodbyes quickly.

"If you get hurt, you're grounded," my dad says, giving me a tight hug. He gives the best hugs. He looks over at Valtu. "And you're a dead man."

Valtu nods gravely, taking it in stride. "You have complete permission to kill me."

My mom hugs me, crying again, and I have to pat her on the head to reassure her. How the hell is she going to do any fighting? Does my mom even know how to fight anyone, let alone immortal witches?

"Are you going to be okay?" I ask her as she pulls away. "You're not the fighting type."

She balks at that with a sniff, straightening her shoulders, and steeling her gaze. "Of course I am. I used to manage the bar at Dark Eyes as a *human*. You think I don't know how to put assholes in their place?"

"Your mother can take care of herself just fine," my dad says but over her head he gives me a look like, *don't worry, I've got her.*

I give him a relieved look, while she goes over to Valtu and pokes her nail into his chest. "Don't you fuck this up."

Valtu throws his arms out. "What the hell?" he says

gruffly. "You know Solon will be with us too, go and threaten him."

My mom smiles at Solon. "Oh, we trust Solon. We just don't trust you."

Solon looks at Valtu like the cat that just swallowed the canary.

"Mom," I warn her. "Come on. How about you get going?"

She takes the hint and they head toward the door with Abe, while Lenore comes over to me, grabbing me by the arm and pulling me to the side.

"You want some magic?" she asks, her hazel eyes gleaming. "You just have to ask yourself for it. You're a witch, Rose. I can smell it on you."

"The others don't seem to notice," I say glumly.

"Because it's altered. It's mixed with you being a vampire. I'm almost the same way, but you can tell I'm a witch because I was born a witch. Your witch powers come from reincarnation. It's a different ball game but in the end, they are still powers, Rose."

She makes a move to leave but now I'm grabbing her hand. "That's it? Aren't you going to tell me how to walk through walls or shoot fireballs or something?"

She gives her head a shake. "I don't need to. Whatever was in Dahlia is still in you. That's the most important thing to remember. All her magic, all her knowledge, you have that inside. Just ask for it when you need it and I promise it will show up."

Then Lenore walks over to Solon, kisses him goodbye, and she leaves with my parents and Van Helsing.

"So..." I say, turning to Solon and Valtu. "What's next?"

Seeing the two of them standing together, both tall, dark-haired and breathtakingly handsome gives me a boost of adrenaline. I may doubt my capabilities at the moment, but I know that the two of them are the most dangerous creatures on the planet.

Or, they were. Fuck. Atlas was able to disappear into thin air. Who knows what the hell Bellamy is able to do now? I considered him all-powerful back in the day and with all these added years, he might be unstoppable. Add in the fact that they're immortal, and all of us might be in over our heads, no matter how much magic or ferocity we possess.

Valtu seems to pick up on my thoughts because he looks at Solon and says, "You remember that time we got captured by Skarde's army and were chained up in that hut in Finland, left there for eternity?"

Solon gives him a tepid look. "Yes."

"Are you still able to turn into that beast?"

He sighs. "Unfortunately not. But I think that's a good thing."

"I don't know, I think a beast might really come in handy right about now."

"In the middle of a spice market?"

"There's a big chance that it's not the place I saw through the vision," I tell them. "We might end up finding nothing but heaps of cheap tarragon."

I can see the relief in Valtu's eyes when I say that. Poor guy. I know he really doesn't want me doing this, but I'm thankful he's keeping his opinion to himself. I know he can be really controlling but there's no way in hell I'd listen to him after all this.

"One more coffee before we hit the road?" Valtu says, going over to the machine. As if caffeine will add extra fuel to the fight.

While he does that, I go to the bathroom and change

into leggings that are a little more fight appropriate than jeans. I slip on my combat boots and then remember the blade of *mordernes*. I had put it in the bathroom, in the cloth bag that the hair dryer is usually stored in. I take the knife and slip it into my boot and the moment I do that, it's like I'm brought back in time.

I close my eyes and Dahlia's life comes rushing back through me. I had remembered everything before but now it feels like I'm living through it again, years flipping through me like pages of a book. And while this whirlwind is happening inside me, I feel a raw power building in my core, like an electrical fire. I feel like a vampire slayer again, which doesn't do me much good if we're battling witches, but the power I felt as a slayer, that unmistaken sense of confidence and skill, of knowing exactly what to do, is something I grasp onto.

I know I made a lot of mistakes as Dahlia, but those mistakes came from my emotions getting the best of me. When it comes to Bellamy, there will be no mistakes, no second guessing, no feelings getting in the way. Just the feeling of wanting him to pay for all that he's done to me, to Leif, and to everyone else whose life he's royally fucked up.

"Rose?" I hear Valtu say from the other side of the bathroom door and for a moment I'm almost confused, because my name is Dahlia, and then I remember—it is and it isn't. "Are you okay?" he asks.

"Yeah, I'm coming," I tell him, giving myself one last look in the mirror. I see all the versions of myself staring back but Dahlia is coming through most of all. It's all in her eyes. That look of never belonging, never fitting in, knowing I was inherently different and that people would treat me as such. Bellamy took that aspect of me and he used it to manipulate me, gave me a focus and made me feel like I was among others that understood me. He used what made me different, preyed on my feelings of loneliness, and molded me into a murderer.

And now, I would take that part of me and use it to murder him.

"I'm ready," I say, opening the door and seeing Valtu on the other side.

"We don't need to do this," he says, looking at me warily. Perhaps I do look a little wild and unhinged at the moment.

"Yes, we do," I tell him. "And I'm ready."

Solon comes over, sipping from his small cup of coffee. He pauses and sniffs the air, then frowns sharply. "You smell like a witch."

I put my hand on my hip and thrust it to the side with flourish. "Ta-da."

He nods, appraising me. "Alright. There you are. Let's get going."

He finishes the rest of his coffee and the three of us leave the room and head through the hotel to the lobby. The hotel itself is in the Sultanahmet quarter and though inside it's very open and calm and airy, with lots of colorful tiles, water features, and plants, outside the city is roaring with energy. If it wasn't for Valtu pulling me back in time I would have been taken out by a swerving motorbike, dirty exhaust blowing in my face.

"Easy now," he warns me. "You're giving me a heart attack this early in the game."

The walk to the spice market takes a lot longer than I thought it would and by the time we cross a busy square and come to the grand building with its domes and three arched entrances, my nerves have had time to fray a little.

"Just over there is the Yeni Cami Mosque, or New

335

Mosque," Valtu points to the sprawling mosque in the background with its massive domes and many spires. "If we were here as tourists and not witch hunters, I'd be suggesting a tour."

"You never know," Solon says, "if we make quick work of it, we might earn ourselves a little vacation."

"That would be nice," I mutter.

We enter the bazaar and are greeted with a cacophony of sounds and an assortment of smells. Stimuli bombards us from every angle, and I know I'm not the only one who is having a hard time shutting a lot of it out and keeping focused, a drawback to having such keen senses. There are so many people bustling to and fro, brushing past us as we try and walk through the halls, and the sound of Turkish and passionate haggling fills the air, along with the scent of mint, sumac, curry, and coffee. Above us black-and-white tiles and mosaics fill the arched ceiling, while the stalls are filled with neat piles of red, yellow, green, orange, every color of spice or tea you can think of, plus dried mushrooms, peppers, and oodles of dried fruits and the ubiquitous Turkish Delight.

"I remember always wanting to eat one of those because the *Lion, the Witch and the Wardrobe* made it sound like the most amazing candy in the world," I admit, staring at the pastel-colored squares dusted with powdered sugar.

"You will be thoroughly disappointed," Valtu comments. He then says to Solon, "Where about did you and Lenore sense the witches?"

"Further along here, toward the back," he says, gazing down the chaotic hall. He looks back to me. "Does any of this look familiar to you?"

I glance around. It's so hard to gauge, everything is so

overwhelming and nearly every stall looks the same. "Yes and no."

"We'll keep going," Valtu says. "And if there's nothing here, then you can have a Turkish Delight, as a treat."

"Thanks," I say with a laugh, but it sounds weak to my ears. Truth is, even though I can't figure out if this is the place I saw through Bellamy's eyes or not, there is something here. I can't seem to focus on it or put my finger on it, but I sense something supernatural, some sort of magic percolating.

Plus a sense of doom. Though I'm not sure if that's my frayed nerves talking or what.

Solon leads the way down the long length of the hall and I do my best to try and hone in on Bellamy. Even though I don't have the book's magic to locate him, I still feel like I'd know his presence if I came across it.

And then I do.

We're near the end of the hall when I come to a sudden stop in front of a stall called Hazer Baba. Right above it, where the arched ceiling curves down to meet the roof of the stall, is a large window in a half-circle, with what looks to be an office or storeroom behind it.

And standing in front of the window is the dark figure of a man in a long black coat.

Atlas Poe.

Staring down at us.

I gasp and point. "There he is!"

Solon and Valtu look but Atlas literally vanishes into thin air. One second he's there, the next he's just dissolved into nothing.

"Fuck," I swear. "He was there. Now he could be anywhere."

"Actually, I'm right behind you," Atlas says.

The three of us whirl around, Valtu stepping slightly in front of me like a shield, while Solon seems ready to pounce.

Atlas is standing a few feet away, patrons walking around him, some glaring at him for not getting out of the way. His hands are flexing at his sides, his head cocked, a stupidly smug smile on his face.

"I'm going to wipe that fucking smile right off your face, you emo piece of shit," Valtu sneers, the veins throbbing at his temple. He's seconds from losing his temper and I reach out to calm him.

"You're going to attack me here?" Atlas says with a haughty laugh. "In front of all these people, in front of all these *humans*?"

A woman walking past him hears that and gives Atlas a wary look, clutching her purse tighter to her and quickening her pace. This is what I've been afraid of. To fight here would only bring a load of unwanted attention to ourselves. Glamours and compelling people can help to an extent, but not where so many live streams are just a click away.

"I don't really give a fuck," Valtu says and before I can stop him he's leaping through the air and blasting right into Atlas. The force knocks Atlas back ten feet, causing him to go flying through the market stands and right through the piles of tea and spices, colorful dust rising up in the air like remnants of an explosion.

I'm stunned, as is everyone else until Valtu starts throwing punches hard enough to deliver a fatal blow and people start screaming and running all over the place.

People also start bringing out their phones and recording.

Oh shit.

Suddenly I'm hit from behind, a blow landing between my shoulder blades that knocks the air from my lungs, and I whirl around to see a dark-haired woman about to deck me in the face. I guess we're fighting old school here.

I duck just in time and throw my hands at her, feeling power flow through my chest and out my fingertips and the force knocks her to the ground. I don't know who this bitch is, she might just be a human defending the market, I don't know, but to not react could be fatal and I'm grateful that Dahlia's power is coming through like this.

While the woman gets up, I look to Solon for support, only to see two men approaching him from different sides. "Solon!" I yell to alert him.

He whips around just as they pounce and from their movement I can tell they're using magic. They land on Solon and he manages to shake one of them off with an elbow to the face, the crunch of bone audible even amongst all the chaos and screaming, but the other one brings out a blade of *mordernes*, Solon's face glowing blue in the light of the knife.

"Solon!" I yell again and I run over to him to help but the woman from behind yells in Latin and then I'm going flying through the air, blasting through rows of neatly stacked Turkish delights and dried fruits and let me tell you, taking dates and walnuts to the face hurts like hell.

I land on my back, winded, looking up at the shopkeeper filming me with his phone.

"Are you okay?" he asks in broken English.

I nod and he leans down to help me up and I give him a grateful smile just as the woman approaches, her hands held out as if she's about to blast me and the shopkeeper to smithereens.

"Stop!" I scream at her, my right palm thrust out.

And she does.

Everything does.

Every single human, witch, and vampire freezes in their place. It's like time goes completely still and the silence is deafening. I look over to Valtu, who has his hands around Atlas' throat, pinning him against the wall and hovering a few feet above the ground, plumes of red sumac and yellow turmeric and green basil suspended in the air around them. I turn to Solon who has managed to deflect the blade and is biting the neck of the witch holding it, trails of blood frozen in motion, while his other assailant lies on the ground, missing his head.

I look at the shopkeeper's shocked face and the mess I just created in his stall, pistachio stuffed fruits and syrup-soaked sweets spilling everywhere.

And then the hair at the back of my neck stands up.

I hear footsteps. The easy, languid footsteps of someone approaching me from the other direction, someone with all the time in the world.

My breath hitches in my throat and I *know*.

"Well, well, well," Bellamy's voice rings out, the only sound in the bazaar. "If it isn't Dahlia Abernathy."

CHAPTER 27
ROSE

That voice.

My name.

I feel as frozen as the people in the market around me and for a moment I feel like I might be in suspended animation as well.

But I'm able to move, to slowly turn around.

And find myself face-to-face with the man who was once like a father to me.

Bellamy.

He stops a few feet away and before I can even make a move to lunge at him, he holds out his palm and pins me in place with an invisible forefield.

"How have you been, my dear?" he goes on, studying me. "I must admit, when I heard you were dead, I was certain I would never see you again."

"Funny how the world works," I tell him, the rage flaring up inside me.

He gives me a lopsided grin. My god, he really is immortal, isn't he? He looks exactly the same as the last day I saw him, maybe even a little younger, like he's in his late fifties now. The only real change I can see is in his eyes. Once upon a time they were wise, calm, and occasionally kind, despite all the awful shit he did to me. They were also a brilliant blue. Now though, now they are black as sin and harboring a malevolence that wasn't there before. Obviously he was no saint, he was a murdering, lying bastard. But now he's brimming with something slick and evil. It's practically oozing out of him.

"You seem confused," he ruminates. "Wonder if I've discovered the fountain of youth?"

"I know you haven't," I deride him. "I know how you got to be this way. You stole my baby brother from my parents."

His brow furrows. "Your parents?"

Oh, right. He has no idea. Which is a good thing, because it means the lengths that my mom and dad went to worked. They kept me and Dylan safe.

"Amethyst and Wolf," I tell him, raising my chin. "Looks like you didn't know about me."

He looks bothered by this and I feel a tiny twinge of pride. I'll take what I can get.

"How can they be your parents?"

"As I said. The universe works in mysterious ways."

His eyes narrow and he breathes in deeply through his long nose, as if smelling me. "Then that means you have the same genes as Leif."

"Same genes as Leif, same powers as Dahlia. I'm the whole package."

"Power?" he says, sniveling. He reminds me of a pig on two legs, wearing a toupee. "The power you possessed as Dahlia was good for one thing and one thing only, and that was killing vampires. Too bad you haven't gotten the urge to use that power on yourself."

I have the need to keep him talking but I'm not really sure why. Solon and Valtu are frozen in time and can't help me. I guess I figure I'll come up with some way to get out of this eventually.

I nod at the market around us. "You picked an awfully public place to do this."

"You're worried I'm blowing your cover?" His grin widens. "They won't remember a thing leading up to this or after, and I've sent an electromagnetic pulse to disable all electronics and technology. No, Dahlia, this is just between you and me now. The way it's supposed to be."

He moves his hand and I cry out in pain, my whole body lifting a few inches off the ground, invisible vices clamped over my arms and legs, pulling me in opposite directions.

"You deserve to rot in the ground," I grind out, fighting through the pain.

"For what? For showing you your true potential?"

"You brainwashed me."

"I was a mere schoolteacher," he comments, his black eyes looking positively inhuman.

"You're a murderer!"

"So are you."

"You made me this way!"

"We all have to wear many hats, Dahlia. That happens to be one of mine. Do you consider it murder when people deserve it? If they've killed others? Do you consider it murder when you do it?"

"You killed my parents!" I scream. "I loved them, and you took them from me. You killed them and blamed it all on vampires, but all along it was you."

"There has to be sacrifices for the greater good. That's how the world works."

"But you did it to *my* world! Then you inserted yourself

in my life pretending to be someone who fucking cared. Someone who looked after me. You used me and manipulated me when I only needed someone to love me!"

I hate how pathetic I sound, Dahlia's insecurities coming through.

"I did care," he says, and I let out an acidic laugh.

He ignores that and continues, "I cared for you like I would my own daughter. Your own well-being was of the upmost importance to me, as was showing you your true potential. You mattered, Dahlia, whether you want to believe it or not."

"Stop calling me that. It's *Rose*."

"If you're so hell-bent on being called Rose, then why do you care what happened to Dahlia's parents? You've got new parents now. Amethyst and Wolf are quite the pair."

"New parents you've also managed to fuck around with," I cry out. "You tried to take my mother, you kidnapped my brother! And just because they're my parents now as Rose, doesn't mean my parents as Dahlia didn't count. They did count! I loved them and they loved me and we were happy. And you came and you ruined it all. You destroyed my family!"

My words screech across the silent market, my heart growing tighter and tighter as the anger and injustice floods through my body, clouding my thoughts.

"As I said, it's all about sacrifices," he says simply with a splay of his palms.

"Sacrifices don't count if they aren't your own!"

His gaze sharpens on me and I get the same feeling from his eyes that I got from the ghosts and demons in Valtu's place.

"Why are you really here, Dahlia?" He blinks slowly. "Sorry. I mean *Rose*. Hmm? It can't be those parents of yours that are just faint memories of a bygone life. And it can't really be Leif. You never met him before. Why would you care about someone you've never met, that is obviously in no distress. You do realize that what you're trying to do is ruin his life? Leif has only known me as his father, Atlas as his brother, Celina as his sister. He doesn't know the sacrifices he made, and he's better off for it. He's a strong, smart young vampire, the only one I can stand to tolerate. You want to take that away from him? He won't let you."

"No," I tell him. "He will know the truth. He will see. We will make him remember what you've done to him."

"We merely borrowed from him to enhance ourselves. We're his family. Without the testing and his contributions, we wouldn't have been able to raise him. It's lonely being a vampire, isn't it? We couldn't very well die and leave him. We had to ensure that we would live forever as well."

What a crock of shit.

"You're just telling yourself whatever you need to hear," I snarl at him. "But I know the truth. You're fucking evil."

He tuts. "Oh come now, Rose. Evil is such a contentious word, don't you think? So...close-minded. I choose to think you mean decisive. It's much more apt."

"If you don't like evil, I have other words. Cowardly, cruel, despicable," I spit them out at him. "Most of all *pathetic*. You're a desperate old white man clinging to his youth, no different than your average sack of shit in a mid-life crisis."

His lip curls into a toothsome snarl and he jerks his hands, making my body feel like it's being torn apart.

I scream. I scream and let the pain and the anger churn through me like waves, creating chaos in my veins. I look up at the ceiling and I pray, wish, *ask* for the lightning to strike him.

With a deafening buzz, the electric energy inside me bunches up and releases right out of the top of my head, shooting up through the market's arched ceiling and then blasting back down through one of the windows.

Shattered glass rains down on us as the lightning strikes Bellamy dead-on and everything turns white for a moment, my eyes reeling from the light. There's a singed smell and smoke and I'm expecting his power to release me at any moment.

But it doesn't.

I'm still stuck, being pulled in different directions.

And then I hear the laugh.

Low, rich, evil.

And then the smoke clears and Bellamy is standing there, not a hair harmed on his head.

"Foolish girl," Bellamy says, his old mouth curving into a malevolent grin.

Then he flies through the air until he's knocking me to the ground. He presses his hands at my chest and my throat and green electricity crackles as it stabs at my skin, burning me from the inside out. It's his magic and it's draining my life force, draining my own magic, until I'm turning into just a husk of what I used to be.

Are my organs going to go up in flames before the rest of me does?

The pain is blistering and I can't even think anymore.

This can't be it.

I'm not done.

All of Dahlia's knowledge is in you, Lenore had said to me.

She was right. I am still Dahlia and there was one thing that Dahlia knew how to do best. I'm losing consciousness, succumbing to the power of his spell while I feel the heat starting inside me, but I have just enough strength to try one last thing.

Bellamy is immortal. Lightning can't hurt him, nor can any of my powers.

But he is only immortal because of the blood of a vampire, and that should make him immortal in the same way that we are.

Meaning there's a fatal flaw or two.

The lightning didn't seem to set him on fire, and I'm not sure I have enough strength or magic left to try and slice off his head. But I do have one thing.

And he had taught me to use it well.

With my last bit of strength I bring my knees half-way to my chest, just enough to reach into my boot, the handle of the blade seeming to leap into my palm. I curl my fingers around it and yank it out with a cry of effort, my muscles straining as every movement feels harder and harder, like I'm moving through tar.

Bellamy looks down in time to see me bring the blade up toward him. It's glowing blue, lighting up his whole face, not from his presence but from mine.

His gaze narrows on it and I feel his power intensify. The wave of power is so strong that it's holding me in place and I'm screaming, trying to move.

Because he knows. He either knows or he fears it, he fears that this might be the thing to undo him.

"To think I wasted all my time on you," he says with an ugly sneer. "Perhaps I should have done the world a favor and killed you along with your parents."

"It doesn't matter," I manage to say, each word broken. "I would have just come back."

The blade starts to shake in my hand from the strain, poised just above his heart. My instincts tell me exactly where to plunge it and I'm grunting, gasping for just one single push of strength to come through.

"I'm starting to think that I didn't just come back for Valtu," I go on with a growl. "I also came back to kill you."

Then with the memories of my parents in my heart, the ones that he killed and the ones that he stole from, I scream and drive the blade of *mordernes* right into his heart.

The blade sinks in with a snap of cartilage and I watch as Bellamy's face contorts from the pain, his power wavering slightly. I don't know what it's going to do, if anything, and from the intensely curious expression on his face, I can tell he doesn't either. But the knife is all the way in and blue lightning is radiating outward like electric veins, coursing through his body and limbs.

"You fool," he says to me. "Do you know what you have done?"

"I did exactly what you taught me to do," I answer.

Then I let go of the blade, all my energy spent and drained, and just when I start to feel my world go black and cold, everything springs back to life with a WHOOSH.

I'm suddenly bombarded with sounds and movement again, everyone back in motion like they'd never been frozen at all. Valtu is choking Atlas, only to have Atlas disappear into thin air, Solon is biting a hunk out of a witch's neck. The shopkeeper who helped me up is looking around wildly for me, and people are still screaming and shouting and running, clouds of yellow and orange spice rising up in the air.

And at my feet lies Bellamy.

On his back with the blade sticking right out of his chest, his mouth open, face bent in horror, the only thing in the market frozen in place.

He's dead.

I bend over him to make sure but his eyes are empty and I can smell death on him like he's wearing cologne.

"Fuck you," I say and then spit right on his forehead. "That's for Leif."

The thought of my brother's name makes me wonder where he is. He's not here in the market with the others, so maybe he's back in the industrial area. God, I hope so, I hope my parents were able to find him—not only find him but save him. What if Bellamy was right and Leif won't go with them willingly?

But my thoughts about Leif are cut short because a child next to me starts to scream and point at Bellamy and I realize that I look like a good old-fashioned murderer.

I'm about to yell at the others to suggest we get the fuck out of here before the cops show up when suddenly I feel someone at my back and my neck is burning and I reach up to find barbed wire placed around me like a noose.

"Help!" I try to scream but the noose tightens, the spikes piercing my skin, warm blood trickling down my neck, and I hear Atlas at my ear.

"Should have known you'd steal my blade," he seethes, his voice ragged and wild. "You're going to suffer for what you've done, bloodsucker."

Atlas yanks at the wire and I scream, blood spilling down my neck as the spikes go in a few more inches, through muscle and bone and if he pulls again I'm—

With a deafening roar, Valtu appears just in time for Atlas to let go of the wire in surprise. Valtu slams into him, knocking Atlas back, and they go flying onto the ground. I stagger backward, my fingers at my neck, hating the feeling of pulling these spikes out of my skin, scared to know the damage it created.

Valtu is in full-on rage mode now. He's bellowing like

an animal on top of Atlas, both of them coated in a layer of sumac powder, like a dusting of blood. I expect him to start bunching him or biting but Valtu just lets out a primal scream and places his hands on Atlas's head.

He twists Atlas' head back and forth and then with an insane amount of power, Valtu rips his head right off the body.

I gasp, forgetting about my neck for the moment. People scream.

Valtu staggers to his feet, looking like a beast, holding the witch's head by a fistful of hair. Blood and gore spill to the ground, the shattered vertebrae trailing out the end. He nearly ripped his whole damn spine out.

"How did you know how to kill him?" I ask, wide-eyed and breathless. Despite the violence I've seen, nothing prepares you for seeing your lover physically tear some-one's head off their neck as easily a flower off a stem.

Valtu frowns as if it's a dumb question and gestures to the head in his hands. "Who wouldn't this kill?"

He's got a point. Still, holy *shit*.

"Little help," Solon manages to say, and we look over to see him still being attacked.

"Allow me," I say, taking my own blade out of Bellamy's heart, then without more than a glance, I whip it toward Solon, who thankfully ducks out of the way. My blade goes straight into the heart of the other witch, where she screams and staggers until she drops dead.

"Two for two," Valtu says with a growl. "I don't think I've ever wanted to fuck you more."

I grin at him, the adrenaline rolling through me. "Keep it in your pants for now."

"Yes, please keep it in your pants," Solon says, walking over and rubbing the back of his neck. "I managed to bite that other guy's head off. Still not as impressive as you, Valtu," he concedes with a smile.

Meanwhile I'm looking around us at all the chaos, the people screaming and stampeding away from us.

"Okay, *now* we need to go," I say.

"I'll try to compel who I can," Solon says, glancing around as we start running toward the exit. "Valtu, try to do the same."

"Bellamy said that they won't remember the moments before and after this," I say, running alongside them. "And that he did like an EMP thing to disable the tech."

And from what I'm seeing as we book it out of the bazaar, past people tapping on their phones angrily or shaking their cameras, it seems that Bellamy was at least telling the truth about that. With any luck, there will only be a few weird stories about what happened in the spice bazaar, but no proof of it happening.

Well, other than some dead bodies. But that's not our problem.

"Do you think they're really dead?" I ask as we burst out into the daylight, pigeons scattering into flight.

"If that goth cunt's head can reattach itself, then I think he probably deserves to live," Valtu remarks as we cut down a narrow alley toward the hotel. "As for Bellamy, I think you did it, Rose. I think you killed him."

"Yeah, but we both thought you killed Saara when you lit her on fire," Solon reminds him. "And you didn't."

Valtu gives him an annoyed look. "At least she's not hell-bent on revenge and is leaving us alone."

"For now," Solon says.

"Then if she comes back, I'll be quick to rip her head off too," Valtu says.

"Look, Bellamy is dead," I insist. "I won't accept any

other response. We found their weakness. Everyone has one."

"Spoken like a true warrior," Valtu comments. "I hope you're proud of yourself because I sure as fuck am."

Honestly, I think I'm proud but it all happened so fast that I'm having a hard time catching up to reality. I did it. I actually fucking did it. I killed Bellamy and his little witchy minions. I got the revenge I wanted.

Then why does it feel so hollow? Like it's not enough? I was expecting this to fill me, make me feel whole, like the final missing puzzle piece. But there's just this vague sense of accomplishment and a relief at him being gone and that's it.

"I'll feel better when I see Leif," I tell them, shaking my arms, trying to dissipate the leftover adrenaline. We're not running as fast now, and so far no one seems to be following us with news cameras and the like.

"We'll get him back, Rose," Valtu tells me. "This was just step one."

"Have any of you heard from them?" I ask.

They both check their phones and shake their head. "No. But I'm sure they're fine," Solon says, though he absolutely has no reason to think that. What if my parents are battling the same kind of situation that we just did? We all nearly died multiple times.

We get into the hotel and go straight to our room. We take turns washing the spices and blood off our bodies, crack open a couple of bottles of red wine, and we drink and we wait. Abe isn't answering his phone, neither is Lenore or my parents and I'm starting to feel really sick to my stomach. I thought we could be popping open the champagne by now but—

Suddenly there's a knock at the door.

All our eyes go wide and Valtu shoots to his feet, hurrying to the door, Solon and I coming after him.

Valtu looks through the peephole then opens the door.

On the other side is Lenore, looking as beat up as I looked earlier, hair a mess, mascara smudged under her eyes, and a bit of blood at her collar.

"Where is everyone else?" I cry out as she steps inside, the door closing behind her. "Where are my parents?"

"Why haven't you been answering your phone?" Solon says, brushing past me and going straight to her, cupping her face in his hands. "Moonshine, what happened?"

Lenore gives him a shaky but reassuring smile and then looks at me.

"We found your brother."

CHAPTER 28
ROSE

I can't believe what I'm hearing.

I have to blink a few times. "You're serious?"

"You found him?" Valtu asks.

She nods. "Yep."

My brows go up impatiently. "And? Where is he? Where is everyone else?"

"They're in Wolf...they're in your parents' room with Van Helsing. He's just giving Leif a look over, judging how mentally sound he is. He'll be here soon and can tell us more." She looks at Valtu. "Can I use your bathroom to take a shower? I feel like hot garbage."

"Sure," he says and she heads in there.

Solon follows, giving us a look like he'll get the details from her, and they close the door.

"Feel better now?" Valtu asks me.

"I think so," I say. "And hey, you were worried too."

"You're right, I definitely was. Your dad's ass is so easily kicked."

I give him a steady look though I have to bite back a smile. "Is this how it's going to be?"

"A vampire not getting along with his in-laws?" he says, coming over to me and putting his hands at my waist. "How utterly human."

"In-laws," I muse, laughing up at him. "I didn't know we had gotten married."

"You don't remember our wedding?" He kisses me softly on the forehead. "I'm insulted."

"But our vows were 'until death do us part.'"

"And death didn't do us part," he says, his dark eyes shining. "Death merely paused our marriage, that's all. We're still married. Maybe you're not Lucy now, but it's your soul that gets married, not your name. And you belong to me."

I can't help but grin and he pulls me into a warm hug and I wrap my arms around him. "So you're still my husband?"

"And you're still my wife," he whispers, planting his lips on the top of my head. "And I've never been so in fucking awe of you, my dove. You did what you set out to do. You got justice for Dahlia. For your parents. For Leif."

At the mention of his name my heart twists a little. "But did I? What if he's not okay?"

"He's probably *not* okay," he says. "But he's with your parents now and it's a start. Bellamy is gone. This is day one. It's going to be a long road ahead. But I'll be with you every step of the way. So will your parents. None of you will do it alone."

"When did you get to be so nice?" I muse, pulling back to gaze up at him.

"Don't worry, I'll be an asshole when it counts," he says with a crooked grin while a lock of his black wavy hair falls across his forehead. I reach up to push it back and he leans down and captures my mouth in his, kisses me, soft, long and sweet.

"Ahem," Solon says, clearing his throat as he steps out of the bathroom.

"Cockblocker," Valtu mutters under his breath as we break apart.

"So, what did Lenore say?" I ask Solon. "What happened out there?"

"Basically that they went to the same place you had been before. Lenore was able to cloak them all so that they didn't know they were coming and basically they just sat and waited until they saw Leif return to the building."

"Really?"

Lenore appears behind him in the doorway, a towel wrapped around her, having taken the world's quickest shower, which is totally doable when you're a vampire.

"Let me tell it, you're getting it all wrong," she says, but she's smiling. "We didn't sit and wait. We actively scoped out the joint. Then Leif appeared. I wouldn't have known who he was, but he looked exactly like Dylan with a beard. Obviously, your parents knew who he was. We watched as he went inside and then I was able to get closer and look. It was just him and a witch, a girl he called Celina. So the rest was pretty easy."

"You just glossed over the battle scene," Valtu remarks.

"Well, it really wasn't much of one," she says, running her fingers through her wet hair and tussling it. "I went in there and was able to disarm Celina just enough to steal her blade and stab her with it."

"You figured out that was the only way to kill them," I say. "So did I."

She gives me an appreciative smile. "I figured it was worth a try. But then I had to deal with your brother." She makes a sour face. "I didn't want your parents to do it because that didn't seem right and the moment they saw him, they went more into protective mode than anything else. Anyway, your brother is one tough cookie, like Wolf 2.0."

Valtu snorts at that and I give him a dirty look.

Lenore goes on. "Eventually I was able to get the upper hand, just enough that Van Helsing injected him with something. I didn't know that neural-paralyzers worked on vampires, but I'm started to think Abe has a whole arsenal of special drugs at his fingertips."

"Who needs magic when you have science," Valtu comments. Then he curls up his lip in disgust. "Fucking hell, I sound just like him."

"Anyway," Lenore continues, "it was enough that Leif couldn't move and we were able to sit him down and explain everything to him. It took a lot of convincing to get him to come with us back here but he's here now."

"So is he still paralyzed?" I ask.

She shakes her head. "No. He's fine, just a little slower than he would be normally, which is good because he's still a vampire. He may have not turned yet but we don't know what the witches did to him and his body, the type of training or powers he might have. It's going to take some time for him to come to terms with all of this, I still don't think he believes any of us, and he doesn't seem to have any sort of instinct with your parents, but Abe said he was hoping hypnosis might help. That's what he's doing now."

"I want to see him," I say. "Now."

Lenore and Solon exchange a look. "I'm not sure that's a good idea," Lenore says.

"Oh come on, he's her brother," Valtu says.

"And according to Solon, she's the one who just killed

Bellamy, the only one he knew as a father. That won't go down so well."

"Then I won't tell him that, not yet anyway," I say.

Lenore nods. "Fine. Come on."

I go for the door and Valtu reaches out and grabs my elbow. "Do you want me to come with you or do you think it's better you go alone?"

I give him a grateful smile. "Actually, I think it's best I go alone. I don't want to overwhelm him."

He gives me a quick kiss and nods. "Good luck. I love you."

This is the first time in a very long time that he's told me he's loved me in public. My cheeks go warm, a giddiness in my chest. "I love you, too."

Then I leave the room with Lenore and as the door is closing I hear Solon say to Valtu, "Well, who knew Dracula was such a softie?"

Lenore is looking at me like she wants to say the same thing to me, but I just nod at her towel. "You can just tell me their room number, you don't have to come with me."

She glances down at her towel and waves dismissively. "Please, this is the land of Turkish baths. Everyone's in a towel. Besides, I just wanted to ask you how it went. How did Dahlia's power feel?"

"Great," I say, then stop myself. "No. It felt amazing."

I fill her in on every little thing that happened, replaying the battle in my mind, wrapping it all up just as we come to a room on the floor above us.

"Here we go," she says. "I'll leave you to it."

She turns and goes, and I knock on the door, my heart thundering in my chest now, suddenly nervous.

Abe answers it, his blue eyes shining through the doorframe. "Ah, I was wondering if you'd come by," he says softly, not opening the door enough to let me in.

He can hear us, so I'd rather talk to you like this, if I'm not being intrusive, Abe says inside my head.

Not at all. How is he? Lenore explained what went down, I tell him.

Well, I tried hypnosis on him, he says. *And that helped a little in that he knows now that your parents are his real parents and he knows that they don't mean him any harm. But I didn't want to go into the deeper, traumatic sections. He doesn't remember the kidnapping or the experiments. It's too much for now for him to process.*

But he knows Bellamy is dead? I ask.

He presses his lips together and nods. *He's been handling it well, considering. But your brother is the type to shove everything deep down and either deal with it later or not deal with it all.*

Gee, sounds familiar, I say, thinking of Valtu.

There are some similarities, he says. *But I think Leif is a tougher nut to crack. Anyway, come in and say hello. He won't attack you. Just don't mention what happened at the bazaar.*

I nod and step through the door as he opens it.

The room is dimly lit, a large suite like ours, and my mother and father are sitting on the couch, talking to Leif who is sitting in an armchair. Though he seems very subdued and is slow to turn his head to look at me, I still approach as if I'm coming up to a wild animal.

I give my parents a quick nod and smile and they look at Leif.

"Leif," my mom says, "this is your sister Rose."

I raise my hand a little in hello and take the seat across from him. "Hi Leif."

Holy crap is this a fucking trip.

I know I'd already laid eyes on him, but to see him again, and up close like this, feels surreal. It's Dylan alright, but it's also a man who is years past that. The haunted look in his eyes can't be compared to his brother, who has never known hardship a day in his life. Leif is just a tightly wound ball of complications, unyielding and impenetrable and in the back of my head I wonder if it's possible to ever save him.

"You're the girl I saw the other day," he says slowly, his words thick. "The one that Atlas attacked. I thought you'd be dead."

I shake my head. "No, it takes a lot to kill me and even when I do die, I always come back," I finish that with a smile.

He frowns. "You always come back?"

"So far, anyway. It's a long story. Actually, it's many long—or short—stories, depending on how you look at it. But I just want to say that I am so glad that you're here."

From the hard look on his face I can tell he doesn't feel the same way.

I go on, "And that no matter what, I'm here for you. I know we'd never met when we were young and you don't know me, but I feel I know you. That might not help to hear right now but I'm hoping in time you'll really know that I have your back."

I don't want to add that it was actually me who instigated this whole thing to get him back and out of Bellamy's clutches. I'll save that for another time.

And I am so fucking relieved that there is going to be another time.

He may be wary of me, he may not know me, he may be experiencing deep loss and confusion and a sense of not knowing who he really is, but I hope that we'll eventually be close. I don't expect the same relationship I have with Dylan, but I hope it's still something honest and real.

Leif doesn't smile but something in his eyes tells me that he accepts me, and that's good enough for now.

THE DRIVE from Portland to Newport is only a couple of hours barrelling down the I-5 and then a quick hop across from Corvallis to the coast, but it feels like both incredibly long and incredibly short.

My dad is at the wheel of our SUV they had left at the airport, Valtu beside him in the passenger seat, and me, my mom and Leif are in the back. It's been five days since Leif came back into our lives and we just landed at the Portland airport. Abe went back to England and Solon and Lenore flew direct to San Francisco.

It's been a tough few days with my brother, that's for sure. Abe has been working with him steadily with drugs and hypnosis and who else knows what, and that's been helping a little. It's at least been helping in that Leif isn't fighting against us or running away or telling us to just fuck off totally. He's only been telling us to fuck off a little. And I can't blame him, considering all that he's gone through.

Somehow though, we managed to convince him to come back to Oregon with us. My parents want to give him a place to stay while he figures shit out, and we also want him to meet his twin. We think meeting Dylan will really solidify the truth. Even though Leif seems to take it all in stride, I fear that he's humoring us and doesn't really believe what we've been telling him.

Even now I keep stealing glances at him and though his focus has been out the window this entire ride, there's a tense set to his jaw that makes me uneasy. I just hope and pray everything goes as well as it can.

Finally we're driving through Newport and pulling onto the street along the beach that will take us to our house, and it feels like I haven't been here for years, even though it's been a couple of weeks. The world I knew when I left this place is not the same as it is now. I'm with Valtu, Leif is back, and Bellamy is dead.

And I feel like I'm finally at one with all the different versions of myself, like all my different lives have finally converged into one. A sum of all my parts.

I am so much stronger for it.

We pull into the driveway and as Valtu gets out of the car he looks up at the house and says, "I was going to give you shit, Wolf, about living the suburban life, but I have to say this is fairly impressive."

My dad grunts in response. "Yeah, well the missus wanted to live by the ocean. If it were up to me, I'd be in the middle of the woods."

"We lived in the middle of the woods the last time," my mom says with an exasperated sigh then gestures to the treed hills on the other side of the road. "And there's a forest right there but I don't ever see you stomping around in it, foraging for berries or whatever you want to do in it."

I give Leif a smile. "You'll have to get used to them. They reverted back into mom and dad mode pretty fast. It's all downhill from here."

Leif doesn't smile but nods, his gaze drawn to the ocean where the grey surf pounds the shore. "It's beautiful," he comments.

"It's moody and gloomy as fuck," I tell him. "But I agree."

We all walk to the house, my mom going to Leif's side, while I wrap my arm around Valtu's.

"Is it weird having me here?" Valtu asks me.

"Weird? A little," I admit. "But I'm glad you're here."

"We don't have to stay with your parents, do we? As much as I would love to piss off your father by screwing his daughter in her bed, I think I want as much privacy with you tonight as possible."

My stomach flips at that, though I have to give him a dirty look for the rest of what he said. "No, we aren't staying here. There are a ton of nice, very romantic hotels right up the street."

"Thank god," he breathes.

We go toward the kitchen and my dad yells, "Dylan we're back. Get your ass over here and meet your brother."

The house is a mess. I know my brother tried a little to keep it orderly but it's a mess. The sink is piled with dishes, despite a perfectly good dishwasher, and there are clothes and vinyl records strewn everywhere.

I can see the vein forming in my mom's forehead as she looks around with wide eyes, but she manages to keep it together as Dylan approaches, looking like he just got out of bed, all bleary-eyed with a stained t-shirt.

"Hey fam gang," he says, giving us a lazy grin.

I rush right over to him and give him the biggest hug. "Dylan, we'd like you to meet your brother. Leif."

I pull back and gesture to Leif who is standing there looking shell-shocked.

Dylan's mouth drops open. "Oh my god," he gasps, one hand pressing against his head. "It's me. But a sexier version of me."

"That's the you if you didn't smoke pot," my father comments under his breath and my mom elbows him.

Leif seems so shocked that he's not even moving, so Dylan walks over to him slowly, peering at him and blinking hard. "Dude," Dylan says, stopping a foot away, looking him up and down. "You're my twin. You're my brother."

And Leif finally nods. "I didn't expect this," he says, his voice hoarse.

"I didn't expect you'd be able to grow such an impressive beard," Dylan says, and everyone laughs, grateful for the break in the tension.

Finally, for the first time, there's just the tiniest hint of a smile on Leif's lips as he stares at his twin and I think, no, I *know*, that we're all going to be okay.

Then Dylan looks at Valtu in surprise, noticing him for the first time. "Wait. Who the hell is this?"

CHAPTER 29
VALTU

I wake up to the sound of pounding waves, my eyes adjusting to the dark of the room. The clock reads two am and I groan. Jetlag is a bitch.

I roll over to look at Rose but she's gone, her space in the bed empty.

Panic floods my mouth.

"Rose?" I say, sitting up, about to get out of bed, when I hear the sink running in the bathroom. I breathe out a heavy sigh of relief and sink back down into the mattress, pressing my hand over my chest as if it might calm it.

Ever since we left Istanbul, but I'm still on edge. Every little fucking thing makes me think that either Bellamy has risen from the dead or Atlas Poe has come back for his head. Or Leif suddenly falls back into his programming or whatever the hell Bellamy and his crew did to him and goes berserk, murdering everyone.

Learn to relax, I tell myself. *Rose can handle herself anyway.*

And that's true. She proved it time and time again.

During her battle with Bellamy, even though I missed most of it because he pressed pause on everyone, she was able to destroy him, using her powers as both a vampire and a witch and though I didn't think it was possible, I fell even deeper in love with her. How could I not? With Mina and Lucy, and even Dahlia, I had never seen them do anything like that, but Rose was able to and she did it so well. She might be able to kick *my* ass and that turns me on more than anything.

Still, I get out of bed and go to check on her just in case.

I knock on the bathroom door and she opens it.

Totally naked.

My eyes roam over her body, dick immediately hard. "What are you doing?" I know she fell asleep with her t-shirt on, whereas I always sleep naked.

"Sorry, did I wake you? I was going to take a shower. I couldn't sleep."

"Me either. Jet lag."

She nods, looking wired. "Jet lag and everything else."

"It's been a hell of a day," I comment, stepping in the room. "I think you should let me take your mind off things."

Her gaze drops to my cock, stiff and throbbing and begging for her attention.

"I can't say no to that," she says with a sly grin. "Though you already wore me out earlier."

"Obviously not enough if you're waking up in the middle of the night. I'm going to fuck you so hard that you'll sleep for days."

She laughs, a throaty, breathy sound and then walks toward the shower. "A fuck that can erase jetlag? I'll believe it when I see it," she taunts, turning on the water.

Fuck, I love a challenge.

I stalk toward the shower, stepping inside the spray of

hot water, then I grab her and twirl her around so that she's pinned against the tiles. Water cascades down her back and I bend down, licking up her spine from the base of her ass to her neck.

"Want me to wash your hair before I take you?" I murmur, sliding a hand underneath the crease of her ass cheeks. "I could get you really clean before I get you so fucking dirty."

She nods, already breathless and I pour out shampoo into my hand, massaging it into her hair with one hand while my other reaches around to her breasts, playing with them. The feel of her nipple hardening beneath my fingers sends a ripple of lust through my cock, and she gasps.

Pulling her wet hair back out of the way, I bite her earlobe, tasting the suds. I nip at her neck then suck a path to where the flesh of her neck and shoulder meet, one of the most sensitive areas of her body, a place where I can always disarm her. She immediately melts under my lips and she moans, pressing her ass back against my cock as she dips her head into the shower stream. "Make sure you use conditioner."

"You're not going to make it easy for me, are you?" I ask.

"Of course not. It's not much of a challenge otherwise," she teases, and I finish getting the rest of the shampoo out of her hair.

Then I take the conditioner and squeeze it out into my hand, running it through her scalp.

"Just the ends of the hair," she says quickly.

"Who's in charge here, me or you?" I say roughly. Then I take my hand soaked in conditioner and slide it down over her spine and to her ass. I gently trace the pucker of her asshole with my finger, teasing her as I go.

"Oh fuck," she says, her breath hitching and she pushes

her ass against me. "You're in charge, my lord. Take what you want."

Christ on a bike.

Her back arches slightly and my finger slips inside her tight hole with ease.

"God," she cries out.

I'm grinning like an idiot as I thrust my finger deeper inside her, sliding in and out of her ass and her body stiffens again, then relaxes. "You still like that, don't you?" I murmur in her ear as my finger slips in. "Because I remember you used to love it."

She nods, making a tight noise of want.

I take the other hand and squeeze out some more conditioner and this time I pour it over her shoulder, so it slides down between her breasts over her stomach and between her legs. I reach forward and rub it in over her clit until she's letting out a sharp cry.

I run my hands back up her body, then slip one hand into the crease of her ass, pulling her cheeks apart and pressing my cock against her slick opening. She groans and pushes her ass toward me, silently begging me to take her.

"Do you still want it?"

She nods and I quickly slap her hard against her ass, the water spraying, my palm stinging. "Use your words," I bark at her, watching as my pink handprint blooms on her skin.

"Yes, my lord," she says. "I want it."

"Ask and you shall receive," I tell her. I shove myself in, sliding in like tight silk and my eyes roll back in my head, a primal moan rising up from my chest.

Fuck.

Rose gasps loudly, tensing, and I push inside, deeper and deeper until my hips are flush with her ass. Then I slide my hand around, pressing my finger on her slick and swollen clit to try and get her to relax.

"That's it," I tell her, my voice strangled and hoarse. "Take me. Take all of it."

"Oh fuck," she cries out. "Oh my god."

"You like it? You like the way it feels, my big fat cock fucking your tight little ass?"

"Yes," she says, her voice shaking slightly.

"You're a tighter squeeze than my fist," I groan into her neck. "I think you might be strangling me."

I slowly pump my hips, thrusting in and out, her body slowly relaxing around me, accepting me. My finger moves faster on her clit as I pump and her body pitches against me, meeting me with every thrust until she's crying out my name.

"Fuck, Val!"

"Let go, my dove," I tell her, my voice breaking off. "Just let go. I've got you."

"I'm going to come," she warns me, her words garbled, and I thrust harder and faster, keeping up the pressure on her clit until her entire body is shaking, out of control and then she's coming. Hard.

Fuck me.

Her body convulses, her ass spasming around me, tight, so fucking tight that I can't breathe, and I bury myself inside her and come so hard it makes me dizzy. I shove my hand over her mouth, stifling her scream that echoes in the shower.

My thoughts are jumbled, my cock spurting inside of her, the orgasm never seeming to end, and suddenly I'm hit with emotions I've been trying to ignore, trying to bury. I'm not the man I was, I can't just erase things, I can't ignore the feelings and thoughts and desires that have been plaguing me for a week now. They come at me now like a riptide, threatening to pull me under and drown me until I face them.

"Rose," I manage to say, my breath finally coming back to me, my cock jerking to completion. I rest my chin on her shoulder and listen to her own breathing slow, my cock still inside her.

"I want a baby," I whisper to her, unable to hold back the words any longer.

She stiffens for a moment, then glances at me over her shoulder. "I hate to tell you this Val, but that was not how you make a baby."

I pull out, turn her around and press her against the wall, just out of the stream of water, bracketing her between my arms. "I'm serious, my dove," I say, my chest feeling tight. "I want to be a father. I want to give you my babies. I want a family with you."

A tear starts to roll down Rose's cheek and I lean in and kiss her, tasting it. The darkness is still there but there is so much light. So much light for both of us. "I want another chance. We can get it right this time, I promise you."

"Yes," she whispers, crying now. "Yes, I want that too."

Relief floods through me, nearly bringing me to my knees. I had been so afraid that she wouldn't feel the same way, that Rose didn't feel the same as Mina or Lucy, or that she was too scared to want for one or try again because of everything that happened last time.

But she wants it. She wants to be the mother of my children and I am so fucking happy that I'm delirious.

"Are you sure?" I ask her, cupping her face in my hands, running my thumb over her lips.

"More than anything," she says softly, gazing into my eyes with so much love that my knees are about to buckle.

Then that gaze turns from warm to hot and, fuck, now I'm going to do my damndest to knock her up.

"Let's get fucking started then," I tell her.

I bend down and scoop her up in my arms, and she laughs as I carry her out of the bathroom, almost slipping on the wet floor. I bring her over to the bed and drop her on it, and yes we're both soaked, but we're going to be wet with sweat after I'm done with her.

I prowl over her and start to kiss her, deep and passionate. I'm going to make her mine in the most basic way possible, claiming her with not just my body but my seed, making her mine until eternity is bored of us.

Our skin slides against each other, her sighs and gasps mixing with my groans, and we're clawing at each other, desperate to get closer, to become one. I reach down between her legs and slip my hand inside her, still so wet, so ready for me. I slide a finger inside, then two, three, and I'm fisting her and she's so tight it almost hurts.

"My lord," she says, her breath catching, her eyes wide.

I grin and move my fist in and out, working her, getting her ready for my cock, and her hands are slipping down my slick chest, over my abs and down to my length, which is so hard it feels like it's going to burst.

"I want you inside me," Rose whispers, her eyes bright with desire, squirming around my fist.

I pull out and flick her clit a few times and her entire body bucks. "Spread your legs," I growl at her and she obeys. I'm about to lick her pussy out but she grabs my hair with a fist.

"Don't fuck around," she says. "I need you coming inside me."

I chuckle. "Yes, ma'am."

I grip the base of my cock and guide it into the entrance of her cunt and start to slide in, her wetness and tightness making it easy, and she wraps her legs around my ass, urging me to go further.

I pull back, slow and steady, then plunge in again and she cries out sharply.

"So good," she moans. "Oh fuck, Val, you feel so good."

"So do you," I grunt, pulling out and thrusting in again. "I'm going to give you everything you've ever dreamed of."

We set a rhythm of long, deep strokes, both of us groaning and gasping, and I can feel her getting tighter around me as she gets closer to her second orgasm.

Her toes dig into my ass, urging me on, and slowly we build up a rhythm, her hands drifting up my back to my shoulders and back down again, skating over my ass, urging me to go harder and faster.

I slam into her again, our wet skin slapping together, and Rose yelps in ecstasy. I let myself go and give her everything I promised, thrusting into her so hard and fast until I think I might drive this bed right through the wall and into the next room.

Finally, I come with her, my orgasm so intense it scrambles my brain and rips a hoarse cry from my chest, my cock jerking inside her and pumping my seed into her again and again until it feels like there's nothing left.

I've given everything I have to her.

I collapse on top of her and she wraps her arms around me and I bury my face in her neck and I swear to all the gods out there, I will never let her go.

Never.

"Do you think that worked?" Rose asks me after a minute, when our heartrates finally slow.

I turn my head to look at her, smiling like a fool in love. "If it didn't, give me a second and we'll try again."

She laughs and kisses me.

For once in my life it feels like destiny is smiling upon us.

Life has never tasted so sweet.

EPILOGUE

VALTU

A Few Years Later

"Signor Aminoff," Maria says to me, clapping her hands together. "*Rose é entrata in travaglio!*"

A wave of nausea comes over me. "Already?"

"What did she say?" Amethyst cries out grabbing my thigh and digging her nails in as she looks between me and the vampire doula.

"She's gone into labor," I tell her. "Please unhook your claws from my leg."

Amethyst lets go of me and leaps to her feet, pleading to Maria. "Can I see her?"

I translate to Maria, who has been helping Rose ever since we found out she was pregnant, who also happens to know very little English. Apparently, Maria hasn't been a vampire that long, so her lack of languages is forgivable.

Maria tells me in Italian that it is up to Rose if she wants to see anyone and she disappears back upstairs.

374

"It's up to your daughter," I tell Amethyst. "I'm sure she'll want you in there."

"She's never going to want me in there! She's going to curse me for giving birth to her in the first place," Amethyst says just as Wolf walks back in the room.

"What did I miss?" he asks eagerly. Then he looks at me. "You okay, Valtu? You look a little pale."

I just raise my hand and nod, trying to breathe through it.

The truth is, I'm not okay. I'm so nervous that it's making me sick. I was better earlier in the day, when Rose told me she was having contractions and I called the doula and the doctor over, but now that the contractions have turned into labor, I'm about to have a complete panic attack.

I have a reason to be nervous too. For the last few years, ever since I reunited with Rose, we've been trying for a baby. I had my vasectomy reversed pretty much right away and I think we both assumed she would get pregnant immediately. After all, vampires are incredibly fertile, especially the young women right after they turn, and it had happened that way for us in the past.

But no matter what, she never got pregnant. It wasn't for lack of trying, obviously. Every day, often multiple times a day, I was screwing her brains out and yet it just wouldn't take. Her body remained in status quo.

Rose had faith, though. Unwavering faith. She said it would happen in due time.

But in the back of my mind, I started to think that maybe there was a reason for this. Maybe it was a good thing that she couldn't carry my child. We were very aware that both of her prior pregnancies ended in her death, as well as the child's death. What if this was sparing her life this time around?

I made peace with it. I wasn't about to do anything that would jeopardize the love that we had. I went to the ends of the earth to make her happy and keep her safe and I wasn't going to throw any of that away, even if having a child was something that I really wanted.

At least, I thought I made peace with it. But nine months ago, Rose came to me with a smile so big it nearly split her face, her eyes dancing with delight, and I knew what she was going to say.

"I'm pregnant," she had said, and the joy and pride in her voice made me realize how badly she had wanted this. And the way my heart swelled at the news, like it had become too big for my chest, made me realize that I hadn't really made peace. I know we would have been fine without children, but knowing she was pregnant cemented how badly I'd wanted them with her.

We had another chance.

And so I wasn't about to take any chances.

At the time we were jet-setting around the world. Rose wanted to travel and I was happy to indulge her. We spent months on a yacht in the Mediterranean, just the two of us, eating fish we'd caught off the boat, drinking retsina in tiny white-washed bars in Crete. We climbed Mount Kiliman-jaro and spent weeks on the beaches of Madagascar. We studied art in Argentina and lived in a penthouse in New York City. We did whatever Rose wanted to, whatever would keep her happy. I just wanted to be with her, it didn't matter where.

We were in Tenerife when she got the news and I knew we had to settle down for good, find a place to raise a family for at least the next ten years.

We decided on Italy.

We decided on Venice.

It was an easy choice to make. There was no other place we'd rather put down roots again. It had been long enough that keeping a low profile in the city would be easy. I couldn't get my job back at the conservatory without raising suspicion, so I changed my name from Valtu Aminoff to Vlad Harper. Seemed fitting enough. Cut my hair a little, grew a beard, then I started offering private music lessons. Most of my students are vampires, but there's a few unknowing humans in there as well.

I also took over the Red Room again, with Rose by my side as a business partner. Bitrus was more than happy to hand over the responsibility and he immediately absconded to the Rocky Mountains of all places, to go live on a ranch, about as far away from a vampire sex dungeon in Venice as you can get. Luckily Rose has really taken to running the room, and most of the vampires call her Madame, which I find amusing.

Van Helsing still lives the scientist life in Oxford, working his life away, though he visits often and has opened another lab in Barcelona, so at least the Doctor gets a little bit of fun in his life. At the moment he's upstairs with Rose and Maria, ensuring a healthy delivery.

Lenore and Solon are back in San Francisco and Wolf and Amethyst have a place around the corner from them, though of course they're here in Venice now for Rose's delivery. Dylan lives in Portland, and probably would have come, but the kid is stoned out of his gourd most days so his parents will probably do a video call with him later.

And then there's Leif. Leif the wild card. Leif the tortured soul.

Leif has a lot of shit to work through, even still. It's

going to take some time before the trauma of his childhood gets resolved, if it ever will. With Bellamy, Atlas, and Celina gone, there's no one left to tie him to that world, but even so, he behaves more like a human than a vampire. Sometimes more like a witch too.

He was living with Wolf and Amethyst until recently, until he decided he'd had enough and needed time away, then he took off back to Europe. Van Helsing said that he wanted to help Leif further, so the last that everyone heard, Leif was living in Barcelona and having sessions with Van Helsing whenever he's in town. I think everyone is relieved that Leif isn't completely on his own, that the Doctor is keeping a good eye on him. We just don't know what his future holds. I know it weighs on Rose a lot to not have the kind of relationship with Leif that she has with Dylan, but I tell her it will come in time.

Everything always does.

"Just breathe," Wolf says, putting his hand on my back, trying to reassure me. "Rose is a toughie. She's going to be okay."

I inhale sharply through my nose and attempt to loosen the vice in my chest. "At the moment, I don't know if I'm going to be okay."

He laughs. "Maybe we should smoke the cigars I bought now. Or do we have to wait? I think it would calm you."

"He just needs a drink," Amethyst says. "And so do I."

She goes over to the bar beside my piano and unscrews a bottle of Scotch, drinking it directly from the bottle.

I groan. "That's like two hundred years old," I protest. "I was saving that."

She shrugs. "And is there a better special occasion than the birth of your child? Which, by the way, I think it's insane that we don't know the sex yet."

Now it's my time to shrug but I hold out my hand for the bottle. "What's the point? It's a baby. Boy, girl, neither —doesn't really matter to us."

"You're still a little too human sometimes," Wolf tells her. "Always liking to put everything in a neat compartment."

She has another swallow and then hands me the bottle. "Neat? You know me. I'm not neat. Boy, girl, I don't care, I just want to know what name the baby will have."

"We've already told you as much," I remind her. "Constantine."

Amethyst groans. "You can't name my grandchild Constantine."

I take a swig of the Scotch. "Oh yes I can. Constantine Aminoff. What's wrong with that? I think it's beautiful for any child."

"It's Constantine *Harper*," Wolf says, taking the bottle from me now. At this rate we'll be finished with the Scotch in no time.

"It's Harper only when we're in Venice," I remind him. "My passport says otherwise."

"Your passport also says you were born thirty-five years ago," Wolf points out.

"*Signor Aminoff!*" Maria's sing-song voice comes out from upstairs.

I give Wolf a look that says, *see, it's Aminoff*.

"*Vuole vederti*," Maria says. "*Sta succedendo!*"

My gut twists.

"What?" Amethyst cries out. "What did she say?"

"She said she wants to see me," I say, trying to straighten up and fight the nausea. The fear is so great but I need to work my way through it for Rose. I can't be losing my damn mind, I'm supposed to be the calm supportive one while she's trying to deliver a baby vampire.

I swallow hard and look at the two of them. "It's happening."

"Oh," Amethyst says, clapping her hands together quickly, while Wolf puts his arm around her, giving her an affectionate squeeze. "Oh, it's happening, it's happening."

"Here comes baby Constantine," I announce, and I quickly head up the stairs before I lose my nerve.

The house I bought this time around in Venice is located in the Castello region, overlooking the public gardens. It's a big and beautiful house, with a lot of history and just a touch of darkness from the shadows of the trees and the gothic architecture. Because we can't have a birth in a hospital—it would be fairly obvious that the baby being born wasn't entirely human—we have to have it in the house. Van Helsing assures me that one day he'd love to open a hospital for vampires, but it's kind of a moot point since vampires have been doing just fine for centuries.

On the second level, Maria waves me over with a smile and I follow her into the bathroom where I can already hear Rose whimpering in pain. They say that vampire births are nowhere near as painful as human births, but even so it's apparent she's feeling discomfort.

I peer around the doorframe to our sprawling bathroom and see Rose in the claw-foot tub, naked and grimacing, with Van Helsing at her feet, coaching her.

"Just a little more," he says, eyes grave with determination. "Just a little more Rose.'

Holy shit this is happening fast.

"I can't," she whimpers.

"You can," I tell her, coming right over to her. I drop to my knees beside her and hang onto her hand. "I'm here."

"Valtu," she says softly, looking at me with dazed eyes, a thin sheen of sweat on her forehead. "You're here."

"I've been here the whole time, my dove," I reassure her, kissing her hand. "Just downstairs with your parents, not wanting to get in the way."

She tries to smile, then scrunches up her nose, smelling me. "Are you drinking already?"

"Hey, this is hard on me too."

"Valtu," the doctor warns me. "Stop distracting her. We need her to do one last push."

I give her hand a squeeze. "Can you give one last push, Rose? One last big push and then baby Constantine is here." I look at the doctor. "Then the baby is here, right? That's it?"

"Yes," he says, his voice clipped. "That's it. Now come on, Rose."

Rose groans and then her face contorts and she lets out a howl as she pushes.

I watch, absolutely fascinated. This is life being born, everlasting life, and it's a product of us, of Valtu and Rose and Dahlia and Lucy and Mina. It's our love mixed together, our destiny coming to fruition. It's all the hell we've had to go through to find each other and all the times we thought we'd never find each other again.

This baby is love eternal.

And the love is ours.

"There it is," Van Helsing says, quickly reaching into the tub as the baby emerges from Rose and is brought to the surface. "It's a boy."

"A boy!" I exclaim. "A boy, Rose!"

She's laughing and crying and reaching forward, waiting for the Doctor to properly clean and dry him off. "Constantine. My baby boy."

381

It's pure fucking joy. Absolutely. I don't even know what to do with myself, I don't even know if I'm breathing. I'm so damn happy, and so fucking proud, if I do say so myself. Not just of Rose but the fact that we produced baby boy Constantine.

And he's beautiful. Chubby, wrinkled, red and so beautiful.

"You did it," I whisper to Rose, kissing her forehead, her cheek, her jaw. "You did it, my dove."

"We did it," she says, giving me a joyous smile that lights her up from the inside.

"You did it," I tell her. "I merely contributed in a highly enjoyable way."

Van Helsing also looks proud as hell. He should be. I know it weighed on him a lot to have lost Lucy and the baby. He grins at us, finding his own redemption.

Then he hands the baby to Rose and she holds him in her arms, rocking him slightly. The baby isn't crying at all, just a few soft whimpers, and I'm struck by what a natural Rose is at this. She was born to do this.

And she was born to be with me.

She coos at Constantine and then glances at me with the softest eyes. "I honestly didn't think this would ever happen," she whispers. "I didn't think life would be so kind."

"But it's happened. And it's kind. And he's perfect, Rose. He found us."

"My heart found yours, Val," she whispers to me before beaming down at Constantine. "And now both our hearts have found him."

I wipe the tear from my eye and lean over, kissing the top of her head.

Then I lean further and kiss the top of Constantine's,

breathing in my baby's smell until my eyelids flutter. Love floods my veins, until I'm completely enveloped by this feeling of being so perfectly complete that it feels like I'm levitating.

It may have taken nearly five hundred years, but I finally have my family.

Finally together.

Finally whole.

THE END

THANK you so much for joining me on this journey to Valtu and Rose's much earned HEA! I am unsure if I will right more in this world, but if I do, Leif and Van Helsing will be the first vampires in line.

If you haven't read Lenore and Solon or Wolf and Amethyst's story yet, please start with Black Sunshine and The Blood is Love, then move on to Nightwolf.

Meanwhile if you can leave me a review for Blood Orange and Black Rose it would be much appreciated! Reviews really help an author out :) ALSO if you want to stay in touch, please follow me on Instagram or Amazon.

ACKNOWLEDGMENTS

If you follow me on social media you'll know I had a hell of a time getting this book out. I was still dealing with the death of my father and brother plus a nice bout of depression and some health problems. The only way out was to cancel my preorder for this book and start 2023 with a clean slate with no obligations to deadlines.

It was a risk. It still is. I worried that my readers wouldn't find Black Rose when it released, or they'd grow distrustful of me. I wanted to do right by everyone but at the same time I had to honor my mental health and what was best for the book.

Then just a few weeks into January, when I thought I would be jumping into this book, my beloved dog Bruce died. He was the biggest part of my life and to have that heavy loss on the heels of the other heavy losses, well...it's taken a lot from me. I relate to Valtu in so many ways, the time that grief steals from you. I have lost so many books and writing time, not to mention trips and events, due to loss. I feel like the last few years of my life have just been ripped away from me and I'll never get that time back. I had so many plans, big publishing and career plans, and then the rug was pulled out from under me and my entire life changed forever.

It sucks. There is no sugarcoating it. There is no "getting over it." Yes, it does get easier but nothing is linear. I'm highly emotional as it is, and my autism/ADHD combo makes me a hot mess in general. After Bruce died, I wondered if I would ever regain my footing again, especially when it comes to writing.

Well, Black Rose was my first step back into it. I didn't think I would ever finish this book. First of all, this was extremely challenging to write, even if my brain was operating at 100%. I knew when I was half-way through Blood Orange that this would be a duet and I knew what the future for my star-crossed lovers would be, but I had no idea how to put it on the page and execute it. I was dealing with different characters, different timelines, and different settings this time around. I knew that what people loved about Blood Orange might not come through since the plot changed entirely. It was a very unique situation and in all my 12 years of publishing and over 70 books, I don't think I've ever written a sequel as challenging as this one.

But it was the only way to write this book and I had to stay true to myself and the vision I had for them. In the end it is Valtu and Rose/Dahlia/Lucy/Mina's love story and I hope I did them justice and gave them the HEA they so sorely deserve.

Most of all, I am so proud of being able to write and finish this book in the way that I wanted. All that grief has been heavy but I am grateful I have been strong enough to let it lift me up instead of weigh me down.

And no, if I had the choice to erase my dad, brother or dog from my life, like Valtu did, I wouldn't do it. The pain may be hard but it's worth it to have loved so much.

Special thanks with this book to Michelle Ackley, Laura Helseth, Betul E, Chanpreet Singh, KA Tucker, Hang Le, and everyone in the Reckless Readers Society! And of course my husband Scott, and Bruce.

RIP Bruce "Boo Boo, Doofus, Mr. Poo" Mackenzie.
#adoptdontshop

About the Author

Karina Halle, a screenwriter, former travel writer and music journalist, is the *New York Times*, *Wall Street Journal*, and *USA Today* bestselling author of *The Royals Next Door, A Nordic King*, and *River of Shadows*, as well as over seventy other wild and romantic reads. She, her husband live in a rain forest on an island off the coast of British Columbia in the summer, and in sunny Los Angeles during the winter months.

www.authorkarinahalle.com

Find her on Facebook, Instagram, Pinterest, BookBub, Amazon and Tik Tok

Also by Karina Halle

A Nordic King

Nothing Personal

My Life in Shambles

Discretion

Disarm

Disavow

The Royal Rogue

The Forbidden Man

Lovewrecked

One Hot Italian Summer

The One That Got Away

All the Love in the World (Anthology)

Romantic Suspense Novels by Karina Halle

Sins and Needles (The Artists Trilogy #1)

On Every Street (An Artists Trilogy Novella #0.5)

Shooting Scars (The Artists Trilogy #2)

Bold Tricks (The Artists Trilogy #3)

Dirty Angels (Dirty Angels #1)

Dirty Deeds (Dirty Angels #2)

Dirty Promises (Dirty Angels #3)

Black Hearts (Sins Duet #1)

Dirty Souls (Sins Duet #2)

Horror & Paranormal Romance

Darkhouse (EIT #1)

Red Fox (EIT #2)

The Benson (EIT #2.5)

Dead Sky Morning (EIT #3)

Lying Season (EIT #4)

On Demon Wings (EIT #5)

Old Blood (EIT #5.5)

The Dex-Files (EIT #5.7)

Into the Hollow (EIT #6)

And With Madness Comes the Light (EIT #6.5)

Come Alive (EIT #7)

Ashes to Ashes (EIT #8)

Dust to Dust (EIT #9)

Ghosted (EIT #9.5)

Came Back Haunted (EIT #10)

In the Fade (EIT #11)

The Devil's Duology

Donners of the Dead

Veiled (Ada Palomino #1)

Song For the Dead (Ada Palomino #2)

Black Sunshine (Dark Eyes Duet #1)

The Blood is Love (Dark Eyes Duet #2)

Nightwolf

River of Shadows (Underworld Gods #1)

Crown of Crimson (Underworld Gods #2)

Blood Orange (The Dracula Duet #1)

Black Rose (The Dracula Duet #2)

9 781088 090305